Say you'll remember me.

PRICE: $20.00 (3798/tfarp)

Say you'll remember me

KATIE McGARRY

Say you'll remember me

HARLEQUIN®TEEN

ISBN-13: 978-0-373-21237-8

Say You'll Remember Me

Printed in U.S.A.

Say you'll remember me

First Teen in Governor's "Second Chance"
Program Chosen; Pleads Guilty for
Robbery and Attempted Assault

By: Jane Trident, Associated Press

The Lexington teen who was arrested for robbing a neighborhood convenience store at gunpoint and possessing an illegal firearm has pleaded guilty and is the first teen selected for Governor Monroe's Second Chance Program.

The program, which is currently under heavy fire from critics, has promised to end the "school-to-prison pipeline." This pipeline is defined by the American Civil Liberties Union as "policies and practices that push our nation's schoolchildren, especially our most at-risk children, out of classrooms and into the juvenile and criminal justice systems."

In an effort to help slow the rising crime rate among teens and the number of these teens funneling into the adult prison system, Governor Monroe kept his campaign promise and has created the Second Chance Program. This program is focused on therapy, specialized educational programs geared toward the individual needs of the teens while incarcerated and a leadership program that will help prepare the teens for when they return to their homes.

Critics point out that the money used for this program is needed to fund other programs in the state. One high-level source, who remained anonymous, stated that the people of Kentucky don't want to see their tax dollars used on teens who can't be helped, and instead prefer for their tax dollars to be used on students who are driven and want to succeed.

Many eyes will be on this program, and many feel that the governor's political future will be tied with the program's success or failure.

HENDRIX

"EVERYONE SAYS YOU HAVE A BLANK SLATE." MY brother, Axle, sits beside me on the ground, arms resting on his bent knees, and he stares at the bonfire I built with my own two hands with only flint and sticks. It's one of the many tricks I learned over the last three months. That and how to survive on my own in the middle of nowhere.

Trees and bears I can handle. It's not knowing who I can trust, now that I'm home, that's the problem. Axle knows this. It's why he's next to me as our friends and family walk around the backyard for the impromptu "Welcome Home" party I told Axle I didn't want.

Someone in this yard is the reason why I spent a year away from home for a crime I didn't commit.

My neck tenses, and I roll it in an attempt to release the anger. It took me close to eight months to find some Zen, and it has taken less than thirty minutes for some of the old underlying rage that followed me around like a black thunderhead to return.

Across from us, two girls I used to go to school with are roasting marshmallows. They're waiting for me to talk to them. That's who I was before: the smooth talker, the guy who made girls laugh and caused them to light up with a few specially chosen words. The right smile dropped at the right time, and panties would be shed. But I don't feel up for conversation and I don't feel like manipulating anyone anymore.

Crazy—I used to thrive when surrounded by people. The more, the better. But after being in juvenile detention for nine months and spending three in the wilderness taking part in an Outward Bound program for troubled teens, I'm more at ease by myself in front of a fire.

"They've all confirmed you're walking out of all this with sealed records," Axle continues.

He's leaving out the part of how those records only remain sealed if I uphold my end of the plea deal—the agreement I made with the district attorney after I was arrested. I agreed to plead guilty, and the DA didn't charge me as an adult and send me to hard-core prison. Considering we had no money for a lawyer to help prove my innocence, the deal sounded like the better of two bad options.

"You're getting a massive second chance," Axle says.

It was rotten luck that got me into this mess, but it happened at the right time. Our governor was searching for screwed-up teens to use for his pilot program. Someone high up in the world thought I stood a chance at turning my life around, but that second chance comes with a price. A price my brother is currently breaking down for me.

"This is a good thing. A blank slate. Not many people get one of those."

Blank slate. That's what I'm scared of. I may not have liked parts of the person I was before I was arrested, but at least I knew who I was. This blank slate, this chance to create someone new, scares me. This is a new type of pressure. At least I had a good excuse for being a delinquent before. Now, if I mess up, it's because I'm truly broke.

The fire crackles then pops, and embers rise into the late May night. My younger sister laughs at the other end of the narrow yard near the aging shotgun house, and the sound is like an eight-eight beat with a high hat cymbal. It's welcomed, and it's the first time this feels like home.

She's sixteen now, grown up faster than I'd prefer, and she's one of the four people I love more than my own life. She's also the only reason I'm still out here instead of holed up in my room. According to Axle, it was Holiday's idea to set up the party.

Old Christmas lights are strung from one towering oak tree to the next, zigzagging green, red and blue across the yard. Most people brought their own chairs and a dish to share. My first meal as a free man and it's hamburgers, hot dogs and potato salad. I don't have the heart to tell her I would have given my left ball for a slice of thick crust pizza.

"She missed you," Axle says, catching my train of sight.

"I missed her, too." Those are my first words since we pulled in the driveway. I used to be the life of the party, but that was before, and as I said, I don't know who I am anymore, so for now, I'm quiet.

"I missed you," he says in such a low tone I barely catch it. "We weren't the same without you."

I take a deep breath because I'm not sure any of us will be the same again.

"Is that jerk still coming around?" I ask.

Axle watches Holiday as she punches my best friend, Dominic, in the shoulder. They're both all smiles, and he places her in a fake headlock, but she easily slips away.

Then, because when one speaks of the devil, the devil appears, Holiday's bastard ex-boyfriend shows up.

His black hair is in uneven waves, he's wearing a Styx T-shirt like he has the right to claim anything related to rock 'n' roll, and he has a smile that makes me want to knock his teeth into his throat. According to the therapy I went through this past year, I shouldn't enjoy my sense of satisfaction at his crooked nose and scar. Those features were courtesy of my fist from my life before. He deserved it then for how he treated my sister. I'm betting he deserves it now.

Holiday beams when Jeremy slinks up beside her and wraps his arms around her waist like he's too familiar with parts of her I'm going to pretend he's never touched. Even though the kid has a slight build, he looks sickly white, especially against Holiday's healthy glow and brown tone.

My sister looks a lot like her mother, at least in the pictures I've seen of Holiday's mother when she was younger. She was a black woman with dancing eyes and a smile that could light up the darkest night. Holiday's skin is lighter than her mother's, but other than that, she's a spitting image.

Jeremy eases my sister away from Dominic, away from the

lights, away from anything good in the world. I can still see them in the shadows, and I consider re-breaking his nose.

"I thought you said she broke up with him."

"She did," Axle says. "Six months ago. But then he came crawling back two months ago claiming he's changed. She took him back last week, and I told her there were rules. I'm going to need you to remember the rules. If she breaks them, then we'll have to stand firm."

A twenty-six-year old roofer, attending night school to be an EMT, and me, a seventeen-year-old juvenile delinquent, are now raising a just-turned sixteen-year-old. That's got to be the picture of dysfunction. "Is one of those rules he can't be within a hundred feet of her? A restraining order?"

"She swears he's changed."

Changed. That's what I'm supposed to be. In the forest, the therapist talked forgiveness. Does it mean I haven't changed because I don't forgive the guy who made my sister cry?

"Did he change?"

Axle's lips flatten, and he tosses a stick into the flames. Within seconds it's engulfed and will soon be ashes. Yeah. That answer is a kick in the gut.

"I say too much, I push her away and into his arms," Axle says.

I'm the living proof of this. I got into it with Holiday over this jerk before I was arrested, and the entire situation exploded in my face.

"I keep quiet, it's like I'm the one auctioning off her soul. No one handed me a playbook on raising a teenager when Holiday's grandmother signed custody over to me. Holiday didn't have rules before. In my house, she does. The rest of it I'm playing by ear."

I glance at my older brother out of the corner of my eye, waiting for him to explain that's how he felt about me before I was arrested. Except, I wasn't falling into the wrong person's arms. I was the asshole parents hated.

"But you're back," Axle continues, "and you can help keep an eye on her. Moving her in full-time means I can finally set some boundaries. Rules. At least limit her time with him."

"Think she'll listen?" I ask. "To the rules?"

"She may not listen when it comes to Jeremy, but she listens to everything else."

Translation—Holiday's not me. "Are you laying down rules for me?"

Axle snorts. "Do you need them?"

Probably, but I only lift my fingers as a response.

"How about you don't screw up again."

"Got it." At least I hope I do.

"What's up, Axle. Drix." A friend of mine from when I used to play gigs at local clubs offers Axle his hand and me a nod. The two of them exchange *how are you*'s and *fine*'s. I alternate between watching the flames of the fire licking up and glancing at them as they talk.

My older brother is now my court-appointed guardian. I did too many stupid things while living with Mom, and Dad's not reliable. Axle is nine years older than me, has a decent job and inherited all the recessive responsible genes neither Mom nor Dad possessed.

Axle and I favor Dad. Dirty blond hair, dark eyes and we both used to be hard-core metal boys. I guess we still are when it comes to music, but not so much with style anymore. He has the tats up and down his arms, and earrings in his ears. Earrings and tats were never my thing, and I used to wear my hair to my shoulders where Axle has always kept his shaved close to the scalp.

First thing that happened when I entered juvenile detention was a shaved head. While mine's not shaved anymore, it is cut close on the sides, has some length on top and naturally sticks up like I styled it on purpose. As Holiday told me when I walked in, I got the good boy cut with the bad boy stride.

Our friend leaves with a fist bump to Axle and a pat on the back to me. *Way to go, bro. You survived time on the inside and then time on the outside in a forest.*

"It's weird not hearing you jump into a conversation," Axle says.

It's weird not being in the thick of things. Not being the one telling the story, sharing the joke, or the one in the crowd laughing the loudest. I used to be the guy who drank to get drunk, threw a punch, then threw too many punches, and then dealt with the guilt in the morning.

Thanks to one year of group therapy, I'm different now. Seven months of that therapy was while I was living behind bars, then the other three months of therapy was in the wilderness. Three months of hiking, three months of paddling along forgotten rivers, three months of climbing up and down mountains, three months of being too damned exhausted to remember who I had been before they handed me a backpack that weighed fifty pounds and too damned exhausted to even contemplate if that was a bad or good thing.

As much as I hated parts of who I had become after I went

to live with Mom at fifteen, there were parts of me I liked. Don't mind so much losing the bad, but there's an uncomfortable shifting inside me at the thought that I also lost the good.

"How does this play out?" Axle asks. "How do I make this better for you? Easier?"

Axle isn't talking about the party; he's talking about living here with him and Holiday. He's talking about how I readjust to parts of my old life and adjust into the new life the plea bargain has created. He's talking about the thing we never mention aloud after the night I was arrested.

That we both think someone we know and love is the one who really committed the crime.

We both think it was Holiday working with Dominic or Dominic on his own, but neither of them could have survived being behind bars. I'm tough. I could handle the fallout, and all that mattered to me was that my family believed I was innocent. They did, but the police didn't, and they had a crap load of evidence that pointed in my direction. This is where Axle would say he's thankful for plea bargains.

"It'll be good to have you playing again," Axle continues, desperate to find the easier. "No one can play the drums like you."

The drums. For months, I've dreamed about playing the drums. Being away from my family and the drums was the equivalent of someone chopping off my arms. Part of the reason I didn't want this party was because I wanted to come home, go straight to the garage, sit in silence on my stool behind my set, then play. Feel the beat in my blood, the rhythm in my heart, the music filling an empty soul. Just me, my drums and the comfort in knowing that at least one good thing about me didn't change.

But the thought of playing the drums also causes my stomach to dip. If I play again, do I become the same asshole that I was before?

"When is the press conference?" I ask.

Part of my penance, part of the deal, is that the state needed ten troubled teens, and out of those ten, they needed a poster child to prove to the public their hard-earned tax dollars were going to stop the school-to-prison pipeline. In other words, the voters need proof that this program could prevent teens, who don't do well in school and get expelled, from wandering in and out of juvenile detention, and after eighteen, beelining it straight to prison.

Last year, Axle had lost his mind when the DA had mentioned if I didn't accept the deal and plead guilty they would charge me as an adult. My brother then begged me to agree to anything they were offering, including them owning me for my senior year of high school. Appearing whenever they want, saying whatever they want, all while I keep my nose clean. Can't say terror didn't seize me at the thought of being charged as an adult. I might be strong, but real prison has never been on my bucket list.

Axle pops his knuckles, and my stomach sinks. I'm not going to like his answer.

"The press conference is tomorrow."

Bullet to the head. "Where?"

"May Fest in Louisville. I guess they already had a general press conference planned, and when they found out you'd be out in time..." He trails off.

Makes sense to go from one prison sentence to another.

"It won't be bad. They said they'll have what you need to say written out. Ten minutes. Twenty, tops. I thought we'd all go together. Spend some time on the midway, bring a change of clothes for you, get it done and then we'll head home."

All in a neat package, to be done and repeated until I graduate from high school. That's the deal, and it's the deal I'll see through. The only reason Axle agreed to take on custody of Holiday, getting her out of her crap situation, was because I agreed to come home and help him take on the burden. Financially, emotionally and whatever the hell else it requires to be a parent, since our biological parents can't find their way out of a wet paper bag.

"Guess I should get a good night's sleep, then," I say.

"You probably should."

But neither of us move. Instead we keep staring at my fire. Both amazed I created this. Both scared of what the future is going to bring.

Ellison

FAIR MIDWAYS ARE MY HAPPY PLACE. RIDES with merry, shrieking people are to my right, and to my left are the bells and lights of games.

Dad and Mom brought me to May Fest so I could be present for Dad's press conference, and they allowed me a few hours this afternoon to explore. I should be in my zone, filled with so much joy I could combust, but I'm not. There are two guys who have been stalking me for the past five minutes, and they're ruining my mood.

My cell buzzes in my hand, and I step away from the crowd and between two game booths to read the text. I'm hoping if I appear interested in my phone, the two boys will keep walking—away from me. I'm also expecting a text from my cousin Henry. He's twenty-four to my seventeen, in the army and *should* be home any day now. It's been too long since he's been in Kentucky, and I miss my best friend and older "brother."

To my complete happiness, it is Henry: I'll be in state to-night. Can you drive down to Grandma's tomorrow?

I sigh because I'd rather he put aside his differences with Dad and come home to stay with us during his leave, but I won't push him on this…for now. Some things are best done in person.

Me: I should be able to. I have nothing planned then. I'm at May Fest now. Dad has a press conference later this afternoon.

Henry: Sounds like hell.

Me: It's not so bad.

Henry: Liar.

Really, the press conference will be boring. The fund-raisers and campaign events are often soul crushing, but ad-mitting so will only add fuel to Henry's current anger at my father, so I switch subjects.

Me: I have good news.

Henry: What?

Me: I'm a finalist for the internship!!!!

Henry: That's awesome! Congrats, Elle!

I'm smiling like a fool at my cell. Since this past spring, the last semester of my junior year, I've been competing for a final spot in the interview process for a four year college in-ternship with a computer software company. I found out an hour ago via email that I'm in the final round, and Henry's the first person I've told. It feels good to finally share the joy.

Because I wasn't sure that I would make it as far as I have in the application process, my parents are on the dark side of the moon with all of it. Mom and Dad have high expecta-tions of me, and lately, they've been disappointed that I haven't truly shone in any area of my life. I'm good at things, and they know this, but they want me to be first place for once instead of third.

So now I need to tell them, and I need to tell them soon, since I'm required to have a signed permission slip for the next phase of the interview process. My parents might not be thrilled that I've omitted some critical goings-on of my life, but I'm hoping they can see past what I've been withholding and instead focus on my win.

"You really are beautiful," a guy with a red baseball cap says from my right. He stinks of too much aftershave and a hint of alcohol.

Fantastic. They followed, and my texting didn't tip them off to leave me alone.

I drop my cell into my purse, grab my bottle of Pepsi out of the side pocket and start walking again, praying that I'll lose this jerk and his friend in the crowd. Yet they somehow have the uncanny ability to twist and weave through the fair's packed midway to remain at my side. I try to ignore them.

Last week in an email, Henry challenged me to be happy, because lately a lot of the fund-raisers for Dad were making me miserable. Nothing makes me happier than thrill park rides, games and, because I'm feeling rebellious, a real Pepsi. My health nut of a mother abhors all things in cans.

Somewhere between exiting off the Himalayan and purchasing my drink, these two guys, Idiot One and Idiot Two, obtained the wrong idea that I wanted their company.

I'm a big girl and can take care of myself. Much to my mother's dismay, Henry taught me how to throw a punch and knee a groin. But I'm not stupid enough to think that doing either of those things is going to impress my parents. In fact, it would infuriate them to the point of implosion.

The two annoying guys are a bit older, walk with that I'm-in-college swagger, and have that sharp-edged jaw of a frat boy with a money-to-burn-and-wallet-wielding daddy. I know the type as Henry was friends with many of them during high school and his two years of college.

"Hang out with us," Idiot One says. "It'll be fun."

"I'm not interested," I respond, "and I would appreciate it if you would leave me alone."

Idiot Two, the non-baseball cap wearing one, steps into my path. "But you really are beautiful. Blond hair, blue eyes, kicking body beautiful."

"I said *no*."

"Have you considered you don't know what you want? Come with us, and you won't have to make a single decision. We'll show you a whole new world. Listen to me, and I'll make sure you have a great night, beautiful."

Won't have to make a single decision. Beautiful. He must believe there's nothing in my skull beyond the beginnings of hair follicles.

My muscles tense, yet my perfectly practiced smile slips upon my face because Mom has told me to never let my anger leak out in public. I hate the word *beautiful*. Hate it. The word *beautiful* somehow gives the world permission to make wrongful assumptions about me, like that I don't have a brain. Beautiful somehow gives men permission to say the phrase as a secret password in my direction, and I should therefore fall at their feet. Beautiful makes people believe they can say anything they want about or to me and that I shouldn't be angry.

Nothing in the universe could be more wrong.

Disapproving of their existence, I force the smile higher and have a pretty good feeling that it's starting to appear as nasty as my current thoughts. I then step out of the path of Idiot Two and over in the direction to my game of choice: Whack-A-Mole. There is a large snake calling my name, and I will be the victor.

Unfortunately, Idiot One and Idiot Two have never been taught kindergarten social cues, and they follow.

"You look familiar," one of them says, and my internal warning system flares.

For most people, I'm a case of déjà vu. One of those big, white fancy furry cats that crosses their path more than once, and it causes their mind to glitch. I'm not nearly famous enough that people follow me on the streets, but I'm more of a mere shadow of a newspaper clipping memory: I'm the governor's daughter.

Best course of action? Push them away. It would mortify my mother, but if, for some strange reason, she learns of this, I'll claim it as an accident.

I glance over my shoulder as I loosen the cap on my Pepsi. "Really? Who do I remind you of?"

"I can't remember. A movie star maybe?" Idiot One brightens like me responding means I agreed to strip naked in the back seat of his car and have sex. Me hooking up with them is somehow a reality in their pathetic lives. I'm half wondering what their success rate is, and if it is high, there should be a mandated course on how girls are to avoid guys like them.

"Which movie star?" I spin on my toes, "accidentally" lose my footing, fall forward and my much-anticipated Pepsi becomes a sacrificial lamb. Brown fluid drips down the shirts of both boys, because I'm just talented that way.

"Oh, my gosh." Hand to my mouth, fake wide eyes. "I'm so sorry. You should go dry off. Get some napkins. There are a million sweat bees here, and if you don't clean up, they'll swarm."

Death stare in my direction complete with splotched red face from Idiot Two. "You did that on purpose."

Yes, I did, and it's hard not to smile when the first sweat bee lands on his arm. *Sting, buddy. Just do it. I'll forever be grateful if you cause him pain.*

"Come on." Idiot One places a hand on Idiot Two. "Let's go."

My fingers flicker in a shoo motion, and I finally turn my back to them. They can either go clean themselves up or die of sweat bee stings. Either option works for me. Now, it's time for me to be normal for a few minutes. Well, to be normal and win. I'm sure normal people are also highly competitive.

The red light in front of me flashes, bells ring and I raise my arms in the air, savoring my victory. I even mimic the dance I performed in my limited and excruciatingly failed days as a cheerleader for Pee Wee football by slightly swinging my hips side to side.

I split my "v," I dot my "i,", I curl my "ctory." Pee Wee football cheer taught me I not only lacked rhythm, but I lacked enthusiasm for my team when it was thirty degrees and raining. But in my defense, how many six-year-olds love cold rain?

The group next to me toss their padded mallets onto the

game. Only one groans as if their loss was monumental. The rest laugh and good-naturedly tease each other. They've been fun to beat. For three games in a row, these two rugged guys and two girls have hung with me. Three times digging into their pockets to ante up, three times we've trash-talked the other in ways that are only done on fair midways, three times each one bites the dust.

Whack-A-Mole is not for the faint at heart. This game is for the serious, and only the serious win, and I'm a serious type of girl when it comes to carnival games and hard-earned stuffed animals. Someone's got to play and win, and it's going to be me.

For a few minutes I forgot I had to be perfect, and being just me felt great.

"Good game." One girl of the group offers me her fist, and the multiple bracelets on her wrist clank. She's my age, has curly black hair in tight rings and friendly dark eyes. Her clothes, I love. Tight jeans, a tank that ends at her midriff and a jeweled chain around her flat, brown stomach that's attached to her belly button ring. She has a daring grin and style. Both I admire.

I'm not the type to fist-bump, and by how long I've hesitated, the girl's aware this is out of my territory. I finally do fist-bump her, though, because I'm not only highly competitive, but I rarely back down from a challenge. For those reasons alone, it's amazing my mother lets me out of the house. "Good game."

Her grin widens, and I hold my breath as she tilts her head in that familiar déjà vu. I silently pray for her to shake it off, and when she does, turning so she can talk to her friends, I blow out a relieved breath.

Most of her group appears to be the same age as her, about the same age as me, except one guy who I'd hedge is in his twenties. By the way they all listen when he talks, it's apparent he has their respect.

I watch them longer than I should because a part of me envies the way they all seem to belong to each other. Henry is twenty-four and loves me, but about the only thing we have in common is my parents, and he hasn't talked to them in two years.

The carnie clears his throat, and I'm drawn back to the sounds of people laughing on rides and the scent of popcorn. I offer the pink-and-black-striped medium snake I've already won to him and motion with my index finger that I'm on the hunt for the massive, big daddy snake that could wrap around my body a few times. To the victor goes the spoils.

The carnie doesn't accept my medium snake and instead hands me a green-and-black-striped small one. "You have to win four times in a row in order to get the big one."

Four times. Good God. At five dollars a game, I could have bought five of these hardened toys, but that's not the point. Winning is the actual prize.

I pull my cell out of the small purse I have crossed over my body. I ignore Andrew's "Where are you?" texts and check the time. I've got an hour to make it back to the convention center, change and be ready for Dad's press conference where it is my job to sit, smile and "look pretty."

If I'm really careful, there won't be time for my mother to berate me for taking off without Andrew. He's a friend of the family a few years older than me, and my mother chose him to "babysit" me for the afternoon. She allowed me to go to the midway with the understanding I was to tag along with him. But I don't like Andrew and Andrew doesn't like me, so I turned right while he walked left and neither of us looked back to see if the other was following. Maybe Andrew will rat me out that I abandoned him. Maybe he won't. Either way, I'm happy with my choices.

Any way I look at it, I have time for at least one more game. I flip my blond hair over my shoulder and give a tempting grin that's meant to rub it in that I not only won, but won three times in a row. "You know you guys want to play again."

You know you hate being beaten by me.

From the expressions of the guys, I pegged them correctly. The girls...I could totally become best friends with because they knowingly laugh at their expense.

"I'll play." It's a small voice belonging to a child, and my smile falls. Long unruly ringlets over a chubby preschool face. She stands on her tiptoes to hand money to the carnie, and he accepts it without giving her a second glance. "I'm going to win this time. I have to. Daddy says it's my last game."

The aforementioned daddy hands another five dollars to the carnie worker and picks up a mallet next to his daughter's spot. Ugh. Knife straight to the heart as he throws me a pleading glance. He wants her to win. He needs her to win. He wants me to help her win.

I totally hate being conned, but if I'm going to lose, it will be to a five-year-old.

"Are you going to play?" the carnie asks me because it's his job to make money. I want to answer no, but because I was once five and my father did the same thing for me, I fork over my five dollars, then tilt my head in a princess-worthy stare over at the boys.

It takes four to play, and I need one of them to lose so this kid can win. They glance at each other, waiting to see which one is going to man up.

"Your ego can handle being beaten by a five-year-old," I say.

A guy in their group that had been hanging back strides up. "I'll play."

For a second, there's a flutter in my chest, the lightest touch of butterfly wings. I secretly wish this guy would chance a look in my direction, but he doesn't. Instead he hands the carnie five dollars and claims the spot next to me.

Wow. I'm definitely okay with this.

He's taller than me and he's in worn blue jeans. His white T-shirt stretches against his broad shoulders, and he's gorgeous. Drop-dead gorgeous. The defined muscles in his arms flex as he switches the mallet from one hand to another, and I've stopped breathing. His blondish brown hair is shaved close on the sides, but the rest of his longer hair is in complete disarray. His freshly shaved face reminds me of a modern day version of James Dean, and everything about him works well. Very well.

I'm staring, I need to stop and he's also aware that I'm staring and haven't stopped. He turns his head, our eyes meet and those butterflies lift into the air. Warm brown eyes. That's when I'm finally scared into having the courage to glance away. But I peek back and sort of smile to find he's now looking at me like he can't stop.

For the first time in my life, I like that someone is looking. Not someone—him. I like that he's looking at me.

"We let her win," I whisper.

He nods, and I lift my mallet. It's tough to not get into position—to be poised and ready to strike. I love this game, I love winning, and losing to be nice is all fine and good, but I have to fight the instinct to go full throttle.

"You're good at this," he says.

"I play this game a lot. At every fair and festival I can. It's my favorite. If there were an Olympic event for Whack-A-Mole, I would be a gold medalist several times over."

If only that were enough to make my parents proud—or to make a living at when I graduate from college.

"Then I'm in the presence of Whack-A-Mole royalty?" The laughter in his eyes is genuine, and I watch him long enough to see if he knows who I am. Some people do. Some people don't. I've learned to read the expression of recognition, and he has no clue who I am.

My body relaxes. "Totally."

One corner of his mouth edges up, and I become tongue-tied. That is possibly the most endearing and gorgeous grin I've seen. He twirls the handle of the mallet around in his fingers, and I'm drawn by the way he makes the motion seem so seamless.

This incredible fantastic humming begins below my skin. To be brutally honest, I'm not sure what attraction is. My experience with boys has been limited, but whatever this is, I want to feel it again and on every level of my being.

The bell rings, my heart jumps and I inhale when the worn plastic moles pop up from the holes. The instinct is to knock the hell out of them, but the tinkling laughter of the little girl farther down causes me to pull back. I hit one. Then another. I have to score something. She needs to think we at least tried.

The guy next to me hits a few moles, but in a rhythm. A crazy one. A catchy one. One that my foot taps along with. The bell rings, the little girl squeals and my hopes of winning the large snake die.

A chirp of my cell, and I immediately text back my mother: Still at the midway. Heading back now.

Mom: Hurry. I think we should curl your hair for the event.

My hair, my outfit. That's what's important to her. I squish my lips to the side. It took her an hour this morning to decide she wanted me to wear it straight. Then it took her another hour to decide what I should wear on the midway, in case I should be recognized. Then there was the painstaking additional hour to decide what I should wear to the press conference.

When I look up, disappointment weighs down my stomach. The boy—he's gone. Not really gone, but gone from beside me. He's rejoined his group, standing with them and belonging. I will him to glance one more time my way, but he doesn't.

That's okay. I'm just a girl on a midway, he's just a boy on a midway and not everything has to end like a daydream. Truth is, once he found out what my world is really like, he'd have taken off running.

But I have to admit, it would have been nice if he had at least asked for my name.

HENDRIX

HOLIDAY SMACKS MY ARM AND WRATH OWNS her eyes. "Why didn't you talk to her?"

I glance around at my family—Axle, Holiday, my best friend, Dominic, and his younger sister, Kellen. I'm searching for at least one of them to have my back and tell her to step off, but instead they're curious for the answer. Even Axle's giving me a questioning gaze, and the last thing my womanizing brother deserves is an explanation from me in my decisions regarding women.

Last time I was home, his reputation was as bad as Dad's, minus the progeny. There are three siblings in this family, and we have three different birth mothers. Dad not only didn't know how to use a condom, but he didn't know how to stay true to one woman.

"I talked to her."

My younger sister throws her arms out and drops her voice to what I'm assuming is to mimic me, but I don't sound like an idiot. "You're good at this." She resumes her normal tone which is entering high-pitched. "Seriously? That's all you've got? Did you get some sort of amoeba that eats your brain while hanging out in juvie?"

I fold my arms over my chest and wonder if my sister can read pissed-off body language.

"You can still catch the girl and talk to her," Holiday continues, proving she doesn't care I'm silently informing her to quit. "Don't make me chase her for you because that would be embarrassing. Embarrassing for you. Not me. I'll have to tell her you sent me, and because you're a wuss, I'll have to ask her out for you like we're in sixth grade."

I find myself missing the middle of nowhere. Trees, bonfires, mosquitoes, mud, bears...company that didn't talk.

"She's out of my league." I haven't spoken truer words in months. She was beautiful. She was poised. She was a cool breeze after a hot humid rain. She was that first ray of sunshine in the dark woods. She was the smell of honeysuckle in bloom. She was the first damn thing that made me forget who I am and what I've gotten myself into over the past year. That means she was out of my league.

Granted, she was out of my league before I was arrested. Everything from her manicured nails, to her brand-name clothes, to her high-end purse, to the way she held herself said she was about a hundred times higher on the social and economic spectrum than me, but the person I was before would have made the play because I was smooth—just like my father.

"She is not out of your league." Holiday hounds me. "She smiled at you. I know when a girl likes what she sees, and she liked what she saw in you."

Tension builds in my neck. Yeah, the girl smiled, but she didn't know what she was smiling at. I'm a pretty façade on the outside. On the inside, I'm a house of cards teetering on a bad foundation.

Axle throws an arm around Holiday's shoulder and edges her away. "Let's get some food. Drix is going to have to talk soon, and we don't want him to do it on an empty stomach. Passing out on TV isn't a great first impression."

Wouldn't want that to happen, would we?

"Hamburger?" Axle calls as he walks backward for the food truck. "With everything?"

I nod. My brother knows me...at least who I used to be.

"I'm agreeing with Holiday on this," comes a deep rough voice to my right. "Pathetic."

I do a slow head turn toward my best friend and cock an eyebrow at an even slower rate.

He smirks at my expression. "We picked a game we always let you win, and you didn't even try."

They picked that game because I used to kick their asses at it, and they were trying to get me to be the old Drix. But I only offer one sloppy lift of my shoulder because I don't know how to explain that it's tough to engage.

"It's creepy hanging with you," Dominic continues. "It's like you're the Walking Dead. I'm half expecting someone to jump out with a samurai sword and slice out your heart."

"Brain," Kellen corrects as she adjusts the Spider-Man beanie on her head. It's a hundred degrees outside, and she wears that hat like it's thirty below. "They'd take out his brain."

"That, too."

Dominic and Kellen stand side by side. Siblings who look and act nothing alike, except for their attachment to me and my family.

Kellen's barely sixteen, the baby of our group. She's blond braids with black bows at the ties, and she wears her beloved fitted black Captain America T-shirt and worn jeans with rips. It's weird seeing her with lip gloss and eye shadow. I'm betting that would be Holiday's doing, but at least Kellen's somewhat the same.

Since we were kids playing baseball in the street, Kellen's been a sucker for a comic book hero. It gives the possibility to her that the world might make sense. Good guys in one corner. Bad guys in the other. It's how Kellen found her way to survive in a very gray household.

Something about her makes me feel protective. Maybe it's how Dominic hovers over her. Maybe it's because Kellen still has the limp from a bad bone break she got when she was eight. Maybe because playing hero to her might make me redeemable.

"I'm the Walking Dead because I didn't play a game?" I ask.

Dominic jerks his thumb toward the game. "Because you didn't hit on the girl."

The girl no longer needs to be part of our conversation. I liked her. She liked me. I'm on parole for a crime I didn't commit. A plus B doesn't equal C in this equation.

"And you only played after we lost. How much did we lose? Three games, five dollars a shot. That would be…"

"Fifteen dollars," Kellen says, the math freak that she is. Don't get me wrong, I respect the hell out of her for it. I'll also admit her nonstop ticking brain scares me. Someone that smart is going to take over the world—in a lab-coat, stroking-a-cat, manic-laughter type of way.

"Fifteen dollars," Dominic echoes. "Times five."

"Seventy-five dollars," Kellen pops in.

"Seventy-five dollars in total. Just to get you to play."

"I never said I wanted to play," I say.

"But I wanted that snake. That girl is walking away with my prizes. You've been gone a year, and you can't help a brother out? That would have completed my collection."

"He needed the pink one," Kellen adds.

"See, my world is now incomplete."

Dominic grins, and I can't help the automatic grin in return. It feels strange on my face, especially when joking with him used to be as natural as breathing.

Where Kellen makes me feel like I need to clear the path, Dominic is a category five tornado; a broad-shouldered brick wall. He has to be for the neighborhood we grew up in. He has to be because his home is even worse, and he considers himself the protector of him and his sister.

The deep scar across his forehead tells one of many war stories. So does the long one on his arm from a surgery when he was ten. He has black hair, blue eyes and is a good guy to have in a tough spot. My best friend is cool on the outside, but deep down he's two pieces of uranium always on a collision course. He's volatile. Too many emotions and nowhere safe to store them. They stew until there's an explosion, and Dominic hates explosions. He hates fallouts. Most of all—he hates tight spaces.

But he loves a guitar, loves music, and from all the letters and emails he sent while I was gone, he loves me. Kellen,

Dominic and I are more than friends. We're family, and I've missed my family.

"You let us down," Dominic continues. "We got beat by some little blonde, and she was a sore winner. And the worst part? I didn't hit on her because she smiled at you, you smiled at her, and I thought you were settling in and returning to playing the game."

"You didn't hit on her because she would have laid you out flat with her no." I mock a jab to his jaw. "That girl was fireworks."

Kellen smiles at the dig, Dominic snorts, and a heaviness avalanches onto me. There's a pause they're waiting for me to fill because that's what I used to do: announce what's next, but I don't have a next. This should be easier than what it is, and I hate that it's not.

"Dominic," Axle calls from a food truck. "Get over here and help."

Kellen starts before Dominic does because where she goes, Dominic does, too.

Dominic steps forward then stops. His shoulder next to mine. Us facing two different directions. It's the first time we've been alone since before I was arrested, and I lower my head as the two million things I've wanted to say to him become stuck in my throat.

With the way he sucks in a breath, he's feeling the same.

My heart beats faster at what he might say and what I might say in return. Did he do the crime? If so, will he confess? What about beyond the crime? Will he bring up how he screwed me over the night I was arrested? Does he have the balls to explain how he left me high and dry, and will he apologize for that? If he does, can I forgive him? Because I've struggled with that—forgiveness. It's not something that occurs naturally for me.

Dominic angles his head so he's looking at me, waiting for me to lock eyes with him, but I can't. I watch the blonde as she walks the midway. She's beautiful. Possibly the most beautiful girl who's talked to me. When she smiled at me, it was like I was being warmed by the sun, and I was her only planet. What I envy is that she seems to know where she's going, where she's headed in life. I've never been so jealous of anyone.

"I'm going to make this up to you," he says.

Sharp pain in the chest. Of all the ways I saw this moment playing out, those weren't the words I imagined. It's not an apology for leaving me behind. It's not an admittance of guilt. It's a promise.

In my final therapy session in the woods, sitting next to a bonfire I created, my therapist asked what would help me transition back into the real world. I told him I needed the truth. He told me there's no such thing, but he did tell me that forgiveness was real.

Forgiveness. In my mind, forgiveness and the truth go hand in hand.

"Why did you leave me behind that night?" I ask because I've waited a year for that answer, and I can't wait anymore. Not if Dominic and I are going to be friends again. "We had a pact—never leave one of us behind, and you left. Why?"

"I thought you went home."

"I didn't, and you need to admit you didn't try to find me. Something big had to have happened for you to have ditched me. What was it?" Or did he really think I was gone from the store and saw that as his opportunity to rob it?

"Dominic!" Kellen calls, and she's juggling several drinks. "I need help."

Yes, his sister needs help, but I need help, too. I look straight into his eyes, and there's no way he doesn't see the plea in them to talk to me, but he doesn't talk. Instead, Dominic pats my back and heads to help his sister.

That night, Dominic had walked me to the convenience store, and dared me to shoplift, but then disappeared, and I passed out behind the store. I was too drunk and too high to know my own name, and he left. Disappearing, leaving anyone he loved behind, wasn't his style, but he was desperate for money. Did his desperation cloud his judgment when it came to me and our friendship?

And that night, Holiday was closer to the crime scene than I had known. Both of them had something to gain, both of them felt as if they had nothing to lose and both of them had motive.

But it's hard to imagine Holiday holding a gun. Dominic, on the other hand, he was capable of aiming a gun, and at the time, he was crazy enough to pull the trigger.

Good thing that bullet missed the store clerk or I would have been charged with more than robbery with a weapon and attempted assault. Manslaughter would have messed up my day—for twenty years.

Do I know for sure Dominic did it? No. There's a chance my sister let her ramped-up emotions control the decisions for her that night and that she talked Dominic into it. But 80

percent of me believes it was him alone—my best friend—
and I don't know how to live with that yet.

Ratting him out to the police was never an option, because no matter what, I love him. Dominic can't handle tight
spaces, and I could. Dominic wouldn't have survived. I did.
I roll my shoulders, but the tightness in my neck doesn't go
away. How can I forgive someone who won't admit guilt?
How can I forgive when I don't know who to forgive?

Axle joins me. "We found a table over by the merry-go-
round."

Soon I have to announce to the world I'm a criminal, even
though I'm not. Sealed records and the truth won't mean anything once I open my mouth in front of reporters. Guess the
therapist was right on the truth. It doesn't exist.

"I need a few minutes to myself." Food doesn't sound appealing anymore.

"I've got your dress clothes in the car. Meet there in a half
hour?"

"Yeah."

Axle returns to our family, and I walk forward, in the same
direction as the blonde. Her path has to be better than mine.

Ellison

IDIOT ONE AND IDIOT TWO HAVE MADE A RE-emergence, and like all things that have died and have been brought back like a zombie, they return more grotesque than before. The dumb duo call out taunts as they follow. Each shout more degrading than the last, each shout causing my blood to heat to the point of melting steel.

"Are you one of those girls?" one calls out. "The type who needs to be shown what to do? Come here, and I'll show you exactly how it's done."

They both laugh, congratulating the other for their wittiness. My fists clench, and I glance over my shoulder. Idiot One slides his hand down to his crotch and says, "Don't you know a guy's—" ringing of a game next to me "—goes into…"

His comment is muffled by the screams of people on the Tilt-A-Whirl, but I can read his lips, spot what he's grabbing at, and tears burn my eyes. I could smack myself. Tears. I'm so incredibly mad my eyes are filling with tears because that's what happens when I get furious, and that only causes me to get angrier.

I swipe at my cell and text Andrew. Where are you?

Andrew: Midway crowded. Still on my way to you.

More frustrated tears that I lowered myself to asking Andrew for help, but it's either that or tell the college boys off in a very public way. My instincts are informing me another Pepsi bath will cause them to morph into Satan's grandchildren.

I scan the area, hoping for an ally, but there's no one who seems interested in the position beyond a few moms whose hot expressions suggest they'd shoot the guys behind me if they had a carry-and-conceal license.

But those moms have children, and their job is to protect them. The rest of the crowd fleetingly glimpse at me then at the jerks, but choose to remain silent. There's this unwritten code in society that tells us not to get involved.

Options:

Stay the course, continue to listen to their taunts and eventually reach Andrew, so I can keep up the appearance of being a sane person.

Destroy my pride and run while people stare.

Grab that baseball on the game ledge, throw the ball straight and hard like Henry taught me, hope it knocks one of them out and then inform the other one in really big words I not only know, but can spell, the exact route he can take to hell.

The third option is my favorite, it's the one that is my most honest reaction down to the core of my being, but doing that will disappoint everyone but Henry. I promised Mom and Dad I would never lose my temper in public, that I would never let my emotions crack beyond the surface.

"Hey, you!" one of the guys calls. "Let me show you a girl's mouth is for—"

Another round of happy screams from a ride, yet I catch the tail end of his statement. My body whiplashes forward as my feet abruptly become concreted to the ground. The sights and sounds of the midway fade, and all I hear is buzzing. I close my eyes as more pissed-off tears fill my eyes. Why won't they go away?

"You okay?" a guy asks.

I open my eyes and focus on the ground. My eyes are red, I know they are. I can feel the puffiness of my skin. I take a deep breath, look up to explain I'm okay, and freeze.

Holy hell. It's the boy from Whack-A-Mole. He's so much more breathtaking this close, and I have no idea how that's possible.

"Are those guys bothering you?" he asks.

My forehead furrows. Yes, they are, but telling him the truth and inviting him into my problems seems wrong.

"Since you're so talkative, I'll start the conversation," he says. "If you want to get rid of those guys then stand here and talk to me, and I'll stand here and talk to you. You can smile like you know me because it's tough to make me smile, and it will seem fake. Then I can try to win you a stuffed animal. Won't be a snake, but it will do. Those losers will catch on we're friends. Eventually, they'll keep walking, and then they'll return to their loser frat house where they'll play with themselves for the rest of the night because they don't know how to properly talk to a girl."

I blink because all thought processes have taken a mini break. Either that or I'm having a stroke.

"Just a smile. Maybe a few mumbled words. Tell me any-thing. Doesn't have to be poetic. Just your lips moving in my direction without your current blank expression."

I blink again, many times, as the sights, sounds and smells of the midway blast back as if someone had pushed the play button on my life. I flash the perfectly practiced public smile I've used too many other times in my life.

"I don't know how to get them to leave me alone." I pause, then the bitterness leaks out as well as a grim grin. "At least not without a baseball and a well-placed throw. Some people shouldn't be allowed to continue their genetics."

The right side of his mouth tips up, and my eyes narrow on him. "I thought you didn't smile easily."

"I have a twisted sense of humor, and I didn't think a girl like you could make me laugh. You've done it twice now. That's a record for the past year."

I bristle, still on the dangerous edge of anger. "A girl like me?"

"Yeah, one that's out of my league. Listen, if you want to get out of this situation without it escalating, let me know. Otherwise, I'll take a step back, and you can do whatever you need. I'm all about helping, but I'm not looking to get into a fight. Your call on how this goes down, but if it's violence, you're on your own."

He says he doesn't want to partake in violence, but there's an essence about him that says he could drop anyone at any time and do it without breaking a sweat.

He's looking at me, I'm looking at him, and the flutter in my chest returns. "Thank you for the offer, but I can take care of myself."

Sure can. Just need that ball, a good throw, and then my mother will be seriously ticked off. I'm tired of people like those guys, and I'm also tired of pretending to be perfect. I rub my eyes at the exhaustion caused by the combination of both.

"Don't doubt you can," he says, "but you really think they're going to back off if you give them a reaction? And if you keep walking, do you think they're going to leave you alone? They aren't some third grade bully who'll run when you sock him in the nose, and ignoring them isn't working either. Guys like them get high off your anger, get off on your fear. Trust me on this one. I've spent almost a year in the presence of some real assholes."

"Why are you helping me?"

He lifts one shoulder like he doesn't know the answer or doesn't care he has an answer, yet he answers anyway, "I have a younger sister. You met her earlier."

It's not an explanation, but it is, and he inclines his head to the game. I move to stand in front of it, and as I go to retrieve money from my pocket, he shakes his head, and pulls out his wallet. "It's on me."

The anger that had been boiling in me retreats because him paying for this game feels old-school James Dean. "Thank you."

"You're welcome, but don't expect much from me. Odds are I'm going to lose."

The urge is to perform a sweep of the area to see where my tormentors have settled. Predators like that don't give up easily on their prey.

"They're off to our right," he says as if reading my mind.

"Next to the popcorn stand, but don't look at them. Don't give them the satisfaction of knowing they have power over you."

"They don't have power over me."

"Good." He lays five dollars on the table. The carnie takes a long look at him and then a long look at me as if we're a defunct science experiment, and eventually places three balls on the ledge.

The two of us are different. Complete sliding scale different. The only thing we have in common, as far as I can tell, is that he appears about my age and that we are both wearing shoes. My sandals to his scuffed combat boots. His sagging jeans with rips and white T-shirt to my ironed khaki shorts and fitted blue top. My diamond earrings and gold bracelet with a heart charm to his black belt that has metal studs and silver chain that hangs from his belt loop to his wallet.

By looks, I should have more in common with the loser college boys, but it's this guy I'm comfortable with. "What's your name?"

He throws the ball, and he's right, he sucks at it. While he has unbelievable power, his aim's completely off. The ball hits the back curtain with a loud thud, then drops to the floor. "Drix."

"Drix?" I repeat to make sure I heard him correctly.

"Drix. It's short for Hendrix. Like Jimi Hendrix."

"That's cool." Because it is.

I wait for him to ask for my name, but he doesn't. Instead he says, "Are you here alone?"

He throws the second ball, and this time he hits the top of the three bottles, sending that one to the ground.

"No. My parents are here. I'm supposed to meet them at the convention center. What about you? What happened to the people you were with? Or are you here alone now?"

"Yes, but no." Drix pulls his arm back, releases the ball and when the ball hits the bottom bottles, my heart lifts with the idea that he won, but only one of the bottles goes flying. The other stays completely untouched.

He turns in my direction, but his gaze roams over my shoulder, then flickers to the left. Drix then glances behind him, and when he returns his attention to me he raises his eyebrows. "They appear to be gone."

That's awesome news, but I'm still stuck on his answer of "yes, but no." Honestly, I'm stuck on him. He's a million questions without a single answer, and he makes me incredibly curious. "My parents weren't thrilled about me hanging out alone at the midway, but I didn't think it would be that big of a deal. It's just Whack-A-Mole, you know?"

"And a ball toss."

"And a ball toss. None of it should have been complicated."

"Shouldn't have been."

"Elle!" Part of me is relieved to see Andrew craning his neck over the crowd. Another part of me is majorly disappointed. There aren't many times in my life I'm left alone. Not many times I'm able to explore new places and people without someone hovering and not many opportunities when I would meet someone like Drix.

"Elle," Andrew calls again. I wave at him, hoping it will buy me a few seconds, and he waves back in a way that tells me he needs me to walk in his direction. That works well for me.

"Is that a friend of yours?" Drix asks.

"Yes, but no." I borrow his answer because it's apropos. Andrew's a few years older. More friend of our family than a personal friend of mine, and I don't like the idea of explaining that my parents think I need a babysitter.

Drix's mouth twitches at my words, and my lips also edge upward. "I just made you smile a third time. Is this a *Guinness Book of World Records* thing?"

"I liked your answer."

"I'm just creative like that."

This time, there's a short chuckle, and I like that sound almost more than I like him smiling. I kick at a rock before gathering my courage to meet his eyes again. "Thank you for helping me out."

"Don't worry about it."

I'm waiting, and I don't have much time. He needs to ask my name. He needs to ask for my number. I'll give him both—in a nanosecond. "I've got to go."

"It was nice to meet you," he says with all the smooth edginess that can only belong to a gentle rebel. It's like his voice was created to slay unsuspecting hearts.

Adrenaline courses through my veins because if I do this and he rejects me, I might as well tattoo a big fat L to my forehead and die of humiliation. "I'll give you my number if you want or you can give me yours…if you'd like. If you'd like to talk again or…hang. My name's Elle, by the way."

Drix rubs the back of his head like what I said made him uncomfortable, and I seriously want to crawl behind the game and die. I'm being rejected.

"Look." He hesitates, and my entire body flashes sickeningly vomit hot. "I meant what I said earlier. You're out of my league. Way out of my league. And it would be easy for you to think I'm a good guy because I stepped in."

And because he paid money to let a little kid win, but hey… who's keeping score?

Me. I'm keeping score.

"I just got home from being gone for a year, and I'm only interested in making friends. Besides, I don't want you to think I stepped in because I wanted your number. I ask for your number, and it'll come off that I'm saving the day to get something out of it. That's not why I did it. I stepped in because not all guys are assholes."

His voice just doesn't melt hearts, his words do, too, and this guy doesn't want my number. As far as rejections go, it could have gone worse.

"Let's go, Elle." Andrew cups both of his hands to his mouth. The sand must be narrowing down in the hourglass.

"Well…" Find something graceful. "Thanks for stepping in when you did…both times."

Drix inclines his head, and his dark eyes soften in such a way that I may as well become a puddle on the ground. "Anytime."

Why doesn't the world have a million guys like this? That should be one of my father's political agendas—create more gentlemen.

Drix turns away from me and walks toward the midway. I stay rooted to the spot because I don't want this moment to end. Some people live their whole lives for the past few minutes I just had, and I want to savor it a little longer.

This time, though, he glances over his shoulder to look at me. I smile. He smiles. That would make it number four. Guess I'm just talented like that, and then with a sigh, I leave.

HENDRIX

"LET ME MAKE SURE I HAVE THIS CORRECT." Cynthia leans forward, places her elbows on the table and has this starry-eyed take-me-to-bed expression that's going to get me into trouble. So far, my brother isn't nibbling the bait, but I don't have much luck left. Axle hooking up with someone involved in my future won't do me any favors.

"You've taken on custody of not only Hendrix, but your younger sister, as well?"

Axle is in the folding chair next to me, and he draws his long legs in as she edges farther in his direction. Cynthia introduced herself as my "handler" when we arrived ten minutes ago for the press conference. She's in a pink dress top, black pants and suit coat, and she's good-looking. Not as beautiful as Elle, though. Not as charismatic either.

My lips slightly edge up at remembering the fire in her eyes when she described her idea of taking out those guys with a baseball. I almost stepped back because I wanted to see her do it.

Have to admit, the girl put the fear of God into me. She had the most intimidating blue eyes. Eyes that made my heart pound, eyes that made me feel like she saw past my skin and into every crack, crevice and shadow. Eyes that made me feel alive. Eyes that also made me want to hide.

Girls like that are one in a billion. Shots with girls like that are even rarer. Another tally mark in the column of things I lost.

Cynthia laughs too loudly, and my brother and I share a side-eye-what-the-hell because Axle's comment about feeling too young to be a dad wasn't funny.

For the fifth time since I put on the white button-down shirt, black dress pants and tie, I pull at the collar. Between the humidity and the pressure at my neck, I feel like I'm choking. The convention center is air-conditioned, but there's also a thousand people worth of body heat.

We're sitting at a table near center stage. When Axle and I first got here, a group of kids were tap-dancing. They've left, so have their parents, and now reporters with cameras are preparing for the press conference. Time feels like it's speeding up while my thoughts are slowing down.

"Yes," Axle says to bring the conversation back around. "To taking on Holiday and Drix."

"You're so giving." Cynthia twirls her black hair around her finger. She's about Axle's age, and I don't know if it should bother me how inexperienced she acts for her job. Flirting with the older brother of the person you're in charge of should be at the top of the Don't Do playbook. "Not many people would give up so much of their life for their family."

I can't argue with that, but I'd still like her to leave us alone.

"How does your girlfriend feel about all this?"

Axle's chair squeaks when he scoots back. "I'm single."

"I didn't know. Sorry." Cynthia appears anything but sorry as she scribbles a few notes. "I know you said your father is out of the picture. How about Hendrix's mother?"

"They both gave custody to me," Axle says.

"I'm aware, but are they both out of the picture?"

"Legally," Axle answers, and I glance at him from the corner of my eye. He and I haven't talked about my mom or our dad yet. I haven't heard from Mom since my first month in juvie. Odds are she's drinking away her problems. That's where she was before I moved in with her, and where she was while I lived with her. Can't imagine that's changed. For Dad—Axle, Holiday and I have never been more than playmates for when he was alone and bored.

"Legally?" Raised eyebrow on her part.

"They won't be problems."

Satisfied with the answer, she moves on. "Do you want to run through what you're going to say again, Hendrix?"

I didn't want to go through it the first time. "No."

Cynthia's cell vibrates. She checks the message then lands her narrowed gaze on me. "You say exactly what's on that sheet. Feel free to read from it onstage. No one expects you to have it memorized. We will open it up to the press, and I have two reporters who have agreed to ask my questions. I have a few prepared answers typed up for you. Memorize those so you can rattle them off. Those I don't want you to read from the paper."

Axle frowns. "That happens? People are okay with you prepping the media?"

She waves his question away. "It's not something we do often, but we do want to seem transparent with this program. With Hendrix only being seventeen, we have two reporters who agreed to take it easy on him and ask simple questions. Oh, and, Axle, make sure you give me Hendrix's cell number."

"I don't have a cell," I say.

"I know." A bat of her eyelashes at Axle. "The moment you get it, Axle, I need that number. I have to be able to reach Hendrix to give him plans. But, of course, I'll use your cell in the meantime. And, Hendrix?"

Axle's phone pings, and a dark shadow crosses his face.

"What's wrong?" I ask in a low tone. Cynthia's close enough to hear, but she's not included in this conversation.

Axle slides his cell to me. The text is from Dominic: Holiday's boyfriend showed.

Fantastic. Last I checked, the ass wasn't invited. "Go."

"Drix," Axle starts, but I shake my head.

"Go. I'm good." My sister is more important than being grilled by my handler.

There's a pout to Cynthia's mouth, and she gives sad eyes when she tells my brother goodbye. Cynthia watches him leave, and when she turns back to me, she giggles over some joke no one told. It all seems forced, and it places me on edge. I drum my fingers on the table.

"You know Marcus would have been a better fit for your

poster child. He was the real leader." I don't know why I say it other than it's the truth. Marcus was my best friend through this past year's entire ordeal.

Cynthia regards me with interest, as if she's shocked I might have something intelligent to add to any conversation. "The position of spokesperson came down to you and Marcus, but the governor and his team believed you would be the better fit."

"He was the real leader."

"You became one, as well."

"I only became one because he pushed me to be better."

She flips her cell phone in her hand as she weighs our conversation. "The home life you have returned to is more stable than his. We believe that means you have a better shot of being successful in your return to society. It doesn't mean Marcus won't be successful, but it will be a tougher road."

"Should you be telling me this?" I ask, if only to annoy her like she annoys me. "Doesn't that break confidentiality?"

"I'm not telling you anything you don't already know."

True story. Marcus and I became tight, and the program's aware of this, even commenting on it several times. Thinking of him causes a sense of uneasiness, as if I'm unbalanced. I haven't heard from him yet. Yeah, it hasn't been long, but after talking to someone day in and day out for a year, I miss him.

"So I spoke with your therapist from the program," she says, "and he told me how you floated the idea of applying for the youth performing arts program at Henderson High School as part of your reentry strategy."

Oddly enough, there's a silver lining to Holiday's boyfriend showing—I never told Axle of my plans to apply to the youth performing arts program for my senior year. I haven't told him yet that there's a scrap of me that's considering applying for college. Before the arrest, my entire life was living one high to the next. No future. Just living in that minute. Going wherever my emotions dictated.

"You know this is a private high school, correct?"

I nod.

"You're hoping for one of the scholarship spots?"

I nod again.

"I know that the program promised to help in any way they could with securing your future goals. Specifically, I know that there had been some conversation of pushing along your application to help you secure an audition, but after much discussion, the governor's office doesn't feel that would be the best course of action.

"The performing arts program is extremely selective, and the competition to gain one of those spots into the school is fierce, especially with a transfer student about to start their senior year. Our involvement would send the wrong message to critics of the Second Chance Program, and alienate parents and students who have worked hard to claim those spots. So, instead, we are highly encouraging you to apply on your own. If you receive a spot in the program and are awarded money to go, won't it feel good to know you did it all on your own?"

She smiles then. Big white teeth against red lipstick. I didn't know I had hope until my gut twists. Getting in on my own. Like that'll happen. Will they trash my application when they see my transcript that's C's and below, or will they deep-six me when they read my essay of what I did on my summer vacation in juvenile detention?

"I agreed to being your poster child, and you guys agreed to get me the audition." I can hold my own in the audition. There might not be much substance to me, but I'm good at music.

My current high school is a holding cell for teens between stints in juvie. If I want more for my life, then I've got to start making some major moves fast. Music was the only good thing about me before the arrest. Maybe music will keep me on track. That youth performing arts program was my best hope at building a résumé that could possibly get me into college. "I never asked for you to get me in. I only asked for the audition."

"Well, we can't," Cynthia snaps, and after she briefly closes her eyes she returns to fake cheerful. "We would love to help, but you're our model for the Second Chance Program. Hopefully, the entire state will know who you are soon and will know that the governor's program is successful. But we can't do anything that will bring criticism to the program. That includes the governor's office calling in a favor. These things get leaked. How the public and media perceive this program is crucial. I'm sorry, but this is how it has to be."

"You think they're going to give an audition to a juvenile delinquent?"

"Your records are sealed."

"But my transcript will speak for itself, as well as any explanation on time gaps in my education. Part of being in the program was your promise to help all of us in our future plans. Since I'm your circus monkey, that promise no longer applies to me? If so, I'm not seeing the benefit of going onstage."

"Being the spokesperson was part of your plea deal. You're choosing to see this in a negative light. You have no idea how this will play out until you apply for the program. Try thinking positively. Good things will happen if you remain positive."

I stand abruptly, the seat beneath me cracking against the floor with the movement. "I'm going to let you in on a secret—hoping and wishing food would appear when I was younger didn't work. Scamming people outside of grocery stores did. So I *do* know how it's going to play out. The boy who has nothing is once again going to get screwed."

Not how I should be talking to my handler, but it's better than the string of four-letter words I'd rather be yelling.

My therapist told me when I couldn't handle my emotions to remove myself from the situation. So I turn away from Cynthia and begin to walk.

"Don't go far," she calls out.

She shouldn't worry. That leash she has me on is so tight it's cutting off blood flow, and it's so damn short, I'm surprised I haven't fallen prone to the ground. At least now I know the score, and once again I'm on the losing end.

Ellison

"NO MORE BRINGING ANIMALS HOME," MOM says in front of an entire room of people, and it takes an amazing amount of self-control to not let my face show how mortified I am by her public admonishment. We're in a private room at the conference center, and the clock ticks down for Dad's press conference.

"The dog you brought home yesterday made a mess in the laundry room. There was mud everywhere, and it growled at me. How could you bring home something dangerous?"

"He didn't growl with me."

"He was feral."

"He was lost." Annoyance thickens my tone. "Someone needed to help him."

"That someone isn't you. I'm serious. No more. I'm tired of coming home and wondering if there's going to be some rabid beast waiting to eat me when I open my front door."

The poor thing had curled up with me. I fed him, gave him

a bath in my tub, fed him again and then he rested his head on my lap and eventually closed his eyes. I loved him from the moment his dark, scared eyes first looked in my direction. "You probably spooked him when you opened the door to my room. He wasn't alone in there but for three minutes."

"Elle," Dad says my name with finality. He's lectured me easily a hundred times: no more bringing animals home, no more talking back to my mother, no more arguing. Just do what I'm told.

"Can everyone give us a few minutes?" my dad asks the room. "Elle, you can stay." Very rarely does my father ask me to leave, since my parents love to keep a close eye on me.

In the mirror, my eyes meet Andrew's, and I try to gauge if he became a tattletale. Andrew is twenty-two, is royalty in this state, and his family and my family are good friends. His grandfather is the current and retiring US Senator. While his grandfather is well loved and respected, Andrew is sought-after, and I understand why. He's gorgeous with his blond hair, green eyes and built body. Plus, he stands to inherit a fortune.

But Andrew and I are complicated. Not only am I the "little sister burden," but at thirteen I confessed my undying love for him. He laughed, I cried and, since then, there's been a sense of embarrassment that includes my face morphing into crimson when I spot his amusement.

Today, I'm able to keep my embarrassment in check. Andrew's been gone a year to study abroad in Europe, and the break has helped me realize he was mean to laugh at a thirteen-year-old. It also made ditching him earlier much easier than expected.

Andrew smirks as he walks over to me, and I immediately

pull my gaze away and pretend to smooth out my dress. He presses a hand to the small of my back as he leans in. Years ago, my heart would have leaped at his touch and at how incredibly close his lips are to my ear, but now all I can think is...*jerk*.

"Don't worry," he whispers. "I didn't tell."

My eyes dart to his in the mirror again, and he waggles his eyebrows. Andrew, even after a year, still finds me amusing.

"I'm assuming you're waiting for me to say thank you."

"Why the bitterness? You used to love it when I babysat you."

Babysat. He needs to be in pain. I check the mirror to see if my parents notice us talking and discover my mother watching us with rapt and joyous attention. Kneeing Andrew in the groin wouldn't meet her approval.

"I'm a big girl," I say under my breath, "and I don't need you anymore."

Full smile with straight teeth. "Been gone a year and I guess you're all grown up, Ellie."

"Guess so. And so you know, I go by Elle. Have now for a few years."

He chuckles and finally removes his hand. "See you later, *Ellie*."

Andrew bids goodbye to my mother and father, then leaves.

I pivot to confirm my sundress isn't riding too high in the back. It's beautiful, it's purple, thick-strapped with no scoop, made of material that feels like I'm being wrapped in soft feathers, and tailored just for me. But sundress does not mean serious. It means pretty, it means fun and this means I will once again smile for the camera and remain silent.

My mother still watches me. Today she slicked back her blond hair and pulled it into a bun at the nape of her neck. She's stylish in her white blouse and blue pencil skirt. People say we look alike, but other than hair and eye coloring, I don't know if we do. She's so poised, and I'm so different from her. She's ladylike, reserved and calm, and I'm…not.

"You look beautiful, Elle." Mom smiles in approval.

"Thank you." The response is so automatic I barely register it.

Mom's spent much of the past three years grooming me and teaching me how to react to people. As it's been explained to me thousands of times, someone is always watching. The media, my father's critics, current and future voters. What I do or don't do is forever a reflection upon my mother and my father.

Perfection. It's what the world expects of anyone in the limelight, especially from our leaders. Absolutely no pressure.

Speaking of zero room for error—there's a piece of paper in my bag of tricks that needs a parental signature: the permission slip to enter the final stage of the internship competition.

Success, at least in my parents' eyes in regard to me, is elusive. I have two left feet, I have no rhythm, no coordination and no athletic grace. I'm smart, I do well at school, but I'm not the kid who can rattle off the capitals of all the nations in the world, or has pi memorized past the sixth decimal place, or cares why I should have pi past the sixth decimal place memorized.

Sometimes it's tough to be the daughter of two extraordinary people and not be nearly as successful as them. While other people my age have found their passion and are on track to whatever greatness they're destined for, I have yet to figure out who I am and who I'm meant to be. But this internship is going to change that; I can feel it down to the marrow in my bones.

I inhale deeply and press my practiced smile on to my face. As I'm about to turn to gain their attention, Mom says, "Elle, come sit. We need to talk."

A hiccup is created in my brain because that was not part of my plan, yet I slip into a seat at the small table and take comfort in the quiet and closeness of my family.

My dad is in a white dress shirt, and his tie is undone. Dad loathes dress clothes. He's more relaxed in jeans and T-shirts, but people aren't fond of politicians in dress-down clothes. When Dad practiced medicine, he said his patients weren't particularly thrilled with the relaxed look either.

What I adore about Dad is how he gazes at Mom—like he's still one hundred percent puppy dog in love as when they met in college.

"Everything okay?" I ask. T-minus ten minutes to a press conference. Not typical heart-to-heart time.

Mom and Dad do that thing where they share hours' worth of conversation in a single glance. Someday, I want that special connection, but I'm not naïve. Their relationship is rare.

"Elle." Mom uncrosses her legs and edges forward in her seat so that her arms rest on the table. "Henry called your father today."

I perk up. Henry and Dad haven't talked for two years. Maybe the Cold War is finally thawing. "That's a good thing."

"Yes," Mom's answer is hesitant, "it is."

"Did you invite him to stay with us? I know he prefers

Grandma's when he's in state, but maybe if you asked him to spend time with us, he'll come home."

A sad shadow crosses my father's face. "I asked."

A ball of lead forms in my stomach and rolls around. I miss Henry at home, and Mom and Dad do, too. Henry came to live with us when his parents died when he was a child, and he became like a brother to me. But two years ago, Dad and Henry got into a terrible argument, and Henry left. To this day, his room is exactly the same as when he walked out, just dusted and vacuumed every two weeks. It's a living tomb.

Mom places her perfectly manicured hand over mine. Her eyes flitter over my flawed nails, thanks to playing the midway games, but she's gracious enough to know that I need a mom and not a campaign adviser on appearance. "He initiated a call, and that's a positive step."

I hope it is because I'm tired of being torn between the two shores of a large ocean. Henry and I talk. Obviously, I talk to Mom and Dad. The three just don't talk to each other. "What did he call about?"

"He's worried about you," Dad says. "He says you're miserable."

I withdraw from Mom and slump in my seat. Henry is a traitor. "I'm not miserable."

"You sure look happy," there's a tease in my father's tone.

A few weeks ago, I called Henry after a particularly rough fund-raiser for my father, and in my exhaustion and lapse of judgment, I might have cried a little too long to my cousin. If I had known that confiding in him would lead to this conversation, I would have never called him.

"Why didn't you tell us you were applying for an internship with Morgan Programming?" Dad asks.

My head falls back. Henry is dead. I'm going to have to kill him. He's the only person outside of school who knew about the internship, and he ratted me out to my parents. "Henry told you?"

"No, but your school called a few months back when you started the application process. I was wondering if the miserable Henry mentioned had any connection to this internship."

Gaped. Open. Mouth. "You've known about the internship?"

"Yes, and I've had the school update me every step of the way."

If I could fit into a sugar cube, I absolutely would. "Why didn't you tell me you knew?"

"Why didn't you tell us?" Mom counters.

All the air rushes out of my body because this is going to suck. "I didn't know if I'd make it to the final stage of the interview process or not." I didn't want them to know if I had, once again, become a failure.

"Do you have any idea what you've applied for?" Mom asks.

"It's a computer programming internship that will start in college and will last four years. I'm a finalist which means the last part of competition is to spend part of my senior year creating an app."

One of my elective courses during my senior year will be an independent study in creating this app, and I'm expected to start that independent study over this summer. Knowing that the last part might not go over well due to my schedule for my father's campaign, I keep that information to myself.

Mom purses her lips, and I can't decide what that means. "Computer programming? When did you become interested in that?"

I shrug because the answer is since freshman year when I took a class that sampled new careers every quarter, and one of those quarters was on programming. I liked it. I also liked drama club and about a hundred other things, so I never thought much about it, but the truth is... "I didn't give it serious thought until I saw the internship announced on the school's morning news. Something grabbed me, and I thought...why not?"

"Why not?" she repeats in a slow way as if the words are new to her.

"Why not," I say again and mentally add *why not, me?*

"Elle." Mom touches her throat in search of the gold locket that contains pictures of me and Henry. "You agreed to help your father with the campaign. In fact, we're paying you to help. You have a ton of scheduled appearances this summer. Then there is the fund-raising and..."

I sink lower in my seat. "I can still do all those things."

"You believe you can compete in this final stage of the application process and still have time?" Dad asks.

"Yes."

Dad shakes his head like I announced I'm attempting a solo trip to the moon. "Your counselor explained that the last stage of the application process is the equivalent to working a part-time job. How are you going to participate in the campaign, which requires traveling, keep up your grades in the fall and compete for this internship? I'm sorry, but it's not possible."

Dad's not seeing the bigger picture. The last stage of the application process is to create an app from scratch. My idea. My conception. My responsibility from birth to production. "Creating the app will be considered one of my classes in the fall, and I have the summer to work on it, as well. I have time."

"Twenty hours a week," Dad says. "That's the minimum the counselor said is expected of you to work on this program. Subtract the hours you'd work on the program at school, and that leaves fifteen hours to be done at home. I'm sorry, but I don't see how it's possible for you to create this program with the commitments you've already made to me and your mother."

The ends of my mouth turn down. "So you're saying I can't apply for the internship?"

Mom slides the locket along the gold chain. "What we're saying is that six months is your shelf life on anything. You try something new, you grow tired of it and then you flitter off. There's something about your personality that loves to chase the new and shiny."

"It's not like that this time." It's not like that most of the time. Shame overwhelms me and I stare down at the table. I don't grow tired of what I try as much as I grow tired of Mom and Dad waiting for me to be the best. When I don't somehow become a brilliant star in the new thing I'm trying out, it's akin to a failure.

"Elle." Dad wants me to look at him, but I can't. The table is the only thing I can focus on without feeling like the entire world is shattering. If I glance at Dad, what's left of my pride will be destroyed, and that's a loss in confidence that will take forever to repair.

"Elle," Dad says again with a more direct and demanding

voice. "I have a press conference. If you want to sit this one out, I understand, but I would like to finish this conversation before I leave. You're my daughter, I love you and nothing makes me more proud than when you stand by my side onstage."

My eyes flash to his then, because I want to make my father proud. I want him to want me by his side.

"We believe in you," Dad says. "But you don't understand commitment. Your mom and I do. We know what it takes to succeed."

Dad grew up dirt-poor and on government assistance. Mom, on the other hand, grew up in the lap of luxury, but her father was emotionally and physically abusive. Life for them was brutal, and they had to scratch, claw and bleed to make it out of their childhoods alive.

"We've had to learn tough lessons with nobody there to help. Your mother and I are trying to give you the benefit of our experiences. We're trying to keep you on an easier path and to give you everything we never had. Trust the decisions we're making for you.

"Plus, I don't know how I would feel if you were to win, and then you decline the internship. This is a large corporation in our state. A lot of eyes will be on you if you win. It would look bad on you and on me if you quit this like how you've bailed on most things."

He believes in me, but he doesn't. Somehow, through this conversation, I'm starting to no longer believe in myself.

"I'll tell you what." His face brightens like I haven't been smashed to pieces. "Let's pass on the internship, get through the summer and if you're still excited about programming,

and if we see a change in your understanding of commitment, we'll allow you to take a coding class in the fall. But
you have to give us a hundred percent this summer. Agreed?"

This is how Dad negotiates. He gives, I give, then we each
win. But my mind is a swimming mess as, for the first time,
this feels more like a dictatorship than a democracy.

Because I can't stand the twisting in my stomach at disappointing Mom and Dad, because I want to take a coding
class, I say, "Agreed."

Dad smiles, a beaming one reserved for me when he's
proud. He checks his watch, stands and kisses my forehead
before going on about how he'll give me a few more minutes
to collect myself before meeting him outside to walk together
to the press conference.

The door opens, then closes. I'm staring at the table again.
It's white, has a couple of coffee mug stains and the table isn't
interested in crushing my dreams.

"We're not doing this to hurt you." Mom's voice is soft and
sweet. If we were home, we'd be lying on my bed, and she'd
stroke her fingers through my hair. I'd be a millionaire if I
had a penny for every time this scene has played out between
us. "We're doing this to help you."

I suck in a breath and slowly release it. The good news
is that my chest aches less, so I guess I will survive the stab
wound that conversation created.

"Most people your age have a focus by now," Mom continues, and I wish she'd stop. Do other people's parents know
when to stop? Do they understand that less is sometimes more?

"Whether it be sports or academics or a hobby. We have
tried so many different things with you—dance, theater arts,

numerous instruments, what feels like a hundred different sports. We have given you a million opportunities for you to find your focus, but you never focus."

"The coding is different," I say. "When I'm programming there's this rush in my blood, and it just feels right."

Mom gathers papers in front of her and places them in a folder in such a slow motion that it's obvious she's thinking her next words through. "We've heard this before, and if your father and I weren't persistent with you helping him with the campaign, you would be graduating next year with a college application that says you have the inability to be focused and responsible. Do you really not see it? One of the reasons you were given a position in the campaign is because we need you to appear focused and driven. By having a steady position with the campaign over the past few years, you look exactly like a determined young lady ready to conquer the world instead of a teen who has no idea what she wants to do with her life. Yes, who your father is could open doors for you, but that's not what we want for you. Don't you want to be the woman who opens doors for herself?"

I nod, because I have never wanted things to happen because of my father.

"Life is cruel," Mom says. "It's hard. Don't be sad because your father and I are trying to help you avoid the roads that cause pain. Do you have any idea how much I wanted a parent who was involved and supportive when I was younger? Do you know how badly your father wished he had the opportunities you do? We're not trying to hurt you. We're trying to help."

Pain. It's something both of my parents understand. My

mother had every possession she could think of, but her father was a monster, and Dad's father died when he was young. While my father had a great mom, he understood hunger pains far more than anyone should. Yes, my grandmother had the land, but sometimes farming the land didn't pay out like they needed, and she stubbornly refused to sell.

Guilt pounds me like a hammer. "I should have told you about the internship."

Mom stands, places her fingers under my chin and forces me to meet her gaze. Her blue eyes are soft, the stroke of her finger against my hot cheek softer. "I love you, and I hate being harsh with you, but the next few months are crucial for your father and me. We need you. I can't help but think that if your father and I were more direct with Henry, like we're being with you today, that he'd still be a part of our family. Henry made terrible mistakes, and I don't want to see you make terrible mistakes, as well. I understand what real pain is, and everything I'm saying to you, everything I do for you, it's to keep you from that pain."

"Henry's happy," I whisper.

Mom grows incredibly sad. "He regrets his choices, and he's too proud to admit he needs our help. I'm starting to wonder if he's trying to turn you against us so he can make himself feel better—to justify his own bad choices. I know you love him, and I would never tell you to stay away from him, but I am asking you to be careful. Don't let him influence you away from us."

A tug-of-war. Mom and Dad pulling on one side. Henry on the other. Problem is, I remember how distant Henry was the summer before he left. Never home. Angry all the time.

Moody. It was as if an alien had taken control of his body. "What did Henry do?"

"He doesn't want you to know, and we promised we wouldn't tell. Someday, he'll come home, and we want to keep our promises. Just think of this as a lesson to listen to us. Henry didn't and he made a mess. You think you know what you want, but trust me, you don't. Seventeen is too young. Just let us make the decisions for you. You'll have the rest of your adult life to make all the decisions you want. But these choices now, they're too big for you to make and the consequences are too dire if you choose wrongly."

After all my parents have done for me, all the sacrifices they made, both of them coming from painful childhoods, I have to listen. Bruises for Mom, and a farm that barely broke even for Dad, yet they both climbed from misery to success.

I nod, Mom kisses my cheek and she leaves. I have three minutes until I have to pretend in public that the last few minutes didn't come close to breaking me.

Focus. Mom says I have none, but I do and I'm going to prove it to them. I have to be perfect over the next few months. Dot every i. Cross every t. Show them how passionate I am about coding and prove to them I have focus. I'll show them responsible. I'll wow them at every turn. I'll do everything they need me to do and more.

In the meantime, I have to lie one more time.

The world is eerily hazy as I cross the room, dig the letter out of my bag and unfold it. This letter doesn't go to the school, but to the company. My counselor won't know anything until the fall which means Dad has lost his mole.

I'll have to tell Mom and Dad, when classes resume, but

until then I have three months to write as much as I can on this code. By then, hopefully, I'll be so far into the project, they'll be amazed that I balanced a schedule full of being on the campaign trail, fund-raisers and this coding that they'll have no other option but to permit me the opportunity for the internship.

By the end of this, my parents will see me as a success.

HENDRIX

"YOU STAY HERE." CYNTHIA, AS IT TURNS OUT, has an intern. She's in college, and she points at the spot I'm standing in as if I'm a six-year-old with ADD. "Right here. Until the governor calls you onstage."

In the convention center, at the front of the stage, there are cameras. Row after row of them, and there are people next to them and people behind them. Also in the crowd are the people who have planned to come and see the governor talk, people who are tired of being in the blazing heat and are taking a break inside, and people who are curious to watch the circus.

Come one, come all. Watch the politician smile and lie. Then watch the poor boy say he's sorry for a crime he didn't commit, and while I'm at it, watch me pull an elephant out of my ass.

"Once you are onstage, the governor will shake your hand." Cynthia doesn't bother looking up from her cell as she talks to me, and with Axle not around, she's lost the sweet voice. "You will then turn to the podium. The speech is already there. Read it, I'll select the reporters, you answer the questions and when you're done speaking, look at me. I'll signal to you when it's time for you to walk offstage, and then you will go backstage and wait in the back room until I tell you it's time to go."

It's the last part that catches my attention. "Why do I have to go in the back?"

"In case a stray reporter would want to talk to you. You only talk to people I approve. If anyone ever approaches you without my consent, you tell them that they are to talk to me. Then you contact me immediately. Got it?"

One more chain locks itself around my neck. "Got it."

Applause breaks out in the crowd, and a man in a suit shakes hands with people as he slowly makes his way to the stage. It's our state's governor, Robert Monroe. I've never met him before. Feels weird since it's his program that saved me from hard time.

He passes me, his wife at his side, neither making eye contact as someone like me isn't worth their time. They then climb the stairs to the stage to join the other people in suits.

"The media loves her," Cynthia says.

"Who?" The intern rises on her toes to try to see around the crowd that's now focused on the next person coming up the aisle.

"The governor's daughter."

The governor's daughter. I've heard about her. Most everyone has heard about her. Holiday used to talk about her all the time. Something about her being beautiful and poised and up on fashion. Gotta admit, I didn't listen. I could care less about someone else's life.

The governor passes by me again, braves his way into the thick of people and when he reemerges, my heart stops. On the governor's arm is blond hair and intimidating blue eyes. It's Elle.

The world zones out.

I'm going to strangle my sister if she knew Elle was the governor's daughter and didn't say a word. *Damn.* I flirted with the governor's daughter. I scrub a hand over my face.

The man I have to impress in order to stay out of jail, the man who can tell my probation officer to flip the switch and send me back behind bars, I flirted with his *daughter.* I helped his daughter, but then I rejected her. Screw me. I can't catch a break.

"Ellison," a reporter calls. She turns her head, and flashes a smile. The reporters and the crowd see what I see—pure beauty in motion.

Elle scans the area, and her smile falters as surprise flickers over her face. But as quick as it's there, it's gone, and she returns to perfection. The upturn of her lips is sweet, it's gorgeous, but it's not the smile that caused me to feel like a moth to a flame. Earlier, I made her laugh, and she owned the type of smile that becomes seared into a man's memory.

Elle's bold. Bold enough to cock an eyebrow at me as she passes. A question as to what I'm doing here. I've been asking myself the same question for over a year. She walks up the stairs for the stage, and my stomach sinks.

To one person, for a few moments, I was the hero. Did I step in to help Elle? Yeah. But I also stepped in to help me.

Because I'm selfish like that. I needed to know, before I made an announcement to the world I'm a thug, that one person saw me as good.

Now I got nothing.

Elle's father walks her to the center of the stage, and the cameras remain on them, remain on her. Her smile stays steady, stoic. Her hand curls into the crook of her father's arm. The governor leans in, whispers something to her and there it is…that smile. The one where those intimidating blue eyes spark.

He covers her hand on his arm, and she raises up on her toes to kiss his cheek. Cameras snap, a sea of cell phones record every second. Then with one last glance at the audience, Elle slips to the back of the stage, next to her mother. Instead of watching the governor as he begins to speak, I watch her, willing her to look in my direction one more time.

Cynthia steps in front of me, blocking my view of Elle. "You ready?"

Adrenaline pumps into my veins, and I scour the area, searching for an exit. Dominic is the one who is claustrophobic, but since being home, I get it. I understand the overwhelming urge to bust out, the need to rip off the chains so I can breathe. But while Dominic's issues are with walls, my issue is my life. It's closing in on me, and there's no escape.

The governor's voice drones over the audio system, and he talks statistics. Numbers that prove that messed-up boys like me can be helped by people like him. He talks about destroying the school-to-prison pipeline, he talks about juvenile delinquents being given another shot, he talks about second chances and blank slates. My heart pounds in my ears.

"I said, are you ready?" Cynthia prods.

No, I'm not, but I walk for the stage stairs regardless.

My name is said, Hendrix Page Pierce, and the crowd claps. For what I don't know. The part of me that's a glutton for punishment wants to gauge Elle's reaction, but knowing I'll see disappointment, I keep myself from looking. Some things I don't need to experience.

I reach the podium, and in a motion so perfect it could have been practiced a million times instead of never, the governor and I shake. He places his other hand on top of our combined hands as if he has to prove he's in control. As if I don't know the score.

He leans forward to say, "I appreciate how much courage this takes."

I appreciate not going to adult prison.

"I've heard great things about you. I heard you're a leader. It's why we chose you to speak on behalf of the other teens like you, whom we're going to help."

A leader. Is he talking about the guy who carried other people's packs when they were too exhausted emotionally or physically to go forward? The guy who gave up his food when others were complaining they were still hungry? The guy who sat up at night with the two younger teens on the trip who were still scared of the dark?

That doesn't make me a leader. That makes me a good older brother.

The governor lets me go, inclines his head to the podium, and Dominic's loud two-finger patented whistle pierces past the polite applause. He's in the back, Kellen by his side, and when Dominic catches me looking at him, he flips me the bird while giving me a crazy-ass grin.

The familiar reminder of my family causes some of the knots in my stomach to unravel, and it gives me the courage to read the words. That's all they are, just words. Words that are unrelated. Words that don't mean anything to me. Words that hopefully won't mean anything to anyone else.

"One year ago, I made a mistake. One that put my life and the lives of others at risk."

The speech talks in circles about the crime, but it skips key phrases like convenience store, gun and stolen cash. "I was on a bad road that was going to lead to more mistakes. Mistakes that could never be forgiven."

I did make mistakes, and I was on a bad road. Living with Mom, I became her. Getting drunk, getting high. Thinking too much of myself, thinking I was as close to a god as a man could get when my mind was in a haze. That's what happens when someone flies too high: they get burned.

"Once arrested, I confessed to what I did wrong, and I was given a second chance."

I lift my head to look at Axle, who is now in the back. He has his arm around Holiday, and she has this beaming light about her like she's proud. I'm not someone she should be proud of, but I want to become that man. I want to be the brother she deserves.

"I'd like to thank Governor Monroe for picking me for his program. In it, I learned how to believe in myself. I learned who I am, and who I am is not the person I was before. I learned I'm capable of more than I could have imagined."

Light applause and Cynthia steps forward. "We're allowing a few questions."

More than two hands raise, and Cynthia points at a man. He introduces himself as a reporter from some newspaper in Louisville. "Can you tell us something you learned during your time in the wilderness?"

I learned I can be alone when I never liked being alone before. I learned the voices in my head that used to taunt me when I was high or alone aren't as bad as I used to think. I learned, sometimes, those voices have something worth listening to. Like stepping in with Elle. That was worth doing. "I learned how to survive. I learned how to make a fire with nothing but sticks and flint. If anyone needs a fire or help after the apocalypse, let me know."

Laughter and I glance over at Cynthia. She nods in approval. One down, one more to go, and I can get the hell off this stage.

"Another question?"

More hands go up, and as Cynthia goes to point, a man next to a camera yells out, "What crime were you convicted of?"

"Don't answer," Cynthia whispers to me, then motions to the man behind him. "Charles, you can ask your question."

"It's a valid question." The guy continues to talk as if she didn't ignore him. "How do we know he wasn't convicted of jaywalking? The type of changes the governor is promising with this program sound good, but how do we know if the results aren't skewed or tainted?"

My eyes shoot to the back of the crowd, straight to Axle, and my brother's face falls because we both feel it coming.

The tidal wave we felt the rumblings of in the distance is about to crest and hit the shore, destroying me in the process.

"What did you do?" the man shouts again, and when Cynthia turns toward me I see the question on her face. Will I do it? Will I answer and save the governor's program?

Blank slate. Second chance. Sealed records. All of it is bull.

Ellison

IT'S A TRAIN WRECK, AND EVERYONE IS WATCH-
ing. Someone needs to do something, and no one is moving.
Cynthia wants him to answer the question. It's also clear, Drix
doesn't want to answer, and I understand why.

"What difference does it make what he did?" I whisper in
hopes Dad will hear, but he's three people away.

My mother shushes me, and Sean, my father's chief of staff,
sends me a glare via certified mail. He and I live in mutual
distrust purgatory. To Sean, I'm supposed to be mute and
look pretty, but Drix helped me, and staying silent is wrong.

"Mom?" I say, and her head jerks at the sound of my voice.
Me speaking onstage without a teleprompter or typed speech
is the equivalent of me biting a newborn. "He shouldn't have
to answer."

"We'll talk about this later," she snaps in a hushed tone.

Lydia, my father's press secretary, walks to the podium with
that air of confidence that only she possesses. She's an intel-

ligent and beautiful black woman who has told me several
times that how you walk into a room defines who you are
before you open your mouth.

Whenever I see her, I believe this. She demands respect
from the moment she comes into view, and I envy her how
people so readily give it. "Mr. O'Bryan, I am kindly asking
you to wait your turn and wait to be called on before asking questions."

I've seen Lydia at work enough to know that the smile
she just flashed Mr. O'Bryan, a loser reporter who has hated
my dad for years, is telling him to shut up. There is a hum
of uncomfortable chuckles from the families, and Lydia goes
on to explain that Drix is still seventeen and that his records
are sealed.

She's saying all the right things, she's saying all I want to
say, but I see it on the faces of the crowd. They want to know
what he did so they can judge. Drix's past defines him, and
that's not fair, especially when it's his future my father is trying to create. Especially when I know that my father's program worked.

As Lydia wraps up, Mr. O'Bryan calls out again, speaking
over her, "I saw Mr. Pierce and the governor's daughter on
the midway together."

Lydia freezes her expression, and the entire convention
center goes silent.

"The point I'm trying to make," Mr. O'Bryan says, "is that
this program has been the governor's main priority for over
two years. Lots of taxpayers' money is going into a program
we have no idea will work, and the first contact we've had
from this program was seen, by me, on the midway with the

governor's daughter. This could be a friend of hers the governor has asked to read a speech to make us happy. If Mr. Pierce isn't willing to tell us about his real past and let us, the press, verify who he is, what he's done and let us judge how far he's come, then how do we really know if this program has worked?"

Cynthia whispers to Drix, and he shakes his head slightly. She's asking him to confess. He doesn't want to, and he shouldn't have to. I begin to run hot with the idea that I'm letting him down after what he did for me.

"Is this true, Elle? Were you on the midway with him?" my mother whispers under her breath, and her glare makes me wish I could disappear. Sean superglues himself to my side, and the way my father is eyeing me makes me feel as if I have somehow betrayed him.

"He saved me." I shake that off because it sounds overly dramatic. "Drix helped me. Some guys were harassing me, and he stepped in to help."

"What happened to Andrew?" Mom demands.

I shift from one foot to another. "I ditched Andrew."

Mom's eyes shut like I announced I kidnapped someone, and Sean pinches the bridge of his nose. "Did Hendrix Pierce get violent with these guys?"

"No. He offered to hang out with me until the guys got the hint that they should leave. Drix never said a word to them."

"He saved you."

"Helped me," I correct Sean.

Sean stares straight into my eyes, and he's making a silent promise to yell loudly at me later. "No, Elle, he *saved* you."

My eyebrows draw together, and before I can ask what he

means, Sean takes my hand and pulls me toward the podium. Drix's head jerks up as I pass, and for the first time since I saw him earlier, he looks at me.

"Excuse me," Sean says into the microphone. "I'm Sean Johnson, the governor's chief of staff and Ellison's godfather."

People watch him, each of them curious, and I know what Sean has done—humanized himself and me. With a few words, he told everyone he's in a position of authority, and that he should be respected. Me? I'm still the pretty girl standing beside him.

"We typically don't allow people like Mr. O'Bryan to shout off like he has, but we're trying to be respectful. In return we're hoping he'll be respectful to the governor and his daughter in the future."

Lots of mothers shoot death stares in Mr. O'Bryan's direction, and I'm okay with this. Mr. O'Bryan needs to be digested whole by a T. Rex.

"Secondly, Mr. Pierce confessed to his crime, has served time for it and he has gone through the governor's program. He has paid his debt to society, and he has learned from his mistakes. To prove it, the governor's daughter is going to explain the events that happened today on the midway."

Sean tilts his head to let me know if I screw up I will never be let out in public again.

The lights are brighter than I thought they would be. Hotter, too. Makes it more difficult to see individual faces, makes it more difficult to figure out how many people are staring at me and if they are happy, annoyed or on the verge of rioting.

My mouth dries out, I swallow, then wrap my fingers

around the edge of the podium. "Hendrix Pierce helped me today."

Sean clears his throat.

"*Saved* me today. I was on the midway, and two college-aged guys began to harass me, and Drix...that's what Hendrix introduced himself as...he intervened."

Multiple flashes of light as pictures are snapped, multiple voices as people talk, even louder voices as people ask questions.

Sean talks into the microphone again. "We will take questions, but I want you to remember you are talking to the governor's seventeen-year-old daughter. I will not allow anyone to disrespect her."

Sean points, and a woman in the back asks, "You never met Mr. Pierce before?"

I shake my head, and Sean gestures to microphone. "No. I was playing a midway game earlier, and he ended up playing beside me, but then we went our separate ways. I left the game, and these guys started to harass me and then Hendrix asked if I needed help. I agreed, and he suggested we talk. He said that if the guys thought we were friends they would eventually lose interest, and they did. Hendrix played a game, and we talked until Andrew showed."

"Andrew?" someone asks.

"Andrew Morton." That causes enough of a stir that nervousness leaks into my bloodstream and makes my hands cold and clammy. Why is it that I feel that I said something terribly wrong?

"Are you and Andrew Morton friends?" someone else asks, and the question hits me in a sickening way. I name-dropped the grandson of the most powerful US Senator…the position my father is campaigning for. Sean is going to roast me alive.

"Yes. We've been friends for as long as I remember." Friends, enemies, it's all semantics at this point.

"Did you and Andrew Morton plan to attend the festival together?" Another reporter.

"Yes."

"Were you on a date?" a woman asks.

My entire body recoils. "What?"

"Are you and Andrew Morton romantically involved?"

I become one of those bunnies who go still at the slightest sound. "I thought we were talking about Hendrix."

"Did Mr. Pierce confront the men?"

Finally back on track. "No, he was adamant that there should be no violence."

More questions and I put my hand in the air as I feel like I'm the one on trial. "Isn't that the point? Hendrix went through my dad's program, and one of the first chances he had to make a good decision, he made one. We're strangers, and he helped me without violence. That, to me, is success." A few people nod their heads, and because I don't want to be done yet… "Mr. O'Bryan—grown men shouldn't be follow-ing seventeen-year-old girls. I'm curious why you didn't step in when I was being harassed. If you saw Hendrix and me together, then you know what happened, and it's horrifying you didn't help. Hendrix made the right choice. You did not."

A rumble of conversation, Sean places a hand on my arm and gently, but firmly pushes me to the side. The raging fire in his eyes says he's mentally measuring out the room in the basement he's going to let me rot in for the next ten years.

My father approaches the microphone with an ease I envy. "Any more questions for Ellison can be sent to my press secretary. As you can tell, it's been a trying day for my daughter, but we are most grateful for Mr. Pierce's actions. We promised a program that was going to help our state's youth turn their lives around, and, thanks to Mr. Pierce's admirable actions, we are proud of our first program's success."

He offers Drix his hand again, and Drix accepts. Lots of pictures and applause, and Dad leans in and whispers something to him. I can't tell what it is, but I do see the shadow that crosses over Drix's face, his throat move as he swallows and then the slight nod of his head.

I don't know what happened, but I don't like it. The urge is to rush Drix, but Sean has a firm hold on my elbow, keeping me in place, silently berating me for causing problems.

Drix stands behind the podium and drops a bomb so huge the ground shakes beneath my feet. "Because Ellison had enough courage to explain what happened today, I'm going to tell you what I was convicted of…"

As Drix continues, it's no longer just the ground that's shaking—it's the entire world. Because the guy who paid to let a five-year-old win at Whack-A-Mole, a guy who stepped in when no one else did, a guy who told me that not all members of the male gender were jerks…he committed a very violent crime, and my world is indeed rocked.

HENDRIX

ARMED ROBBERY IS A CLASS B FELONY IN THE state of Kentucky, punishable by ten to twenty years imprisonment. Whoever robbed the convenient store with a Glock ran off with 250 dollars. That's enough money to settle a cell phone bill and to fill the tank to an SUV. The payout doesn't seem worth the risk, but I'm the one who did the time, so that makes whoever did it smarter than me.

Two hundred and fifty dollars. It's still a kick in the gut.

Axle pulls into our neighborhood, and lights flash behind us as Dominic follows us in his car. Holiday's asleep in the cramped back seat of Axle's aging truck, and Dominic drove Kellen.

Me and Axle, we've been quiet. There's not much to say. The whole world now thinks I robbed a convenience store at gunpoint. Won't be long until someone does an internet search and discovers the trigger was pulled, the shot missed and that kept me from being charged with manslaughter.

"They painted you as a hero," Axle says in a hushed voice. We pass box after box of the same house that are all stained yellow by the streetlight. It's ten, and the night got darker once we turned down our street. "That's what people are going to remember. You swooped in and helped the governor's daughter when no one else would. That's something to be proud of."

Maybe. But I caught the expression on Elle's face after I made the announcement. She wasn't thinking about heroes anymore. She was thinking about a masked guy high on drugs waving a gun in someone's face.

I glance back at my sister, and I take comfort that she's in my life again. Holiday—the girl with the big heart and even bigger voice. Just like her namesake, Billie Holiday. "You want me to carry in Holiday?"

"She's not six anymore," Axle says as he coasts into the driveway. "She can walk."

But she doesn't look like she just turned sixteen. In her sleep, she reminds me of huge eyes, huge hugs, hours of coloring pages and her begging me to let her paint my nails pink.

There was a girl in the program, younger than Holiday, but she also had big eyes. During the day, she had an attitude a mile long, but at night she'd become terrified of the dark. First few nights, she didn't sleep, and that made the hike the next day hell for her, especially carrying a pack that was a fourth of her body weight.

She was falling behind, she was getting down and with each new level of spiral she hit, her mouth got nastier. On the fifth day, she tripped. Mud in her hair, a tear in her athletic pants, blood on her knee and something in me shifted when her bottom lip trembled. I understood how she felt. Sometimes the weight of my problems and my pack was almost too much to bear.

I heard that she had never cried during her stay in detention, and five days into the woods, she was being cut off at her knees. I thought of Holiday then, and before this girl had a chance to break, I walked over to her, grabbed her pack and offered her a hand to stand back up. She took it and lost the attitude as she walk alongside me. After that, a lot of the younger people on the trip followed me like I was the Pied Piper.

"You're right. Holiday *can* walk," I say, "but I'll take her in."

"I'll get her. Why'd you tell everyone? Your records are sealed. Only reason I agreed to this circus was because they promised no one would know what you were convicted of."

Cracking of pleather in the back seat and Holiday's groggy lids open, but her face remains pillowed by her hands.

There are some people you don't say no to, not without there being consequences. The governor asked me to tell as a "personal favor." He said it like it meant he would owe me, but I don't believe that for a second. I rub the governor the wrong way, and he has the power to send me to prison. People like him don't owe anyone; they own. Telling Axle that won't make him feel better, so I lie. "Seemed like the right thing to do."

Axle kills the engine and shakes his head at the wheel.

Dominic and Kellen lean against the back of his run-down 1980-something junker that's put together with gray tape.

Their dad doesn't leave for his third shift job until ten thirty. Neither of them will enter the house until he's gone.

I glance over at my front stoop, and my heart stops. "Holy hell, he came."

Axle's head rotates to the house so fast that I place a hand on his arm to calm him down. "It's not Dad. It's Marcus."

My brother's chest deflates, and I'm out the door. Marcus was my breath of sanity in the program. My cell mate. My fellow outdoor warrior. The guy who had my back. My friend. While some followed me around, I followed him.

Marcus rises to his feet, a six-foot-two towering black man, and his smile pushes the darkness of my neighborhood away. He's barely seventeen, and due to a messed-up situation, he's a year behind me at school, but it doesn't matter. I call him a man because that's what he is. Both of us offer our hands for a shake, but pull in for a hug. A hard hug with pats to the back.

"You said I could stop by anytime. Hope you meant it."

"I'm glad you're here." I step back and take him in. It's only been a few days, but seeing him here feels like a lifetime has passed since I saw him last. He looks a bit different with his hair shaved close to his scalp, and I had no idea his ears were pierced. Fake diamonds are now in both lobes. Marcus is the same height as me, but has the build of Dominic.

"How's home?" I ask.

The smile fades. "I'm here, aren't I?"

I nod because I get it. "How bad?"

"Bad." His somber expression jacks me in the head hard. Marcus is as rough-edged as they come, but this year broke him down, built him back up and I know he's just as scared as I am of screwing the second chance up.

"Mom's moved up in the world," he says. "Went from dating a dealer to a gangbanger. Hanging at home isn't healthy for my probation."

When the plea deal was offered to Marcus after he stole three BMWs in a single night, then crashed one of them while high, his mom promised the program she had changed her life. Guess she did change, just not how Marcus needs. I understand having a crap mom. Marcus, unfortunately, doesn't have an older brother who gives a damn like I do so I told him he could borrow mine.

I owe Marcus my life. His friendship kept me sane during this past year. His friendship kept me from losing my mind. His friendship, even in the darkest moments, gave me hope.

Slamming of car doors and Axle automatically has his hand extended to Marcus. They haven't met, but I talked about Marcus in letters and emails. I don't make connections easily, so that makes Marcus welcomed.

"I'm Axle."

"Marcus. Things were hot at home, and I needed some place that was cool. Drix said I could crash when needed."

Axle shrugs like it's nothing to find a stranger on his doorstep. "Air conditioner is broke most days, and I can't promise it'll be quiet, but our home is your home."

Marcus tilts his head to the house. "Mind if I use the bathroom? Bus broke down on the way here. It would have been faster to walk."

Axle goes to unlock the door, and my eyes land on the guitar-shaped material case next to a backpack. "You really weren't messing with me, were you?"

Marcus grins again. "I'm full of it, Drix, but music isn't something I lie about."

The light flips on in the living room, and Marcus meets my eyes. "Thought about what you said last week about making plans. If you try for that youth performing arts program, I will, too. Let's get in and show those rich pricks how to play."

He picks up his pack, and I lift his guitar. "Is the program going to help you apply?"

Marcus shakes his head. "They told me they'd help me get into a trade school, though. As I said, let's show those rich pricks that talent beats money."

Gotta get the audition first, but I keep that to myself. Marcus has a shred of hope, and that can't be easy after getting out of the program to find no home fire burning. "Meet me in the garage. I want to know if all this self-hype you've been rattling about for a year is real."

He slaps me on my back. "I see you quaking in those boots. You know you can't keep up with talent like me."

Axle holds the door open to our house, Marcus enters, and before Holiday goes in, I pull on her sleeve for her to stop. The front door shuts, and my sister looks up at me with those big dark eyes. "Everything okay?"

I keep my voice pitched low because our windows and siding are thinner than paper. "Do me a favor and offer him some food. Some of the leftovers from last night maybe."

She nods and goes into the house not asking why because she understands. There were times in her life she hadn't been fed either, and pride has a way of making you deny your aching belly. If Marcus is anything like me—which, from what

I know about him, he is—he might not accept the offer with me in the room.

Dominic and Kellen watch me from the street. I don't know if I'm ready to play music with Dominic again. Music, chords, strings, melodies…that was a shared bond between us, but I don't know where he and I stand anymore. Not until he tells me the truth about what happened that night—even if it's only an explanation on why he left me behind. Not until he thanks me for what I might have sacrificed for him. I should invite him, it's what he's waiting for me to do, but I don't and instead head to the garage.

It's not a place where we park. A car hasn't been in here for years. What's in there is more sacred than any church I've stepped foot in.

Using the key, I unlock the knob, then use my shoulder to shove the aging and stuck door open. I flip a switch, and the shop light overhead flickers, cracks and snaps to life. The scent of dust, mold and motor oil fills my nose, and I briefly close my eyes with the familiar mixture.

In front of me are guitar stands, cords, amplifiers, speakers, a keyboard, a piano and cases filled with guitars. There's an electric, a bass, an acoustic and anything else to be thought of, and it's heaven.

In the back, covered with a tarp, is the only place where I've felt like I've belonged. More than the house, my room or even my bed. Behind the drums, I used to feel like I was flying, like I was free. Anywhere else, it's like I was constantly a snake trying to shed dead skin.

I pull off the tarp, a cloud of dust rolls into the air and there's a tightening in my chest. Last time I saw my drum set was after the gig. I had broken it down, then placed it in the back of a truck. *Axle.* This is Axle's work. Only he would spend the time to have tracked down my drums. Only he would have set it back up and covered it up with such care. My throat thickens, and I rub at my face to push the emotion away.

The last words we had said to each other before the arrest had been in anger. He mad at me. Me mad at him. I was the idiot. He was justified. I thought I was smarter, better, but I was too stupid to listen.

I was playing the drums for a band that was going places. Locally, we were becoming royalty. Regionally, we were making a name. Nationally, we had people starting to look at us. The fame filled my inflated ego, and I partied and behaved like I thought a rock star should.

That last fight we had was Axle trying to tell me what an asshole I was becoming, and I told him he was jealous. Now my gut twists. Yeah, like I was someone to be jealous of. There's so much I wish I could take back.

My sticks sit on the stool, and my fingers twitch with the need to pick them up, but what does it say about me if I do? That I'm weak? That I'll return to paths I don't want to go down again? I felt like a god behind the drums, and when I was behind the drums, I made every bad choice available. But the thought of playing sends a rush through me that's greater than any high provided by a needle stick or inhale of smoke.

I slip my finger over the cymbal, careful to move slowly enough and soft enough to not make a sound. Smooth but worn, cold but warming under my touch. A winding inside of me at the thought of hearing the high-pitched crash.

"You should play," Axle says, and I withdraw, shoving both of my hands into my jeans pockets.

No, I shouldn't. When I was behind the drums I had no self-control. When those sticks were in my hands, I went to another level in my brain, another realm of consciousness. It was raw freedom, and that freedom made me feel invincible. I was addicted to that feeling, addicted to thinking that I could never die.

But I did die—at least the old me did—and I don't trust myself to allow that sensation of flying and freedom that comes with playing the drums again. I wasn't strong enough to handle who I became with those feelings before, and I don't trust myself now. I've got to be better than who I was. I deserve that and so does my family.

"It'll piss the neighbors off. We'll do acoustic." I'm also good at the guitar, and playing the guitar never gave me that manic rush playing the drums did. Maybe I can keep music if I go down another path because the feelings associated with the drums lead me to hell. "Where's Marcus?"

"Eating and chatting with Dominic about Fender guitars. And the late excuse is sad. We've always played late." My brother leans his shoulder against the door frame. "That's nothing new."

"Don't want to wake up Holiday. I saw she was tired. She'll want to head to bed."

"You playing would make Holiday's year. Since you've been gone, there hasn't been a beat. No one will touch those drums."

"Because they're cursed?" I meant it as a joke, but seriousness leaks through.

"Because they belong to you." Axle goes silent like his words are somehow meant to sink in and make everything okay, but they just bounce off me and hang in the air.

He pushes off the frame and enters the garage. "The rest of us know how to play, can do the counts, but none of us can hold it steady like you. We can't shift fast enough with the change up in rhythms and still keep the beat. We couldn't release the sticks like you do to get the same sound. When you played, Drix, it was all emotion, all heart. It was the type of beat I could feel in my blood."

Yeah. I used to feel it in my blood, too. Playing consumed me, and that was my sin. "I was becoming Dad."

Silence. The heavy kind. The type I dread. A pit in my stomach because part of me said it so he would disagree. It hurts he's not offering up a denial.

"You didn't commit that crime," Axle says, "but I was relieved when you were arrested."

Concrete fist straight to my head, and I hear bones snapping.

"You needed that year away. You needed that program. It gave you something I couldn't. You were going one hundred miles per hour toward a cliff, and I couldn't get you to stop."

Because I wouldn't listen.

"I know coming home is tough. I know you don't know how to fit back in. It's okay not to fit back in. It's okay to be the person that's come out on the other side."

I crack my neck to the side. "That's it. That's the problem. I don't know who I am."

"But you know who you aren't. That's a big step."

I pick up the banged-up guitar Axle bought me for my

birthday when I was younger, claim one of the hundreds of picks left out and sit on a stool. My fingers begin moving before I give conscious thought to the motions. I'm listening to the notes, closing my eyes with the vibrations, twisting the tuning pegs searching for the perfect pitch.

After a few seconds of silence, Axle grabs his acoustic guitar, sits on a stool across from me and starts tuning his instrument by ear, as well. I've dreamed, literally dreamed, of this moment for a year. Me making music again…there's not another feeling like it in the world.

"I'm thinking of applying to that youth performing arts school," I say as casually as I can. Marcus is a good guy, but he can have a big mouth. If I don't spill, Marcus will. "The application deadline is in a month."

Axle's fingers freeze, then he's smart enough to keep tuning. "What instrument will you audition with?"

"They have to accept my application before the audition."

"What instrument?"

When the hell did he become an optimist? "The guitar."

"You're a beast on the drums. Don't throw that gift in the trash."

I don't want to, but I don't trust myself. "We all switch up playing something one time or another. It's time for me to give up the drums."

"The drums are who you are. The rest of that bull you had going on before you were arrested, that was the aftermath of ego. That was you allowing Dad to play with your brain. Dad's on tour, and I told him if he rolls back into town, he's not welcomed here. The house is mine. Custody of both of you is mine. He's gone. Playing the drums doesn't make you

Dad. How you decide to behave once you get some fame, once you succeed, *that's* what's going to separate you from Dad."

Dad taught me to play drums. He was the one who hooked me up with a band that had success. He was the one that showed me how a real man celebrates his success—with a needle. "I can't risk it again. I don't want to return to who I was from before."

"You won't."

My hand lies over the strings to stop any sound. "You don't think I know the drums aren't to blame? I know it was me. I know I made the wrong choices, and I'm scared as hell that I'm going to choose wrongly again. Getting back into any type of music scares me, but it's the only thing I'm good at. It's my only shot of doing something worthwhile. I can choose to look at it that music destroyed me, but I'm not. I felt like a god when I played the drums, and I don't trust myself to feel like that again and make the right choices. I'm trying here, Axle. Try with me."

"I'll try with you." Marcus walks into the garage, half of a ham sandwich in his hand. "Not sure what we're trying, but as long as it doesn't violate parole, I'm in."

Marcus unzips his case and extracts his electric guitar and wiring. Outside the garage door, in the shadows, there's movement. First Dominic hopping the fence to go home, then Kellen leaning against the fence between our house and hers, watching me.

Guilt feasts on me because playing without Dominic is sacrilegious, but so is how Dominic is dumping on our friendship by not opening up to me about why he left me behind after I passed out the night of the robbery. I've done my part, a year of it, and it's time for him to tell me the truth. Only then will he and I play.

Ellison

FORGET MY MOTHER AND SEAN, MY FATHER IS
never going to let me out of the house. The three of them
took turns yelling at me, berating me, making me feel like
the sludge of humanity because I wanted to play Whack-A-
Mole. Because, as my mother explained, I lied by omission.

Now, all of them, along with other selected staffers for my
father, are downstairs in his office, each trying to figure out
how to contain me, the media abomination. I messed up yesterday, and I'm quite aware there's no way my parents will
ever allow the internship now.

I'm in my room, on the floor, laptop in lap, and I'm trying
to find my happy place. I'm coding, and the code isn't running correctly, but that's okay. I find it calming to take something apart that doesn't work, discard the broken parts, find
ones that do work, and then piece it back together to make
something functional—to make something new.

My cell buzzes, and I consider ignoring it, just like I'm

ignoring any social media account and the news. Another buzz—it's the fourth one in a row. Most of my friends have texted, wanting the behind-the-scene details to everything they're seeing on the news, but I've remained silent. Another buzz, and I'm plain annoyed at the spamming. Though the urge is to throw something, instead I set my computer gently on the ground, and I swipe my cell:

Henry: You okay?

Henry: Answer.

Henry: Answer now.

Henry: Answer now or I'll call your dad again and tell him you snuck out four months ago to go on a date.

Henry: I'm dialing.

And I'm texting, quickly, because I need more drama like I need a hole in my head.

Me: I'm okay and it wasn't a date. It was a group of guys and a group of girls. That's it.

Henry: There were boys, correct?

Me: Yes.

Henry: It was a date.

Did I wish it was a date? Yes. Was it a date? I sure as hell hope not. Some boy who spent most of the evening looking at my breasts and who kept trying to touch me instead of talking to me isn't what I want a date to be.

Me: I hate you.

Henry: I can live with that. I saw the news. Who was the asshole you were with?

Me: There were two guys harassing me. I don't know who they are.

Henry: Them I'll figure out. I'm talking about the guy there's a picture of you looking all googly-eyed at. You're too young to look at anyone like that.

I groan. It's long, it's painful and the back of my head hits my fluffy bed. The media is having a field day with a picture of me and Drix. No wonder all my friends are demanding details. I go to an all-girls school, and besides the times I've snuck out with friends to go to parties where there were boys, I don't date. I'm pretty sure I'm not allowed to date. It's not that I've been told that as much as there's been this unspoken agreement. Boys are a complication.

Me: At least you agree with Mom and Dad on something.

I stare at my cell, waiting for his response, and my lips lift because I shut him down. Then I frown as another message appears.

Henry: Were you on a date with this Pierce guy?

Me: I really did just meet him. And I wasn't looking googly-eyed at him.

Henry: Do we have to have the sex talk now? If so, here it is—you're becoming a nun.

Neanderthal.

Me: I'm not Catholic.

Henry: Semantics.

The last thing I want to do is talk boys with Henry, and I silently thank the doorbell gods above when the loud chime rings through the house.

Henry: Can you come down to Grandma's today?

I'll probably never be let out of the house again. Me: I'll try for tomorrow. Doorbell. Gotta go.

Barefoot, I pad along the plush carpet of the hallway, down the curved stairs, then cross the hardwood of the foyer.

I open the door and the late spring heat creeps in. When I lift my head with my practiced smile to greet whichever member of Dad's staff has been summoned, my eyes widen and sweet nervous adrenaline floods my veins. The type that tickles and makes me feel like I'm floating.

It's not Dad's staff. It's dirty blond hair sticking up in a sexy way, defined arms, broad shoulders and dark, beautiful eyes. My mouth drops open to speak, but absolutely no words are formed. There's no way this is real. I want it to be real, but my mind can't seem to find a reason why this is at all logical. Standing on my doorstep is the main lead of last night's dreams. It's Drix.

HENDRIX

ELLE WAS BEAUTIFUL YESTERDAY—PERFECTION from a magazine—but today she's *my* type of perfect. Cutoff jean shorts, a T-shirt that clings to her curves, blond hair piled upon her head in a messy bun and she wears black horn-rimmed glasses. Gotta admit, it's the sexiest sight I've seen in over a year.

Those blue eyes go from big, round shock to narrowed and, once again, intimidating. "What are you doing here?"

I hook my thumbs into my belt loops and wonder the same thing. "My brother received a phone call from a guy named Sean Johnson an hour ago who said I needed to show."

Her mouth moves to the side, and I follow the action more closely than I should. Elle has lips made for sin. The kind I would have worked my magic a year ago to spend an evening kissing. Me and sin, though, aren't friends anymore, and I'm supposed to be avoiding temptation.

"That sounds like Sean. Super control freakish and bossy." She widens the door and steps aside to create a path for me.

"Come in, then, and I'll track him down for you. Though it wouldn't be hard for you to find him yourself. You just have to close your eyes and feel for the dark energy of the Force."

Sean Johnson's the guy Axle talked with the most after we signed on for the program, and Axle would agree with the dark Force association. My brother said that the guy wasn't an ass, but was pushy. "A good friend of mine is a *Star Wars* fan."

"I've seen it a few times. It's good, but it's not my thing, you know? My cousin loves it. I had my tonsils taken out when I was ten, and we watched every movie back to back."

I walk into the house. "Was it torture for you?

She brightens like she's listening to the best chorus of a song in her head. The type of chorus that touches your soul in a way you know you'll never be the same again. "No. It was with Henry. Anything with Henry is worth doing."

I get it. Anything with Axle is worth doing, too.

Elle closes the door, and I freeze. And I thought the outside of this sprawling house was a formidable fort of red brick. The inside of this place makes me feel like dirt on the bottom of someone's shoe.

"I texted Sean." Elle pockets her cell. "He said to give him a few minutes."

"Okay." Behind Elle is a massive staircase leading to the second floor with an open air hallway. Dark hardwood below me, walls with white crown molding, huge heavy solid oak closed door to my right, and to my left is a dining room with a long table and chandelier.

I finish the scan and find Elle watching me. Curiosity plain on her face. She's studying me the same way I'm trying to figure out her.

"Did you know who I was?" she asks. "On the midway?"

"No."

She watches me with a soft expression, and I will her to believe me. I liked being her hero, and I don't want that to go away. After the longest silence of my life, she finally says, "So you're the one?"

I nod because I guess I am.

"I've heard a lot about you."

"All the bad's true."

A ghost of a smile plays on her face. "Actually, I heard a lot of fantastic things."

"You're kidding me."

"Not at all." She leans her back against the corner completely unguarded. After spending a year with people who literally stabbed others in the chest with a knife, her openness is unnerving and leaves me in awe.

"My dad received tons of updates over the past year, so he'd know who to choose to help promote the program. You were in the running from the very start."

"Because I pled guilty?"

"Because they said you were smart, caring and a leader."

I don't know what to do with any of that. "You seem to know a lot."

Her expression turns serious. "Of course I do. Dad discusses everything about you over dinner."

I blink, and Elle flashes a supernova smile. "Now, that I'm kidding about. At least on the Dad talking to me part. He hardly ever discusses business with me."

"Then how do you know any of this?"

She cutely shrugs her shoulders like she should be embarrassed, but she's not. "I was curious about the program, and I may have eavesdropped a few times."

"May?"

"I'm going to plead the Fifth."

I chuckle with that and she laughs with me.

"Don't tell my dad, okay? He's still mad over the midway debacle. Anyhow, they obviously never used names, and I only heard about twenty seconds' worth of stuff because there's only so many times I can walk past Sean and Dad in the kitchen without them noticing."

"Your secret's safe with me."

Clicking of heels and with her eyes attached to her cell, Cynthia rounds the corner from the hallway next to the stairs. "Thank you for coming, Hendrix. Sean would like to speak with you, but he's in the middle of a meeting at the moment. Would you like anything in the meantime? Something to read? Drink? Lemonade, maybe?"

"We can have someone do your taxes while you wait," Elle pipes in with that spark in her eyes that's the equivalent of a gravitational pull. "Half of the people currently in this house are CPAs, including Cynthia."

Cynthia frowns at Elle. "She's joking, of course."

"Am I?" Elle asks. "Really?"

Cynthia returns her attention to her phone with an irritated sigh, and Elle mouths, "I'm not joking."

My lips tug up, Elle smiles and when Cynthia huffs at the exchange, I fake a cough to cover. That only causes Elle's smile to widen.

"We do have lemonade," Elle says, "and before you try to be all, 'I don't want to put anyone out,' just let me get it.

It'll make life easier on everyone if they feel like you have something to do, and before you ask, they consider lemonade something to do."

Cynthia has a just-accept-it expression, and I like the idea of anything that keeps me talking with Elle. "Okay."

Cynthia returns in the direction she came. "I'll come to get you when Sean's ready."

Then Elle and I are alone...again. Pieces of her blond hair fall out of her bun as she angles her head in the direction away from the foyer. "Shall we partake in some lemonade? It's good. Made out of water, sugar and the secret ingredient of lemons."

"You like telling me secrets." This conversation is too easy, too comfortable and it feels very dangerous. The ingrained instinct is to step closer, and watch her reaction. If her eyes darken with hunger, then I'll keep going forward, and I'll keep talking so she'll laugh and I'll laugh and eventually let us both become intoxicated with each other's company until...

I roll my neck to snap myself out of this. There is no until. Not with her. Not with anyone. Not anymore.

Why couldn't it have been this easy at home? With Axle? With Dominic? I've been practically on my knees begging for at least one thing to be effortless since being home, and I'm screwed because it can't be with her. "You think it's okay to be alone with me?"

"Cynthia didn't seem overly concerned, so I'll take my chances."

"I have a criminal record."

"I'm sort of aware."

"I was arrested. I served time in juvenile detention."

"The criminal record implied that."

"Do you talk to all ex-cons this way?"

"Considering I only know one, yes."

That brings me up short. "Are you scared of anything?"

"Lots of things." But damn if she doesn't even blink as she stares me down as if she answered no. Despite her answer, this girl is fearless.

The intensity in her face fades and is replaced by some sort of awe that causes me to want to look down at myself to see what has changed her mood. She walks over, and shocking the hell out of me, Elle reaches out and takes my wrist into her hand. Her fingertips pressing against my skin.

My pulse pounds with her soft touch. Cool fingers against my hot skin. A brush of her long painted nails along the edge of my leather cuff and every cell in my body sizzles to life. Yeah, it's been over a year since anyone has really touched me, since I've had any physical comfort, but even when I had been with another girl, I've never had a reaction like this. Never felt like my entire body was engulfed in flames by a single caress.

"This is seriously cool," Elle says. "Where did you get it?"

The cuff. Elle is examining my cuff. Not offering an invitation to take her home for the night. "My brother Axle gave it to me a few years ago."

I haven't worn it since I was fifteen. After that I was too cool to wear a gift from my brother. But I found it last night before going to bed, and feeling out of place in the world, I needed the reminder I fit in anywhere.

Using the slightest pressure, Elle coaxes me to turn my arm so she can further investigate the worn brown leather that's tied together by multiple black cords in a lace pattern. I'm pliant, moldable as she moves me one way, then the next. I briefly close my eyes as each brush of her skin against mine feeds this liquid warmth into my veins.

"Does the etched-in pattern mean something?"

It does. It means everything. It's a symbol Axle drew to represent me, him and Holiday. A branded mark I should have paid more attention to when I was younger. "Yes."

Elle studies my expression, and she earns respect when she drops the line of questioning. "Well, I think this piece is utter brilliance. It's unique, and I have a thing for the unique."

She flips my wrist over to look at the lacing again, and she slides a finger over the thick threads. "It's all brilliance, but this... I can't even begin to explain how much I love this."

As her finger continues to slip up, her wrist comes in contact with my hand. The pads of my fingers lightly brushing her skin. My heart jumps out of my body, and Elle had to feel it as she jolts with the impact. Her entire body a joyous shiver, and both of us freeze.

Her chest moves faster than before, her breaths shallow, and when she returns her gaze to me, those eyes have melted into the deepest blue of the sea. Neither of us move. Just my pulse pounding, just her fingers pressed against my skin, just my thumb drifting of its own volition, enjoying the smoothest, softest being on the planet.

"Elle?" rings out a voice, and both of us leap away. I scrub a hand over my face as I turn my back to her. What the hell was that? I've been messing around with girls since I was fourteen, and no one ever made me feel as alive as that.

But Elle? She's a risk, and I can't afford to take risks anymore. I've changed, and it's time to play it safe. It's time to realize I can't chase anything that makes me happy anymore.

ellison

MY BODY BURNS AS IF I'M WILLINGLY HOLDING on to a flame, and a beautiful tremor runs through me like an earthquake. But this earthquake is the best adrenaline high ever. Drix touched me, and I'm flying.

The door to my parents' room on the second floor opens all the way, and Mom appears in the open hallway. I smooth my hair away from my face as I try to organize my cluttered mind.

"Elle," Mom says again, "Fantastic news. I just spoke to the Ladies Auxiliary group at the army base and…"

From the top of the staircase, Mom finally looks upon us, and pauses, her eyes flickering between me and Drix. My stomach cramps. Not what I need—a mother on high alert.

"Who is this?" Mom has the straightest posture on the planet as she marches down the stairs.

When I go to talk, I begrudgingly have to clear my throat. "This is Hendrix Pierce."

Mom cocks a deadly eyebrow. "Hendrix Pierce?"

Drix's full name felt weird against my lips, but it felt safer to introduce him this way, because then maybe Mom won't be able to see past my skin, notice how fast my blood pumps and how my heart races. "He's the person from Dad's program. You saw him yesterday."

Mom's mere blink informs me she's already aware of this, and her question and repeat of his name had more to do with why he was here, with me, alone, more than who he was.

"Sean asked him to come. I guess they need to talk to him."

A reassured nod, and Mom lets out an exasperated sigh. "Well, then, do you mind walking with me? Your father needs me in his meeting."

I can't decide if I'm more relieved or embarrassed Mom isn't acknowledging Drix's existence even though he's standing no more than five feet from us. Mom's heels click down the hallway, and I follow because that's what's expected of me. Outside Dad's office door, my mom pauses. "You're flushed."

I'm in hell. "So?"

"Tell me the truth, did more happen between you and Mr. Pierce than you led on?"

"I swear I have not lied or held the truth back at all since the press conference."

"Do you have some fascination with him for saving you?"

He *helped* me. "I ran down the stairs, and I was surprised to see him. If you recall, our last meeting was the press conference. Seeing him on our front porch stunned me."

She studies me as if searching for a lie, and it's killing me not to fidget, because once again, I'm lying. I am flushed, and I am fascinated, but why do those emotions have to belong to my mother? Why can't they belong only to me?

"You need to talk to Andrew," she says.

My eyebrows rise so high that they might have lifted off my head. "Why?"

"Andrew feels terrible about what happened yesterday, and he wants to apologize. He's realizing his attitude with you over the past several years may not have been the nicest and that may have contributed to you running off at the midway."

"Seriously? That's all you've got? His attitude hasn't been the nicest?"

That glare is enough to shut me up with superglue.

"Next time you see him, give him an opportunity to apologize—in private. Men don't like to grovel, and they don't like doing it in public. He's sorry, and he wants to make it up to you. Now, what were your intentions with Mr. Pierce?"

My intentions? Anything that pertained to me being in the same breathing space sounds awesome. Preferably with his fingers touching me again, but that wouldn't be a smart admission, so I say, "I offered him lemonade. It was Cynthia's suggestion."

"Lemonade will do. Please see fit to keep some space. We don't want him to get the wrong impression of you, and I would appreciate it if you would please fix yourself up in the morning when your father has meetings here."

I breathe in so I don't sigh loudly. Mom enters Dad's office and closes the door behind her.

HENDRIX

ELLE RETURNS WITH A FARAWAY EXPRESSION, like she's wrapped in her own thoughts. Probably how I look most of the time. She smiles in my direction. It's a nice smile, but it's not the one she's given me before—the one that hits me straight in the chest.

"Ready for some lemonade?"

We walk down the hallway, and through the huge plush family room complete with big fluffy furniture, and a massive curved screen television that I'd bet is 3-D and can read my mind. We then pass through a sunroom before eventually reaching a kitchen that's the size an industrial chef would wet his pants over.

Elle pours lemonade into two glasses, and her eyes sweep over me as she returns the glass pitcher to the fridge. I know she likes what she sees, I like what I see, too, and that's a problem for both of us. I round the island, putting the large granite block between us, and Elle slides a glass in my direction.

I catch it and sweep my thumb over the condensation already developing. *Conversation.* I need to try conversation with Elle and attempt to neutralize what happened between us. "Your mom seemed nice."

"No, she wasn't. She was rude to you, and I'm sorry."

Damn... "That was direct."

"But it's true. Have you seen what's going on online and in the news?"

My gut twists like I drank poison. "No, what happened?" Part of me doesn't want to know. Another terrorist attack, another shooting, another...

"Us. Me and you. What happened at the press conference?"

"We made the news?"

Elle focuses on her glass. "I've heard we've made the news. I've also heard we're trending on social media, but I don't personally know these things. I haven't had the heart to see it all for myself yet."

If I stick my head in that huge oven, will it kill me faster than using one of those fancy knives in the butcher block to slice open an artery? Trending. Screw me. Now everyone in the world will see me and think *criminal.* This is my penance for loving the attention of being a drummer in a band on the way to great things—I go from being close to a god to scum. Guess the higher you go, the tougher the fall.

"You really haven't seen it?" she asks.

"I was up late, slept in and woke to that phone call bringing me here. And I don't do online."

She blinks. "Really?"

"I've been in juvenile detention for seven months, then in

the woods for three. I didn't have much of a need to update my status."

"That could have been interesting, though. Selfie with a bear."

I can't help it. My mouth edges up just enough that it could be considered a smile.

"Were you online much before?" She leaves off *before I was arrested.*

"Why? You planning on Facebook stalking me?"

There's laughter in those dangerous blue eyes. "Maybe. How else will I find out if the reason you didn't ask for my number is because you have a girlfriend?"

"Turns out bears don't like being hit on, so no girl for me."

She giggles with the joke, and I like that she gets my sense of humor.

"I was online," I say, "before. I used it to figure out what girls were in bad moods so I could avoid them at parties, and what girls would be easy for the hook up."

Elle had started to drink and chokes. "And you called me direct."

Telling her that didn't make me feel good. In fact, it makes me feel like a dick. "You need to know who I am. At least who I was."

"Why?"

Why? "Because I had to talk myself out of asking for your number. I did the right thing by walking away on the midway. Now I'm in your house, and I need to keep talking myself out of asking for your number."

"Why?"

Is she not listening? "You think it's smart for a guy like

me to kiss the governor's daughter? You need to know who I was before, so you'll stay away from me, and before, I wasn't a nice guy."

Elle studies me too seriously and long enough it causes me to shift my footing. "You want to kiss me?"

Who wouldn't want to kiss her? "That's not a good thing." At least not for her. "I'd only be using you for your body, but I'd try to convince you it was true love to land you in bed. Then I'd never call."

"Wow. You really *are* terrible. Do you cross old ladies across streets in between returning stray sheep back to their herd?"

The girl any guy would happily have a lobotomy for, so he could spend one evening with her, walks into my life, has no problem giving me hell, and I can't touch. The past year wasn't my penance for my sins. This moment is. "Did you miss I'm a bad guy?"

"A bad guy encased in bubble wrap with warning labels included. Yes, I saw you in one of my prevention videos at school. Beware of boy warning you off of kissing—he's the nightmare all parents shiver in their beds about at night."

"I'm being up-front of who I am."

"Please," she says. "You're a kitten."

My eyes bug out of my head. *"Kitten?"*

"You know you want my number."

There's a tease in her voice that goes straight to parts south, and my blood courses with desire. That's the problem. I do want her number, and I do want to kiss her.

"How about you let me continue to be the good guy. You keep pushing, and I'm going to give in and be the guy that says pretty things to get close to your body."

"Why can't you be both?" she asks. "The guy who wants to kiss me and the good guy?"

Because I don't know if those things exist in the same universe. Because a girl like her never gave the time of day to a guy like me. "I'm beginning to think you want to be kissed."

Her cheeks blare bright red, and that causes me to stop breathing. She really does want to be kissed, but then she winks. "You're fun to mess with."

An unexpected chuckle on my part, and I drink from my lemonade. Fire. Cracker.

What would life have been like if I had met her before the past year? Would I have used her or would I have seen the gorgeous girl in front of me as someone worth getting to know? I'd like to think I would have seen her worth, but I was a jerk before who was more concerned with what made me happy in the moment, not the future, and I would have talked her into bed.

"Well, if you're determined to not use me for my body," she says, "use me for my mind. Ask me something."

I can do that. "If *Star Wars* isn't your thing, what is?"

She surveys me like I'm a textbook. "Computers."

Wasn't expecting that. "Computers?"

"Don't sound so shocked. That thing between my ears? That space within my skull? It's filled with more than blond hair and air."

Point awarded to Elle. "Fair enough."

"What about you?" She plows forward in a way that tells me that question-and-answer session is done. "What's your thing?"

That's the million-dollar question. "For the past couple of

months, my thing has been walking around outside with a pack on my back."

Elle bobs her head back and forth as if that was a given. "Besides that."

"There's not much else. I love my friends, my family."

Elle taps a finger against the counter. She's on the hunt, and I don't care for being the prey. "That's it? Really?"

"Yeah."

"I think there's more."

"You'd be wrong."

"Do you like books?"

"I read." But it doesn't move me.

"Obsessed with any movies? Wait in line overnight for tickets? Have a secret website devoted to a character?"

"Like them like anybody else."

"What about music? Do you like music?"

I scratch the back of my head and move the glass on the counter for something to do. Yeah, I love music.

"You like music," she states.

"Yeah."

"Do you listen or do you play?"

"Both." Not sure how you can play without loving to listen.

"What do you play?"

I should tell her the guitar, my new instrument of choice. "The drums."

Elle leans her elbows on the counter and laces her fingers together. "Should I be scared of you?"

My eyes snap to hers. Demanding an answer, she doesn't look away. Intimidating blue eyes behind kick-ass glasses.

"You keep trying to prove you're this big, bad boy. Should I believe what you say or should I judge you by your actions?"

I don't want her to be scared of me, but according to what I was convicted of, I should say yes. Play the part. A sickness shreds my insides. "I am bad."

"Yes, because bad boys do what you've done for me."

She has it all wrong. "I used girls for their bodies and did it without an ounce of guilt. I did drugs, I drank and I used to beat the hell out of guys because the fight felt good. I wasn't someone you would have liked."

"When you finished that statement, you left it hanging as if there was an unsaid 'but.'"

"I wasn't a good guy."

"Fine. You weren't a good guy. But according to your speech at the press conference you had a year to figure yourself out. Did Dad's program work?"

It did. I don't know how, and I won't know how until I'm faced with making some of the same choices. I'm hoping I'm strong enough to go down different paths, but I doubt myself. "I won't hurt you if that's what you're asking."

It's not a great answer, but it's the best I've got. One second of her eyes boring into mine. Two seconds. Three. My pulse pounds in my ears.

"I think you've changed."

I pray she's right.

Elle sips her lemonade, then holds her glass between her hands on the counter. "You didn't have to tell everyone what you did. I overheard Sean and Cynthia talking about it. She said it was part of the agreement for what you did to stay sealed and that the only reason you told everyone is because my dad asked you to share."

My skin shrinks on my bones as I'm backed into a corner. "Does anyone in this house realize how much you hear?"

"No. Most people in this house don't think much of me, at least with anything that matters. Sometimes, I'm convinced they think I'm as useful as paint. Will you tell me why you told everyone what you did?"

She's quiet for a few beats as if giving me a chance to collect my thoughts and jump into the conversation. There's no jumping as I don't know what to say.

"You can say no," she says. "You don't have to do everything they tell you."

That's where she's wrong. "Yeah, I do. It's part of my plea deal."

Her forehead wrinkles, and I don't like it. She shouldn't wear worry. "I know you don't know my dad, but he's not a politician because of power or because he likes bossing people around. He's a politician because he wants to help people. My dad wants to make the world a better place. If you didn't want to tell the world what you did, he would have been okay with it."

"You spoke up," I say.

"That reporter was crucifying you, and you were good to me. You deserved better."

Deserved better. People don't get what they deserve. At least not people like me.

"Let me guess. You're going to save the world like your dad, too." There's more bite to my comment than I intended, and I hate how she flinches. Asshole. I'm an asshole. That's a part of me that could have stayed behind in the woods, but nope, I had to bring that back with me.

I open my mouth to apologize, but the steady staccato rhythm of her fingernails tapping in rapid succession causes me to pause. I don't know much about life, but I do know a pissed female when I see one. That wildfire raging inside her, if it's anything like Holiday's...it'd be smart to find the nearest exit.

"Do you think I'm not capable of saving the world?"

Mouth open again, but her glare cuts me off. Speaking now would be bad, and as she tilts her head in a cutting way, not speaking is bad, too. I. Am. Screwed.

"I'm capable of saving the world."

Both hands in the air. "I believe you."

"Sure you do. That's what people say, but then I'm only asked to pose for the picture."

The world halts. Elle's cheeks are red, remnants of the anger that just boiled over, but there's hurt raging in those blue eyes, and the urge is to make her better. But I don't know how to make her better. I've never been the guy to make anyone better. I'm just the guy who knows how to make himself feel good.

I scan the room, half hoping the answer genie will appear out of thin air, but besides the buzzing of the fridge, like always, I've got nothing. That's wrong. I got the truth.

"Look..." Who knew telling the truth could be so hard? The truth is stripping and raw and creates a tightness in my chest. "My family was at the press conference, and all I could think was how I didn't want my sister to see me as..."

...a criminal.

A thing to be hated and judged. "I didn't want anyone to know what I was convicted of. When that reporter started shooting off his mouth, if I talked then, people wouldn't have cared who I want to be and they wouldn't care about your dad's program. All they would have cared about is that I did something wrong, I didn't serve the time they wanted and that your dad was stupid to give me a second chance."

Because that's how people work. Somebody does something wrong and people are salivating to point it out. There's no forgiveness, just vengeance. Hang the person by the rope in the center of town and have a picnic around them with the family. It's what they did in the Wild, Wild West. We do it now, just a more technologically advanced version.

"Then you spoke up and people saw me differently. If you had the courage to come forward, I could, too." If Elle saw me differently, maybe Holiday would see me as redeemable, too.

A rush of regrets saturates every cell in my body, and I try to shake it off. To survive the past year, I had to be numb. Even now, to do what needs to be done, I've got to keep from feeling too much for too long. Emotions—feeling—needing to feel, it's what got me into trouble.

"You say I don't have to do everything they ask of me—" I lay it out for Elle "—but your dad saved my life. I say listening, paying attention, doing what he says…it's got to be better than when I made decisions for myself."

"That's why we chose Hendrix for the program, and why we chose him to represent it for the next year." Sean Johnson enters the room. "He's smart and learns quickly."

Sean's in a polo shirt, khaki pants and is put together like I'd expect a rich politician to be. Hair in place, a smile that's chemically white and straight teeth. I met him a few times before I went to juvenile detention, but my thoughts were so warped then that he felt more like a nightmare than real.

"Listen to Hendrix, Elle. You can learn a few things from him." Sean stops at the edge of the counter and levels Elle with his eyes. "The advice your parents give isn't to punish you. It's to help. If you don't want to take it from me, then take it from him. You need to start listening."

Ellison

NOT JUST LISTEN. SEAN WANTS ME TO OBEY. They all do. I'm starting to question my own sanity because every person I've had contact with has told me to listen and do what I'm told to do. I sag. Maybe they're right, and if they are, what does that say about that part of me that's screaming when I do conform?

Footsteps in the foyer and multiple voices carry through-out the house. The meetings are over, Sean's here and that must mean it's time to learn my fate. My mother's laugh-ter rings out, and she and my father walk into the kitchen. Something has put Mom in a splendid mood, and I'm not sure if that should freak me out. Did I mess up so badly that her mind fractured?

Without any pleasantries, my parents join us at the island. With his loose faded blue jeans and a chain hanging from his belt buckle to his wallet, Drix stands out, and he steps back as if wishing he could blend into the wall.

"Thank you for coming, Hendrix," Dad says, and offers him an inclusive smile. Drix merely inclines his head in greeting. I don't blame him for staying quiet because I'm also choosing silence as my line of defense. "Sorry you had to wait, but we needed to wrap up a few things before we spoke to you and Elle."

Sean unrolls a national newspaper, and staring back at us is the front page. I pinch myself to make sure I'm awake because that headline, it's not a nightmare—at least I don't think it is. The headline is one word alone: "Hero."

Below the headline is a picture of my father and Drix looking at each other and shaking hands. There's also a picture of me and Drix. I'm gazing up at him, he's gazing down at me. We're on the midway and we're both smiling.

"Congratulations," Sean says, and I don't know who he's talking to. "You're famous."

Hero
USA TODAY Network Jackson Jenner,
The Lexington Tribune

Kentucky Governor Monroe's Second Chance Program is being hailed as a huge success by supporters and critics yesterday when the governor introduced one of the first graduates.

Hendrix Page Pierce, a native of Lexington and convicted of a crime last year, has spent the past year in the Second Chance Program. The first seven months were in an intense therapy and education curriculum while being held at a juvenile detention center, then the last three were in an Outward Bound program designed especially for the program's participants.

Yesterday, Pierce proved to the state of Kentucky and the nation that second chances are possible and that people can change. The last time Pierce was on the streets he committed a violent crime, but now, not even a week since being released, Pierce proved himself a hero when he saved the governor's daughter, Ellison Monroe, while she was harassed by two men at the May Fest midway.

Witnesses have stepped forward and multiple cell phone videos have surfaced since the press conference showing how the men stalked the governor's daughter and continued to harass her as she tried to flee from them.

Pierce, not having any prior knowledge of who the

governor's daughter was, approached Ellison Monroe and protected her without violence.

The police are currently searching for the two men and, if found, charges are expected to be filed.

(Story continued on page 2)

Ellison

"EVERYONE HAS A JOB," I SAY. "THIS HAPPENS TO be mine."

My feet dangle off the dock, and my big toe barely skims the water. There's been a drought, and the water level is down. Typically, I could cool my entire foot in the large pond, but this isn't my lucky day. It's been a week since the press conference, and my parents have mellowed out enough that I finally felt comfortable asking for permission to visit Henry. They, of course, said yes, making me feel silly for waiting as long as I did.

Henry sits beside me and messes a towel over his dark brown hair that's cut close to his scalp. He jumped into the dark water. I didn't. My thoughts are too complex for me to be wet, too heavy for me to float, and I sort of have an irrational fear of drowning.

"That's the point, Elle." Henry dries off the skull tattooed on his biceps. My father hates that tattoo with a passion.

"Most seventeen-year-olds are flipping burgers, working retail or serving ice cream. They ask if you want sprinkles on top or fries with an order. They *aren't* fleecing grown men for money, and they *aren't* living in hell posing for pictures."

I'm two hours away from my home in Lexington and at our grandmother's farm so I can soak in whatever time I can with Henry. He's stateside for now, but for how long, he has no idea. But that's how the army works—one day you're here, the next day you're gone. As long as Henry keeps returning and what he does makes him happy, I'm okay with what my parents consider his bad employment choice.

"Dramatic much?" I nudge my dry arm against Henry's wet one. When he nudges me back, drops of water he hadn't toweled off fall on to my tan shorts and dark green lace tank. "You make what I do sound so scandalous."

The wind ruffles the leaves on the trees surrounding the pond, and the sound is like millions of people clapping at my witty comeback.

I love this place. It's one of the lone spaces in the world that seems to *get* me. I love the towering oaks, the old worn wood of the dock and the even older tiny and broken farmhouse at the top of the hill. My father's family has owned that house and this land since 1770-something. The Monroes are rooted in Kentucky, so deep there isn't a back strong enough to yank us out.

"Scandalous." Henry throws the towel over his bare shoulder, and I can't help but notice how he resembles my father's side of the family. Dark hair, dark eyes, chiseled jaw and sharp features. Someone who people automatically pay attention to and respect when they walk in the room. "I think scandalous is a good word for when you hate what you do."

"Hate's a strong word."

"Are you changing your mind and telling me you enjoy what you do? That you like being the *belle of the ball* at your dad's fund-raisers?"

No, but... "I do get a very awesome allowance, and Dad bought me a car. Mom and Dad told me to think of working the campaign trail and going to the fund-raisers as a part-time job with great perks."

"Doesn't change that you hate it."

"I have a feeling I'd also hate handing out Happy Meals and wiping down tables finger-painted in profanity with ketchup. And last I heard, they only pay minimum wage."

Henry cocks his head in agreement, but he's worse than a dog with a bone. "But it does rip out a piece of your soul each time you pose for the camera."

What he's saying is true. I've been helping my father on the campaign trail and fund-raisers for the past two years. I don't do much besides smile, nod, make polite and useless conversation and look pretty in photos.

To prepare for these functions, my mother and her stylists fix me up, and I'm transformed from plain me to the girl people enthusiastically stand in line to take pictures with. It's unsettling when someone changes me from who I am to someone I'm not, so when I glance in the mirror it's like falling through the looking glass to another side of me that shouldn't exist.

In my bedroom at home, I'm glasses, jeans and my hair is up in a ponytail. Outside of my room, I'm wearing the latest fashions, in full contact mode, and people feel the need to tell me things that are so cheesy that it's physically painful to not roll my eyes. They'll tell me I have hair so golden it must have been hand spun, have blue eyes that rival the ocean and possess a beauty so unusual that even grown men can't help but stare at me longer than should be legally allowed.

People look, but they never see *me*.

"Being on the campaign trail isn't so bad." It's an honest answer. "Sometimes it's awesome. How many seventeen-year-olds can say they're helping to change the world? Besides, it's just for one more year. After I graduate, Mom and Dad promised I can quit working on the campaigns to focus on college, which they are paying for."

My parents aren't stupid, rolling-in-it rich, but before my father was elected to office, my father's medical practice did well enough, and Dad had saved for my education. They saved for Henry's education as well, but he left school one week after returning to Harvard for his junior year.

Henry came home and had a fight with my father that was so loud my mother whisked me away from the house. When we returned, Henry was gone, only to reappear three months later after joining the army.

Mom and Dad had never been so angry. Mom cried, and Dad wouldn't speak to anyone. When he finally did, he mumbled about how Henry was one of the most intelligent people he knew and that he had trashed his entire future. Mom and Dad were miserable. They fought, we fought, I cried and they cried, and I hid in my room.

Henry was twenty-one, I was fifteen, and sometimes it still feels like yesterday. Even after all these years, Henry's relationship with Mom and Dad is strained, and I'm my family's version of a United Nations Peacekeeping Delegation.

"Fine," he says. "Working on the campaigns is a fast-food job on crack, but what do you call the fund-raisers?"

I smile then, and it's only about ten percent bitter. "It's called working for the family business."

My cousin turns his head to look at me. "Is that what the cool kids are calling it now?"

He can be such a pain in the butt. "If Dad owned a restaurant, would you give me a hard time if I was a waitress?"

"Your dad doesn't own a restaurant."

"If I worked in his medical practice, would you give me a hard time?"

"It's not his medical practice now. He put his part of the practice in a trust while he's in office. But let's say the practice was still his, then yes, I would pay you a hundred dollars I don't have if you told me you were working for your dad's medical practice."

"Liar."

Hand in the air as if swearing on a Bible. "Honest truth."

"You don't like me working for Dad."

"No, I don't like you raising money and campaigning for him. If he wants a life in politics, that's his choice, but he should have never dragged you into it."

I sigh, because I hate this cyclical conversation we're wasting our precious time having when we already don't see each other nearly enough. When Henry was ten, his parents died, and my dad took him in and raised him as his son. Henry's my blood cousin, but I love him like a brother, and he loves me back with the same ferociousness.

"I'm seriously sick and tired of explaining this to you. This is a family business. Dad doesn't have enough money to finance his own campaign, which means we need donors, and I'm good at asking for money."

"Then work for commission at a sales job. I got a friend who owns a car lot—"

I cut him off. "When I was eleven, Dad asked both of us if we were okay with him running for governor, and we both said yes. I was sitting next to you on the couch, and you were excited about the idea."

Henry's only response is to glower at the water, and I'm currently mad enough that I'm perfectly content with a monologue. "He asked me last year if I was okay with him running for the US Senate seat, and I said yes again. He made it perfectly clear that his involvement in politics was going to have an effect on me, that there would be media pressure, and I don't care. Dad is a good man, and he is doing great things. Our country needs more people like him."

"Does your dad have any idea how playing perfect for him tears you up?"

I don't want to answer because I'm not just playing perfect for the public. I also might not be mentioning to Mom and Dad how uncomfortable the fund-raisers make me. But I do like being useful to Dad, and I do like knowing that helping him is helping those in need. So I go for a nonanswer. "In case you haven't noticed, Dad is doing a fantastic job with this state. We're ranking higher in education. Our unemployment rate is the lowest in years…"

"Nine out of ten house dogs sleep more during the day."

Evil side glare on my part.

"Numbers and percentages are just that—theoretical things people assign whatever value they want to it. You gotta remember there are real humans behind the numbers."

"I know that."

"Do you?" he shoots back, and any worthy comeback I would have had with anyone else dies on the tip of my tongue. I will not strike verbal blades into someone who willingly places his life on the line to protect my freedom.

But that doesn't mean I won't give up. I'm too competitive for my own good, and then I have this stupid pride that I can't seem to shake. "I only attend a handful of fund-raisers a year, and they aren't nearly as bad as you think."

Yes, at the fund-raisers I have a list of people to go around and make pleasant conversation with. Yes, I take pictures with donors who have asked for a few minutes of time with me because I'm the pretty daughter of the governor. Yes, I smile a lot when I don't feel like smiling. Yes, I pretend to be someone I'm not for the span of a few hours to make others happy.

Yes, I usually end up going home exhausted and feeling like I'm an alien in my own body because I spent the entire evening impersonating whoever it is a perfect governor's daughter should be. Yes, I may have called Henry crying about a particular tough fund-raiser, and he hasn't let that lapse in judgment slip.

"Your dad uses you, and your mom isn't much better."

His harsh words cause me to flinch, and I stare at the glimmering water below to help calm the anger simmering beneath my muscles. Maybe if Dad and Henry sat here by the water together they could work things out. "What happened between you and Dad?"

Like the hundreds of other times I've asked, Henry stays coldly silent.

"Whatever it is," I say, "whatever may have happened, you know it won't change how I feel about you."

Henry, of course, ignores me. "I wouldn't be pushing you so hard if you were happy."

"I am happy."

"Because they tell you that you are and you believe them."

Anger snaps so loudly within me I'm surprised the ground beneath us didn't tremble. "Explain to me what I have to be unhappy about?"

"You angry now?" he pushes.

"Angry?" My mind is spinning. "Is that what you want?"

The light in his eyes is nearly my undoing. "Yes. You're at your best angry."

Mom and Dad say I'm at my worst. "I have a family who built a prominent medical practice, who owns a beautiful home, a mother who adores me, a cousin who loves me, friends, a fantastic school, and I have one of the world's best fathers. My father listens to me. In fact, he listens to everyone. He gives a voice to the voiceless with the laws he's been enacting. I know you and Dad have your issues, but he's a great man, and I won't let you tell me differently. How's that for angry? And so you know, you don't get to push your problems on to me."

The ice in his eyes drops the temperature surrounding the pond twenty degrees. He loves me, I know this, and if he is able to look at me with his current expression, then I can't imagine being his enemy. "You're happy?"

"Yes."

"You have everything?"

"Yes."

"Then why did you sign their name on the permission slip so you could remain a finalist for the internship?"

I seriously need to stop telling him things.

Birds chirp in the background during our silence. I don't know how to explain to him how much Mom and Dad love me. I don't know how to explain that when they see me, they see all the horrible things that went wrong in their lives and how they want me to have and do better. "Mom and Dad are overprotective."

"I think you mean controlling. You're not twelve. You're not fourteen. I bought that bull protective story then, but I'm done buying it now."

When I was young enough to believe in fantastical worlds beyond my own, Henry would tell me stories of how the beams of sun shining off the pond were really millions of tiny fairies waving hello, and if I swam underwater fast enough I could catch one.

The story was great until one day I swam under the water too deep for too long. After he saved me and I had coughed up half the pond, Henry broke the news to me it was a made-up story.

As long as I can remember, Henry has been my guardian angel. Watching over me at every turn. But as Mom explained to me, Henry has his own issues. Losing his parents greatly affected who he has become: protective of me, but rebellious of Mom and Dad.

It makes sense. I was never a replacement, but he saw my parents as trying to be permanent substitutes. Mom said Henry once accused them of trying to wipe out his parents' memory. Nothing could be further from the truth.

I love Henry, more than he can imagine, but since Henry left home, he has tried to make life a battle with him on one side and Mom and Dad on the other. Can't he see we're all on the same side?

I suck in a deep breath and readjust so I'm facing him. "Sometimes I have bad days, but that doesn't mean I'm unhappy. Do I love being on the campaign trail? No. But they do pay me for it, and it helps Dad. Do I love the fund-raising? No. But I love Dad. If he knew the fund-raising was tough on me, he'd never let me to do it. I believe in him, plus he's my dad. I don't help him because he's using me or forcing me. I do it because I want to help."

Henry shakes his head as if he's disgusted. "Then what was that phone call a few weeks ago?"

"It was a bad day. If you're going to freak out every time I have a bad day and call to talk, then I'll stop calling."

A twitch in his jaw informs me he doesn't like that solution. "I just want you to be happy."

"I know." Because he loves me.

Henry rubs his neck, and when he looks over at me the sadness in his eyes causes a lump in my throat. "I promise I'll listen better and keep some of my opinions to myself. Just do me a favor. Don't shut me out, okay?"

"I won't."

"Then tell me the truth about you and this Pierce guy."

My head falls back and I groan. "There is nothing going on between me and Drix."

Would I love for there to be something between me and

Drix? Yes. Is there something between me and Drix? No, and he made it perfectly clear in my kitchen that he would be keeping a safe six foot distance from me at all times. Am I still hoping that maybe we can be friends? Yes, because I like Drix. Talking with him was easy and there isn't a lot easy in my life.

"Nothing?" Henry pushes.

"Nothing."

"That picture on TV made it look like you were into him and he was into you."

"Can I borrow your knife? I sort of want to stab you."

Hands in the air. "All right. Consider me backed off. Want a grilled cheese sandwich?"

I laugh because that's the only thing my cousin knows how to cook. "I would love a grilled cheese sandwich."

"Then let's go." He stands, offers me his hand to help me up, and the two of us walk barefoot in the grass toward the small house where my dad used to live.

HENDRIX

I PUT IT OFF FOR OVER A WEEK, BUT I RAN OUT of excuses so now I'm sitting at the small table in our kitchen with the application to Henderson High School Youth Performing Arts Program in front of me. I had to go old-school, and print the application at the library this morning. Two mile walk there. Two mile walk back. My house is like a third world nation without a computer and internet. What a lot of people don't understand—technology costs money.

All I've accomplished is my name—first, last and middle. That's because I lost my Zen, and it requires all of my focus to stay in my seat. The rising and falling of Holiday's voice along with her asshole boyfriend's voice in the backyard is the equivalent of someone peeling off my skin.

"I'm not ready," Holiday says. "So quit pressuring me."

"You're being a tease."

The pen drops from my hands in an effort to keep from snapping it. One year of therapy and I'm hanging on to a stripped guitar wire of every piece of advice given to me on how to rein in my temper.

Breathe. Focus. Find empathy within the situation. If all else fails, leave.

Breathing ain't working, I get double vision every time I try to focus, and I don't have an ounce of empathy for this bastard. My final option before reverting back to the guy who spoke with his fists is to leave, but I can't. Only way out of this deep level of hell is to walk past my sister and her dumb-ass boyfriend who are in this messed-up combination of making out in the driveway and arguing, and I don't trust myself to not kick his ass.

From the window, they're a tangled mess. Anytime she pulls away, he yanks her back, and anytime he steps in another direction, she wraps herself skintight around him.

"I'm not a tease." My sister has this grating whine to her voice. I've heard other girls use it before—on me—but I've never heard that eye-clawing sound from her.

"I'm just being honest," he says, and somehow she accepts that as an apology. Holiday slings her arms around his neck, clinging to him like her life depends on his presence.

"Just being a dick," Dominic mumbles. "Did you hear how he called her fat?"

I heard, and I'm trying to not break my parole by killing him. Maybe I could get off on temporary insanity.

They lower their voices to whispers, and as their conversation continues, their arm motions get bigger until she starts to shrink from him while lowering her head. Dominic drops from the counter, picks up one of the folding chairs, lifts it high in the air and drops it to the ground. The chair bangs repeatedly against the floor. Holiday bolts away from Jeremy and pops her head into the back door. "Is everyone okay?"

Dominic straightens the chair. "Sorry. Just clumsy."

Her eyes narrow on him, and when she looks over at me, she spots the paper on the table. "Are you doing it? Are you applying?"

"Yeah."

"Awesome." And then she's gone again.

"Why is he still alive?" I ask, and the glare I give Dominic is probably illegal in fifteen states. Odds are, I went to jail for Dominic for a year. If he can't fess up he did the crime or explain why he abandoned me that night, the least he could do is make this bastard go away.

Dominic doesn't kill Jeremy. He doesn't tell me the truth. He returns to sitting on the counter. The two of us are in purgatory. He's still pissed I won't ask him to play music with me, I'm still pissed he won't tell me the truth, yet I feel like the one who killed a damn baby unicorn because I'm the one disappointing him.

Groggy from a nap because he's taken on more roofing jobs to cover bills and then was up late studying, Axle stumbles into the kitchen and rubs his chest. "Holiday and Jeremy making out again?"

"Fighting," I say.

"Imagine that. How's the job search going? I need both of you to make me some money. Either that or you gotta stop eating. Your choice."

"No one wants to hire a felon." Even though my records are sealed, trending on social media negates the in-theory private parts of my life. Yeah, the headlines are calling me a hero, but while people say they are into forgiveness and second chances, they only mean it from a distance. Ninety-nine percent of people want someone *else* to take the chance on the ex-convict.

"Fantastic." Axle leans against the counter, and the dark circles under his eyes indicate he needs a few more hours of sleep. "What about you?"

"No felony excuse here. They just don't like me," Dominic answers.

"Great." But we all know Dominic busts his ass unloading freight at the warehouses, getting paid under the table so the company doesn't have to document him as a worker. Axle and I also know he's been trying to save money for a surgery that will help Kellen's leg. She's in pain, and he can't stand her hurting.

"You have custody of Holiday now," I say. "Make her break up with him."

"We push Holiday too hard on Jeremy, it'll drive her straight into his arms."

"She's already there, and if they aren't shoving tongues down each other's throats, they're tearing each other apart. I say we break them up."

My brother looks out the window and witnesses the horror movie being played out in 3-D. "Last year, she was in a bed with that kid. Now she's in my driveway where one of us can watch. I consider clothes on an improvement. Plus, not sure if you noticed, but there are less bruises from all those 'accidental' falls she used to take during their last round of being together."

Yeah, I noticed.

"Here she's got a curfew," Axle says. "Here she has rules. Here I dictate how much time she spends with him and where she spends it. It's not the best solution, but it's the best I got."

Last year when I beat the hell out of Jeremy because he hit my sister, Axle didn't see her for three weeks. I was arrested, she ran away from her grandmother's that same night, and she blocked Axle out. Axle doesn't want to risk that type of response from her again.

"I'm just trying to contain this," Axle says. "Until she figures this bastard out."

The guy claims he's changed, and she bought it hook, line and sinker. Problem is, if she stays on the hook, she's not going to be a fish that survives the aftermath of being reeled in. She's going to be the type that dies on dry land.

"You think someone else is going to love you?" Jeremy raises his voice beyond a whisper, and Axle grabs on to my biceps when I stand.

"We try to run her life, we lose her."

We lose her. My sister. Holiday. I'm tired of losing things. I shrug off his grip and go to the back door.

"What are you doing?" Axle demands.

"Showing her someone else does love her." I lean out. "Holiday."

She angles her head in my direction, and her tight black ringlets bounce with her raw fury. She hated it when I stuck my nose into her fights with Jeremy last year. Don't guess she likes it now, but I'm doing things differently. "I got paint swatches for your room. Can you tell me what you want? If I'm buying paint it has to be before Axle heads to work. I already walked four miles today, and I'm not walking anymore."

A slow smile spreads across her face. "You're going to paint my room?"

"Nice," Dominic says behind me like I need his approval.

Holiday says something I don't hear to Jeremy, he points at me like I'm the knife sticking out of his side, but then she reaches up and kisses him. The smug-ass expression the bastard wears tells me he's claiming this round as his victory. Keep smiling, asshole, because she's leaving you someday for good.

When Holiday walks in, we head for her room. Earlier this morning, Dominic and I replaced the water-damaged drywall as Axle fixed the leaking roof. Axle and I agreed to give Holiday this room. I'm upstairs in the attic that has a ceiling so low I have to tilt my head when I stand, and Axle sleeps on a futon in the living room.

Three people in a house built for one. Reality is there are six people in residence since we've become a safe haven for Marcus, and Dominic and Kellen will crash here when their dad hates the world, which is most days.

Our house is a 1920s shotgun. As explained to me by my dad as a kid, someone could take a shotgun, shoot at the front door and the bullet would go through every room and head out the back. Except for when I moved in with Mom at fifteen, this is where I've lived all my life.

Even though some of the wiring may have been updated in the '50s, the appliances updated in the '80s and the walls painted yellow by me and Axle when I was in middle school, the place reeks of old. But it's home, and there was an ache in me whenever I woke to find myself not here.

At the door to her bedroom, Holiday lifts my cell from my

back pocket, and flops onto the twin bed. The cell's a gift we received yesterday via personal courier from the governor's office.

"Why did they give you the phone?" she asks.

"Because I'm going to be traveling more than they originally thought, and they want unlimited access to me." To continue to be their dancing monkey, but now in a more pronounced way. According to Sean, people loved what I did, and that causes everyone to love the governor. It's what he referred to as a win-win.

"That's cool. When do you leave again?"

"Tomorrow." I'm heading with the governor's team to western Kentucky for some fund-raiser. I gather the remaining tools on the floor and place them back in Axle's toolbox.

"I followed Ellison for you on Instagram and Twitter," Holiday says. "Did you know she has thirty thousand followers? She gained ten thousand followers in days. That's crazy."

"I don't have Instagram and Twitter." I don't have any social media.

"You do now. Don't worry. It's not like a real account. I called it DrummerBoy202, and I set up a fake email account for it."

"Why?" Is all I got.

"Why not? Do you think I can meet Ellison? I've been following her on Instagram since she set up her account. Don't tell her, but I'm one of her regular commenters, that is when I can get on a computer at the library. She posts the best pictures and always has something real smart to say."

The hammer falls with a clunk into the toolbox, and I'm slow as I turn toward my little sister who might have limited time left on this earth. "You knew who she was on the midway?"

Holiday finally drags her eyes off my cell, but then ducks behind it. "I mean I may have been following her, but... I just linked it together who she was."

Screw that. "Holiday."

With a huff, she sits up like she's the one who's annoyed. "Okay, yeah, I did. But you didn't and nobody else did, so what difference does it make?"

What difference does it make? My fingers twitch with the need to throttle something. "She's the governor's daughter." The man who holds my entire future in his hands.

Holiday flashes a bright smile. "And she thought you were cute. By the way, you need to apologize to Jeremy."

My teeth click together, and I have to breathe in and out several times before I can open my mouth without asking what the...is wrong with her. "For what?"

Holiday regards me for a mere second before returning her attention to my cell. "He's still mad at you for when you beat him up before the arrest."

"He hit you."

"He said he was sorry to me, and you gave him a scar."

I should have ripped off his balls and shoved them down his throat. "He *hit* you."

"He's changed. I broke up with him and he's changed, and I would think you, of all people, would understand that because you've changed."

Walk away. That's what I need to do—walk away. I slam the toolbox shut, and when I make it to the narrow hall, Holiday yells out, "Jeremy's been there for me when nobody else has. I know he didn't treat me well before, and I know we have bad days now, but he's better, and he's changing and he's there."

And I wasn't. Not during the past year and I wasn't reliable before. But I'm here now. It's what I want to tell her, but I don't because it'll be empty words. At least they will be to Holiday. I wasn't a bad brother before, but I wasn't a good one either.

"I'm proud of you," she says. "With what you did on the midway...with Ellison."

Air out of my lungs, past my lips and I lean my back against the doorway. "I would have done it for anyone. I would have done it for you."

Holiday puts my phone on her bed and picks up the worn stuffed octopus she's had since she was a toddler. It's more holes with lost stuffing than anything else, but it's loved. Just like everything else in her room. "I know you would have done it for me."

In a heartbeat. Back then, though, I would have done it with fists.

"I hope you don't take this the wrong way, but while I know you would do anything for me or Axle or Dominic and Kellen...the old you..." Holiday twists one of the tentacles around her finger. "The old you wouldn't have stood up for someone he didn't know, and I think it's cool that you did stand up for a stranger."

Holiday glances up at me, gauging my reaction, and that makes me want to hit myself. I rap the back of my head against the door frame, then nod in defeat because my sister...she's right.

"Guess that program did work." I try for a joke, but it falls flat. Funny how easy it came with Elle, and it's difficult with anyone else.

Holiday lifts one shoulder and loops another tentacle around another finger. "I don't think Mom's noticed I'm gone yet. At least Grandma hasn't said anything about it, but I thought for sure Mom would have been home by now and would have seen that my stuff was gone. I thought if she saw that I left that she'd tried to..."

Find her? Call her? Notice that her mother, who's in her nineties, wasn't taking care of her daughter anymore? Holiday's grandma lives around the corner. She's a wonderful woman who couldn't keep up with Holiday. When I think of Holiday's grandma, I think of hot food, the scent of freshly baked cookies, soap operas on her TV and her dry smile that would stretch along her wrinkled face. A proud black woman who looked after me, Holiday, Axle, Dominic and Kellen until she could hardly take care of herself. We watch over her now, but we let her think she's still watching over us.

As for Holiday's mom. She's a waste of space. It wouldn't have taken much for her mother to try to search for Holiday, but giving a damn isn't Holiday's mother's style.

I cross the room one slow foot at a time, then sit on the corner of the bed. I understand crap moms. I understand our crap dad, too. "What color do you want to paint your room?"

Holiday scoots closer to me and places her octopus on my leg and her head on my shoulder. I lock up as it still catches me off guard when someone touches me, but it's Holiday. She's the affectionate one in our family. "I don't have to stick with yellow?"

"Your room. Your choice."

"That's cool. But you don't have paint swatches, do you?"

"I'll get you a million paint swatches.

She chuckles. "Jeremy's changed. Give him a chance."

I'm starting to get what Axle's saying and not saying. Holiday trusts Jeremy because he's been around, and she doesn't trust me and Axle because we've only been around when it was convenient. Trust—she has to trust us before she chooses us.

Holiday wipes the drywall dust off her sheet, then blows out a breath. "Ask me, Drix."

It's a still night in my windpipe because I don't want to ask her, and I sure as hell don't like her knowing I have my doubts. That's not going to help build trust. "Don't know what you're talking about."

"Yes, you do. Things aren't the same. We all look at each other differently. We're all waiting for someone to spill that they were the one who robbed the store, and I want you to ask me because I don't want you wondering if I'm the one."

I'm shaking my head, placing my hands on the bed to push myself off, but Holiday lifts her head and clamps a hand on my shoulder. "I regret my last words to you that night."

I don't want to do this. Because her talking about her last words to me before I was arrested means I have to think of my last words to her. I'd rather cut out my own intestines.

Holiday got into a fight with her asshole boyfriend because he was going to Florida for two weeks, and he'd only take her if she had enough money to pay for her part of the room. Holiday came to me, begging for the money, begging to help her convince her grandma to let her go because otherwise, she knew Jeremy would cheat.

Her instincts were right. That jerk didn't want her to go on his vacation because he was after as much tail as he could get—not too different how he acted in our neighborhood. Having a girlfriend hanging on him would ward off girls. The money—it wasn't about her going, it was about keeping her home. Bloody fifteen. It's a doomed age for the Pierces.

I told her to break up with the asshole, and she told me she hated me and that I was a worthless man-whore. Her words hurt so I told her to go to hell, and she told me she didn't care if she ever saw me again. Then when the asshole showed his face toward the end of the argument, he yelled at me, made the mistake of smacking Holiday, and I beat the hell out of him—came close to cracking open his jaw. This made him the ever-loving martyr in Holiday's mind.

I look down at my hands, still expecting to see his blood dripping from my knuckles. Half waiting for the torment in my heart to tear me open because I had felt joy in causing him pain.

"Ask me, Drix."

I'm silent.

"You won't ask because you think I was involved. You know how desperate I was. You know I was capable of anything that night. You know I had crossed the line of crazy."

"Doesn't matter who did it. Not anymore. I did the time. It's over."

"If it's over, if it doesn't matter, then why do you avoid Dominic?"

I stand, but Holiday grabs my hand. "I didn't rob the

convenience store. I didn't do it, and I didn't ask anyone else to do it. I swear to God I never stepped foot near that store that night."

I collapse back onto the bed, but this time Holiday grants me my distance. I look over at her, and she looks over at me. We sit there, in silence, and I pick up her octopus. Oliver is his name. I used to hide it from her when she was little as a game, and she'd spend hours trying to find it. Life was easier then. Hard in its own way, but easier.

Holiday didn't rob the store. One person down, one more to go. "Did Dominic do it?"

"I don't know. He confessed he was the one that walked with you there and that he had dared you to go in and shoplift. He also said when he didn't see you go in the convenience store that he thought you chickened out and went home. He said he didn't know you were so high you passed out behind the store. That all puts Dominic there and puts what he thought was safe distance between you and the store. We all knew he had a gun he bought off someone in the neighborhood. He was doing a ton of stupid stuff, and I wouldn't put it past him."

To feel alive, Dominic had been after adrenaline rushes because on the inside he felt mostly dead. Plus Dominic is the primary caregiver for himself and his sister, and money doesn't appear at the bottom of an empty milk carton.

"But I don't think Dominic would have let you take the fall for him. That's not who he is. He loves you."

She doesn't know he's terrified of confined spaces. I do, and because of that I would have never ratted him out.

"Do you think we'll all be the same again?" she asks.

"Do you think we can go back to being the family we once were? Because I miss it. I miss when I was here and all of you were here and no one was high and no one was arguing and we were a family. I used to go back to grandma's and pretend that's what it was like all the time. Not just once a month. Not just every once in a while. That it was like that all the time. I liked pretending I had all of you, all the time."

"You have us."

"But I want all of us together, not separate. I want us to be a real family. You, me, Axle, Dominic, Kellen and now Marcus. I want a real family. I don't know what that would look like, but it has to be better than what we had before and what we're doing now."

A real family. Society says that's a mom, that's a dad, that's a smiling family in a shiny house behind a white picket fence. We don't have that, but we do have each other, and that makes my stomach bottom out.

Holiday's asking if I can get past not knowing the truth. She's asking me to forget the past and focus on the future. She's asking me to forgive Dominic. I inhale deeply. "I'll try."

"I guess that's all I can ask for."

That's good because trying is all I have to offer.

"Hey, Drix?"

"Yeah?"

"I know what girls think when they smile a certain way, and I'm not letting this go. Ellison thought you were cute."

Not having this conversation. I stand, and Holiday fol-

lows, grinning from ear to ear. "Can I help with your application?"

"Yeah." I'll take all the help I can get.

ellison

MOM JUST INFORMED ME HER STYLIST HAS TO dye my hair. As it turns out, people with my shade of blond aren't taken as seriously as people with a different shade of blond that comes in a bottle. Mom also made an appointment at the eye doctor for new prescription contacts—colored contacts. Ones that will make my eyes pop. All of this is done courtesy of answers from a focus group, and I'm having a hard time wrapping my brain around certain truths.

One—that a focus group was created with the purpose of asking questions about me.

Two—some of those questions seriously asked what shade of blond and blue makes people like me better.

Three—that anyone thinks changing my appearance to please anyone is okay.

"What do you think?" Mom asks. "I think you're going to look gorgeous when we're done."

It's a rhetorical question. This is where I say yes, and Mom is happy. I can say no and make her disappointed. So I give her a, "Sounds good."

"Great! Now, let's continue." Mom holds up a picture on her tablet. "Who is this?"

I rest my elbow on the dining room table and prop my head up by my hand. My brain is melting and is in the process of draining out the side of my ear. It's been the same thing for the past week…names, faces, why the person is important and then an endless stream of possible questions I could be asked and the appropriate answers, and I'm wondering if melted brain fluid can be collected and poured back in at a later date.

Next to me, my Southwest chicken salad sits practically untouched. It's a down day in my house. I'm in yoga pants and a cotton T-shirt. Mom is wearing the same, but just her own style, and Dad's wearing his favorite pair of jeans Mom complains are too old and need to be thrown out. He also wears one of his numerous shirts that claims he's a University of Kentucky fan.

We finished dinner a half hour ago. Dad, in theory, went to get more to drink, but I have a feeling he got sucked into ESPN. That gave Mom the excuse to focus us back on work. "Really, Elle, I know you know who this is."

Another old, rich white guy. They all look the same at the moment. Gray hair, aging face, black suit. Why not mix it up? Wear something else? Try some color? It's like they want to make it easy for their family when they drop dead in their Sunday best. "Senator Michael Jacobson."

"No."

"US Congressman Michael Jacobson."

"No."

"Party Chairman Michael Jacobson."

"It's not Michael Jacobson. It's like you aren't even trying anymore."

Sad part? I am trying.

"Who is this, Elle? He's going to be at the fund-raiser tomorrow, and if you're going to attend more of these things, you need to be able to make proper conversation."

It's sort of scary because for the first time in my life, there is complete and utter silence in my brain. Not even a backup thought to maybe breathe in air. This is brain dead.

"Dwight Stevenson," Mom says with exasperation, and my forehead hits the table with a loud thud. I knew that… about an hour ago.

"He has been one of your father's biggest donors this year, and he has expressed an interest in meeting you."

Mom's said that for easily fifty of the people we've gone over tonight. I turn my head so that my cheek is pressed against the wood of the table. "Why do these people want to meet me?"

"Because you have a gift, Elle." Dad walks into the dining room, and in his hands are several binders, but it's a magazine that he drops onto the table. "There's something about you that makes people feel at ease. You make them feel included."

Because people like things that are pretty.

The magazine on the table is one of those gossip ones everyone reads the cover of as they stand in the grocery store line. I lift my head, flip the magazine around, and spot a small picture of me in the right-hand corner. It's a close-up, me in the purple sundress and wearing one of those smiles that means I'm on display.

"Sean stopped by to bring us these," Dad says.

These. Meaning more than one magazine, yet Dad only chose to bring this one along. I sigh at the title underneath: Bluegrass Beauty. How original. "They compared me to grass?"

Mom snatches the magazine and goes to the page marked by a sticky note. There's a long and awkward silence that makes me wish I had something to do as she reads.

"It's a page article on you, but they do mention your dad a few times. There's a great picture of you and your father, and they do talk about your keen fashion choices."

"Did they actually use the word keen or was that your one million dollar addition?"

Mom raises an eyebrow, but then her lips twitch when I wink at her. She continues to silently read, and the many worry lines she's collected over the years become more pronounced.

The article must contain more than just my "keen" fashion choices, and my heart clogs my throat. I'm wagering that it mentions how the Bluegrass Beauty had to be saved. Stinking fantastic. "Does the article at least mention Dad's program?"

Mom's sad eyes meet mine. She understands why this bothers me. "Yes. They credit Hendrix's actions to his being reformed in your father's program."

I try to breathe the embarrassment away. "That's what's important, right?"

Dad and Mom share their patented long look. I gather my hair to the side, start to braid it and pretend they aren't having a private, silent conversation about and without me.

Mom rolls up the magazine and places it in her lap. Done

in such a way that it's like she's hoping I'll forget the magazine and the millions of other copies in the world exist. There's something in there she doesn't want me to see. Something, I'm sure, I won't want to see either.

Dad reclaims his seat next to Mom. From the opposite side of the table, they become the solid front that is their marriage. Their fingers automatically link together on the table.

"From the initial reaction," Dad says, "we think the media is going to grab on to you and it's only going to get bigger. More pictures, more articles—"

"More public appearances on behalf of your father," Mom interjects. "My phone has been ringing off the hook."

"Elle," Dad says, and I force a smile on my face when I glance up at him. "Are you sure you're okay with all this? Taking on more fund-raisers? Becoming more active on the campaign trail? Because we can keep you at the same commitment level you had before."

I do like being involved, but I don't like the idea of changing my appearance, nor do I like being fodder for gossip. But I'm sick of being a failure. Sick of not being taken seriously. Maybe if I do this, my parents will be proud.

"My job as a politician is to serve," Dad continues. "My job is to listen to my constituents. The form of government is best in which every man, whoever he is, can act best and live happily."

"Aristotle," I say, because my father has taught me well. He nods with pride, and I finally find the energy to sit taller.

"I'm under intense scrutiny. It comes with the territory, but you don't have to live under the microscope. You can choose to stay out of this. Your mom and I won't hold it against you."

Won't hold it against me. Will they continue to love me? Yes. Will they be disappointed in me and possibly not grant me the internship? Probably. "Aristotle also said the price good men pay for indifference to public affairs is to be ruled by evil men. I don't want to be indifferent. I'm ready for this."

Dad lets go of Mom's hand as he leans on the table as if it's just the two of us in the room. "Then what's your platform when you talk to people? Top three, and keep the pitch short."

I angle forward as well because now we're talking business. I've spent days researching Dad's platforms so I can sound intelligent during the fund-raisers. "Push for higher turnout among younger voters, and find a way to help handle college costs and student loan debt."

"Number three?"

"Your Second Chance Program. It worked, and I want to see the program implemented in other states and expanded in our own state."

Dad frowns, and my stomach drops. "What?"

"There are some magazines," Mom trails off. With a deep breath she starts again. "There are some articles suggesting that you and Hendrix Pierce are in a relationship."

As my mouth slacks, my cheeks burn hot. From embarrassment, from anger to just plain frustration... "I've seen him a grand total of three times. Once on the midway, at the press conference and when he showed here for you guys to talk to him."

"We know," she says in that condescending it's-only-a-nightmare-so-go-back-to-bed Mom voice. "But there are some people in the press and on social media who are extremely focused on the pictures of you and him on the midway."

My head falls back, and my fingers cover my throat as if that could save me from this picture that's been following me around. It's a picture of him smiling and me smiling and while I have secretly loved that photo to the tips of my toes, it's also annoying that so many people are making judgments about my life on one picture that they know nothing about.

I rake my fingers through my hair, undoing the loose braid. "What difference does it make what they think?"

Mom's shoulders droop in defeat, and the magazine reappears. She flips it to the middle, slides it to me, and the biggest picture of all the others is of me and Drix on the midway. That hesitant and beautiful smile dances along his gorgeous face, and the best part of it? He's looking down at me like I'm some sort of magical dream. I've seen that picture a hundred times, yet it still causes my heart to flip and my blood to tingle.

I fiddle with the edge of the magazine, and when I believe I have control over my facial expression, I lift my head. "This picture isn't new."

"No," Dad says, "it isn't. But if people think the two of you are together, that will become the story. Not how Hendrix entered my program and through the course of one year, changed his path from one that was broken to one that will guarantee him success.

"This program works. Not just with Hendrix, but with the other young men and women who went through the full year. We're keeping tabs on them, watching them, and we

SAY YOU'LL REMEMBER ME   163

are amazed by how well they're doing. We need any media coverage on Hendrix to be on that program."

And if I talk about the program, the story will revert back to me and him on the midway. It sucks, but it makes sense. "So I don't talk about the Second Chance Program, and instead focus on voter turnout and the insanely enormous cost of higher education and student loan debt."

"That and not calling anyone in the press a stalker. In fact, I'd prefer if you didn't call anyone names."

"He deserved it."

"He did, but that left a mess for Sean to clean up." Dad pushes the binders, all of them, in my direction. "If you're up for it, you can talk about my clean energy initiative. Our latest poll shows that is a top three priority for younger voters."

I wince because clean energy are fighting words in a coal-mining state, but the future is the future. I accept all the "light" reading material that will keep me well rested for the next twenty years. "I'm all for saving baby seals."

"As with the other information packets we gave you, bullet points are on the front page. The following pages are the details."

And that's where the devil likes to play.

"There's more, Elle," Mom says.

I slap both hands against the table. "Okay, this is where I'm putting my foot down. I can't possibly read any more stuff. You've already given me a multivolume encyclopedia set to memorize, and I still have to work through the documents you sent me via email—"

"Not that," Mom intervenes. "It's about Hendrix."

The world goes into slow motion. Like I'm standing in the

middle of the road, and I'm watching a tractor trailer come at me at a hundred miles per hour. "What about Hendrix?"

"He's going to be traveling with us and will be at some of the same events as you."

I gathered that last week.

"Obviously, you should be nice to him, but..." Mom trails off.

"But..." I encourage.

"When we are at events, we'd like you to keep a polite distance," Dad finishes. "If the press, if anyone sees the two of you together, even if it's just as friends, the story of the two of you in a relationship will continue and the conversation that needs to be happening—the conversation about the Second Chance Program—will never be discussed."

"It's not a big deal." Mom stretches her arm across the table as if she can reach me. "It would be one thing to ask this of you if you were close with Hendrix, but as you said, you've only had contact with him a few times. Be nice when you see him, but keep your distance."

I feel like a rose wilting on the vine in fast-forward. Mom's right, this shouldn't be a big deal. In the realm of reality, it's not, but there had been daydreams and dreams at night and lots of possible what-ifs I knew would never come true, but still crushed is crushed. "Okay."

"There's one more thing," Mom rushes out, and I brace myself for impact.

"What?"

"Andrew's going on the campaign trail with us," Dad says.

Once again, I figured that out last week when he showed a few hours after Drix left. Andrew, Dad and Sean were in their meeting for hours. Makes sense, though. Andrew is the grandson of the current senator. Politics is in Andrew's blood as much as it is in mine. "And?"

"We don't want anything like what happened at May Fest to happen again," Mom says. "This time when we tell you to stay with Andrew, you stay with him."

"Like glue, Elle." Dad pins me with his gaze. "We've already had this conversation, but I'll say it again. You need to trust us and the decisions we are making when it comes to you and your future. What we say goes. Period."

I get it. I messed up. I didn't tell them about the internship, but I should be able to walk down any street in the US by myself and not be harassed. But my parents gave me instructions and I disobeyed. I did ditch Andrew when they were under the impression I wasn't alone. Fair enough. It sucks, but fair enough. "Okay on Andrew and okay on listening."

Mom lets out a relieved breath. "That's good to hear because you're going to be spending a lot of time with Andrew."

My head tilts, as I broke a major rule to negotiations—read the fine print before signing on the dotted line. "What do you mean by a lot?"

"If you're in public, he's in public," Dad says. "And you're within breathing distance of the other. As I said, you two will be like glue."

Dizziness. I'm seventeen, I still have a babysitter and it's the one person I dread the most.

HENDRIX

"THE SUITS THE GOVERNOR'S OFFICE PUR-chased for you should arrive soon." Cynthia is head down in her cell again. I'm beginning to think she can't talk if she isn't texting. "I'll text you when they're in, and you'll need to collect them from the front desk. Please hang them in the closet. We don't want them to wrinkle."

We're in the lobby of a fancy-ass hotel that's probably as old as the state. Everyone around me is dressed like they're attending a funeral or a business event. I'm in a pair of ripped jeans and a black T-shirt. Even the hotel workers are looking at me like I'm about to pull a gun.

I checked in an hour ago, and Cynthia summoned me. They call, I show. While I hate it, it's something I have to learn how to handle.

"What do you mean suits?" I overemphasize the *s*.

Cynthia's fingers fly over the screen. "You're going to be attending many events over the next year. We can't dry-clean your clothes after every event. Multiple suits is more efficient. We also included some dress-down options for you. Feel free to wear your own style during time periods between events as we travel. We feel the media will enjoy those pictures."

"Glad I have your approval," I mumble.

Cynthia cocks an annoyed eyebrow, but still types on her cell. "In the meantime, meet me here at eight, and I'll walk you around the fund-raiser."

Her cell rings. She holds up a single finger as she answers, then tucks the cell away from her mouth. "And remember what I told you about Elle."

To stay away from her at the fund-raiser. According to Cynthia, Elle's been informed to stay away from me. Cynthia said a lot more. Many words meant as comfort, to hide the truth that the governor and his aides believe I'm toxic. But still... staying away from Elle is what needs to be done, and it's the last thing I want to do. Being with Elle is the only time I feel like the world isn't turned upside down.

"Eight," she says. "Fund-raiser. We will walk." And I'm dismissed.

Any mention of the fund-raiser creates the urge for me to throw my fist through a wall. I miss the sound of the wind going through the trees of the forest, the chirp of night crickets and a time where the hardest decision I had to make was which tree to piss on.

In the forest, all I wanted to do was go home. Weird how I find myself wanting to go back. I should head to the weight room, lift until my muscles hurt and I'm too damn tired to think, but the walls are closing in. I need space. I need freedom.

I go out the revolving door, and the bright sunlight hurts

my eyes as the humid summer heat seizes my lungs. Breathing in is like sucking in water, and it won't take long for my clothes to stick to my skin. Regardless, I take a right and head for the running path that zigzags through a tree line. It's not a forest, but it's better than inside.

A few feet into the canopy of green leaves and the muscles in my neck relax. At this rate, I'm going to end up one of those guys who lives by themselves in a one-room cabin eating only berries and nuts. Talking to squirrels when I'm lonely.

The trail continues through the trees, but it doesn't hide the rest of the world like how I wish. Airplanes overhead, rumble of car engines on the state road, the tap of someone else running on the path up ahead. A break in the trees and sunlight glitters off water. Now this is what I need. Silence, a lake and time alone. Recharge, reenergize, and make it through this nonsense without losing my mind.

A slamming of a car door, and my head jerks to the right. Farther down the edge of the water, a guy in a beat-up Chevy sloppily weaves what should be a straight line from the front to the back of his truck. He leans over into the bed and his shirt pulls up. What catches my eye is what is tucked into his belt at the small of his back: a handgun.

"Drix." It's a whisper, and Elle slips out from the shelter of a tree trunk. She's in a tank top, athletic shorts and in her hand is her cell with earbuds still attached. Her tan skin glistens with sweat, and she's so damn beautiful it nearly hurts.

Within a few steps, she reaches me, and we're shoulder to shoulder. "He's drunk."

Yeah, he is, and he's armed. "You should head back."

Elle frowns. "Don't you mean we? If this guy is trouble for me, then he's trouble for you."

Tension sets into my jaw, and I work it. Elle stares at me, waiting, and when I stay silent, she crosses her arms over her chest with an annoyed huff. "That's what I thought."

"Thought what?"

"That my dad's team got to you, too. The whole 'the two of us can't been seen together' because, in theory, people are more obsessed with the appearance of us dating than the real issues that affect the real world. People are so stupid. I meet a guy and he's nice to me, and therefore people assume I'm going to give up my entire identity, pledge my undying love to you and bake you cookies every few days as an eternal thank-you."

"You mean we aren't getting married next week?" I ask. Her mouth pops open in shock, and that causes me to grin. "By the way, I like chocolate chip, and I'd appreciate it if you'd iron my clothes. I like my pants pressed at the seams, and I'm not a fan of starch."

She smacks my arm, and I laugh, enjoying the smile on her face. "You're awful."

"I tried warning you."

She lightly hits my arm again. That picture of the two of us was everywhere, but then the world moved on. Gotta admit, I liked the picture. Like how it captured Elle's smile. Like how it captured that smile happening toward me. Don't know why. Maybe because it's a reminder that for a few minutes, I was her hero.

"Are you planning on ignoring me now because they told you to?" she asks.

My grin runs away. "In public? Yeah."

She scowls.

"Reminder—I'm on probation."

"Are you going to ignore me in private, too? If so, I'd appreciate the heads-up, so I don't make a fool out of myself thinking we were actually becoming friends."

I should be ignoring her in private, as well. That'd be the smart thing to do, but evidently I'm brain-damaged. I enjoy the peace being with her brings, and I'm not ready to give that up. "I'm still standing here talking with you."

Elle kicks at a rock on the ground, then peeks up at me. "Is talking with me going to get you into trouble?"

Probably. "I'm willing to live dangerously."

Elle softly laughs, and the sweet sound dances along my skin and warms my blood.

"So I'm dangerous?"

"Yes." That body of hers is lethal. So is that beautiful, smart mouth and easy way about her that keeps me drawn in. My eyes roam her from head to toe, and the blush that forms on her cheeks only causes her to be more appealing.

Elle sucks in a deep breath and tears her gaze away from me to the drunk. "I hate running on a treadmill, and I'm so tired of stupid boys ruining my plans."

"Am I included in that?"

She gives me a look that's full tease and reprimand. "Yes, guys who constantly do nice things ruin my day. No, I'm talking about stupid guys like that one. I needed this run, otherwise I'm going to combust with stress. My parents are insisting on me playing perfect tonight."

Nice guy. Did she just call me a nice guy? "You're the first girl who's called me nice."

"Well, I haven't seen much of the bad you keep referring to. Or am I misunderstanding? Do you mean you're the bad boy at school who thinks he's bad, but not? He just dresses bad and does that swagger thing that makes all girls dream of him at night." She waggles those perfect blond eyebrows, and I'm losing myself in the game.

"You know you dream of me."

Lust darkens in Elle's eyes, and that causes a rush in my veins.

Bad. I could be bad with Elle in very good ways. I could give in to temptation. I could crowd her space—press my body against hers. I could put my leg between her legs and walk her until her back is against that tree. I could run my finger along her neck, watch as she closes her eyes, as her chest moves faster with excitement. Lean down, breathe in her sweet scent, and allow my palm to mold into the side of her waist. I could skim my lips along her cheek, hesitate at her mouth and after a brief few seconds of her pulse racing and my pulse racing, we would kiss.

Elle wets her lips as if she's reading my mind. As if she wants me to make this fantasy a reality. She's turned toward me. My body has, without my consent, turned toward her. Our shoulders still touching. Our chest centimeters apart. Magnetism pulling us in. A natural attraction that begs to be unleashed.

Blood pounds at my temples and…another bang of a car door and Elle jumps, placing distance between us.

The drunk lifts a cardboard box out of the back of his truck, and he stumbles to the water.

"What's he doing?" Elle asks. I don't know, but the mood between us shifts as a sense of unease creeps into my gut.

Elle places her hand on my biceps, and my heart rate picks up speed. From her touch or from the same sense of panic that's invading my bloodstream that appears to be hitting Elle's.

"Something alive is in that box." Her words like a wrecking ball in my chest. Elle edges forward, and I snake my fingers around her wrist, keeping her there. "We have to help."

"He's packing, and he's loaded in alcohol." My thumb sweeps over her skin. Elle's beautiful, and she's impulsive. A deadly combination. "We approach him, he'll shoot."

A splash, the box is in the lake and nausea strangles me. The box is floating, but it'll sink fast.

"The police," she whispers. "We'll call the police. There are plenty of them at the hotel for the fund-raiser tonight."

But the ache in her eye tells me she's smart, and knows they won't reach us in time to help the life trapped in that box. I nod my approval, release her wrist, and Elle swipes her finger across her cell.

The engine of the truck roars to life, and dirt flies off the back wheels as it lurches away from the lake. My heart thrashes past my rib cage, and I'm running. Over logs, through thickets, my feet stomping against the brush near the lake. Elle hot on my heels.

The box shakes, a sickening whine echoes across the lake, and the box sinks halfway into the water. Shirt over my head, boots being kicked off my feet midstride, and I dive in. The water's freezing, knocking the wind out of me, but I push through it as I kick.

Arms cutting through the water, propelling me forward, but the box is almost under.

"Grab it, Drix!"

A lunge as the box is swallowed into the dark. It's gone, and I suck in a breath as I go under. Kicking down, eyes wide open, blackness and then my hand hits something solid. I shove the bottom of the box up until it breaks through to the surface. I go under with the uneven weight, the lake deeper than I thought, and I tread water with my legs.

The box pitches back and forth as whatever in it shifts. Weight. Dead weight. My heart slices in half, and using my shoulder to anchor the box, I swim to shore. My legs drag with the heaviness of my soaked jeans. Elle wades in at a run until she's chest deep. My lungs burn, and right as my toes can touch bottom, she meets me and grabs the box.

I stumble forward for land, and Elle's already on the dirt, ripping at the tape sealing it shut. "Please don't be dead, please don't be dead. Please."

Her voice is thick, filled with grief, and I can't let her open the box. I can't let her see what might be inside. She slashes through the last piece, and I snatch the box from her, opening the flaps with my back to her.

"Jesus," Elle says in a whispered rasp. As a prayer. As a plea. "Just Jesus. Who would do this? Why would anyone do this?"

In the corner of the box is a small wet ball of fur, and it's not moving. I drop my head and silently swear. I should have gone after the son of a bitch. Should have ran out, regardless of the danger, should have socked him in the damn mouth and made him bleed. Should have made him black out. Should have hit him hard enough he'd have trouble remembering his name.

If I was half the man I was from a year ago, I would have done it, and I hate that I paused. Hate that I thought the scenario through because waiting was wrong.

"What's in the box?" Elle asks.

My mistakes. That's what's in the box.

She moves around me, and as I go to close it, Elle's arm hits mine as she reaches in.

"Leave it," I say, but she doesn't listen. I'm beginning to realize, Elle never listens. Does whatever she wants, whenever she wants, regardless of how the outcome's going to hurt her.

"No." The gut-wrenching moan that comes from her as she lifts the animal causes me to swear again, fall back to my ass and for my eyes to burn.

"I'm so sorry we didn't save you," she whispers. "I'm so sorry."

So am I. My mouth turns down, my throat thickens, and I rub my hands over my face.

"I'm sorry," my voice hoarse. I clear it, but it still doesn't work. "I'm sorry, Elle."

"Drix," she whispers, but I can't look at her. Can't witness her disappointment. Can't live with that failure. "Drix, the puppy...he's alive."

ellison

ME: I'M ON MY WAY.

Drix: Door propped open.

Drix and I exchanged numbers. It's weird how that one little victory gives me a thrill. I'm officially floating on a cloud. Granted, he asked because there is currently a smuggled puppy in his room, but he still asked.

Drix's room is two doors down from mine. Close, but not close enough. My parents made it perfectly clear I'm to keep my distance from Drix, and being caught coming and going from his room will be the equivalent of me being placed in boiling water. My parents also clearly informed me I was to no longer take in stray dogs. I'm also supposed to be playing perfect and no longer lying by omission. So far, me listening isn't working out, but I'll deal with that tomorrow.

Today, though, I've weighed my odds. The chances of me being caught with a puppy in my room are far greater than me being caught sneaking into Drix's room. I've also taken emotional stock. Seeing this puppy, spending more time with Drix, it's definitely worth the risk.

As Drix said, he's left his door ajar, and I lightly knock before entering. Using my back, I press the door shut, and nervous adrenaline skips into my veins. I just entered a guy's hotel room, and we're alone. This is a first for me, and there's this tickle under my skin. "Drix?"

"In here."

I walk the short hall, past the bathroom, and stretched out on the king-size bed with the smallest, cutest little ball of black-and-white fur, is Drix. The TV is on, pillows are piled up at the top of the bed, and Drix is leaned up against them. In the crook of his arm, on his own pillow, is the puppy who is fast asleep.

Yes, the puppy is adorable, but that's not what one million percent captures my attention. That would be Drix. He must be fresh from a shower. His blondish-brown hair is wet and is tousled in breathtaking spikes, like he ran his hand through it and it came out perfection.

And his naked chest. Holy mother of God in heaven, Drix doesn't have a shirt on. His jeans are on, because if they weren't I probably would have turned beet-red and ran into the wall as I tried to not look yet look because how could I not? Drix is ripped. Completely and utterly ripped. Muscles defined, lean stomach, tanned skin and very, very beautiful.

"How is he?" I ask as if my mouth hasn't completely dried out.

"After a brief stint of exploring everything in the room? Exhausted."

The puppy lifts his head at Drix's voice, and I melt. His

teeny tiny ears perk up, and he has a curious and confused expression. I kneel on the edge of the bed and hold my hands out to him. "Hey, buddy? How are you feeling?"

He does a head swivel toward Drix, as if seeking approval to chat with me, then stands on all fours. The puppy stretches each little leg individually and yawns so loudly I yawn with him. He stumbles off the pillow, and I flop onto the bed so he doesn't have to walk as far to reach me. Our noses touch, and then he takes an interest in my glasses. I'm completely in love.

"I told my mom that I called in the drunk driver," I say. "And, as promised, I left you and the puppy out."

As soon as we saw that the puppy was breathing, I made the call to 911, much to Drix's dismay. I don't understand why we wouldn't report someone so dangerous. Drix just mumbled something about not trusting the police.

To appease him, I kept his name out of it, and I also didn't tell the 911 dispatcher about the puppy. I gave them the license plate, car description, description of the man and how erratically he was behaving. Drunk driving should be enough to put this man in jail.

"How'd she take it?"

"Fine. She asked me a few questions, but told me I 'did well.' She also told me that I shouldn't leave any of the hotels we stay at anymore and instead should use the indoor gym to work out, so that sucks."

I comb my fingers through the puppy's baby-soft long hair. "He's part border collie."

"And part what else?"

"I don't know yet." I'm not sure I'll have enough time to spend with him to figure it out. "I've made some calls to animal rescue groups. Hopefully we'll hear something before we leave. We'll have to get him something to eat. I bet he's starved."

"I gave him some water and part of my chicken from my sandwich. He gobbled it up."

"Chicken?" A cocked eyebrow on my part. "Can puppies eat meat?"

"Puppy chow wasn't on the room service menu. Maybe that's a dining room-only thing."

"Ha," I say drily. "You're so funny." The puppy turns his head one way, then another, so I can scratch behind his ears. "Can you imagine the headlines if this got out?"

"Governor's daughter caught in hotel room shacking up with juvenile delinquent. Love child expected next summer."

"Good Lord. Am I an elephant? Last time I checked, human babies pop out in nine months. We'd easily have the twins by next spring."

Drix chokes. "Twins? Are you trying to kill me?"

I bat my eyelashes and fake a pout. "You wouldn't leave me and the babies alone now, would you? What would the press think then?"

"They'd think your father revoked my probation and threw me in prison."

True. That's if Henry didn't kill Drix first. My parents aren't the safe-sex-talk type of people. They were the refuse-to-sign-the-permission-slip-for-sex-education, have-sex-before-marriage-and-we'll-be-very-disappointed parents. I'm still not sure how to put a condom on a banana. "I was talking about the puppy."

"Governor's Daughter Saves Puppy. I can see how you'd hate that headline."

"They'd say, Governor's Star Protégé Saves His Daughter and Puppy."

"You helped."

"Saving me and the puppy is a sexier headline."

He has that skeptical expression most people have when I speak, and I hate it. The puppy slips away from me and bounds up the bed to Drix. I scoot up along with him, and if I wanted, I could rest my head on the pillow, but I don't because while I'm brave, I'm not that brave.

Hanging out with Drix is easy, and I like how one thing in my life is effortless. "Did you honestly not see any of the headlines about the two of us?"

The annoyed set of his jaw tells me he did.

"Governor's Daughter Saved by Unlikely Hero."

Drix laughs bitterly. "Misfit on the Midway Changes Hearts."

"Fair Fraught with Danger, Governor's Daughter in Peril."

"That one was a piece of work. I personally liked the ones that made me sound like a superhero. Crusader Comes to the Rescue."

"Governor's Daughter in Torrid Affair."

Drix's head snaps in my direction. "I didn't see that one. I saw a few that questioned whether or not we would hook up, but I didn't see that."

I flip to my back, my head on the pillow, and I stare at the white ceiling. This has nothing to do with courage and everything to do with frustration. "That was my mother's initial fear."

"Her cold shoulder makes more sense now."

"Yeah." I lay my hands over my chest and stomach and feel the rise and fall of my breath. "I was on that midway because I wanted to be normal for a few minutes. I didn't intend to be gossip for the media, and I never intended for what happened to be a constant examination at dinner of what I did wrong. Walking the midway wasn't supposed to become a stain on my record to discount anything going on in my brain. I just wanted to be normal."

HENDRIX

THE CROWD AT THE BASEBALL GAME ON THE TV cheers, and the announcer says something about a home run. Elle looks so damn lost that the part of me that feels lost too wants to scoop her up and hold her tight.

I lean over the fancy-ass bed that's bigger than Holiday's room, rummage through the drawer of the end table and turn off the TV. Neither one of us needs additional noise. If she's anything like me, she's got enough voices mouthing off in her head. I roll onto my side and watch as she stares at the ceiling.

Sadness rolls off her in waves. A few weeks ago, I would have said she was a rich girl who has it all, but then I saw how people treated her during the press conference, saw the rage on her parents' faces when we reached the back room, I heard them yell, and I've seen on the internet how Elle's entire life has been played out one Tweet at a time.

"How long has your dad been in politics?" I ask.

"Forever. He's always been involved with helping his political party, but he gave up practicing medicine and ran for governor when I was eleven."

"Do you like it?"

She shrugs. "It's not mine to like or not like. Dad loves being the person in the thick of change. He asked my permission to run, I agreed because Dad has some brilliant ideas of how to make the world a better place. I'll admit, the media is an added weight I didn't expect, but it's worth it. My dad really is making positive change."

I can't argue with her there. I'd be sitting in an adult prison if I hadn't been chosen for this program. Instead, I'm home with my family trying to make up for lost time. And Marcus… no doubt he'd be out of juvenile detention again, but even he admits he'd be a gangbanger, hooked on drugs or dead if it wasn't for the program.

"Do you like working for your father?" I ask. "I heard you're involved and make speeches for him."

She squishes her mouth to the side and the movement of those pink lips is perfect. "Who's Facebook stalking who?"

She's right. After I left her house, I sat at the library and learned as much as I could on Elle. "Do you like working for him?"

"Next question." Her expression hardens, and I search her face. She doesn't like it, yet she does it. I understand that. Understand it perfectly.

"What if you tell them you don't want to do it?"

"I can't. There're expectations of me, and I have to meet them. This is my job, a part of who I am. At least right now. It won't be like this forever. Just one more year of no mistakes and then I can wear glasses all the time."

"Your dad doesn't let you wear glasses?"

"The focus groups have issues with my glasses, so I have to wear contacts on the road to make me more likable."

"I like your glasses," I say, and that causes Elle to turn her head in my direction.

"Liar."

I cross a finger over my heart, and a sad smile spreads over her lips. "You'd be the only one. In a few minutes, I'll have to head to my mother's suite, and there's this professional who is going to do my hair and my makeup. They'll pick out my clothes, my shoes. Someone will take a picture and post it for me on Instagram because I don't run a single one of my social media accounts. Then next week Mom is going to take me to a salon where someone will dye my hair to an acceptable blond people will take seriously, and then she's taking me to get new contacts that will make my blue eyes bluer."

Blue eyes bluer. There's a string of curse words running through my brain and not one of them is suitable for Elle. "You don't need to change."

The puppy gnaws on her fingers, and she scratches behind his ears. "Do you think we should name him? My parents will never allow me to have a dog, and I've been dying to name one. We should name him something ferocious like Spike or Dragon Slayer."

Anger causes me to sit up. "Is that what people are telling you? That you need to change? That's bull."

Those intimidating eyes narrow in on me, and warning flags are going off in the back of my head suggesting I should sprint for shelter. "Is it? Because the last time we talked, I believe you were explaining to me that you were going to do everything my father told you to do, yet when I take that advice, it's bull?"

"That's different."

"How?"

"Maybe you forgot I'm a criminal. If I mess up, I go to prison. I don't get any more second chances or a team full of people who can make my mistakes disappear."

"Are you kidding me on the mistakes? I play Whack-A-Mole, and it becomes a national headline. I'm not allowed mistakes. Perfection is the name of this game, and if you think that's easy, you are sadly wrong. If I mess up, I ruin his career, and I ruin any chance I have of doing what it is that I really want with my life. So don't act like pressure is something only you own. There's plenty to go around."

ellison

DRIX GLARES AT ME LIKE SOMEHOW MY BUR-
dens are laughable. Maybe in his world they are, but my life
is important, too. "Drix, you don't get to make me or my
problems feel small. No one does. I'm not friends with people
who want to make me feel bad about myself, my dreams or
my goals. I get enough of that garbage at home and from the
media. I don't need additional help."

I keep glaring at him, and he keeps those dark eyes on me.
Like he honestly thinks I'll give. "What are you expecting
from me here, Elle?" The stare-off still going strong.

"For you to apologize. Like I did with Mom, and I'll continue to do when I'm wrong or someone else I feel responsible for is in the wrong. It's not that hard if you think about
it. Two words. Three if you really want to draw it out."

There's a hard glint in his eye. Pride. I get it, because pride
is my favorite sin, but I don't have time for this nonsense.
Not even for Drix. I scoop the puppy up in my hands, but

before I can roll off the bed, Drix places his fingers on my wrist. "Don't go."

My pulse reacts under his touch, but I try to play it cool. "That's not an apology."

His thumb sweeps across my pulse point and pleasing goose bumps form along my skin. "Maybe not, but, regardless, I'm asking you to stay."

I want to stay and being asked to remain in his room somehow feels bigger than an apology. There's a softness in his eyes that asks for forgiveness, and I give, relaxing back on the bed and permitting the puppy to trot back over to Drix. Traitor.

"Do you always grow horns when you're mad, or do you save that for me?" Drix stretches back out, too.

I sort of hate myself that my lips turn up. "Evidently just for you."

"You could have warned me about the blood loss from your nails. Next time, I'll carry around a first aid kit. Maybe a needle and thread for the deeper cuts."

And here comes the soul-sucking killing of my pride. "I'm sorry I lost my temper."

"I didn't help," he says, and I notice he still won't fully admit he's sorry. "And I don't want you to apologize to anyone for who you are. Never do that."

I open my mouth to respond, and he cuts me off. "My father is a musician."

My forehead wrinkles as I have no idea what that has to do with anything.

"He's good. Very good. Possibly one of the best."

The puppy circles the blanket next to Drix three times before dropping back into a ball to go sleep in the shelter of his body. I'm grateful this happens because, from the expression on Drix's face, he needs this puppy more than me.

"My dad knew he was good. Before I was born, he had a number-one hit on Billboard."

I brighten. "Really? What song?"

Drix's head hits the pillow, and he rolls his head to look at me. "Does it matter?"

From the pain etched on his face, I shake my head. No, it doesn't.

"My dad loved being in the spotlight. It made him feel like a god. He loved the attention, loved the parties, loved the people, loved the life. It gave him a high that he was always trying to chase. And he was willing to do anything, give up everything, hurt anyone to keep that high."

The puppy jerks as if he had caught himself going to sleep, and Drix reaches down and places a hand over him. To comfort himself, the dog or maybe both, but either way, at this moment, they need each other. "I became my dad."

My blood is pins and needles as this feels like I'm about to learn something huge. Is this the bad he keeps referring to?

"I used to play the drums with my family. We were good, and I loved it. One time, Dad rolled back into town between gigs, and he listened to me play. He saw my potential, and he hooked me up with a band that was going someplace.

"Because Dad was on the road so much, I lived with my older brother, and he disagreed with me joining this new band. I was fifteen, and Axle thought I was too young to be on the road, too young to handle the life the road had to offer. I thought he was wrong, so I moved in with my mom because she didn't give a damn what I did.

"Musically, I thrived in that band." A faint smile spreads across his face. "After I joined them, things started happening fast. We went from playing crap holes to venues that could draw crowds. Record labels started to come and watch us, and they talked about possible deals. I loved playing and I loved the crowds, the attention, the parties, and I loved feeling like a god."

His smile fades, darkness creeps into his eyes, and my stomach cramps.

"I was one person before joining that band, and then I became somebody else. I didn't give a damn who I hurt. The only important thing in my life was myself. I was at that convenience store drunk and high because I thought I was invincible."

Drix is courageous because he meets my gaze. I couldn't do that. I couldn't bare my soul, hang my mistakes out for someone to see, and do it while staring at someone plain faced.

"I lost myself, Elle. I don't claim to know who I am anymore, but I'm not that stupid kid who thinks he's a god, and I have your dad to thank for that."

I nod because the sincerity flowing from him is genuine, and he needs to know I understand.

"But while I'm grateful to your dad, don't talk to me about changing who you are. I like who are. Since being home, you're the only person I feel comfortable with. Maybe I'm drawn to you because I envy you. You know who are. I want that. I want to know who I am, too."

My parents say I'm too young to know who I am. They say I haven't tried hard enough to figure myself out. Maybe they're wrong.

Bolder than I have ever been in my life, I reach out and place my hand over Drix's. My fingers curl around his, so he knows I'm here and that I'm not going anywhere. "You may not know who you are yet, but what I have experienced with you is amazing."

Drix turns his hand around so that we're palm to palm, and my heart skips beats when his fingers glide against mine. I'm staring at our hands, so is Drix, and it's like magic.

His fingers don't lie still. They move slowly along mine in this exotic caress that's causing my entire body to run warm. I like his hands. They're strong and they're rough, yet they're tender. I could stay like this, on this bed, with him touching me for the rest of my life.

"I'm not going to lie." Drix's voice is rough as he speaks. "There's stuff that went down after being arrested that's left me bitter. But that doesn't have anything to do with you or your dad, but with how screwed up the justice system is. The system doesn't work for people who are poor. The school-to-prison pipeline is real. It's also real that people who can't afford representation serve time they don't deserve. It feels better to have someone to blame. But sometimes I blame the wrong people at the wrong time."

Even though I love how his fingers are brushing against mine, I knot our hands together and squeeze. Drix squeezes back, and my heart mirrors the motion.

He's holding my hand. I'm holding his. Neither of us are pulling away. Drix caresses his thumb along my skin, and it's such a slow movement, such a purposeful movement, that it's as if he's memorizing every part that he's touching. As if I'm glass, and if he presses too hard, I'll break or he'll break, or maybe he's just as scared as I am of this moment shattering.

Drix's head is on a pillow, my head is on the pillow and we're eye level to one another. The material is cool against my warm cheek, and a tremor of nerves sweeps through me. His dark eyes deepen into a chocolate brown, and I melt. My grandmother once told me the eyes were the window to the soul. If it's true, Drix has the most beautiful soul in the world.

A million questions float in my brain. What's happening between us? Does he also feel this gravitational pull for my body to come closer to his? The need for me to put my arms around him? The desire for him to enfold me into his chest? Does his body also have this growing curious pulse that's awakening cells that have been in constant hibernation? Is he also thinking what it would be like for his lips to be near mine? What it would be like for our lips to touch?

Drix's hold on my hand tightens in such a pleasurable way I close my eyes as my breathing picks up speed. I want all of those things. I want Drix to want all of those things, too, and when I open my eyes again, Drix is staring at my lips. My lips. And there's a hunger in his expression that sends a pleasing shiver through my core.

Kiss me. Please kiss me.

Drix edges forward as if I had said the words aloud and he's willing to grant me my request. My fist kiss. Hendrix Pierce is going to give me my first kiss. My entire body hums and vibrates along with the pulse of my heart.

My cell rings, and I jump out of my skin, breaking the connection between me and Drix. I'm out of breath when I answer and silently curse myself because it's my mother, and me being out of breath will trigger her warning bells.

"Hello?"

"Elle? Are you okay?"

I wince. "Yeah, I was reading…Dad's binders…memorizing bullet points—" I'm incapable of sounding coherent "—the phone scared me."

"Oh, okay." And I now have a happy Mom. "You were supposed to be in my suite five minutes ago so we can start on your hair."

"On my way." I end the call and wonder how to handle this because this is new to me. Very, very terrifying and awesomely new. "I've got to go. Do you mind keeping the puppy in your room? I wasn't kidding about my parents killing me if they find me with this puppy, and they're still angry about what happened on the midway."

"He's fine. Cynthia said I'll only be at the fund-raiser for a half hour. I'll put Thor in the bathroom with a blanket and put the do-not-disturb sign on my door."

My eyebrows raise. "Thor?"

"You have something better?"

Pure joy floods my system. "I like Thor. I'll see you at the fund-raiser. Or not see you…" My face, smile, heart collapse to the floor. "Ignoring you at the fund-raiser is wrong."

"You really *are* concerned about the world being fair."

"Aren't you? If we all did the right thing, instead of what other people say we should do, the world would be different. It would be better."

"It won't hurt my feelings if we don't talk during a rich people party."

It won't hurt my feelings either, but the fund-raiser would be a lot more enjoyable if Drix was by my side. He goes to stand, but I put out my hand, scared he'll wake the sleeping puppy, scared if he does stand and comes too close he will kiss me, and I'm not sure I can handle that.

Of course, I'm not sure what I'll do if he doesn't because this is all happening way too quickly, and there's an inkling inside me that questions whether or not we were about to kiss at all. As if I had made it all up inside my head. "Are we friends?"

Drix looks me over, then says in a smooth voice, "Yeah, we're friends."

Another ping of my cell, indicating my mother's impatience. If I wait much longer, she'll hunt me down, and then she'll skin me alive for catching me in Drix's room. "So we'll talk later, then? After the event?"

"I'll leave my door open."

His door open...for me. The absolute thrill racing through my bloodstream is the highest I've ever been in my life, and I can't wait for the fund-raiser to be over because Drix and I are friends.

HENDRIX

"YOU BROUGHT A DOG INTO A HISTORIC HOTEL? Are you *insane*?"

As it turns out, Cynthia is part demon. Red-faced, spit flying out of her mouth, and I'm half expecting a few new limbs to pop out of her body.

"The hotel manager has contacted the campaign, and they are livid."

The entire conference room full of people stop talking and turn their heads to look at me. I'm leaned up against the wall, my white dress shirt untucked and my tie loosened. Because Cynthia told me that the media has been preferring my "street style," I'm in my own pair of jeans sans my wallet chain. This isn't the first time in my life I've been busted, and Cynthia has to be aware being caught with a puppy isn't my worst offense.

In a half hour, we're all attending some summer festival in some town in Kentucky I didn't know existed until four hours ago. This is what my life has become: go to where I've been instructed, read from a script, be a robot, but then at night, I spend time with Elle.

Cynthia stares me down as if she's scary enough for me to offer an explanation. I cross my arms over my chest. I went to juvenile detention for Dominic. I can take on a pissed-off, pampered, fresh out of college, twentysomething wannabe politician with too much eye makeup.

"That's it?" she yells. "You say nothing? There are pictures online with you taking a puppy out of the hotel and getting into your brother's car. You are representing the governor. You are supposed to be a model of…"

She open and closes her mouth as she searches for the right words. "You are not supposed to be smuggling puppies in and out of historic hotels where dogs are not allowed and where the damage that mutt could have done could have been close to criminal. That hotel is on the list of historic registries."

Thor's lived with me for two weeks, and besides taking a piss once in Holiday's room, a dump in the kitchen and eating my pair of combat boots, he's been good. In the hotel, Thor only messed in the bathroom, and I cleaned, literally, that crap up.

"Where the hell did you get a puppy from, and why on earth did you think it was okay to bring it into a historic hotel? Is this a joke to you? Is this entire deal you've made with us a joke? This picture of you and the puppy is starting to make national headlines, and I have to answer to the governor as to why you had a puppy at a *historic* hotel on *my* watch!"

I can count in single digits my number of cares over someone taking a picture of me carrying a puppy out of the hotel.

I had the bugger wrapped in one of my shirts, but he popped his head out right as I made it through the front doors and into Axle's car. It wasn't the media who took the picture. It was just a person who saw me, saw the puppy, clicked a button, pushed Tweet, and two weeks later the media found it online.

The media and the world have wrong priorities if this is news.

"Say something!" Cynthia demands. "Say something, or so help me, I'll tell the governor that this entire deal was a mistake."

The chain around my neck tightens. "I found a puppy. I took it in. What's the big deal?"

Cynthia spins on her feet so quickly her hair catches on her thick coat of lipstick. "Big deal? I have no idea if that thing did damage to the hotel! You should have told me. Even better, you should have never brought a puppy into a *historic* hotel, and you should never break any rule! You are on probation!"

The door opens, Elle's dad enters the room, and my gut twists. It's not just me who's uncomfortable. Everyone else in the room looks down and fidgets in a wave as he walks toward a table that has his computer. Cynthia, I can handle. The governor's disapproval, I'm not excited about, but once again...a puppy isn't the worst thing I've done, and I'm banking on him seeing it that way. Historic hotel or not.

Elle's dad gives me an analyzing glance then talks to Cynthia. "I saw the picture. Was there damage to the room?"

Cynthia sighs and places her hands on her hips. "The hotel says the towels were dirty from Hendrix obviously cleaning up after it. Other than that, no, but they are reinspecting the room, and they'll blame any damage in that room on us. The hotel is mad. They released a Tweet expressing how Hendrix bringing a dog was disrespectful, and that they are demanding a public apology."

The governor is a bear of a man—tall, the physique of someone who has worked out their entire life, someone who demands respect because he enters a room. The way he watches me makes me feel like he can read my mind, and that's scary for both of us. But I'm not going to bend, not even for him.

"I found a puppy," I repeat. "I took him in. That's it."

"It's a big deal!" Cynthia yells at me.

The governor pulls out his cell and texts. How damn silent can a room full of people be, and why the hell is a puppy a federal offense?

"You're right, Cynthia, it is a big deal, but it's not a big deal for Hendrix. Bringing in stray dogs is someone else's style which means this is someone else's fault."

Cynthia's entire body flinches with his words, and I'll admit to letting out a breath I hadn't known I was holding. I didn't think I'd go to jail over a puppy, but I had been imagining a warning that would put me on edge. Like do it again and we'll throw your ass out of the campaign, and you can finish out an additional year behind bars.

A knock on the door of the conference room and when the door opens, I briefly close my eyes. Just damn. I shoot a glare straight at Elle who is walking in. She's no longer in the glasses, blue jeans, and the white lace tank from last night, but in a blue dress that looks like it was made perfectly for her every curve. It flows with her, and makes her look like she's walking on a breeze.

Yeah, she's gorgeous, but I prefer the real Elle and not as she is right now: makeup, hair, clothes, perfection. A walking, talking magazine cover.

While she's currently most men's fantasy of a breath of fresh air, she's about to give me heartburn. The girl isn't afraid of a thing as she glares straight back at me.

For the past two weeks, we've talked on the phone, via video chat, and have hung in person late at night in hotel rooms as we ate room service and watched movies until we could hardly stay awake. Friends. Just friends. Each and every time I talk to her, I want to talk to her more. I want to sit with her more. I just want to be with her more, and she needs to let me take the fall.

"You wanted to see me?" Elle says to her father.

"Yes." His words the equivalent to a slice of a razor. "Everyone needs to leave."

People file out, and Elle stands near the wall next to the door, staring at the floor with that same pissed-off expression I've seen a few times. She knows what's about to happen as well as I do. Elle told me she would be blamed, and I can't let it happen. I'm the delinquent. I'm the person who makes mistakes. Elle is the girl with a big heart.

"I did it," I say. "I was outside walking around, I saw a guy dump a box and I was curious. The puppy was in there, and I brought it in. I didn't know it was going to be a big deal." And I say the words I hardly ever utter. "I'm sorry."

"Drix didn't do it." Elle lifts her head, and it's like watching a ram kick its front legs as she glances over at her father. "I'm the one who found the puppy, and I knew you'd be mad if I picked up another stray. When I saw Drix in the hallway, I asked if he would watch him."

"And then take it home?" her father pushes, and I wince internally at the anger simmering underneath his suit and tie.

"Yes," she says. "I made phone calls, and I got the dog into a no-kill shelter, so I asked Drix to take him there and he agreed."

"Because how can he say no to the governor's daughter," her father says, and I'm shaking my head. I saved that puppy, and if Elle wasn't there, I would have given him shelter.

"Sir, with all due respect—"

"It's okay, Drix," Elle says. "I'm the one who's wrong in this scenario."

"Yes, you are." Her father raises his voice. Not a lot, just enough, and that angry darkness from before the arrest raises its groggy head. No one should be yelling at her. "Do you have any idea what Hendrix has gone through in his life? Do you have any idea how thoughtless your actions are?"

Elle only tucks her hair behind her ear, meets my gaze and says, "Do you mind giving me and my father a few minutes alone?" Her steady voice is perfection, as if she's reading a speech.

I tilt my head. *You're interrupting me taking the fall. Step back. Let me handle this.*

Elle arches an eyebrow that's a darker shade of blond than the last time I saw her. It's not a big difference, but I notice. I also notice her new contacts. Still blue, but that blue is brighter and not the deep blue I dream about at night.

I prefer her lighter blond, deep blue eyes and glasses. I prefer hair in a messy bun and those wisps of strands curving around her beautiful face. I prefer her real smile when she laughs at a movie over the fake one she puts on for everyone else. I prefer the faint scar over her right eyebrow she got while climbing rocks with Henry when she was eleven more than the makeup that currently covers and conceals. I prefer her as she is, and I prefer for her to let me to continue to keep her out of trouble.

"Please leave, Hendrix," the governor says, "and please accept my apology. My daughter has a habit of not thinking her actions through. I understand that my campaign staff and I ask a lot of you, and you have done an amazing job, but please know that Elle is not an extension of me or my staff. You are under no obligation to her whatsoever."

No obligation. Elle opens the door, and those fake, bright blue eyes beg me to leave. I go through a million scenarios in my mind, try to figure out what words I can say to convince her father that the puppy is on me, but even with a photo, he's made his decision.

Judge, jury and executioner and I get it. It's what happened to me the moment I was arrested, and like me, she's willing to take the fall. Hating myself, respecting her, I leave, and the door doesn't even close all the way before he begins to yell.

Ellison

"HEY," HENRY SAYS OVER THE SPEAKER OF MY cell. "Are you still there?"

I suck in a breath and stretch because while my body is still in the same spot as when I accepted Henry's call, my mind has wandered far.

I'm on the bed, in my hotel room, waiting for tonight's event. Dad informed me it would be wise if I stayed here until summoned. That was his way of grounding me while on the road.

My laptop is on, and the program for coding the app is open, but I haven't typed anything in. My mind is every-where else, not on the code, and I need it to be on the code or possibly the conversation with Henry.

I'm officially in deep with my father, and he told me that he thinks they've been too lenient on me. He thinks I'm not making good choices. He thinks they need to start making more choices for me. He thinks I shouldn't take the coding classes this fall. Both of my parents are terrified I'm going to turn into Henry.

"Yes, I'm here," I say. "What were you saying?"

"That you sound miserable. What happened?"

I'm silent because I'm still too raw from Dad's rant, and I don't really need Henry laying into me, too, because Dad's mad.

"Elle," he urges, "talk to me."

I roll my neck, but that doesn't ease any of the tension. "Why? So you can use it against me later because I'm having a bad day?"

Silence on his end. "Guess I deserved that."

Guess so. "I'm sorry. It's been a rough day."

"It's okay. But I do want you to talk to me, and I promise I won't bring it up later."

I tap my fingers against my computer. I want to talk to him. I want the pain to go away. My throat burns, and I press the space bar as if that will magically make my world better.

Who do you think you are? my father demanded of me many times. *Who do you think you are to ask Hendrix to help with something so selfish? I expect better from you.*

Better. I'm supposed to be better. I'm always supposed to be better. Because who I am isn't good enough. Will it ever be?

"I miss you," I say. "Sometimes I wonder if it would be easier if you were still around."

"I miss you, too, but it wouldn't be easier with me around. It would probably be harder. I wasn't really me when I was around your mom and dad, and I used to feel like I was suffocating. If I was around, I'd be bringing you down with me."

Suffocating. I lift my head and look at myself in the mirror on the hotel wall. Reflecting back is more of the girl who should be getting ready for a photo shoot than me—the girl comfortable in glasses. At least, before the coloring of my hair, I used to be able to return to the old me. Now I seem to be turning into someone else instead of just borrowing a personality for an hour.

"Hey, Elle, I'm getting paged. I'll call you later."

"Okay. Be safe."

"You, too."

And he's gone, doing whatever it is that his job in the army requires of him. My cell chimes, and I sigh. Henry is going to get in trouble for not saying how high when they say jump, but I pause when I spot Drix's name instead of Henry's.

Drix: You okay?

No.

Me: I'm good. ☺

Drix: I heard your Dad yelling through the door.

Roiling in my stomach. Fantastic. People heard.

Me: Everything is okay. Promise.

Drix: You shouldn't have let him think you were responsible. I'm good at taking falls. You should have let me taken care of it.

Me: Dad was right. I should have never asked you to take on the puppy. It was thoughtless of me.

Drix has so much more to lose than I do, and he's currently paying a media price.

I expect Drix to rapid-fire text back, but he doesn't, and there's a shifting of disappointment in my stomach. Any conversation with Drix is welcomed, even if it is me apologizing.

A knock and I pop my head up. Drix and I have been so much smarter than standing in the hallway knocking, as that could lead to someone seeing us, so it must be Mom, Dad or someone from the campaign. I move slowly for the door, look out the peephole and nobody's there. Yet, there's a knock again.

I pivot with the sound, then stand in front of the adjoining door. Another knock and my eyebrows rise. Could it be?

Me: Is that you?

Drix: Open the door and find out.

My heart beats hard, and my fingers shake as I twist the knob. The door opens, and Drix is standing on the other side. His right arm resting above his head on the door frame, his blondish-brown hair in those messed up spikes as if he just adorably rolled out of bed. He's in a black T-shirt stretched beautifully along sculpted muscle, and those jeans ride dangerously low.

"Hey." I'll admit to being breathless.

"Hey," he says in that deep, smooth tone of his. "Can I come in?"

Definitely. I scoot back, and he enters my room. My room. In the past two weeks, I've gone to his room, and now he's in my room and he's seeing my mess and now he's looking at my computer...but I want him here. I like being with Drix, I like talking with Drix, I just like Drix.

He surveys the room, probably taking in my choices of dresses for tonight's fund-raiser hanging on the portable closet in the corner. I'm aware normal people don't bring so many clothes for such a short time, and I'm also aware how crazy this must all look to him.

"What did your dad say?"

"Honestly? That I'm a bad influence on you."

He laughs, I don't, and Drix sobers up. "You're kidding."

I shrug like Dad yelling at me doesn't sting. "I've been told I should stay away from you entirely as Dad doesn't trust me. He said I haven't been making very good choices lately, that you've been doing a good job and that he doesn't want me influencing you."

Drix does another scan of the room, I'm sure searching for a place to sit. Shoes are in one chair. The desk is overtaken by hair products and makeup. Obviously, I'm a slob.

"You can sit on the bed," I say. Since the day we brought Thor into our lives, we haven't sat on a bed together. Mostly out of my choosing because just sitting next to him on the floor where our arms occasionally touch is enough to cause me to be dizzy.

He sits on the edge of the mattress. I grab my laptop, snap it shut and hold it close to my chest. Drix eyes me and the laptop, but says nothing about it as I place it in my bag.

"What are your bad choices?" Drix asks.

I tuck my hair behind my ear. "Spilling drinks on guys who won't leave me alone, ditching Andrew on the midway, playing Whack-A-Mole."

"Be careful of that slippery slope. Once you go midway games, you're a goner."

The ends of my mouth edge up, and Drix watches the movement so closely that I blush. I playfully push his shoulder as I pass him to go sit on the other side of the king-size bed. Drix doesn't rock at all with my shove, yet touching the muscles of his biceps sends an electrical current through my bloodstream.

When I drop my hand, Drix snatches it. My entire world stills as he holds my fingers in his, and I'm absolutely hypnotized by those dark brown eyes. "I'm sorry you got in trouble, and I hate you took a fall for me."

"I asked you to keep Thor. It's my fault."

"I would have kept him anyway. If it weren't for you paying for his bills, he'd be in a shelter now. He'd probably be dead with the help he's needed."

Thor is underweight for his age and requires a special diet. I'm paying for anything associated with Thor, and Drix's family is giving him a home. That is until he's well enough to be adopted.

"I should have fought harder for you," he says. I open my mouth to tell him it's okay, but Drix squeezes my hand. "I should have fought harder."

The seriousness in his eyes, the deepness of his voice is like he's making a solemn pledge, and this type of promise is like nothing I've experienced before. I take a deep breath and tell him the truth. "Dad wouldn't have believed you."

"Not many people do."

I blink at his response and he lets go of my hand.

"What does that mean?" I ask.

"Nothing. What was your dad talking about with the coding?"

I drop on the bed and flop back. Oh my God, the entire worlds now knows I'm a huge freaking failure. "Did you hear everything?"

"Bits and pieces. Don't worry, no one else did. I stayed outside the door, and the glare I gave kept people moving."

I giggle; I don't know why, but I do. Maybe it's the tragic irony of how I sometimes catch the way people stare at Drix. Like he really is big, bad and scary. The terrifying wolf walking around in human clothing getting ready to eat babies, but those people are all wrong. Drix is beautiful inside and out. "Thank you."

"Tell me about the coding."

"I told you, I like computers."

Drix only stares at me as if I should keep talking, and while I intended that to be the end of my explanation, I honestly consider telling him more because even though we come from completely different places, something tells me he'll understand.

"Fine," he says. "I'll go first. I'm applying for late admission at the youth performing arts school at Henderson High School."

Joy blossoms within me because Drix never ceases to amaze me. "That is awesome."

"Yeah." He runs a hand over his hair, and the motion creates more of those lazy spikes I love so much. "Your turn."

Whish. All that joy rushes out of me like someone had blown out a single flame.

"I overheard a lot about programming," Drix continues, "and how now you're not allowed to do it anymore because of Thor. I want to know how important this is to you because I'm still willing to make this right."

I place both of my hands over my face. "There is no right. We both saved Thor. We both made the decision. We both dragged a puppy into a historic hotel. I was the wuss who was scared to be seen with it, and you're paying the price."

"It's a puppy. They'll get over it. It's not like you robbed a convenience store."

My hands slide off, and I turn my head toward him. "That's not funny."

"Yeah, it is."

It's not, but there's a tingling in my chest with how he smiles at me, but then this weight descends as I think about programming and my father and how he's disappointed in me. "I've lied to them."

Drix eases on to his side and lies opposite of me. "Your parents?"

"Yes. I've lied, I keep lying, and I can't seem to stop, and they're very angry at me."

"For Whack-A-Mole?

Yep. "For everything at the fair, for taking in Thor, for applying for an internship with a computer programming company that would last four years during college and not telling them." For my secret friendship with Drix, but that one feels obvious.

"Maybe you should knock off a convenience store."

"It's definitely not funny this time."

"I'm not joking on this round. Your parents need a reality check. I don't think they understand what real-world problems are."

"Lying isn't a problem to you?"

"Sometimes people lie to survive. Sometimes they lie because that's the only choice they have or the only choice worth taking. Have you considered that's what you're doing?"

I rub my eyes because I don't know what I'm doing. I don't know who I am. I don't know anything anymore. My eyes burn and my eyesight is blurry and I don't want to cry. Not in front of Drix. Not in front of somebody who knows what, as he just said, are real problems.

"Hey," Drix says. I can't look at him, and he needs to be okay with me not looking at him. One frigging person in my life needs to be okay with me being upset and withdrawn for two flipping seconds. "Elle, it's okay."

That's the thing—it's not okay. I'm seventeen years old, I don't know who I am, and I don't have any idea how to get my parents to take me seriously. I'm trapped, and I can't breathe.

There's shifting on the bed, his body moving toward mine, and nausea creeps along my stomach. I expect Drix to force me to pull my hands off my face, demand for me to look at him, and he'll be one more person pushing their way into my world, but that's not what happens.

Instead a strong arm slides under my back, another arm goes under my knees, and a surprised breath leaves my mouth as he lifts me and then cradles me in his arms. At the top of the bed, he holds me close, he holds me tight, and I rest my head in the crook of his neck.

Drix is warm, Drix is solid, and he rests his head against mine as he says, "It's okay to cry, Elle. Sometimes, this past year, I cried. Sometimes hurting happens."

And it does. The pain inside me at losing so many dreams with the possibility of never knowing if I'll be able to fight for them is too much to bear. The pain of looking in the mirror and having no idea who is staring back is enough to make me feel a little insane. So I rest into Drix, hold on to him, and I cry.

HENDRIX

EVERY EYE IN THE ROOM IS ON ELLE, AND I'LL admit, I'm one of the many who can't stop staring. She's in a long fitted emerald green dress, her hair is pinned up, and there are perfect spiraled tendrils that flow around her bare shoulders. She's the most beautiful creature in the room, and there is an easy and fluid grace with the way she moves as she greets one person to the next. She's busy, yet she takes the time to find me as she works the room. Each and every time she briefly looks in my direction my heart stops.

Her eyes will glitter like fireworks, that smile shines like the sun, and then because she and I aren't supposed to be near each other, she'll turn her head, granting her attention to some other lucky bastard.

But she doesn't smile at them like she smiles at me. Her eyes don't dance with them like they dance with me. I feel like a fraud in a suit I could never afford after working for a year straight, but each and every time Elle gives me that one second, a rush of energy keeps me here. I'm willingly en-during hell for the chance that her eyes will meet mine one more time.

The muscles in the middle of my back tighten. I'm playing with fire, and I'm going to get burned. I've got to be smarter than this, but when I look at the doorway, I only want to stay.

Today, I held Elle as she cried. In years past, when girls cried, I ran in the opposite direction. But Elle—she's different. She makes *me* different, and that makes me want to stay, if only to keep seeing her, even at a distance.

I shake another hand as Cynthia says a name I won't re-member. She's been by my side the entire time, beaming be-cause I've remained longer than the half hour they demanded.

To be honest, it's been tough to concentrate on the people Cynthia introduces me to. My attention is split between Elle and the jazz band on the stage. The band is good, but they aren't great. Hearing that steady beat has created an itch under the first layer of my skin I can't reach. Since being home, be-sides playing guitar with Axle or Marcus, I've avoided music, preferring silence, but I can't avoid it here, and listening to it is like being a heroin addict who is taunted with a needle full of the high.

"How are you handling the transition from the program to your life at home?" the man asks. I think Cynthia said he had something to do with finance in some part of government.

"It's going well. My family encouraged me to enter the program, and they have been very supportive of the changes I've made since returning home." The rehearsed answer slides more easily now that I've said it a hundred times tonight.

"What are your plans for your future?" the woman on his arm asks.

"College," I say, but I have no idea if that's true. Before the arrest, I never thought of going to college, but it's the answer Cynthia said will make people happy. That's what I'm learning that this year will be about—making everyone else happy.

"I have one more year of high school," I continue. "For now, I'm searching for a part-time job, and I'm helping my older brother raise my younger sister."

The woman touches a hand to her chest as if that's the most heart-wrenching thing she's heard, and the man tips a glass full of golden liquor in my direction. "Keep up the good work, Mr. Pierce. We'll be watching, and we look forward to you doing great things."

No pressure there. They leave, and Cynthia mumbles we should take a breather, which means something important or unimportant has popped up on her cell.

From across the room, another man walks up to Elle, thirties maybe, and she greets him with the same polite smile as she has with everyone else. Like the other times, he talks, she nods, he talks some more, and she chats along with the conversation, but there's a strain that hasn't been there before. Her eyes more narrowed, her smile stretched.

He moves. A centimeter at a time until he crowds her space. Elle subtly steps back until she hits a chair. That dark shadow that lives inside me growls as Elle's polite smile dissolves and her body goes rigid. Her shoulders roll back like she's considering taking a swing, and fire sparks from her eyes. I've been in more than a few fights in my life. Most of them because I was a bastard, so I'm well versed in that stance.

Elle glances around, the same way she did when she was on the midway when those guys were stalking her. I step forward, but Cynthia angles in front of me, blocking my view of Elle. "Where are you going?"

I roll my arms to keep myself in check. "Elle's uncomfortable."

Cynthia glances over her shoulder, and spits out a word she'd give me hell for saying aloud. She's texting again on the cell I'm convinced is physically attached to her hand. "Elle isn't your concern tonight. In fact, Elle isn't your concern at all. I thought we had this conversation. If you and Elle are seen together, even as friends, it will appear like there is something more, and that will be the headlining story, not the governor's program. We need the press to focus on the important issues, and today I've been entirely too busy turning that picture of you with a puppy at a *historic* hotel as another headline of you saving the day."

The man extends his hand to Elle, and after another scan of the room, she accepts. Sludge oozes into my veins as it's like watching a naïve calf being led to the slaughterhouse. Several other couples dance to the bad beat, and they make room for Elle and this bastard.

Elle's jaw juts, and rage radiates from the proud way she holds herself as he takes her into his arms. He crushes her to him as if she's a rag doll. His hand slides along her side, breezes past parts high he shouldn't be near, then rests his hand too close to parts south on her back.

My ears ring, and as if hearing the warning bells herself, Cynthia's arm shoots out to block me as she puts her phone to her ear.

"Where the hell is Andrew?" she spits. "He's supposed to be watching over Elle."

The girl on the midway would have nailed this man in the nuts, and I find myself wishing she would because otherwise I'm going to have to get involved.

"Andrew," she says the name again. "Where is he?"

Andrew—the jerk she dumped on the midway, the jerk who is supposed to be attached to her side at public events. Yeah, Elle's given me an earful on him, and I've seen him around. He's more interested in what's at the bottom of a liquor bottle than helping Elle. He's currently failing at his job, and I'm more than happy to meet him in a dark alley and teach him with my fists how to care for Elle.

The anger that controlled me for so long before the program rears its ugly head. "You've got ten seconds, Cynthia."

She holds the phone away from her mouth. "You can't intervene."

"Five."

"Andrew is on his way."

"Three."

"You go over there, and any progress we made on this program will be ruined."

"One."

"You do this, and it will ruin you. The governor overlooked the puppy, but he will not overlook you insulting one of the most influential people in politics. You are still on probation, and if you cause a scene tonight, it will negatively affect your future. Do you understand?"

As I take my first step forward, Andrew approaches Elle. Giving a light bow to her as if it's a couple hundred years ago in a castle, he cuts into the dance with a laugh and a smile. Jealousy becomes a new monster as she offers him a relieved lift of her lips.

I'm her hero, not this jerk.

She accepts his offer to dance, and the only solace I find is that his hand is in a respectful place, his body isn't pressed to hers, and he doesn't focus on Elle, but on the rest of the room as they talk and dance.

Every muscle in my body is still poised, ready to rip apart, ready to kill, and that reaction belongs to a part of me I tried to leave behind in the forest. I pinch the bridge of my nose and breathe. I need out of this suit, I need air, I need freedom.

"You've done enough tonight, Hendrix," Cynthia says. "Why don't you go back to your room?"

The criminal is no longer needed and has been ordered to return to his cage. Like the chained animal I've become, I obey.

Ellison

MY HEART DROPS AND MY THROAT TIGHTENS.
Drix is gone. I don't know why it saddens me, but it does.

The song ends, Andrew releases me, and we both politely
clap for the jazz band. The scent of Terry Clark's strong and
sour cologne smothers me, and I search for another smell for
comfort. The scent of spilt champagne, the bacon in the hors
d'oeuvres, the trace fragrance of Drix's rich scent that stayed
with me long after our afternoon together.

Reclaiming my game face is key, and I need to control the
turmoil in my mind because more conversations are waiting
to be had. More smiles, more handshakes, more hugs, and
I tremble. The thought of another man touching me after I
was mauled by Terry Clark's eyes, by his words, by his hands
causes nausea to twist my stomach.

Terry Clark. Talking with him was hell, and dancing was
worse than death, but I didn't know how to say no without
offending him and he is not a man I can offend. In fact, he

was on the short list of people my parents told me to keep my mouth shut around.

This was the type of scenario that caused me to call Henry crying months ago. It doesn't happen often, but it does happen. Perfection. I will be perfection, and I will gain my parents' approval. I will convince them to let me take coding this coming year. I will earn that internship, but I had no idea perfection meant selling a portion of my soul.

"You look pale," Andrew says. "Let's go outside for a few minutes. Give you a break."

Andrew offers me his elbow, and I loop my hand around his arm.

"Just a few seconds, Ellie, and I'll have you out of here. Fake it for a bit longer."

Right. Appearances. They're important. More important than the tears I'm not allowed to shed because I'm angry. More important than the fact that my skin feels tainted, that my body feels used and that I want nothing more than a scalding shower.

More important than an entire room of people who just witnessed that show and did nothing because Terry Clark has lots of money and he has a lot of power and he and my father often butt heads because my father doesn't like to be owned.

Andrew leads me through the entrance marked No Entry, the one the waiters and waitresses have used. We go down a long hallway, then out the exit. My heels click on the concrete of the loading dock, and my cold skin is shocked by the humidity of the hot, dark night. I release Andrew and gasp for air as if I'm a fish out of water.

My hands run over my arms. Fingernails scraping. Like that

will be enough to rid the memory of Terry Clark touching my skin, of him "accidentally" brushing the side of my breast and of him squeezing my butt before he left me with Andrew.

You're so grown up now, Ellison. A woman. I bet you gain the attention of many men. Bet you've had experience with many men. Your father is smart to use you.

Flipping pervert. "That man needs to die."

Andrew chuckles, my hands begin to shake, and I want to hit myself when a renegade anger tear slips down my cheek. Men suck, and Andrew belongs in that category.

I spin and stick a long pointed fingernail into his chest. "You think this is funny?"

"No," he answers, yet he's all mocking teeth. I have never wanted to slap anyone so badly in my life. I take that back. I have wanted to slap several people in my life, and Andrew is, once again, on the list.

"Take off your jacket," I demand.

He proves he's the devil when he permits that evil smile to widen. "Why, Ellie, I'm honored you're still crushing on me, and while I'd like to strip for you and get it on, we're going to have to wait until you're eighteen. I have a no-minors rule, but the moment you blow the candles out on your cake, I'm game."

"You're sick, and I go by Elle."

He shrugs one shoulder, still smiling. "You're the one telling me to take off my clothes."

"I want your jacket so I can sit and not ruin my dress, you moron."

That grotesque smile doesn't wane as he slides his jacket off and dangles it in the air by two fingers. I shove the middle of his chest with my fingernail, and he rocks before I snatch the jacket. Lightweight. Andrew is tall, and he looks solid, but unlike Drix, he moved.

I spread his jacket over a bench and sit. Every muscle in my body sighs in relief, especially my ankles that are tired of maneuvering in heels I'm sure are a form of capital punishment in other countries.

"I was there when your parents told you to stay away from Terry Clark," Andrew says.

I take off my shoe and consider throwing it at him. "He approached me."

For 1.2 seconds, I consider reminding Andrew that my parents threatened him with death if he left my side tonight, but I don't. Doing so would make it sound like I needed his help, and admitting that makes me feel weak.

"The Elle I knew a year ago would have given Terry Clark a verbal beat-down and a slap that included claws and his blood. But I guess your dad is right—you've matured. Seems a lot changed while I was gone."

I circle my ankle to ease the tension. "When did he say that?"

"Before the fund-raiser began. I overheard him talking to your mom."

My head snaps up because I wasn't expecting that response.

"Your dad thought you were going to fight him on that damn dog you convinced the felon to take on, but he said you stood there, took your punishment and agreed to everything he laid out for you without argument. Both of your parents were impressed. Have to say, I am, too. I thought everything with you was always a fight, but I guess you're learning how to play the game."

Andrew's monologue is salt on a bleeding wound. I'm being torn apart. Between who I am to the core of my being, the person who would have stood up for herself, and the person I've been asked to pretend to be. Have to admit, I'm ashamed, at least when it came to Terry Clark, that I did keep silent.

Mature. What does being mature mean? Mature feels an awful lot like being tamed, and so far, I'm not caring for the view from my cage. "Why does being mature mean I have to let people treat me like crap, all while I smile and act like I'm grateful for being dumped on?"

"If you look at it that way, we all might as well hang ourselves by a showerhead now." Andrew removes a package of cigarettes from his pocket and knocks them against his open palm.

"You shouldn't smoke," I say. "Studies have proven it will kill you, and if that doesn't change your mind, studies have also proven it causes you to age faster. You seem a little too self-obsessed to be okay with wrinkles at twenty-five."

"This is Kentucky. It's politically correct to smoke."

I shoo him away with a flick of my fingers. "You're wrong, but if this is how it has to be, then go be politically correct farther down. I don't want to smell like smoke, and I don't want to die from secondhand lung cancer."

He does what I ask by positioning himself downwind of me, places the cigarette in his mouth, and cups his hand over the lighter. I watch as the flame sparks to life. A few puffs in and ashes form at the tip. Andrew places the lighter in his pocket, draws in a deep inhale then releases a long stream of smoke.

"You really going to do this, Elle? You want in on the political game?"

"No on the game, but changing the world is a good thing. I don't mind helping Dad. He does amazing things for people who need help."

"You should join the Peace Corps if you want that daydream because politics is a game. Even you can't change that."

While the Peace Corps is admirable… "I believe in my dad. I believe in what he's doing. Guys like Terry Clark are awful, but my dad is someday going to make people like that obsolete. No more playing their games. No more letting money have power. He will protect the people."

Andrew flicks the ashes. "You think that's how it is?"

"I know that's how it is. Dad came from nothing, and he remembers where he came from and how hard it was. Dad wants to help people."

He watches me as he sucks on the cigarette again. With the exhale, he shoots the smoke into the starless night. "Here's the truth even your parents won't tell you because they don't have the heart to kill that innocent optimism that even I find attractive—you can't fix things without compromising yourself and your beliefs."

"I have a hard time believing that. My father stays very true to his beliefs."

Using the hand with the burning cigarette, Andrew points in the direction of the ballroom. "You think your dad likes Terry Clark?"

"I know he doesn't." My father loathes that man.

"Yet this is your father's party, and Terry Clark was invited. That man treats all women like dirt, but he's on the invite list to every fund-raising function because he has money and he owns a lot of people in the right spots, and your dad is smart. He knows if he wants the programs that are going to make the world a better place, then he has to make deals with the devil himself. Terry Clark included. Your dad takes money from Clark, and with the amount of money Clark gives, he expects his phone call to be answered."

"Dad doesn't bow down to Terry."

"Not on all things he doesn't, but he bends on some. In order to win, you have to lose. That includes your precious morals you wrap yourself in."

"That's not how it should be."

"*Is* and *should* are two different things. You know this— at least deep down you do. You kept your mouth shut with Clark tonight because you instinctively know how to play the game. Just like your dad."

"My father is a good man."

"Your father knows how to get things done. He knows how to take care of the greater good. That, Elle, is politics."

"How Machiavellian of you."

"I'm assuming you're referring to me being smart."

"I was aiming for deceptive. You know, the bad part?"

"Morality is subjective. Being king and making sure your country is safe and solid means making tough choices. Your dad knows how to make the choices for the greater good."

"My father fights for everyone."

"Your father invited Terry Clark."

Pure fury and my voice rings out into the night. "If my

father saw what happened tonight between me and Terry, he would have stepped in."

Andrew meets my glare, holds it for a few seconds, then drops his cigarette, grinding it out with his shoe. "We've been gone for too long. Are you ready?"

I stand, Andrew reclaims his suit coat, shakes off the dirt, puts it on, then offers his arm. Another part of my soul sends a warning shock at the idea of caving in and accepting his offer. "I need a few more minutes on my own."

"Suit yourself. But if your mom and dad ask where you're at, I'm not covering for you."

Andrew returns to the hotel, and I lean my head back wishing the clouds would part and I could find some stars. Searching the night sky can negate all the things that weigh me down and make me feel I'm drowning. Some people hate knowing they're such a small piece of the universe, but I prefer it. Makes my problems seem less encompassing.

Footsteps and I glance over my shoulder. A shadow rounds the corner, and I ease closer to the door, my fingers gripping the handle. While I'd like my few minutes alone, I'm not suicidal.

But then a familiar face enters the light, and so much happiness explodes from me I could be compared to a supernova. "How did you know I'd be out here?"

Drix is no longer in the suit from earlier, but in a pair of jeans that hang loosely off his hips, and he's in the same snug T-shirt as when he was in my room. "I didn't. I needed to clear my head."

"Are you all right?" I ask.

"Yeah." Drix rubs the back of his neck. "Sometimes I have

demons that like to ride me hard, and being outside helps scrape them off."

I want to ask what the demons are he's referring to, but if he wanted me to know, he'd tell me. "I don't know about you, but that fund-raiser was pretty brutal."

"You okay?" he asks as he shoves his hands into his pockets.

"I will be. I'm not interested in Andrew."

His eyebrows methodically rise, and I can't read if he thinks what I said was crazy or interesting.

"I've told you about Andrew, but I thought I should clarify that Andrew and I are barely friends, and most days I lean toward thinking he should be neutered."

"This is you being direct again."

"I thought it would be easier than lying in bed tonight, staring at the ceiling, wishing I had said that to you. Then imagining a million scenarios of how I could drop it in conversation later because, while I danced with him, I like you."

I like him. I said it out loud, and while it's obvious I like Drix as a friend, I like him as more than a friend. There's this surge of excitement and fear, and waiting for him to respond is absolutely painful.

"I was thinking." Drix watches the ground, not me, and I hate the distance that's between us when we were so close earlier. "Maybe your family and your dad's staff have it right. Maybe we should stay away from each other."

Blood drains from my face. "But I like you."

"I'm no good for you."

"You're wrong."

"I'm right." Drix steps back, widening the gap between

us, and the action feels so heartbreakingly dismissive. "I'm drawn to you, but if this goes bad, I have too much to lose."

His words strike me like a sword. "That doesn't sound like you're bad for me. That sounds like I'm bad for you."

"I'm on probation. I mess this up, they don't pat me on my head and send me to my room. I go to prison. Not juvenile detention. Prison. And the last thing I want or need is prison. This isn't a game. This is my life. Two weeks ago, when we found Thor, I almost kissed you. *Kissed* you. The governor's daughter. And, Elle, if I'm alone with you again, I'll do it. I'll kiss you and I'll want to keep kissing you and I'll want to keep holding you. My life falls apart if this goes wrong."

"Then we don't let it go wrong."

His arms go out from his sides as if I should be understanding something I'm obviously not. "We don't get to decide which way it goes."

"Yes, we do. We decide. We make it happen."

Drix scrubs a hand over his face, and just the fact he's struggling hurts. "That asshole touched you tonight, and you let him."

My body goes numb, and it's hard to catch a thought. That man did touch me. In ways that weren't okay, and…as much as I hate myself…I did let him. I didn't push his hands away, I didn't scream, I didn't slap his face. I compromised myself.

Drix looks like a bomb ready to detonate, and I'm the one keeping the wires from meeting. But there are no wires, there are words, and the wrong ones could cause the explosion.

"He touched you, and I wanted to hurt him. He made you uncomfortable, and I wanted to make him bleed. I can't feel this way. I can't have feelings for you. I can't be the one to smash an asshole's face in when he treats you like a piece of meat."

"I didn't ask you to," I whisper.

"No, you didn't, but this is me when I feel. This is who I was before the arrest and who I don't want to be. As much as I want nothing more than to be around you, as much as I want to touch you and kiss you and hear your laughter and your voice, I can't. You and me—it can't happen. Not in public. Not in private. I lost one year of my life, and I can't lose any more."

I'm frozen, and Drix breathes hard like he ran a marathon. "I lost a year. A year with my family, a year with my friends, a year I don't get back. And I meet you. This incredible girl and it kills me that I'm still losing on bull I had nothing to do with. I'm sorry, Elle, but my family needs me, and I don't want to be the guy who beats the hell out of somebody because they touch you. I can't be that guy anymore, and I can't put myself in the position to be tempted. I'm not strong enough. Not yet."

Drix finally raises his head and looks straight at me. His eyes are thunderclouds on the verge of rain. My heart aches. I'm losing something amazing before it was even mine. This is it. This is over. The first guy I ever really liked and who liked me back said it's over.

Air is a struggle as my lungs collapse, but I clear my throat because this is what I've been trained to do. Mask the hurt, keep going. "The animal society said they'll place the puppy's information on the website for adoption next week. I can stop by, get him and take him to the shelter if you don't want to wait until they find him a home."

I think of the cute fur ball I held two weeks ago. I think of how I had hoped to see him again before we turned him over to strangers. It's easier to focus on him than the sadness. "The no-kill rescue organizations said they don't have an open spot. So the animal society is our only shot. I hate it because they can't guarantee he'll stay alive."

"He'll be adopted," Drix says.

I close my eyes. "I'd give anything if he were mine." We should have never named him. He became mine then, and losing another dream right now sucks. "I have to go back in, but I'll come get him when I'm back in town."

"What about your parents? They're already mad at you."

"That's my choice."

Drix steps forward. "I'll take him to the shelter."

Frustration causes me to choke. "I get it, Drix. You have a lot to lose. I understand, and you're making the right choice. Taking the dog, not taking the dog, it doesn't matter. It doesn't make it better that the best guy I've ever met, the only person I honestly want to be around, can't be around me. So don't worry about it. I'll take the dog."

"We named him. His name is Thor."

"No, it's not. He'll become whoever his new owners want him to be."

He flinches as if my words were a slap. "I'll take care of him."

Fine. If that's what he needs to do. Because ripping off Band-Aids is the most humane, I gather the hem of my dress so I won't trip and place my fingers on the door handle. "Good luck with everything. You deserve the best."

And I make the mistake of meeting Drix's eyes. There's

pain in them, and I hate that because Drix deserves better. He deserves that smile I've been graced to witness. But I can't be the girl to put it there, not anymore. "You deserve to be happy."

I turn away from Drix and go back in to find Andrew.

Hearts and Minds
Kylie Pleasant, USA TODAY

Ellison Monroe, daughter of the current Governor of Kentucky and candidate for the open US Senate seat in the state, is capturing the attention of more than the constituents of her state, but also of the nation.

The seventeen-year-old, on the verge of starting her senior year of high school, has shown herself as not only on the cutting edge of fashion, but as a champion for issues that are important to her generation.

"For years, as children, we are told to be seen and not heard," Ellison said in her latest speech at the University of Louisville, "but it's time for us to shed those old rules and learn that our voices are important and need to be heard."

With social media accounts that have followers in the thousands and are growing daily, Ellison is becoming a force of nature that is having a positive effect on her father's approval rating among younger voters.

Page 1/Page 2

HENDRIX

THOR'S CURRENT FAVORITE ITEM TO CHEW ON are Holiday's shoes. Never mind that I've given him old socks tied around empty water bottles as toys, Thor keeps returning to the pair of high heels. With his head down and butt up, he growls, attacks and chomps on the shoe like he's taken down a water buffalo.

Holiday fell in love with him at first sight—otherwise Thor wouldn't be alive. Axle's not happy with the additional mouth to feed despite the fact that I'm buying the cheapest food I can find, and I haven't taken him to a vet since Elle was involved. Keeping him is stupid, but it's all I have left of Elle.

Two weeks have passed since the fund-raiser. I've gone on trips, she's gone on trips, but they haven't been together. Don't know if I should be relieved, but each time, I'm kicked-in-the-balls disappointed.

Holiday, Axle and I are in the living room. Holiday is on her stomach rolling a ball to Thor. When it passes him, he bounces on it with both paws, but when it rolls away, his focus returns to the torn-up shoes.

I'm in the recliner that's older than me, and every muscle in my back aches. Axle got me a job on his crew hammering in shingles for roofs. When I work, it's twelve-hour days, hot as hell and doesn't pay near enough. I sweat buckets and come home dehydrated and famished. I make less than Axle's paycheck, but it's money.

Axle's taking a catnap on the futon. As a part of his training to become a paramedic, he just got off a forty-eight hour ride-along that included extracting a family out of a car that flipped eight times. He was also on duty during a kitchen fire in 110-degree heat index.

The window unit pushes in cold air and a standing fan helps circulate it to the other rooms. The central air unit imploded two days ago, Axle's car died, Holiday grew a foot overnight and needed new clothes, and roofers/paramedics-in-training might as well work for free.

Each time I go to an event, I hear the governor talk about the upswing of the economy. I hear him talk about bettering people's lives. I can't help but wonder whose lives are improving because it's not the lives of the people who sweat all day. His economic improvement strategies aren't for the people who are forgotten.

The evening news continues, and as I grab for the remote to change the channel to one of the other six we get through the antenna, Elle's face appears. Bright blue eyes that aren't hers, and dark blond hair that's from a bottle. The remote falls back to my lap.

"The Bluegrass Beauty is making headlines again," the

news anchor says. "Today, it was announced she will be next month's cover model for the largest magazine in the nation. The magazine's editor said Ellison Monroe is the epitome of grace, charm and intelligence for this generation of women, citing not only her fashion choices, but Ellison's involvement in social issues."

Pictures of Elle at various events fill the screen. Each time Elle is breathtaking yet I don't see happiness. That smile might fool other people, but it doesn't fool me. It's her polite one, the one she uses on everyone else.

"Ellison returned to Kentucky earlier this week from a photo shoot in California and is scheduled to be leaving again soon for Washington, DC, where she'll be traveling with her parents and Andrew Morton, the grandson of Kentucky's current and retiring US Senator."

Cue pictures of Andrew and Elle together. Her on his arm and both dressed to kill, them dancing together at the fundraiser I had attended, them smiling at each other onstage during her father's speech.

Jealously is a mean bastard.

The camera returns to the news anchors, and they face each other. "Does this mean Andrew Morton and Ellison Monroe are dating?"

"That has been a very popular question asked of the Monroe camp. Each time, the press is asked to give Ellison her privacy in such matters."

"That doesn't sound like a no." A huge sugary smile that causes me to close my fist.

"No, it doesn't, and the public appears to be rooting for Ellison and Andrew to become a couple. Andrew is a few years older than Ellison, and insiders have suggested the couple is waiting to make an announcement about their relationship when she turns eighteen this week. On a side note, there are rumors Ellison has been ill since her trip to California. A close family friend confirmed her parents brought a doctor to the house, and IV fluids were administered."

"Like many other Kentuckians, our thoughts and prayers are with Ellison. In other news—"

I turn off the TV and stand. Elle's sick? Holiday glances up at me, and so does Thor. Axle cracks his lids open, too. Elle's sick, and I can't do a damn thing to find out if she's okay.

It's like someone reached inside my chest and is squeezing the life out of me. Elle is sick, and I can't check on her because I told her I was better off without her. I need a release, and a long time ago, that used to be playing the drums.

"Want to go hit something?" Dominic enters from the hallway, echoing the thoughts in my head because that's where Dominic used to live—in my mind. We were so close that people would mistake us as fraternal twins.

His presence causes me to be off balance as I didn't hear him enter the house. The kid is the Grim Reaper with his black hair, battle scars and cold blue eyes.

Axle's gaze darts between me and Dominic, and he rubs at his eyes as he sits up. "You okay, Drix?"

"No," Dominic answers for me, "he's not. Come on, let's go hit."

"I told you and everyone else, I'm not playing the drums."

"I wasn't talking drums. Though you're an idiot for not playing. You want to make some money? Gigs. We could make bank playing gigs, and we need a drummer for that."

Dominic doesn't flinch from the death written on my face. Ignoring the last part of his statement and focusing on the first, he has to be high if he thinks picking a fight with some random guy on the street is in my best interest.

"I'm not talking about that either." Once again reading my mind. "Come on. Trust me."

Trust him. Weeks home and Dominic still hasn't talked about the night I was arrested, and I still don't know how to be around him.

"You should go," Holiday says to me, and I feel like an asshole. I promised her I'd try.

I take a step in Dominic's direction, and, smelling trouble, Axle shoves off the futon. "I'll come."

"No, you sleep." Because Dominic and I need to have it out, and I'm pissed enough that doing this might feel good. I'll worry about regret later.

Dominic goes out the back, and I follow. He ignores our garage, cuts through our yard, jumps the rusting chain-link fence at the dip from the years of us hiking over it, and he beelines it for the garage in his backyard that's all busted windows and a sagging roof.

Above us are gray clouds, and heat lightning flashes across the sky. Dominic leaves the door open behind him, and I pause in the door frame. With no electricity, the garage is dark, highlighted only by the rays of dull light streaming through the broken glass. Dust floats in the air. My eyes adjust, and Dominic surveys a worn punching bag.

"So you weren't talking me hitting you?"

A faint smile marks Dominic's mouth. "I had a feeling that's what you were hoping for." But then the same blackness of the sky covers his face as he turns to me. "You want to take a swing at me, do it. I'll stand here and take the hit. No swing back."

Lead solidifies in my gut. This kid has taken more hits than anyone in life should, and I could never add one more. No matter how mad I am. "I don't know how to get past this."

Dominic launches a right hook at the bag, and it swings. "I know."

He catches the bag. I lean a shoulder against the frame and cross my arms over my chest. I told Holiday I'd try. I told her I'd attempt to mend our family, but there's so much anger swirling around inside me that it seems impossible to speak.

I scan the dirty garage, then Dominic's broken house. When I was in the forest, the anger didn't exist. Maybe I'm a better person behind bars.

"I was thinking," Dominic says. "We should go out like we used to. I talked with Jenna and Renee yesterday, and they were asking about you. Renee told me to tell you she's around."

Around as in she's down to hookup. Renee was good for that. I used to be good for that, too. Renee and I were cut of the same cloth. Neither of us liked attachments. We were on the hunt for anything that made a high run in our veins. Renee's a beautiful girl, probably one of the smartest girls at our school, but I don't want the hookup anymore. I want Elle. "I don't want the hassle."

"There's no hassle with Jenna and Renee. They know you're on probation, and neither of them believe you did the crime. Hell, Jenna's dad's serving time downstate for a crime he didn't do either. He had the same damn public defender you did, and he also took a plea deal. One year looked better than ten. The girls know and understand the score—no drugs, no alcohol. Just two girls, hanging out, relieving some stress. You're seventeen, Drix. Not fifty. Let's live."

"No, thanks."

"You like the girl." Dominic's blunt admission causes my muscles to lock up. "The governor's daughter. Don't deny it. I saw the look on your face when you told us how you got Thor, and I saw the same look when you saw her on TV. You finally fall for somebody, and she's out of reach."

Thunder rumbles close enough that the ground vibrates. I don't deny it, and I don't look away when he briefly meets my stare. There's a give inside me because Holiday's not the only one who wants her family back. I do, too. I want my best friend back. I want to shoot the breeze with him until 3:00 a.m., I want to binge play our battered and bruised Xbox, I want to tell him about Elle.

"Which was it? Did she want nothing to do with you because you're a poor boy, or did she turn her nose up to you because you have a criminal record?"

Neither, and I'm not having this conversation with him. I went to jail for him, and he can't even thank me. He can't look me in the eye and tell me he's sorry. I turn to go back to the house.

"Hey!" Dominic calls, but I ignore him.

"Hey!" Pounding of feet behind me and my arm is wrenched back when he grabs my biceps. Anger pummels my bloodstream when he whips my body in his direction, and we're nose to nose.

"I don't want to hit you," I seethe, "but keep pushing me and getting in my face, and I'll lay you out."

Dominic raises both of his hands and shoves my chest at full strength. I rock, and my arms automatically come up. I fist his shirt and push him into the concrete block of his garage. The air rushing out of his lungs with the impact.

"Do it," Dominic yells. "If it'll make you feel better, do it."

"Make me feel better?" Lethal rage pours into my muscles, and my fingers shake with the need to do exactly what he's asking for. "Rewind time and redo it all. How about you don't dare me to shoplift because you were pissed I was going someplace with the music and you weren't? Because you had to feel big and you wanted to make me feel small. How about you had been the best friend you claimed you were and noticed I was too lit to be on my own? How about instead of robbing the store yourself you had made sure I made it home? How about when you heard how I'd been arrested, how I woke in a drunk tank, how I called Axle scared as hell, you stepped up and confessed?"

"Is that what you want?" Dominic asks, back still pressed against the wall, not giving a damn my fists are still pressed against his chest. "You want me to take responsibility for your choices?"

I shove him into the wall again. "I want you to take responsibility for *your* choices. I saw the evidence. They laid it out for me. Same height, same build. Black T-shirt with the word Renegade written in white. I know you did it, and I want you to admit it to me. I want you to tell me you're sorry. I want you to thank me for not letting you go crazy behind bars in a small room because that's how much I love you. I want you to acknowledge our friendship is worth you admitting the truth."

Dominic leans forward, and there's danger in those crazy blue eyes. "I didn't do it."

As if struck by lightning, my entire body jolts, and my fingers yank free from his shirt as I stumble back. "What did you say?"

"I didn't rob the convenience store. You went to jail, brother, but it wasn't for me."

Ellison

I'M STILL LOSING ON BULL I HAD NOTHING TO do with. Drix's words continue to echo in my mind. He said so much to me, many things, but some of his words feel weighted... *I had nothing to do with... I'm used to taking the fall...*

Rain taps against the windows, and I finally find the strength to throw off the covers I had yanked over my head. My head is foggy, and as I sit up my body is heavy. I hate California. I hate California rolls. I hate flying from California to Kentucky after eating California rolls. I hate whatever virus I contracted, and I currently hate my revolting body.

My mouth is a desert, and the water bottle on my bedside table is empty. No doubt I could text Mom for more, no doubt I could open my mouth and whisper her name and she'd come running, but maybe moving out of this room of the Black Death will help me recover.

I open the door and go down the stairs, my feet cold against the hardwood. The house is unusually quiet and unusually empty. Bet there's a black flag hanging on a pole out front, warning the world of the plague.

In the kitchen, there are multiple vases of flowers on the island. With a cold bottle of water from the fridge in hand, I pause when I spot my name on the cards. My forehead furrows, and I open the card attached to the red roses.

Elle,
I hope these roses bring a smile to your face like you bring a smile to mine. I miss you. Get well soon.
Andrew

The card falls from my grip, and I place a hand over my mouth. I haven't barfed in hours, but that note made bile crawl up my throat. Like he honestly cares. Wonder who forced him to write that note and why.

Searching for another sign of life and proof that the aliens I dreamed about last night didn't invade earth and kill everyone but me, I wander through the house in the direction of Dad's office. If there's nobody there, then the world is definitely lost. There's always someone in this house at work.

Not a good sign when one of the double doors is open. I step in, and it's eerily empty.

"Mom?" my voice is pathetic and scratchy. "Dad?"

I should head back upstairs and check my cell, but I'm too tired. Instead, I choose the next best thing—the phone on Dad's desk.

When I was a kid I used to love to play in Dad's massive, cushy leather chair. I'd go round and round until I was so dizzy that if I laid on the floor the earth tilted. I drop into

Sean. I'm coming in."

I'm still losing on bull I had nothing to do with.

Between fevered dreams about aliens and complete human annihilation, I dreamed of Drix and those words.

I'm still losing on bull I had nothing to do with.

What does that mean? Was it just words that fell out during so many other words? But that doesn't feel right. Drix is methodical. I open my mouth and thoughts tumble out. Drix, on the other hand, thinks. Overthinks. The opposite of me.

I pick up my head, and the world has a fuzzy haze. My body's hot, and I drink half of the cold water. I move the mouse on Dad's computer. The time and date appear in the corner, and it's like someone kicked my already sore stomach. Crap. I've lost not just time, but I've lost track of days. The big trip to DC is this weekend.

It was supposed to be parties and fund-raisers, and Dad said I might meet the president. The *president*. I would have had thirty seconds. I was going to fill those thirty seconds with something profound, something amazing...something that would have left my father proud.

I sigh as another wave of dizziness hits. I'm obviously not making Dad proud today.

I'm still losing on bull I had nothing to do with.

"What did you mean, Drix?" I whisper.

I pull up Solitaire on Dad's computer, but three clicks in and my brain starts to hurt from focusing, so I turn the chair away from the screen. Behind Dad's desk are binders. A ton of binders. Dad loves to have all of his political stances printed out with bullet points. It helps keep him organized and on task, but he'd better hope the environmentalists never find out how many trees he's killing.

In a corner of binders on the floor is one labeled Second Chance Program. Below it is another binder labeled Hendrix Pierce.

I'm still losing on bull I had nothing to do with.

"Congratulations, Elle," Dad says as he enters the room. Even though it's Wednesday, he must be having a down day as he's in a T-shirt and jeans. "You hit one of your first milestones of your career in politics."

I use my toes to slowly spin in his direction. "Did you congratulate me on being sick?"

"Politician plague. Shake enough hands, kiss enough babies, and your immune system will finally meet its match."

Dad stops short of his desk, and his face falls. "You look bad, Elle."

I try to flash him my perfected fake smile. "Why, thank you."

Dad rounds his desk and places the back of his hand against my forehead. "You're burning up."

"I'm fine."

The I'm-sorry glance he's giving me says it all, yet he still talks, "You're not going to DC."

Not what I wanted to hear. We had big plans for my birthday in DC, and that's what I was looking forward to the most—spending time with Mom and Dad.

"I win this election and you'll be in DC all the time."

If he wins the election... "Am I doing okay? With the election?" Has doing close to everything he's asked of me and being miserable the entire time been enough for him to forgive me?

Dad tucks my loose hair behind my ear. "Your mom and I are proud. You've followed every direction, and Sean came by to tell me we're leading in the polls. Hugely. You've played a big part in that. Even Sean's impressed."

I sit a little higher. At least I do in my head—in reality I might have slumped lower in the chair. Regardless, I love my dad. Just love him.

"I know your mom and I have been tough on you, but we know life, and we understand hard life. I came from nothing, you're mom had so many demons she had to slay to make it out emotionally alive, and look what we have now. We love you, more than we could have imagined loving anyone. We want the best for you."

My mom and dad didn't want children. They were so emotionally scarred from their childhoods that they weren't convinced that adding to the human population was a good idea. But then there was me. I was a surprise—a happy surprise, I have always been reassured, but a surprise. One, as Mom has said, they have worshipped since seeing two lines on a pregnancy test. I believe them, but sometimes their love is a little intense.

"Let's get you back in bed before you puke in my office."

I start to move, but then my eyes fall on Drix's binder again. *I'm still losing on bull I had nothing to do with.*

"Hey, Dad?"

"Yes, I'll carry you."

"No, that's not what I was going to say." But doesn't sound like a bad idea. "Why did you choose Drix for the program?"

Dad's eyes narrow. "Why do you ask?"

"I'm curious. How did you know he was the one to take the risk on? Your program was going to succeed or fail on his shoulders. How did you know he was the one? You promised to help end the school-to-prison pipeline, so why did you think Drix was the one to prove it?" I fan myself as a wave of unwanted sick heat hits my head. "When so many things hang in the balance, how did you know you were making the right choice?"

Dad leans back against his desk and crosses his arms across his chest in a relaxed position. I must be doing something right because he's going to answer. Typically, my father blows these types of questions off—at least with me.

"If I talk to you about this, then it stays between us. Part of doing this type of job is learning how to keep information to yourself."

"Got it."

"Do you understand the pipeline theory?"

I read about it when Dad proposed the program, and people thought it was a waste of money. "Teens act out at school, sometimes being thrown out over something such as cursing, sometimes something worse. While out of school they commit a crime. They go to juvenile detention, and even though they have classes there, they fall behind in their studies. They get out, don't do well in school because they are behind, act out, get suspended, commit a crime while on suspension, and end up in juvenile detention again. Rinse and repeat until they turn eighteen and end up in adult prison."

"That's the gist. How did I choose the spokesperson? By making an informed decision. We looked at teens from several different stages of the pipeline. Ones who had already been in and out of the system several times, to some who were on their second offense, and then there was Hendrix. First offense, a *serious* first offense, and a history of suspensions at school for fighting. His home life had instability, and teens like him have greater chances of staying in the system once entering."

A painful squeeze in my chest. Fighting. Drix said he was scared of returning to who he had been. "But why choose *him?*"

"He didn't fight the charges. Within forty-eight hours of being arrested, he pled guilty. He showed signs of remorse, showed signs of concern for his future, and had an older brother who stepped up and promised to help once Hendrix was released from the program.

"Unfortunately, there isn't a lack of teens to choose from, but with so many eyes on an unpopular idea, we knew we had to be conservative with our choices. Make choices with teens who had a better chance at success so we could expand the program to all. Any teen we picked was a risk, but Hendrix was a controlled risk. We had a feeling from day one if we removed him from the situation he was in, showed him who he could be and then returned him to his brother, he'd succeed. His success and his willingness to be the face of the program will pave the way for other teens to escape the pipeline."

Individual attention. Individual care. Individual plans created for the individual teen. Lots of money, and anything involving lots of taxpayer money isn't popular, even if it helps save lives. But my dad, he's not the guy who makes the choices for the greater good. He understands society won't work until the voiceless have a voice.

That's good because my dad is my hero, and I'd be crushed if he was anything less.

My fever-induced slow-moving brain rolls through Dad's explanation, and my eyebrows knit together. "Drix didn't have a trial?"

"No."

"How do you know he did the crime?"

"As I said, he confessed."

My head begins to pound, a blinding pain, and I rub my temples.

"You just turned a scary shade of white, Elle, and I don't like it. Your doctor said you shouldn't push it."

"You're my doctor.

"Exactly. I'll feel better if you're lying down."

Me, too.

I'm still losing on bull I had nothing to do with… I'm used to taking the fall… Drix's words are like their own virus mutating in my mind. Drix confessed, so what do those words mean? What could he possibly mean?

HENDRIX

"KELLEN!" DOMINIC YELLS AS WE ENTER HIS house. "I think she headed to your house to hang with Holiday."

Dominic pops his head into the living room, bathroom, their Dad's bedroom and then when confirming we're alone, the two of us climb the rotting and aging stairs to the attic Kellen and Dominic share.

The house is hazmat clear, meaning their Dad is gone. Dominic carries too many physical and emotional scars from a man who is supposed to love and care for him. Hopefully the son of a bitch won't return for a few hours because he could never keep his mouth shut around me, and I could never keep my mouth shut around him. There aren't enough years in the forest that can heal me of that illness.

Once upstairs, the heat trapped by the roof causes my clothes to stick to my skin. Dominic kicks the small trunk that has held his belongings since we were kids in my direction. "Open it."

I drop onto the thin twin mattress that serves as Kellen's bed, and Dominic sits his ass down to floor level onto his mattress that doesn't have a box spring or a frame. Resting my arms on my bent knees, I clasp my hands together because I don't want to open this box. If Dominic didn't do the crime, I have a sick feeling of where this is headed, and suddenly the truth doesn't seem so important.

"I'm not talking until you open the box, and you're not leaving until I talk."

Because Dominic is stubborn, I undo the combination lock, flip the top back, and, after moving around the crap on top, I rake a hand through my hair. The gun Dominic bought on the street a few weeks before I was arrested is there, and so is a stack of cash.

"It's only half the money. Kellen said she dropped the other half. Far as I'm concerned, it's yours. It's been tainted with the blood you bled this past year taking the fall," Dominic says. "So tell me, what do you think the police do with guns they confiscate from crimes?"

Hell if I know, but that's not what Dominic is really talking about. It's a reference to the fact that the gun used in the crime was found next to my passed-out body, and last I heard that gun was still in police possession. Dominic still has his gun which means he didn't do it, and he just basically said Kellen did the crime—damn. "Kellen did it?"

"Kellen did it." Silence as we stare at each other until he finally looks away. "Look, I'm capable of stupidity so I don't blame you for wondering if I could have pulled something that insane off, especially at the time, but how could you think I would let you go down for something I did? You're my brother, and I don't treat my family like crap."

I drop the top of the chest into place and meet his pissed-off glare. "You want to go there?"

"I've been there, and I've been waiting for you to finally arrive."

"You and I got drunk that night." I spell out the play-by-play. "We smoked up until I couldn't remember our names, and then you start pulling that dare nonsense. If I remember correctly, when I said no, you told me if I didn't play along it's because I sold you out for the band. You said if I didn't shoplift, I was more concerned about myself, and not you."

"I never said I wasn't a jealous asshole." Direct and brutally honest. Dominic and Elle would get along...either that, or hate each other.

"Jealous asshole or not," he continues, "I would have never let you go down for a crime I committed. And if I had known in time, I would have never let you go down for Kellen either."

I roll my neck, then lower my head as if that could help with the weight pressing down on me. "I would have never let you do that."

"She's my sister. My responsibility. It wasn't on you to take that fall."

I raise my head and see the truth tattooed on his expression, but there's no point arguing. "It doesn't make sense. They told me the guy who did the crime was the same height and same build as me. Kellen's tall, but there's no way you could mistake her for me."

"Did you see the footage?"

I shake my head. The police only showed me a still frame, blurry image of the shirt—the type of shirt Dominic used to wear. When they described the person they had on video, I knew in that moment, or at least I thought I knew, it was Dominic. They found that shirt next to me, along with the gun. "It was your T-shirt."

"The same one I bought at the dollar store? The same one they had a hundred of? They railroaded you into that plea deal, brother."

Yeah, they did, but I still would have pleaded guilty for Kellen, and as much as I hate to admit it... "Accepting the plea deal was my best option. That public defender got my last name and case information wrong every time he walked in my room. My fate was in the hands of a man who couldn't remember what I was being arrested for. I was screwed from the start."

Axle had asked for another public defender, but all public defenders were overloaded with cases, and the lawyer I had was actually giving me more time than he did with his other juvenile cases. He wasn't a bad guy—just underpaid and overwhelmed. As someone told me in juvenile detention, public defenders have so many cases that they "meet 'em, then plead 'em."

"Why did you leave me behind?" I push. "When I passed out behind the convenience store—why did you leave me?"

"Honest to God, Drix, I thought you went home. I knew you were mad at me for daring you to shoplift, and when you staggered through the alley and made the turn for the store, I was pissed at myself for daring you. I did go after you. I checked the store, the parking lot and the alley, but I obviously didn't check hard enough. I thought you abandoned me, so I went home."

The two of us both screwed up, and it's time to let that part of that wretched night go.

"Why did Kellen do it?"

Dominic rubs his hands together. "It's my fault. Things with Dad were bad. Worse than normal. It was getting harder to keep Dad's fists on me and not her. When I got home that night, Dad got me good. Cracked me in the back of the head hard enough to draw blood." Dominic angles his head and the scar resembles grated skin.

I swear under my breath, and blackness tightens my muscles.

"I have to admit, I saw stars. I thought the bastard finally won and had killed me. Kellen dragged me up here, and she was a mess. Choking on her own tears. Pacing the floor. The kid was losing it, and I was in and out of consciousness. To calm her down, I lied. I told her I was going to get another job, save money, and when I had enough, we'd leave.

"She was scared. She knew there's no way I could make that much money when I could barely afford to take care of the two of us. I passed out, Kellen stole Dad's gun and went shopping for cash in an effort to speed up the imaginary timeline to get us out. You know me, Drix, I'm a disaster, but even I know not to steal from Dad. If you're interested, I got a nice burn mark on my back for the missing gun. I considered shooting Dad in the head when he gave me the burn." The frightening smirk on his face makes him look possessed.

"But I obviously changed my mind. Two of us in jail didn't seem smart."

"You should have told me things were getting worse with your dad."

"When?" Dominic's eyes widen in a challenge. "When you were on the road playing in a band with your new best friends? How about the few times you came home and only cared about getting laid and getting high?"

I pop my neck to the side and hope to God Dominic can grant me forgiveness. I stare at him. He stares at me. He screwed me over that night, but I also screwed myself and let down my best friend. "Never said I wasn't an asshole either."

The right side of Dominic's mouth turns up. "I guess that's why we're friends."

Guess it is.

"I know you thought I did it," he says, "and I know you thought you were saving me from hell in a small room. If thinking that kept you strong behind bars, I wasn't going to take that from you."

Dominic's right. Though I had anger, on the nights I thought I was going to lose my own mind, I thought about what being behind those walls would have done to my best friend, and it gave me the courage to keep myself from fracturing.

"How's Kellen?"

That weight I'm carrying appears heavier on him. "Messed up. Lost it for a bit after she found out you confessed to the crime. Cried all the damn time and that set Dad off. Kellen wanted to tell the police, get you out of jail, but I wouldn't let her. You want to be pissed at me on that, I deserve it, but it's Kellen. I couldn't do that to her. You want to be pissed at me for not taking the fall for my own sister even after you took the deal, I deserve that, too."

Dominic touches a faint scar on his wrist. That scar haunts me, and I don't think there's a day it won't. "For months, I considered confessing, but I couldn't leave Kellen alone with Dad, and then when I thought about being locked in a room…" He meets my eyes, and I see the same terror as when the doors are shut and the windows are closed. "I couldn't."

"I'm glad you didn't." Kellen doesn't have claustrophobia, but she wouldn't have survived this house without her brother. She's fragile to begin with. Juvenile detention would have done her in, and Dominic would have died. If not his body, then what was left of his soul.

"Kellen feels guilty, brother, and the longer you're mad at me, the worse it's getting. Life has got to get back to normal, or the kid is going to break. I can't let that happen." The desperation in his voice picks at barely healed scabs.

"Why not tell me all this when I got home?"

He works his jaw. A signal he's weighing his words. "I was waiting."

"For?"

"To see if you were the same asshole who left here a year ago or if I was getting my best friend back." Dominic stands, relocks the trunk, shoves it in a corner and hides it under a blanket. "I knew immediately we didn't get the asshole back, but you didn't come back the guy I claimed as my best friend either. It took me a while to figure out who you are. I needed to make sure if I told you the truth, your focus would be on helping Kellen."

It's scary to hear him verbalize my fear: the terror of not knowing who I've become. "Who am I if I'm not who I used to be?"

His forehead furrows like the question surprises him. "You're better."

Better. While the word creates a sense of relief, it also feels a lot like the suits—makes me feel like I'm wearing a sign that points out I'm a fraud. "How do I help Kellen?"

"I promised her I wouldn't tell. She's not me and you. We can handle pressure. If she's aware someone else knows what she did, she'll crack. She needs her family back and acting normal again. Holiday and Axle do, too. We're all on eggshells wondering if the changes we're seeing are real or if you're going to change your mind and go back down that dark road."

No more dark roads. Not for me. "I'm in this."

Dominic studies me, then nods. "Good. So you know, I'm clean more times than not. I won't claim I'm sober, but I won't do anything to ruin what you've fixed in your life."

The drinking, the drugs... I don't miss it. I didn't have the same type of withdrawal other people in detention had, didn't have an itch under my bones for a hit of any kind after I was clean. I met guys whose bodies and minds belonged to a substance other than themselves long after the drug was physically out of their systems.

But I liked the high. I liked feeling lost. I liked not feeling like me. While high, there were no emotions and no thought. While high, my life fell apart. There are no more highs for me.

Dominic leans back against the wall. "Why aren't you playing the drums?"

"Not going there."

"Me, you, Axle, Kellen and this Marcus kid could make money, but we need a drummer. Hell, Holiday would be a huge draw with her voice if Axle would let her onstage."

I breathe deeply, doing what the therapist told me to do when anger creeps into my blood one drop at a time. He taught me if breathing didn't work, to remove myself from the situation, so I scoot to the edge of the bed ready to bolt. "I can't do it."

"Why?"

Another breath. "Because you're not the only one scared I'll go down that dark road. I know the drums aren't to blame, but I don't trust myself. I felt high behind the drums, and I'm scared to let myself feel that high again."

"Playing the drums is a part of you. A good part of you."

"Next subject."

"Drix—"

"I said next subject." The words come out harsh, and I give him a warning glare.

Dominic only shrugs his shoulders like the ominous turn was comparable to an annoying fly. "Tell me about the girl."

Not a better change of subject. "There's nothing to tell. She's the governor's daughter."

"We've been friends since we learned to piss in a toilet, and I've never known you to fall for a girl. There's plenty to tell. Consider telling me about this girl as your first step in making us a family again."

Ellison

MOM AND DAD ARE IN DC, AND I'M CONSIDER-
ing disowning them. I hold the thermometer to the camera
on my laptop. "Ninety-eight point six. Normal. My temperature is normal."

When they left my temp was normal, but, no, I couldn't go.

On her end of the video chat, Mom tilts her head. Her
blond hair is pulled up into a twist and she has on diamond
earrings that dangle. That means she's headed to something
fancy. Something fancy I'm not attending that includes the
president.

Yes, I'm bitter.

Behind her, people are moving about in her hotel room.
Dad is close enough that he occasionally adds his opinion to
whatever Mom and I are discussing.

"Martin said to not push yourself and that you needed to
rest," Mom says. Martin has been Dad's friend since medical
school, and he took over Dad's medical practice. "You have

a full schedule when we return, and those events are important to your father's campaign."

"Yes, I can see how meeting the president pales in comparison."

"It was never a hundred percent certain you would meet him, and if you did, it would have been brief. When your father wins the senate seat, you'll have plenty of chances to meet him."

I slump back on my bed against my pillows.

"What did your father say?"

"Eyes on the prize," Dad calls out in the background. "I told her to keep her eyes on the prize."

On the bed next to me, my cell vibrates again, and I ignore it. It's been an avalanche of texts from friends terrified I'm dying since the media announced to the world that I'm sick and that a specialist (Martin) was called to the house.

I called my friends Megan and Jennifer from school today in hopes they could get the word out that the plague did not end my life, but obviously people still want to hear specifically from me that I'm breathing. "Did you find out who leaked I was sick?"

Dad pops on to the screen over Mom's shoulder. "Sean's working on it. Are you sure you're okay staying at the house by yourself? Maybe you should stay with a friend."

"Or you can have a friend stay with you," offers Mom. "But let me talk to their parents first, so they understand your father and I are out of town."

Which means Mom wants to approve of the person I'd choose for a sleepover.

"Maybe you can ask Megan or Jennifer? I can text their moms now."

Either will be fine, but… "I'm fine on my own." Truth is, I am still tired, and while I love my friends, I don't have the energy to talk 24/7.

I level my stare straight on Dad. "How did the media get the note Andrew sent with his flowers? To be honest, that seriously creeps me out. I thought we could trust the people coming in and out of our house, and the thought that someone is watching me and telling the media everything doesn't make me feel safe."

Mom's smile falls as she looks up at Dad. He takes Mom's cell, he's on the move and a door clicks shut. Dad sits, and I can tell he's on a bed. "I need you to be honest, Ellie, are you scared being there by yourself?"

It's physically painful to not roll my eyes as this place is wired tighter than Fort Knox. "I feel safer without anyone here. I'm more worried that someone we know isn't respecting me or my privacy."

"Sean thinks someone at the florist where Andrew ordered the flowers called the media. Other than not ordering flowers from there again, there's not much we can do."

My cell vibrates again, and I ignore it again. Dad's watching me, waiting on a reply.

"I trust every person who enters our home," he says. "No matter what, your safety comes first."

My cell pings indicating an email. I pick up my cell and open the email when I notice it's from Sean. "Sean just sent my schedule for when you guys return, and he told me to spend my bed rest learning my speeches. He dared me to do one of the speeches by heart. Tell him, dare on, and I'm going to win. He also says you should have been downstairs five minutes ago and that I need to tell you I'm fine, otherwise he said you won't care you're late."

Dad doesn't laugh like I expect, instead he remains dead serious. "He's right. You're my daughter. You come first."

Andrew can suck it. I know my father. He does not. "I'm good, Dad. I promise."

"Your mom will feel better if you weren't alone. Plus she feels guilty we aren't going to be with you on your birthday."

"The whole birthday thing doesn't bother me. We'll celebrate when you return." And because it's my dad and we're close, I choose honesty. "As for being alone, I don't feel comfortable staying with anyone right now. I trust my friends, but I'm not sure I can trust the other people in their house. Plus, I'm still tired and I don't want to host. I want quiet."

Dad nods. "Being in the public eye is a tough life. Rest up. We've got big events when we return, and I need you at a hundred percent."

"Will do."

"When we get back, you name whatever it is you want to do for your birthday and it's yours. I'll have Sean schedule the time off. I love you."

"Love you back."

Dad winks and then he's gone. I have the best dad ever. I truly do. I turn off the video chat, open Sean's email on my laptop and scroll through the events. Most of them I knew about, but my level of presence and activities at the events have increased which gives me an awesome thrill. I'm needed, what I'm saying is making an impact, and that's amazingly cool.

Speaking at the Daughters of the American Revolution—check.

Attend the Louisville Bats Game—check.

My head tilts to the side as I read the overview of events at the game. *Elle will be in attendance with Andrew. Elle and Andrew are scheduled to appear on the Kiss Cam.*

I'm sorry? I'm going to do what? Actually, no, I'm not. No. Way. In. Hell.

My cell is in my hands, and there's one ring for video chat, then there's another. I'm so angry my fingers shake, and if Dad doesn't answer soon I'll have no choice but to get in my car, drive all the way to DC and scream very loudly for a very, very long time.

The call is accepted, I inhale deeply, so I'll have plenty of air for my raging rant, and I'm dumbfounded into silence when Sean appears. "Calm down, Elle. It's not as bad as you think."

"You want me to kiss Andrew. Yes, it's exactly as bad as I think."

"A friendly peck. That's it. Seconds of your life."

"Where's Dad?"

"You're overreacting."

"Where's Dad?"

"Your father was already running late because he was listening in on the phone call with you and your mother, and then he talked to you privately. He's busy."

"Then I'll talk to him later." I go to hang up.

"If you do everything I ask of you from here until the election, I'll not only convince your dad to let you take the coding classes, but I'll convince him to let you apply for the internship."

I blink because I'm confused why he knows about this.

"Once your dad wins, they plan on moving to DC—you included. But if you do all that we ask, with no attitude, I'll lean on your dad to let you and your mom stay in Kentucky until you graduate from high school."

A rush of air out of my mouth because I hadn't fully realized what winning would mean. Dad and Mom would move, and they'd want me to move with them.

"Plus, your mom and dad have seen the schedule and have approved it. They know about the Kiss Cam and you know how protective they are of you. They see this for what it is— nothing big. This is you overreacting and letting your emotions run away with you. A quick kiss on the cheek, that's it. Something playful. The crowd will think it's fun and cute."

Maybe I'm still sick because I'm overwhelmed with the need to vomit again. I don't know how to, nor do I *want* to, explain to Sean why this is big for me. I've never been kissed. "Why can't Mom and Dad kiss?"

"People want young."

"Then make someone else kiss."

"When are you going to understand? Drix is winning the minds of the state by proving your father has ideas and programs that work. But you, Elle, are winning their hearts."

I open my mouth to offer another better alternative, but Sean cuts me off. "Are you in or out? I need to know now. You will have a strong media presence at the game. It's assumed you'll take part in a tradition. It's insulting if you don't, and people will notice. Plus it's already on the schedule. If we have to call and tell them it's not happening, that will be the bigger news story. Are you going to throw me attitude, or are you going to do exactly what I need you to do?"

My lips turn down as pure sadness drowns me from the inside out. "Fine."

"Thank you. I appreciate how mature you've been. As I said—"

I hang up on Sean. I may be making the "mature" decision, but no one ever said I had to be "mature" with him. I close my eyes and take a breath in and a breath out. I will not cry over this. I will not cry over Andrew. I will not cry over Sean. I will not cry over any of this.

My cell rings. No doubt Sean attempting to reconnect, and I deny his request. Seconds later, he tries again, and I deny his request again. Each and every denial my silent expression of how much I hate him. Sean calls again, and I hang up on him again. I can do this all night. After the fourth time, he gives up.

I told Dad I wanted time alone, but the silence in the house I found comfort in before has disappeared. It's now deafening, and it causes me to feel hollow.

I open my texts. Maybe Mom and Dad are right. Maybe I should invite a friend over. I scroll through my messages, thinking of who would be the least dramatic. Who will be willing to watch movies and go to bed before midnight.

Names roll through the screen, and then my brain has a hiccup. I scroll back and my heart stalls. It's Drix and he texted me yesterday. An hour between two texts.

Drix: I heard you were sick and I want to make sure you're okay.

Drix: Maybe this will help. He likes hanging at my home.

I put my hand over my mouth as my heart explodes. There's a picture of the cutest ball of fur on the planet. It's Thor.

Oh my God, Drix kept Thor.

HENDRIX

MY SISTER IS BAKING.

I can't find my cell.

I'm a broken and live wire.

Touch me, push me too far, and I'm going to explode.

On the counter are two sheet cakes my sister made from box mixes. She's frosting one and instructing Marcus how to frost the other. She's been at these cakes for most of the afternoon, and she hums to herself or sings along with the radio in that cool demeanor of hers as if two big sheet cakes in this small house is normal. Holiday's up to something, and it's slowly driving me insane.

"Where is my phone, Holiday?" She was the last one to have it. My cell has internet, hers just makes emergency calls.

"I gave it back to you. I can't help it you're forgetful."

If I lose this cell, I'm screwed. If Holiday's up to something, I'm screwed regardless. Maybe I should move to Montana. There aren't many people in Montana. There, I could be happy.

Thor weaves through my legs, then runs around me in circles. He's my shadow, following me everywhere I go, and I take him with me whenever I can. Currently, he longs for a walk. It's reaching late afternoon, that's what he and I do—walk for over an hour down by the creek. I'd like to take him out, but I need to find my cell first.

I open drawers in the kitchen and search them in the faint hope I set the cell on the counter, and it fell into one of the drawers. Forks, spoons, knives, various other utensils clank and bang together and then the pounding of wood against wood when I slam the drawer shut.

Holiday glances at me from out of her eye and then immediately focuses on frosting the cake. She begins to sing an old Beatles tune that's a favorite of mine, and Marcus joins in. They sound good together, complementing the other. Holiday has a soulful voice. Rough, edgy and smooth all at the same time. I used to love listening to her sing, used to love playing the beat for her when she sang. Right now, I'm not caring about her voice. I want my cell. "Where is it?"

Thor swings his gaze between me and Holiday. Because he's a good dog, he sits on my foot, then barks at her. *Get her, boy, then while you're at it, fetch my cell.*

She bats her eyelashes, pretending she has no idea what I'm referring to. "Have you checked your room? Maybe it fell out of your pocket up there?"

I've checked my room. Four times. I've checked every pocket of pants I own and every other pair that are not on people's bodies. "That phone is part of my probation. They call, I answer. That's how it works, and right now, I can't answer because I don't have it. The last person who had my phone was you, so where is it?"

I know Holiday is the one responsible, I can feel it deep in my gut, but still I search. In case I'm wrong, hoping I'll find where she's stashed it.

My sister does what she's done all day—shrugs one shoulder like that's an answer, and the level of crazy she's driving me to is undefinable. Skin peeling off my muscle, muscles crawling along my bones, in the way that only younger siblings can push older siblings out of their minds.

The back screen door opens, and Dominic pokes his head in. "Here."

A knife full of frosting drops from Holiday's hand as she spins, and it hits the counter. Her eyes go wide. "No, that can't be. The cakes aren't done."

Dominic's eyebrows rise. "Not my problem."

"But I have a plan and this is not part of the plan."

Dominic does a slow side eye to me, then studies my sister. "You've got to learn how go with the flow."

Sinking feeling along with the annoyance that they act like I don't exist. "What are the cakes for?"

Holiday flashes a smile at me. "One is for your birthday."

"I *had* a birthday. Six months ago." In juvenile detention.

Marcus turns with a can of frosting in one hand and a spoon full of frosting in the other. My mind is tripping over itself because a six-three stack of muscle with a tat on his right arm is baking, and he looks damn happy doing it. "You didn't tell me you had a birthday."

"Everyone has birthdays."

"You should have told me you had one in detention."

This entire house has gone insane. "And what were we going to do about it?"

He grins and it's almost contagious. "Sing, man. We would have sung."

Because that's what I would have needed. An entire cell block singing to me on my birthday.

"Well," Holiday says, "we're celebrating your half birthday, so suck it up."

Tension in my neck and I roll it. "I don't want another party."

"I don't want another party," she mimics in a low voice. "You know, you can do fun. That's not against the law. Anyhow, today is officially your half birthday, so we're celebrating because I like cake, and I was robbed of cake this past year when you weren't here."

"What's the other cake for, and what are you and Dominic talking in code about?"

Holiday sighs, then levels a hard stare at Dominic. "For real? Here?"

"Here. Axle's thirty seconds away from flipping cars. By the way, I told him it was your idea."

Her lips curl into a snarl. "Coward."

"Sticks and stones, sweetheart." Dominic fishes my cell out of his back pocket and tosses it to me. I consider taking a chair and breaking it against the floor just to make myself feel better.

"Why do you have my phone?"

"Did."

"What?"

"You said do. I don't have it anymore. You do, so now it's a did."

"I'm going to kill you."

"Ellison Monroe is out front talking to Axle. You better get out there. Axle's going to excuse himself to murder Holiday, and I don't think leaving a rich politician's daughter to fend for herself in your front yard is smart. The girl is pretty, but I'm not getting a street-educated vibe."

"It was your idea, too," Holiday sings as she returns to icing cakes.

I'm caught between that fogginess that happens when someone clocks you in the head and the overwhelming instinctual need to protect Elle. My feet are moving, so the latter wins. I hit the screen door with enough force that it bangs against the siding. I round the house, and I can't decide if this is a nightmare or the best dream.

Standing in my front yard, chatting with my older brother is the most beautiful girl in the world. Khaki skirt that's showing off some mouthwatering thighs, a fitted blue top that appears tailored to each and every gorgeous curve, her long hair pulled into a high ponytail with loose curls, and I'll be damned if she's wearing those sexy glasses which means the color of her eyes are the real deal.

It's Elle.

Dominic catches up to me, and he talks low and fast. "Four texts from your account. That's it. Holiday wrote them, I approved them before she pushed Send. We said something about Elle being sick and wanting to know if she was okay. We texted her a picture of Thor. We waited, and we wouldn't have sent another text if she didn't reply. But she did. Holiday knew it was her birthday and asked if she had plans. She didn't, so Holiday invited her here."

It's Elle's birthday. She's spending it alone. I had no idea.

"Her family isn't in town, brother, and she said yes. I heard what you had to say the other night, saw the look on your face when you talked about her. You like this girl."

I lean into him. "I walked because I don't trust myself. I can't screw up again."

Dominic places a hand on my arm, and it's a strong grip. "You won't. I told you, you're better than you were before, and if for some reason you do start to backtrack, I've got your back. I didn't before, but I do now. It's not enough for your body to be back home. I want your soul back, and the only time I saw a glimmer of that was when you talked about this girl."

"This was not your call to make."

"It wasn't, but she's here, and you've got a choice. Send her away and be the asshole that forced her to spend her birthday alone, or we order some pizzas, get some chicken wings and eat cake. Your choice."

Elle's gaze travels over my brother's shoulders, and when she spots me, she brightens. Not the expression I've seen on TV. The real one. The one I'm starting to believe might only belong to me. I'd give up years of my life if that were true. That somehow I'm deserving enough to be the guy who's worthy of her smile.

"Which one is it?" Dominic asks. "What type of man are you going to be?"

The right decision would be to send her home, hurt her feelings, cut open myself and bleed and make sure I don't piss off the governor and return to jail...or...spend Elle's birthday with her, soak up that smile, bask in her laughter, live for a few hours without the constant knots in my chest because only Elle has the key to unravel the chains that keep me locked up in my past sins.

Number two is selfish, number two is what she's chosen, but what type of guy am I if pick number two?

Follow directions, not follow directions.

Pick my own path or start my own?

Hurt her, hurt me, or maybe be seventeen, if only for a few minutes.

What type of man am I going to be?

That's the question. That's always the question...

Ellison

"DOES YOUR FATHER KNOW YOU'RE HERE?" AXLE'S question causes me to rip my eyes off Drix and back onto his older brother. For the brief few minutes since I've arrived, Axle and I have exchanged pleasantries.

Hi, I'm Ellison.

I know. His "I know" the equivalent to "Go home." *I'm Axle, Drix's older brother.*

Drix has mentioned you before. He has a lot of wonderful things to say about you.

Drix has talked about you some, as well. Axle went out of his way to make sure he didn't mirror my "and he said something nice about you."

Is Drix here? Like I was six and knocking on a door for a playdate.

And that's when Drix appeared, and my heart did a bit of a tap dance, but then that one question sent me crashing back into sick reality. *Does your father know you're here?*

I see so much of Drix in Axle—the dark eyes, and I can spot the same blondish-brown even though he wears his hair shaved close to his scalp. But Drix doesn't have tattoos, and Axle's arms are covered in them, and he has small hoops in his earlobes.

At the beginning of the summer, being nearly alone with this man in a neighborhood that has a high crime reputation would have frightened me, but I have a hard time finding that fear. Drix is nearby, plus this is Drix's beloved older brother. I may not be wanted, but I'm safe.

Protective. That's what I overheard Cynthia call Axle, and I agree with her assessment. "My parents don't know I'm here. I was invited and I accepted. If the invitation is no longer valid, I can leave."

Axle scans me from head to toe. Not at all in a perverted way that's been done to me by too many filthy men over the last several weeks, but he is taking in my wealth. The bracelets on my wrist, clothing on my body, sandals on my feet, then his eyes drift to the street.

"Nice car."

"Thank you."

"You leave it parked there, and it'll be jacked in about fifteen minutes."

The familiar anger creeps out from those doors I can't seem to keep locked, and I lift my chin. "If you'd like me to leave, it would be polite to say it instead of inferring your passive-aggressive feelings."

His eyebrows rise in this weird shocked motion, and I remain persistent in eye contact. I don't do passive-aggressive.

"Is there a problem here?" Drix's low voice is like a rumble of thunder. "Because from a distance, it appears like you're pissing off my guest."

Axle's head falls back, then he angles his body to make me, him and Drix a neat little triangle. "Her parents don't know she's here. Do you think that's a wise choice on your part?"

My lips squish to the side as I'm starting to feel like a yo-yo. "I've already explained to your brother I was invited, and I assumed you had taken our last conversation into consideration when you extended that invitation, but now I'm beginning to feel like maybe I should leave. But know that if I do, you are to never text or talk to me again. I'm not a toy, and you are not allowed to jerk me around."

"Drix didn't invite you. His sister did by stealing his phone." Axle sharply tilts his head in my direction. "Tell her."

I glance down to see if my skin is turning black-and-blue because my pride was just beaten and bruised. I'm a joke. I was invited here as a joke. It's my birthday, and I blink repeatedly because there is no way in hell I'm going to allow them to see me broken.

Keys out of my purse and I spin on my toes for my car. All members of the male species are stupid. Each and every single one. A complete waste of my time and I'm the idiot who had the moronic belief one boy was different from the rest.

With a push of a button, my Volvo blinks to unlock, and when I touch the handle, a body presses against the door and becomes dead weight. I look up, and Drix is staring down at me. "You move extremely fast."

My fingers wrap dangerously around my keys. "I highly suggest you move away from this car before I raise my knee and make your life extremely painful for the next two minutes."

Drix's lips twitch, and there's a spark in his eye that's informing me he's laughing at me in his mind, and that causes my blood to boil. "Last chance to move, Drix, and I would take me very seriously if I were you."

Instead of heeding my warning, Drix hitches his thumbs in his pockets in a too relaxed position for someone who is about to be nailed in parts he should be protecting. "I want you here."

I hate the small part of me that melts with those words, and I still own enough pride to cross my arms over my chest, refusing to give.

"Axle's right. I didn't invite you. My sister and best friend stole my cell. I didn't type the words, but I agree with what they wrote. I want you here."

"I'm not a joke," I say.

"No one thinks you are."

"This feels an awful lot like a joke. Contact the rich girl, invite her over on her birthday and then laugh it up when she finds out she came running after a setup text. What's wrong, Drix? Was not everyone here to see the big reveal? Or is it a joke that doesn't get old?"

"Then I'll go with you," Drix says. "If you don't want to hang here, then we'll go someplace else. I don't care where. I'll leave that up to you, but don't walk, Elle. Just—" he lowers his head and when he lifts it again, his brown eyes bore into mine, and I'm close to hypnotized "—don't."

"You're confusing."

"I don't mean to be." Drix inhales as if he's struggling. "A year ago, I would have said as many pretty words as it took to convince you to do what I wanted, but I don't have much prettiness inside me anymore. I'm raw, and I'm telling you the truth. I want you to stay."

I pull at the ends of a strand of my hair, and I welcome the pain over the conflicting emotions crashing into each other at every pressure point in my body. "What about your brother? What about what you said the night of the fund-raiser? What about—"

"My sister made you a cake."

It's like someone pushed pause on the treadmill I was running on. "What?"

"My sister. Holiday. You met her on the midway. She made you a cake for your birthday. Two cakes, actually. Big ones. Sheet cakes. One chocolate. One vanilla. My best friend, Dominic, has promised pizza and chicken wings. He doesn't offer to pay often, so I'd jump on this train. They want to meet you, and I...I want you here."

"What about your brother?"

"Axle's only concerned about me. Same way your family is concerned about you. Give him a few minutes, and he'll warm up."

"Why should I stay? Why should I believe you?"

Drix shrugs. The same heart-stopping lift and lowering of his shoulder from the midway. "Why did you come?"

My mouth pops open, and no sound comes out. I came because of Thor. I came because it's my birthday, and I didn't want to be alone. I came because...because it's Drix.

"Stay, Elle. Just stay."

HENDRIX

WITH HER HANDS IN THE BACK POCKETS OF HER tan skirt, Elle wears that polite mask as she walks away from her car. I had her park behind our house and next to the garage. The front of the house isn't much to see, the back not much better. Suddenly the idea of Elle hanging here leaves a pit in my stomach. We don't have foyers and dining rooms with crystal chandeliers. Lemonade at my house is just a drink, not an event.

Elle skims a finger along the hood of Axle's car. "If car crime is a big deal around here, do you park in the garage?"

"No."

"Why not?"

Because what's in the garage is more important than any car. Since the night of the press conference, I haven't entered the garage. I've played acoustic guitar with Marcus when he shows, but no garage.

My brother has gone in there; so have my best friends and

my sister. At night, I've lain in bed and listened to them play, listened to them sing, listened to them laugh, and the sound was like shredded glass against my skin. It was also medicine on my soul.

Two parts of me pulling in two different directions. Both parts demanding they know what's best for my future. I don't end up going anywhere, though. I stay stuck in the middle.

Not eager to take Elle into the house, and in an effort to give Axle a few minutes to chill, I stride over to the door to the garage, undo the lock, flick the light on and step inside. Elle follows, a few steps back.

The flourescent light overhead buzzes, and Elle's sandals quietly clap against the garage floor. "Wow. There are a lot of instruments in here."

There are. Elle drops her small purse onto the floor near the door and returns her hands to her back pockets. She walks past the stands that hold Axle's, Dominic's and Marcus's electric guitars, and Kellen's bass. At the piano, she pauses.

"When I was a young, like five or six," she says, "my parents took me to some congressman's or senator's or somebody important's home. If you think our house is big, this place would blow you away. The moment I walked in, I thought I was in Cinderella's castle. But then again, it was through a child's eyes, so who knows how massive the place really was.

"Anyhow, we were in this sitting room with antique everything, including the furniture. My mom and dad talked with the other couple for what felt like days, and I was only allowed to eat one cookie and have one drink and I was incredibly bored."

She regards the piano like it's a religious relic she's drawn to and terrified of. "I asked Mom if I could look out the window, and on the way there, I saw this beautiful piano. Chestnut color, hardwood, shiny, had one of those long open tops where you can see inside, and the piano had beautiful white and black keys. I wanted to touch and hear the sound it would make."

I understand the feeling. Have felt it my entire life. This itch beneath your skin that can only be scratched by playing a chord, feeling that musical vibration down deep into the marrow of your bones.

The piano she stands in front of is nothing like the possible baby grand she's describing. This is an upright acoustic Dominic and I bought for twenty bucks off a guy who was full-blown tweaking and had a shady white truck of stuff he was unloading to anyone with green. We were fourteen, and it took Dominic and me an hour to push the piano on wheels to this garage, but it was worth every blister and near heat stroke.

After listening to the notes, their pitch and harmonies, Dominic began playing as if he'd owned that piano his entire life because that's how the son of a bitch is—pure talent.

Elle flashes a sly smile. "It was like I had an angel on one shoulder and the devil on another. The temptation to touch in direct contrast to my mother's reminder that I was to be seen and not heard."

I could definitely see her mother's face when she said it. "What'd you do?"

"I touched."

My eyebrows raise. "You touched?"

"I touched."

"Born insurgent from the get-go."

"Don't sound so shocked. You're talking to the Whack-A-Mole rebel and the stray dog–saving mutineer. I totally have a bad side."

I laugh, the type that takes me by surprise, the type I've only been able to do with Elle, and she grins along with me. But then the smile falls, and it's like watching a single candle that brightened an entire room be snuffed into darkness. "My mom was so mad. She slapped my hands. First and only time in my life she's struck me, but I remember the sting on my skin, the cold shock throughout my body and her words. She was so ashamed of me, so disappointed, and then when I looked over at my dad, I could tell he felt the same way."

A rip in my chest at the ache in her eyes. Elle's always beauty, always impeccable manners, always this picture of perfection, but in this moment, there's only pain.

"I have never touched another instrument since."

It's like someone staked my heart. "Never?"

She methodically shakes her head. "Never. I'll be honest, I don't listen to music much either. Whenever I hear it, it makes me feel…guilty. Like I've done something wrong."

Guilty. Yeah. That I understand, too, but for Elle, it's a shame. Music is life. "You can touch the piano if you want. It's more against the rules here to keep your hands to yourself."

Elle glances up at me, and I waggle my eyebrows. I love how she blushes.

"I'm serious. Play."

"I don't know how."

"It doesn't matter. None of us knew how to play any of these instruments at some point. First step is finding the courage to make a mistake. Playing music will mean mistakes. Sometimes those mistakes lead to new sounds, new rhythms. Music is not perfection."

And it's part of why I miss it so damn much.

She withdraws her hands from her pockets, but it's like a force field has formed between her and the keyboard. Instead of reaching forward and pressing the key that will cause a hammer to strike a wire that would play a sweet note, she takes a step back and tucks her hair behind her ear.

The need to mirror her motions is too strong. For every step she takes, my body automatically takes one as well, but not to widen the gap, but to be near. Damn if I'm becoming her puppet, and she controls the strings.

"I was supposed to be in DC this weekend," she says. "I was supposed to be meeting the president tonight."

"That sounds important."

Elle nibbles on her bottom lip as she continues to stare at the piano like the keys are razor-sharp teeth and if she makes the wrong move, it will jump forward, snatch her and bite.

"I have to kiss Andrew."

Serrated knife cut to the throat. "What did you say?"

"Sean sent me my itinerary for when everyone returns from DC, and Andrew and I are scheduled to go to the minor league baseball game in Louisville. It's been scheduled for Andrew and me to perform for the Kiss Cam."

Jealousy smothers me as if I fell into an algae-thickened pool. A breath in. A breath out. I'm the one who sent her away. I'm the one who told her we wouldn't work. I drove her straight into the arms of that bastard. "You're with him, then?"

Her face twists in disgust, and she drops a hand to her stomach like she's about to puke.

"That's sick. On so many levels. Having him as my first kiss is the last thing I want."

Did she just say...?

"I tried calling Dad, but Sean answered. I was mad and he knew I would be mad and he said words and I said words and then he said more words and somehow I agreed. Now I'm kissing a guy I absolutely hate in front of the entire world."

A slight tremble to her lower lip, and her hand shakes as she twists her hair. "I don't know what's happening to me. I want to take coding classes, and I want an internship. But now, I don't know who I am. I've somehow become the girl who allows men to touch my body in unwelcomed ways because they have power. I'm now the girl who stays silent when people say things that are offensive, and I'm the girl who gives her first kiss to a guy who makes my skin crawl. I don't know who I am anymore, but I do know I don't want to be this girl. I just want to be me. But according to Sean, I don't get what I want unless I compromise, and I don't want to compromise."

The rims of her eyes are filling, and she blinks like that will make all the hurt, all the pain go away. I understand her pain, understand her desperation. There were nights when tears spilled down my face. Late at night, in the dark, staring at a ceiling, missing my family. Hating myself for giving attention to anyone who used me and for ripping apart the people who really cared.

I understand trying to please someone you think loves you. To keep that love, you keep twisting and bending yourself to become who they want you to be until you eventually break. There's a hole in them, a hole they need filled, and they want you to become the circle that will fit into them to make them complete, even though you're a square. It's an awful place to be, the person responsible for someone else's happiness, because being human, we're going to fail.

And by being human, we'll take the lashing when we never meet expectations.

When I joined that band, my dad stayed in town, he talked to me, spent time with me… I thought he loved me, and I ruined myself to keep that attention.

I don't know how to explain this to her. I don't know how to tell her that tearing herself apart for someone else will end up killing her. As I told her earlier, I ran out of fancy words after being arrested, but she's in pain. Knowing Elle, that pain is feeding into anger, and she'll need a release.

I have a feeling Elle's not into long walks through a bad neighborhood, then to a worse area along the creek. The type of walk I've taken nearly every night since I've been home. I have another feeling she's not into building a fire with two sticks and some flint.

My heart pounds. I know what I need to do, and for her, I'll take the risk. With her, maybe I can handle the high I feel behind the drums. Maybe I can trust myself. I pick up the piano bench, haul it over to behind my drums and shove the stool out of the way. "Come here."

Elle's eyes crinkle as she tries to understand what I could be asking her to do. I don't want her to think. Thinking in this moment is bad. She needs to feel. If she feels, then she'll be able to take all that's bottled inside her and give it away.

Maybe if I allow myself to feel, too, I can finally give away some of my pain.

Terror, fear and excitement become a potent drug as I pick up my drumsticks for the first time in over a year. Last time I touched these, I was on a path to self-destruction. My decisions, my behavior, my past all colliding and causing an explosion.

But a year ago, I didn't know Elle. A year ago, I never thought of anyone but myself. According to my family and Elle, I've changed. Maybe it's time to be man enough to figure out if that's true. "Come here, Elle. I'm going to teach you how to play the drums."

ellison

DRIX TWIRLS HIS DRUMSTICK IN HIS HAND BE-
fore pointing it toward me, then jerking it back toward him.
I just got called out. Challenged. I sigh because I'll hate myself if I cower back like a scared mouse. As if my ankles were
shackled together, I cross the garage. Drix slides back on the
bench and motions for me to sit in front of him.

I fold my arms over my chest and appraise the drums as
if there were spiders scampering along them. "I'm going to
make a fool out of myself."

Drix bobs his head back and forth. "Probably."

My mouth pops open, and when he flashes that heart-
melting grin, I smack his arm and then straddle the bench to
sit in front of him. Drix slides up the seat, his body pressed
into my back, and air rushes out of my lungs with the contact.
The insides of his thighs are touching the outside of mine.
His heat penetrates through his jeans to my skin.

Drix reaches around, and his hands cover mine. His thumbs

work open my fists I had no idea I had formed. I give, and he places a drumstick in each palm. His fingers skim my skin, and it's such a beautiful tickling touch that my entire body hums. Then his large, calloused hands tenderly close my fingers around the sticks, and he covers my hands with his.

"Everyone thinks the key to playing the drums is a firm grip, but it isn't." Pleasing goose bumps form along my neck as his breath whispers against my ear. "You want a light grip. It's not about muscle, it's about momentum—the tighter you hold the sticks, the slower you'll go. The sound comes with the opening and closing of your fists and of your wrists."

He leans his head over my shoulder and raises our combined right hand. We hit a drum to the right and then a drum to the left. His deep voice drifts over me like smooth silk. "These are the tom-toms."

He guides our right hands toward the floor and hits another drum. Every muscle in his arms flexes, and I'm quickly losing the ability to breathe. "This is the floor tom."

Moving our left hands, Drix hits a smaller, thinner drum, and it has a quicker, snapping sound. "This is the snare drum."

I shift on the bench in the desperate search to stay upright, and Drix somehow settles closer to me. Can he feel my heart beating at every pressure point? Can he feel the excited tremble of my body, the quick rising of my chest with my rapid breaths? Does he know, besides when he held me in the hotel room, this is the closest I have ever been to a boy?

His foot nudges the inside of mine and ushers it to a foot pedal. The touch of his leg twining with mine so intimate, I shiver. Drix gently pushes the pedal. "This is the bass drum, and these—" he moves his left foot to the inside of mine and delicately slides it toward another pedal "—are the hi-hat cymbals."

I try to wet my dry lips without Drix noticing, but with his face so close, I had to be unsuccessful. "What's the large cymbal called?"

Drix raises our right hands and strikes the cymbal with such force that I flinch and then laugh. The type of laugh that starts in my stomach and is so joyous in sound that it feels like I'm flying. Drix laughs with me, his body creating a fantastic pressure as it shakes against mine.

"That is the crash cymbal."

Drix releases my hands and rests his hands on the top of my thighs. I briefly close my eyes at the gentle touch. The tip of his index finger brushes against the line between my top and inner thigh. On purpose, not on purpose, I have no idea, but oh my God, my heart is going to explode.

My hands begin to lower, but Drix removes his right hand from my thigh to force them back up.

"What do you want me to do?" The question barely a whisper.

Drix angles his head, his mouth so close to my earlobe I swear to God his lips brush against the sensitive skin as he breathes out, "Play."

As if I had become weightless, a feather prone to the desperate breeze, I rise from the bench. Reverently shaking my head back and forth, and my grip on the sticks loosens. "I can't."

A strong and firm hand on my shoulder and Drix exerts enough pressure I return to the bench. "You don't have to know how to play. You just play. No perfection here, Elle. Just you being you."

Just me being me. But who is that anymore?

My hands quiver as I timidly hit the tom-toms. Other than their hollow sound filling the garage, nothing happened. No mother yelling. No slap of pain against my hands. No disappointed stares. No shame.

Handling the sticks how Drix had gently positioned them in my hand earlier, I strike the snare drum. The sound causing me to sit straighter, more determined, and everything within me lifts to a higher level. My spirit, my lips, my cheekbones, my hands.

This. I can do this.

As if through their own volition, my hands move the sticks, hitting them against the different drums. My feet stomping on the pedals. No beat. No rhythm. Just noise, dissonance and freedom. The sound fills the garage, fills my soul, fills me. It's loud, it's overwhelming, it's chaotic, and it's peace.

I finally pull back, my chest rising and falling rapidly, adrenaline coursing through my veins, and I angle so that I can face Drix. "That was fantastic!"

Drix's dark eyes stare at my lips, and I draw in a shallow breath, but I can't release it. That hunger in his eyes, I've seen it before in my direction, but never had I felt that same hunger inside me...until now. Do my eyes look as wild as his? Does his heart beat as quickly as mine?

Drix tugs the sticks from my hands and drops them to the floor. They tap several times before rolling to a stop under the bench. The only other sound in the room is the buzzing of the light and the pulse in my ears.

He cradles the back of my head and stares intently into my eyes. "Can I be your first kiss?"

A million butterflies take flight in my chest, and the sudden motion makes me dizzy or maybe it's how fast I'm nodding. "Yes."

Drix's thumb brushes my cheek as he tilts his head and lowers it to mine. His lips so close to my lips. Just a breath's distance, and when I inhale, I'm consumed by his dark, rich scent.

"Me and you, Elle," he whispers. "This belongs only to me and you."

Yes, it does.

And he kisses me. His lips pressing against mine, and careful of my glasses, his fingers clutch my hair. Drix's other hand rubs gently along my back. It's soft and sweet, and warmth floods through me, and there's this need for closer, to press near, for more.

Drix draws my lower lip into both of his, and I part my mouth. My heart beats hard at the idea of going further, beating hard at how I never want to stop. Drix accepts the invitation, our kiss deepens and I lose myself in the haze of it all.

My skin tingles with his touch, my mouth burns against his, my mind reels with his strong presence and touch. A strange falling sensation in my head and I pull back and gasp.

Breathing. I was forgetting to breathe.

I rest my forehead against Drix's, and we both scramble for breath. Because this was the most intense moment of my life, I whisper his name.

I don't know why, I don't know what I'm trying to say, but he seems to understand as he kisses my forehead and gathers me into him. My head on his shoulder, my arms wrapped around him, his arms wrapped around me. An embrace that is warm, that is safe. An embrace I could stay in forever.

"What is this, Drix?" I whisper. "What is this between us?"

"I don't know," he says against my neck. "But I'm not ready to let it go yet."

Neither am I.

HENDRIX

THERE'S A KNOCK ON THE DOOR, AND ELLE pulls away from me and slips off the piano bench. But she doesn't watch the door. She looks at me instead. Her gorgeous blue eyes shine. I rise to my feet, stretch out my arm, and hold out my hand to her. I should say something. Explain how I want her standing beside me when my family plows in, but this action feels stronger than a declaration. "If you want to keep us a secret from them, we can, but they won't say a word to anyone about us. My secrets are their secrets. It's how it works."

"Your brother doesn't like me."

Another knock on the door, and I call out, "You can wait," while keeping my hand outstretched. "My brother doesn't like anything that's going to hurt me. You make me happy. Give him a few minutes and he'll see that."

"He won't tell Cynthia?"

"If I tell him to keep quiet, he will. That's how we work. This family, we protect each other. I'm the one that messed up and walked from them when I was fifteen. But as I said, you want to keep us a secret, I'm fine with your call."

The right side of her mouth quirks up, and she gives me this blinding grin. "Is that your way of asking me to be your girlfriend?"

"I guess it is." I can't help smiling along with her.

"You know when I first met you," she says. "You told me you don't smile very often."

I did say that, and for the year leading up to meeting Elle, I couldn't remember smiling. For six months before that, my smile wasn't from joy, but from a fake and deluded sense of happy. "What can I say? You're magical."

She winks, and that confidence that belongs only to Elle returns as she places her hand in mine. "I am."

Another bang on the door to the garage, and my sister shouts, "I'm coming in now!"

The knob turns, and sunlight and my sister's head poke in. "You played the drums. I heard you. I mean, I heard something. You might be rusty, but you played."

I squeeze Elle's hand. "Elle played."

Holiday's eyes widen so big she looks close to a cartoon character. "You let someone else play your drums?"

"Is that a big deal?" Elle asks.

I lift one shoulder, but Holiday answers, "It's a huge deal. A massive deal." Her hand splays over her heart. "I've never played his drums, and he, in theory, loves me." Holiday's head jerks to the side. "Shut up. Shut the freak up. You're holding her hand. You're holding Ellison Monroe's hand. He's holding your hand. Are you two together? Like a couple? For real? You are. You're together and I did this. I'm the one who sent the text and the reason Ellison came here. It was me. I did this!"

"It's a secret," I say, and she rolls her eyes in a "duh."

"Of course, but still, you owe me because I did this. But anyhow, you're together and Drix played and I want him to play again."

"Yeah." Dominic walks in behind Holiday. "But this time with a steady beat."

No way. Elle playing was one thing, but me playing is something else. "I was going to show Elle the house and get her something to eat."

Dominic approaches Elle and holds out his hand. "I'm Dominic. His best friend. Nice to meet you. The house is a dump, but it's better than mine. Honestly, you ain't missing much, and pizza's on the way. Do you like chicken wings?"

Elle blinks several times because that's how someone reacts to a train wreck that is my family, but she releases me and shakes his hand. "I'm Elle, and I've never had a chicken wing."

Dominic recoils. "What are you? Amish?"

"I bet Amish eat chicken wings," says Holiday. "They shun electricity. Not food."

"Po-tay-to. Po-tah-to. Same thing."

"It's not."

Dominic picks up his electric guitar and says, "I'm always right, Holiday. Get used to it. Now, let's do this."

Axle and Marcus walk in together, laughing. Half of Marcus's black shirt is stained with cake mix, and when Holiday points it out, he takes her hand and twirls her like they had been in mid-dance. Holiday giggles, then playfully shoves him away. Marcus winks, and I nod my head when he looks over at me. His family is toxic, but mine isn't and I'm not afraid of sharing.

Axle rolls up the main garage door and a light breeze sweeps into the building along with a ball of fur. "Your dog whines when you leave. Figure out how to make it stop."

Thor races toward me, his paws clicking against the concrete. Elle explodes into a supernova as she crouches down and holds her arms wide-open as if the dog could hug her back. Thor goes straight to her, and she loves on the ball of black-and-white fur as he licks her face. "He's so big."

True. I doubt she could even pick him up, and Thor's impatient not understanding why he's not in the air. With a tongue hanging out, he looks over at me, and I crouch and scratch him behind the ears. The sense of pride when I see him confuses me, but I go with it. I put my arm around Elle and kiss her temple, causing Thor to break into another round of licks for Elle.

My family suit up with their instruments with the seriousness of a soldier going to war. Dominic pats Kellen's back as she picks up her bass guitar. He gives her some instructions of how to switch fingers on chords and encourages her to keep going, even when she gets behind. He then turns on his amp. She rolls her eyes behind his back because she's a seasoned player, and he's an idiot.

Holiday settles behind the piano, and my older brother stands in the doorway, his hip cocked against the frame.

From the start, my life with music has belonged to Axle. When I was six, Dad was in town; he picked me up from Mom's, bought me a Happy Meal, and when he dumped me at his house, he promised he would teach me how to play guitar when he came back later that night.

Dad left me alone. I sat in the hallway, knees drawn up, arms wrapped around them, and watched as the rays of afternoon light slanted into rays of evening light. The house was hauntingly quiet except for the sound of the refrigerator humming, and I thought about calling Mom. She might have been drunk and passed out, but she was there. Always there.

Then there were clouds. Dark clouds, black clouds and thunder rumbled in the distance. Lightning flashed across the sky, and each strike felt like a shot through my stomach. Tornado sirens rang out, wind hit the house, and something banged against the side. I shook, head to toe, and the lights flickered, then blackness.

Tears burned my eyes, and I rolled into a ball. I didn't want to be alone, I didn't want to die, and I didn't want to be in the dark. The wind howled, a screeching of a freight train, the ground trembling beneath me and a scream. The wind screaming, me screaming, the glass exploding and shattering throughout the house.

"Drix! Drix, where are you?" Arms around me and my screams were muffled into a shoulder covered by flannel. A hand behind my head, I was in the air, then dropped into the bathtub. The cold porcelain biting into my back and then a hard body on top of me.

"It's okay," Axle shouted over the wind. "It's okay."

And we lay there until the storm passed. Him over me. Me clinging to him. The wind died down. The rain slowed to a pattering on the tin roof, then stopped. Axle eventually pushed off me, helped me up, and the two of us slowly crept through our small house. Taking in the shards of glass in the living room, in the kitchen, but the walls were still standing.

Axle cleaned the glass off the counter, set me on it and looked me over for blood. "I told you after Dad bought you dinner to have him take you back to your mom's."

I rubbed my nose as Axle used a kitchen towel to clean up a cut on my knee. "He said he'd teach me how to play guitar."

Axle's head snapped up, his dark eyes meeting mine, and I saw something then I've seen too many times since. My hurt mirrored in him. "You don't need him, Drix. If you want to play guitar, I'll teach you. Whatever it is you need, I'll give it to you. Neither of us need him."

My older brother takes in my arm around Elle. He nods. I nod. Elle is my choice, she's choosing me, and now Axle will defend her like he defends me. I slide my hand from around her shoulder and caress her back. "How do you feel about listening to some music?"

Her answering smile owns me entirely. "I would love that." Good. All of this is good.

Ellison

AN APP THAT HELPS PLACE STRAY ANIMALS IN foster homes and eventually their forever home—that's what I decided upon. It's ambitious, but I'm starting to figure out that ambitious might be who I am. It's a Wednesday, a rare day off for both me and Drix, and I'm at his garage again as this is the only place besides the occasional hotel room during a campaign stop where we can be alone.

Thor is laid out on his side dreaming puppy dreams—if he's allowed to be called a puppy anymore. I'm convinced he's part border collie/half bear. His feet twitch as if he's on a run. He's big now. Too big for me to pick up, but not big enough that he doesn't try to sit on my lap. While he likes me, he worships Drix. Though he'd never say it, Drix worships him in return.

As I try to program, I'm also listening as Drix talks about timing. He throws out words like four-four, three-four, six-eight, and nine-eight. I'm only half listening, and I'm pretty sure he's aware. He's this new force of nature behind the drums, and he wants me to love them as much as he does, but I'm not sure it's possible for anyone to love it more than him.

I close my laptop and rub my eyes. "My brain is going to explode."

"From which part?" he asks. "The four-four?" He plays that beat. "Or the nine-eight?" He pounds that count as well, and I have to admit, he's extremely sexy. Sometimes, Drix can be quiet and internal, but the more time we spend together, it feels like he's beginning to fly.

He stops playing, grabs the folding chair I'm on and drags it closer to him. In seconds his lips are on mine, and my body is the equivalent to a struck match. His hand is in my hair, and he tilts my head so that he can kiss me deeper. Right as I reach over to touch him back, his cell rings.

Just like that, he's gone, and somehow I miss his heat even in the sweltering summer afternoon. My fingers brush my now swollen lips. This. This is what being with Drix is like. A couple of weeks have passed since we first kissed, and I love kissing Drix. We haven't done more than kissing, as kissing is my comfort level, and Drix seems fine parking it here.

But *here* is a very lovely place. Here includes lots of kissing, and that I adore. I also love his hands on my body, I love how he smiles, I love his voice, I love how he talks to me, I love just being near him, and I wish I could spend more time with him than what I currently do. The only time we're alone besides the campaign trail is when Mom and Dad are traveling without me, which may only be one day a week.

"It's Drix." He answers his cell, and he reaches over and

sweeps a stray hair away from my face. His fingers linger along my jawline, and pleasing goose bumps rise on my arms.

His head inclines as if he's surprised by whoever is on the line. "Yes." A pause and a then he blinks. "Yes. That sounds great." Pause number two, and whatever it is that's being said is putting live electrical wires under his skin as he jumps to his feet and paces.

"Yes. Yes. Understood. I'll be there and thank you." Another round of pausing. "Okay. Thank you. Goodbye."

Drix turns off his phone and stares at it as if it might ring again. He then blows out a long breath, and the anticipation threatens to eat me alive. "Everything okay?"

"Yeah." He glances around the garage, and then he looks at me in complete shock. "I got the audition."

I can't breathe. "You got the audition."

"I got the audition." Drix throws both hands in the air, and before I can get to my feet to celebrate with him, Drix takes two steps, and I yelp when he swings me into the air.

My feet off the floor, his arms two steel bands around my waist and he has me angled so that I'm looking down at him. I frame his face with my hands, and I drink him in with complete awe. Hendrix Pierce, the boy who a year ago was on a path to complete self-destruction, is creating a future molded just for him. "I'm so proud of you."

"I knew I wanted this," he says, "but I didn't know how much until now. I *want* this, Elle. I want this spot in the school. I want to graduate from high school, and I want more. I can get out of this neighborhood. I can break the cycle. *I* can do this."

"And you will." I don't know much about music, but I

know when I'm in the presence of magic, and Drix is magic. Anytime Drix plays an instrument, anytime he's behind his drums, he's the most magical person in the universe.

I lean my head down, my lips whisper against his, and then my entire body shakes at the clanging in the corner. My hands push on Drix's shoulders for release, but he keeps me steady against his body and off the floor as if I weigh nothing. "Chill. It's Holiday."

Thor pops his head up. At least I'm not the only one being awoken out of sweet dreams by loud sounds.

Drix's sister dumps a bag of trash into the metal can and then places the top back on. "You two are so epically cute together, and just to let you know, Jeremy is on his way over."

Drix lowers me to the floor, immediately takes my hand and guides me around all the instruments and out of the garage. With a bark, Thor is up and following. "I told you, he's not allowed here while Elle is visiting."

Jeremy: Holiday's boyfriend who every male here hates with a passion and who Holiday appears to have some sort of emotional attachment with. She says she's in love, but I'm not sure if I buy it. When someone brings him up, the smile on her face never reaches her eyes. In fact, she dulls out at the sound of his name.

I'm not seasoned enough to make a complete judgment on what love is, but I am secure enough in myself that I never want that to be my version of love.

"He won't say anything, Drix." Holiday wrings her hands together. "And if I don't see him now, I won't see him at all today."

"Ask me if I care," Drix mumbles as he pulls me into the

house. Dominic, Kellen and Marcus are at the table poring over sheet music, and each offer me and Drix a colorful greeting, but I don't have much time to offer anything back as Drix pulls me past them, down the narrow hallway and into the living room.

Once there, he drops my hand and collapses back against the wall. The TV is on, the evening news, and I have this awkward feeling that I'm taking up too much room because I have no idea how Drix and I just went from complete heaven to this cold place of purgatory. As if feeling the same way, Thor sniffs, probably wondering if a stranger has entered Drix's body.

Light footsteps and Holiday creeps out of the hallway and into the living room, reminding me of how I used to feel when I'd sneak out of my bedroom at night, knowing my parents were going to be disappointed I was scared of the dark and of the monsters in my closet.

"Drix," she says. "Please let me see him. It'll just be for a few minutes, and I need to see him and tell him I'm sorry. We fought earlier today and—"

Drix cracks his head to the side. "I thought you said you hadn't seen him today."

"I meant I didn't see him today when he was in a good mood. He's going out with friends tonight, and I need us to leave on a good note, so I won't worry about him going out."

My soul twists with her words. It's such a horrifying, dark and demented shadow that's cast over Holiday that I step closer to the window for light. Is that how love feels to her? Because that's not okay. "What will happen if he goes out mad?"

Drix's eyes shoot to mine, and Holiday looks down at her

feet. A pit forms in my stomach, and I wish I could disappear. "Oh."

Oh. He'll cheat on her.

"He's not a bad guy," Holiday suddenly says. "He's just real emotional, and I know how to calm him down. I'm the only one who can. Even he admits it, and he tells me all the time he doesn't think he can live without me. That without me, he'll fall apart. He says I'm the only good thing in his life."

The kitchen goes quiet, and she's staring at me with such hope that I'll tell her I understand, but I can't because it's like she's speaking a completely different language. If I open my mouth, I know I'll also be speaking in a tongue that will be incomprehensible to her.

Suddenly, my skin feels like it's shrinking because being in the same room with Holiday is a type of suffocation. With her brothers, she's light and love and confidence and beauty, but with the mention of this boy, she turns into a black hole, and that happiness Drix just had about the audition has been lost into the void.

Thor jerks his head toward the door. The hair on his back rises, and he growls. A menacing bark following every low rumble. A knock and a part of me feels like I should run while another part feels like I should throw myself in front of it to save Holiday from the Grim Reaper.

"Drix?" she asks.

He's completely closed off. Head down, arms over his chest, one foot crossed over the other. "Elle has to leave in twenty minutes, so you have fifteen. You stay in the front yard as I don't want him to see her car around back, and you two stay within sight."

Thor keeps growling, keeps barking, and there's no way that dog is letting anyone out.

"Thor," Drix says, and the dog automatically glances back at him. Drix snaps his fingers and points at the floor. With ears back, Thor trots to the designated spot. Drix lowers to a crouch, pets the dog, and my heart hurts. It's almost as if he's touching the dog to keep himself from going out the door.

Holiday walks out and my stomach flips. Silence. There's only silence in the house beyond the low voices of the news anchor on the TV. Then there's two more voices coming from outside. One is Holiday's, the other is her boyfriend's, and within seconds those voices are raised and ominous. Like a lightning strike before a storm. They're fighting.

"Why did you let her go out?" I ask.

"Why are you here, with me, working on a computer program? All three things your parents know nothing about."

I flinch with his verbal attack, but he keeps going.

"Don't take it hard because I'm not judging. I'm acting like a dancing monkey for your dad, and I'm keeping you and me a secret for the same reasons you're keeping quiet."

"I don't understand."

"We all have somebody in our life we can't say no to. Whether it be because they're our parents, like you, or a person in authority, like me, or because that person makes them feel secure, like Holiday. Some choices, we have to make on our own. I can't choose who Holiday loves. As much as I hate it, that's on her, just like my choices are on me and your choices are on you."

My spine straightens. "My situation is different. They're my parents."

"Ellison Monroe and Andrew Morton are turning heads again."

At the sound of my name, nausea crashes into my system, and the urge is to vomit. On the screen are pictures of me and Andrew. Us together at fund-raisers, us together walking red carpets, us together in what should have been private moments outside of evening events. His jacket is around my shoulder on a cool night. And then there's the pièce de résistance—the picture of Andrew leaning forward to kiss me at the ballpark.

What they don't show is that I averted my head and kissed his cheek. His cheek. Sean's still mad at me, but I don't care. I couldn't stomach kissing anyone but Drix.

"You choose to be seen with him, Elle."

"He's there to protect me."

Drix stands, and he levels his dark, ice-cold eyes on me. "Then why aren't your parents and your father's campaign staff telling the media he's not your guy?"

Hurt pricks at my heart and that causes anger to awaken within me. "You think I'm with him? Is that it? You think I'm cheating on you?"

He methodically shakes his head back and forth, pinning me in my spot with that frigid stare. "I think that's who your parents want you with, and this is their way of making it happen. I also think you're choosing not to see it."

"You're wrong," I say, but it was more a whisper when I intended it to be strong.

"I'm not judging you," he says softly. "I'm doing what I've been told to do, too. We're both on a leash."

"So what are my options?" I snap. "Holiday has options.

She can leave him, and that is the best choice. Where's my best choice?"

He merely shrugs like I haven't asked the most profound question in my life. "Sometimes there isn't a best choice. Sometimes we're given two bad choices. That, Elle, is how life works."

No, he's wrong. I'm not on a leash. My parents are guiding me, they're helping me, but I still have control and I'm going to prove Drix wrong.

HENDRIX

SITTING ON A STOOL IN THE GARAGE, I MESS around on the guitar. Just a few rolling chords to help soothe the edginess and anger rumbling deep inside. I hurt Elle tonight, and while I regret it, I also don't. Seeing her with Andrew cuts me deep. Each and every time. She doesn't see it, but I do. I see how that's the man her parents want her with, and it kills me because I want to be her man, not just in private, but in public.

"Hey," Marcus enters the garage, picks up a battered acoustic Axle bought at the Music-Go-Round for him and takes the stool next to me. "How are you?"

I shrug while my fingers continue to move over the strings. No need to talk about Elle or Holiday. Our house is so small that we hear when the mice take a dump.

"Yeah," he says. "I feel like that on most days, too."

Marcus listens for a few minutes, watches my choices on the strings, listens to the broken melody and slowly begins to join in, playing the same chords, but on a higher scale. The melody we play is sweet and sad, it's broken and raw. It describes me. It describes Marcus. I wonder how many more people in the world could relate.

"You didn't apply to the youth performing arts school, did you?" I ask.

"What do you think?"

I think he should have. "You're talented enough."

"Maybe."

I place my hand over the strings to stop the music. "Why didn't you?"

It's his turn to shrug. My stomach drops because I see it—fear—and I hate that it's taken up residence in a guy who I consider one of my best friends. In a guy I'd bet who has never feared another human being in his life.

Marcus strums a few more strings, then stops, but the last note continues to vibrate. "I don't know." A pause. "Did you ever feel like life before was easier?"

I nod because I know what he's talking about. Before being arrested, before going through the program, before looking too deep into myself to see all the hurt and anger that had been controlling my decisions without my knowledge. Back when I didn't care that the path I was going down was leading to an implosion.

"Every day I wake up, whether it's here or at home, and I wonder if I have the strength to not mess up, to keep going. Each morning, I know it would be easier to go for the high again. It would be easier to not care, but I do care, and I don't miss the high, but I'm also scared of failing.

"Each night I don't return to the life I had before, I thank

God for it. It may not seem like much to some people, but just getting through a day feels like I've survived the bloodiest battle of a war, and I'm proud. I didn't have it in me to try for the youth performing arts program and fail. Not when it's so tough to just survive the day."

I watch Marcus and can't help but wonder if he's a mind reader because he just said all my fears aloud, but the difference between us is I'm more scared of my life remaining in this daily battle to survive.

Marcus is stronger than this. I know he is. During the three months in the forest, we would hike for most of the day, sometimes it felt like in circles, and then we'd set up camp. Every few days, though, we'd come across some obstacle course, and we'd be expected to run it through.

One of the courses was to climb up a sheer cliff and then rappel back down. I was tired, I was weary, and my mind had settled into a dark place. I didn't see the point anymore. Not in walking, not in setting up camp, not in completing another obstacle, and all I wanted to do was give up. On the program, on my family, on myself.

But Marcus, he didn't give up. He never gave up.

He had already climbed the cliff, he had already rappelled back down, and so had everyone else. I sat on the ground, my equipment beside me, and I wasn't going to do it. Throughout the day, counselor after counselor came and sat by my side. They tried talking to me, joking with me, and demanding of me. They even sent for my therapist, and I stonewalled him by my silence, too. I was done, and it just wasn't with the program, I was done with myself.

I reached a point that I didn't care if I lived or if I died because living hurt too damn much. It hit me that morning exactly what they were trying to teach us. That the cliff? The walking? The setting up, then tearing down and then doing it all over again? That's what life was. Life was up and then back down. Life was hard, life was tough, and life meant there would be hurt, and it was up to me to keep going. Life was for the strong, and I wasn't strong enough to survive.

"You want to eat?" my therapist said. "You've got to try."

"What are you going to do," I bit back. "Starve me?"

I saw the answer there on his face. They wouldn't. They couldn't. It was an idle threat, and if I wanted I could have stood up, headed back to camp and stared all those all-knowing adults in the eye and eaten every piece of food in the camp, and they wouldn't stop me because they couldn't. The state would never risk a story of starving a teen.

"That food will taste better if it's what you've earned," he said.

I shrugged. "Food is food."

The disappointment that covered his face kicked me in the nuts, but I still didn't move. He left, I sat, and the sun began to dip in the western sky. Everyone, even the adults, left the cliff. Left me alone, and from the distance, I could hear the laughter and chatter of the other teens as they set up camp. I could smell the smoke from the fire, and my famished stomach cramped with the delicious scent of meat being cooked in the pit.

Alone didn't feel good. Alone was awful. But alone felt safer. So did any wall that was slowly being built up around me.

A stick snapped, and I shot a look over my shoulder. I unloaded an f-bomb at the sight of Marcus. He dropped down beside me, and I expected him to give me one of his two thousand lectures he'd given to drag me through detention, but he didn't talk. He just sat, and the two of us watched that cliff like it might come alive and eat us both.

The bell for dinner rang, more excited conversation and laughter drifted on the breeze from behind us, but Marcus didn't move. Just stared at the cliff.

"You should go eat," I said. "The younger ones don't think to keep enough for anyone else."

"You don't eat, I don't eat."

His declaration caused me to swear. "I don't have it in me."

"The cliff?" he asked.

I shook my head. "Everything. I'm going to get out, I'm going to go home, and I'm going to screw it all up all over again because that's who I am."

Marcus released a breath and stood, my gear to climb in his hands. "Get it on."

I opened my mouth to argue, and he shut me down with a glare and a harsh tone that even I knew not to mess with. "Get it on."

I stood and I did, still having no intention of climbing, but it shocked the hell out of me as he also suited up. "You've already done it."

"Yeah." A look straight into my eyes. "I did, so follow me, and I'll show you the easiest way up the cliff. Because, sometimes, that's what we need. Someone to show us how to get there."

I blink several times as emotion still tears me up when I think of that moment. My throat's constricted and it burns and I breathe out to try to contain myself. The guitar is heavy in my hands and on my lap. I climbed that cliff, and when I reached the top I'm not ashamed to admit I wept. Something broke in me, and that's what I needed. The pieces had to be shattered, so I could repiece myself back together.

Marcus saved my life that day. He saved me, and it's time for me to repay the favor. I'm going to get into this program, and I'm going to get him in, too. He dragged me through my fears before, and this time I'll be the strong one.

"You know I'm not going to give up on this," I say. "You're only a junior so there's no reason for you to not apply next year."

"I had a feeling you'd say that." He begins to play again, and this time, I'm the one who follows his melody. "Dominic and I are talking about taking Kellen and Holiday to the lake soon to get Holiday away from here while you and Axle are working out-of-town jobs. He thinks it would be better if I ask Holiday as she won't see me as trying to put a wedge between her and Jeremy."

"Are you?"

He chuckles. "Yes."

"Thanks for having my back with her." And with me.

"Anytime."

Marcus and I, this is how it's going to be—a friendship where neither dominates or controls. A friendship where we're both going to have bad days and the other will carry the one down on his luck until he's strong enough to stand again.

ellison

IT'S SEVEN AT NIGHT, AND DAD'S CAR IS IN THE garage which means he's home, and if he's home, he's working. There's so much adrenaline coursing through my veins that when I open the door to my father's office, I partly wonder if I'm going to rip the massive wooden door off its hinges. Instead, it bangs against the wall, and every head in the room shoots up and stares at me like I've lost my mind. Maybe I have, but sometimes losing yourself is needed in order to discover the real deal.

"You have to announce that Andrew and I are not a couple."

Dad had been in the process of picking up his phone, and he drops it back to the base. "Another time, Elle. I have work I need to do."

Dad picks up the phone again, his aides start to chat, and I'm left standing in the middle of his office on his red-and-black Oriental rug feeling as if I'm having an out-of-body experience. Did he not hear what I just said? "I'm sick and tired of the media acting like Andrew and I are a couple. We aren't. I want you to set them straight."

The receiver is to Dad's ear, and he glances up like he's surprised to see me. "I said another time. I've got a firestorm on my hands."

A firestorm? There's always a firestorm, and I'm confused how this is complicated. "Just say yes. That's it. Tell me you'll clear up the misunderstanding."

Dad jerks his hand in a motion for someone to enter and then begins speaking on the phone. He then nods his chin as he makes eye contact for me to leave, but I don't want to leave, not until he gives me the answer I'm searching for.

My mother appears on my right and puts her hand on my shoulder. She tilts her head toward the door, and this is one of those moments where I follow. Once I'm out, Mom closes the door to Dad's office with such care that it's like she's laying an infant down to bed.

"Your father is having a rough day, and you need to let him deal with some things. Where have you been?"

"At the mall." The lie comes too easily. "I saw the story about me and Andrew on the news. This needs to stop."

"Did you buy anything?" she asks.

"No. I want Dad to tell everyone that Andrew and I aren't dating."

"Did any media follow you to the mall?"

Oh my God, I could scream. "Mom, I'm not talking about the mall anymore. I'm talking about me and Andrew."

She sighs like I'm a bother. "You want your father to announce you're not dating."

Finally. "Yes."

"No."

"What?"

"The moment your father opens his mouth and answers any question about you, then that makes your personal life up for discussion, and that is not an option for us."

"They're already discussing my personal life. If they're going to do it, at least they should get it right."

Mom's eyes sweep over me from head to toe. "Have you met a boy?"

I blink several times because that question threw me to the ground and because the answer is a blaring yes. As I open my mouth to answer no, nothing comes out except for a squeak. My mother smiles. "You met a boy. Who is it?"

"I have not met a boy."

She purses her lips. "Then what difference does it make what the media says?"

"It matters to me." I press a hand to my chest. "What they're saying are lies about me."

"And that's what the media does. They take pieces of the truth, and they twist things to make a story that will give them higher ratings. Often, they are so hungry for the next big story that if they get a small inkling of the truth, they run with the story before fleshing out all the facts."

The air squeezes out of my lungs. "But they're lying about me."

Mom's blue eyes become sad, and she places a hand on my cheek. "I understand how upsetting this is for you, but if your father speaks out, it will only cause the media to start hunting for more on you. Just be patient. You're the headline now, but wait long enough, and someone else will be the headline later. That's how this all works."

Frustration causes my throat to swell. "What if there is a boy?"

Mom tucks my hair behind my shoulder. "Is there a boy?"

I care for Drix so much that if I look at her she'll know, so I lower my head and shake it. "But what if there was?"

"Then he'd have to be patient and understand that being with someone special like you isn't going to be like dating anyone else."

Drix said I have a choice, but I don't. I'm absolutely and completely stuck.

HENDRIX

MY BODY RESTS AGAINST THE SEAT, AND MY temple is cool against the window. The August heat was so intense I doubt there's water left in my body. Every muscle is already asleep, but my mind is halfway awake. Axle hums along to Fall Out Boy on the radio, I'm guessing to keep himself awake on the ride home. Our job was an hour away, and I nailed in more shingles than I can count in the past ten hours. I'm tired, Axle's tired, yet I'm semi-awake in the passenger seat.

Elle. I'm waiting on Elle. She's been gone a week. First traveling with her Mom to New York for a shopping trip, and then to DC with her dad. She was supposed to return sometime today, but her flights kept getting delayed due to storms on the East Coast.

My cell's in my hand as I wait for it to vibrate, for me to know that the past week of being without her is almost over. I've got a crazy hum in my brain, beneath my skin, that begs for me to hold her again. One week apart was too long.

Axle's car slows and I open my eyes. He's heading off the freeway and we're almost home. I check my cell in case I had fallen asleep, but it confirms I didn't miss anything. Dammit, Elle, where are you?

"Still nothing?" Axle asks.

"Nada."

"From neither Elle nor on the audition?"

"Nothing," I confirm. This week, I auditioned for the youth performing arts high school, and I nailed it. I played both the guitar and the drums, and it's the only flawless thing I've done in my life. Now I wait.

"So you and Elle," Axle says like he asked a question, and I circle my neck.

"Don't start." My brother likes her, but he's concerned with good reason. We're the definition of doomed. Star-crossed and all that bull. But I'm not ready to give her up, and it appears she feels the same way about me.

"Not what you think," he says, "so take a step back. Though since you brought it up, dating the governor's daughter without his consent is stupid. Dating her with his consent would still be borderline stupid."

I scrub both hands over my face. I'm too damned tired for this. "Drop me off. I'll walk home."

"But that's not why I'm bringing her up."

I roll my head against the headrest to look at him. Axle's focused on the road. One hand on the steering wheel with his fingers tapping out the strands of the chords of the song on the radio. "Are you being safe with her?"

Damn if that wasn't direct. "I know how to use a condom."

"Considering you don't have any baby mamas at the door

screaming for money, I've guessed that, but I saw how you and Elle kissed goodbye last Sunday. I also saw the look on her face when she pulled away, and I saw the same expression on you. This ain't a hookup, and I don't want a conversation with you down the road where you explain you forgot to use the condom because you were swept up in a moment. Moment or not, you cover up, you got me?"

Couldn't get it any more loud and clear if he screamed it point-blank in my ear. "No babies. I understand." I pause, playing out the next statement in my head because I'm not the kind of guy to talk girls in a locker room. "How I feel about her—she's different."

Axle switches hands he's driving with. "I know. Different looks good on you, Drix."

"I said, *she's* different."

He glances at me out of the corner of his eye as he pulls into our driveway. "I heard you."

Axle turns off the car, followed by the headlights, and neither of us move to exit. Our front porch light is on, and light also pours from our living room. Shadows moving behind a curtain and there's a strange tug at my heart because this house is finally becoming a home.

"Have you ever been in love?" I ask.

"Once."

"What's it like?"

He flips the car keys around his finger. "Like you didn't know a piece of you was missing until they smiled at you, and then you realized what it felt like to be whole."

The front door opens, and Holiday waves at us to come in. She's smiling, and that's a good indication she listened and spent the day with Dominic, Kellen and Marcus instead of her asshole boyfriend. They offered to take her to the lake, and as she steps onto the stoop, a part of me rests at seeing her bathing suit straps poking out from beyond her T-shirt. Point for the home team. For today, she chose her family.

We leave the car and head straight for the garage to unload our tools. The two of us talk trash. How I was faster than him pounding in shingles, but he nailed straighter than me. We argue over playlists in case we land a gig. I want anything with a strong beat. He's insistent we add slow songs for couples to dance. I tell him slow songs are for wusses. He tells me I'm an asshole. I tell him to kiss my ass. We eventually finish up and trudge toward the back door of the house.

All I want is a shower, hot food, a bed and then for Elle to call. There'd be nothing better than to listen to her sweet voice until I fall asleep.

"I call dibs on the shower," Axle says.

"Try for first and I'll kick your ass," I say, and he chuckles behind me.

Back door open, I step into the kitchen and loud voices ring out, "Surprise!"

Startled, I go still, then glance around the room. It's my sister, Dominic, Kellen and Marcus. I narrow my eyes, since I don't get what the surprise is. "What's going on?"

Holiday rocks on her toes. "You got a letter today. From the youth performing arts program."

My heart stops in my chest. "Where is it?"

"I already opened it. You got in and this is your surprise party."

I hold my breath because I don't know if I heard her right. "I did what?"

"Got in." My entire body vibrates at the glorious sound of Elle's voice, and Dominic and Marcus split apart to show her coming in from down the hallway. Each and every time I see her, she takes my breath away, and this time it's no different.

Her long hair is loose around her shoulders, and the blue cotton dress she has on makes me think of all the ways I'd love to take it off. Elle extends her hand, and in her fingers is a letter addressed to me.

"You were supposed to come in the front," Holiday says. "I had it all planned out. Elle was going to be standing their waiting for you with the letter, and then you two would kiss and be happy, and then we'd all join in and jump up and down with you, but you ruined it. Front door, Axle. What part don't you get of front door?"

"When have we used the front door?" Axle claps a hand on my shoulder. "Congrats. You deserve this."

I don't say anything in response as I'm too busy memorizing every part of Elle. The letter. I should read the letter. Confirm the words myself. "I got in?"

Elle nods. "Yes."

The room sways as a wave of emotion slams into me. My mind's a mess, too many thoughts colliding all at once. Then another wave smashes into me, and it feels a lot like guilt. I hurt people, and now I'm getting this. I hurt people, and I don't understand why good things are happening to me now. I hurt people physically. I hurt people emotionally, and my eyes immediately go to Holiday. "I'm sorry I wasn't here for you."

All of the chatter ceases, and Holiday blinks. "What?"

"I'm sorry I wasn't here for you when I was in jail, and I'm sorry I wasn't here for you before. I let you down, and I'm done letting you down. I promise you, I'm going to be here. I'm going to go to this school, and I'm going to make something better out of who I am. And then me and Axle, we're going to get you to someplace better. Help you be whoever you want to be. I promise you can trust me."

Thor runs into the kitchen and through my legs, and I don't know what to say anymore. *I got in.* I got into the youth performing arts program. One year ago, I was a selfish bastard, and I pounded my way through life one hit and punch at a time. One year ago, I was a wreck, handing over my life for a stick of a needle or swallow of the bottle. One year ago, I was on a path to death, and now I have a real chance at life.

Emotion burns me up from the inside out, and I don't know how to handle it. The therapist said to talk, he said to leave if I couldn't contain myself, but this feeling isn't anger. It's something that resembles a ball of fire. It's powerful, and it causes my eyes to sting and my hands to shake.

I look over at Elle, and my voice is unrecognizably hoarse. "I got in."

She's smiling at me, pure softness in that joy. "You got in."

I step toward her. One foot, then another, and when I reach her, Elle falls into me. Her arms around my neck, her fingertips sliding along my skin, her warmth surrounds me, and all the chaos in my mind ceases. There's quiet and peace, and that ball of fire isn't raging, but instead is burning. Slowly, deeply, in such a way that I'm fine with being consumed.

"You deserve this," she whispers. "You deserve to be happy."

Is this what this is? Happy? If it is, I want more of it. Never in my life have I had a taste of a drug that's as potent as this moment. Feeling whole with her in my arms, this triumphant feeling that I can take on the world. No more wasting away. No more letting someone else control my life. I'm the master of my own destiny.

"I love you, Elle." I lower my head and I kiss her lips.

Ellison

"MY BROTHER DECLARED HE LOVED YOU IN front of our entire family." Holiday's many bracelets clink together as she moves. "And Drix doesn't love easily. So him loving you makes us sisters."

Holiday and I sit on top of a picnic table that the boys dragged from the back of the yard to the driveway so we could have the celebration pizza and chicken wings outside. The August night is one of those rare ones where the heat feels like a comfortable blanket. The sky is black, the stars are bright, and my parents are still in DC for two more days. Right now, they think I'm safe at home tucked away in bed.

Thor sits at my feet, his eyes glued to me, tracking my every minute movement, and a bead of salvia falls from his mouth. "I'm not giving you any."

"Drix does," Holiday says. "Drix gives that dog anything he wants. I'm warning you in case you guys grow up, get married and have babies. When the zombie apocalypse happens, he's saving the dog before he saves any of us."

I snort, drop what I'm promising myself is my last chicken wing on the plate and lick my fingers. My mother would be horribly appalled at the number of chicken wings I've eaten, but she's not here, and I'm enjoying doing what I like more and more. "Guess it's good I plan on being strong enough to protect my children, and, so you know, I've always wanted a sister."

Holiday's grin widens, and I'm on cloud nine. Drix told me he loved me, and I could have kissed him until the end of time. But then Axle cleared his throat, a subtle reminder we had company, and I separated faster than a tick to a flea collar. Drix only winked at me. Winked. Not sure what that wink meant, but it felt like a thousand promises of future plans that involve his arms around me.

Kellen and the boys are working on their version of a Beatles song. They're gathered near Drix's drums, and he's trying out different beats to see what tempo they want to use. Holiday often sings with them or will play the piano, but hangs back when they get into discussions.

Tempo, as she told me, *doesn't concern her. Pitch is her thing.*

Not being a music person, I have no idea what that means, but it sounded poetic.

The timer she brought out with her from inside beeps. "Are you ready for dessert?"

"Sure. What are we having?"

"Birthday cake."

"Really? Whose?"

KATIE McGARRY

There's a glint to her eye that makes me feel like I should run. "Yours and Drix's."

"We already celebrated that," I say so slowly that turtles could have run past.

"We celebrated it the normal people way because Drix threatened to use all the hot water in the shower for a week if we celebrated your birthday *our* way, but now that he's in love with you, you're family, and we're celebrating correctly." Holiday slips off the picnic table and goes into the kitchen.

I nibble on my bottom lip and try to decide how scared I should be. "Drix?"

All of them turn their heads in my direction, and Drix pokes his head around his cymbal to see me.

"What does it mean to celebrate my birthday like your family?"

Axle chuckles, and the smile that stretches across Dominic's face causes an anxious spiraling in my stomach. Drix mutters a curse, stands and leaves his sticks on the piano as he walks to me.

"Someone catch me up," Marcus says. "What's going down?"

Axle whispers something to Marcus, and he laughs a little too loud. Drix reaches me at the same time Holiday walks out of the house, once again, with two huge cakes in her hands.

"No way," he says. "It's not happening."

She merely shrugs one shoulder, like her towering brother with a storm cloud for a face doesn't faze her. Holiday drops the cakes onto the table, and instead of frosting, she takes cans of whipped cream, and one after another, covers the top of the cakes.

"I apologize," Holiday says. "It's not icing, but it's the best I got at the moment. These were marked down to fifty cents each."

Drix continues to glare at Holiday, arms crossed over his chest, big, bad brother mode. "It's not happening. Not to Elle."

"Well—" Holiday empties out the last can "—I say it is, so that's how it's going to be. Besides, this isn't for her, it's for you."

And with that, my eyes practically fall out of my head when Holiday digs into the cake with her fingers as a claw, looks at me and then smashes the cake into Drix's face.

I can't breathe. All bodily functions cease. Drix wipes away cake and whipped cream from his eyes, and a vein pops out of his forehead. Oh my God, he's going to kill her.

Holiday watches her brother, digs for another batch of cake, and my hand snatches out to grab on to her wrist. "What are you doing?"

"We don't eat cake here on birthdays. We fight with it."

"You fight with it?"

"Yeah, we—" Holiday doesn't finish as Drix wraps an arm around her with one hand, grabs a handful of cake with the other, and she squeals as he smashes the cake in her face, then into her hair.

My mouth drops open and chaos ensues. There's cake and bodies and screams and battle cries, and before I can even begin to comprehend what's happening, something cold yet warm and wet slides down my scalp. My shoulders shrug up, my arms rise, and when I look left, Dominic winks at me. "Welcome to the family."

Cake, I have cake on me. Cake in my hair. Cake on my skin. Cake on my clothes and whipped cream melts down my neck. Oh my God.

Dominic runs off and slams cake onto Axle's neck. To the right, Holiday and Drix work together to baptize Marcus. If you can't beat them…

With a fist full of warm cake, I duck and weave through a firefight between Dominic, Kellen and Axle. Drix is laughing as he pins Marcus with cake in the face. Holiday doubles over in laughter, and I keep my hand behind my back. When Drix spots me his smile falls. "Aw, Elle. I'm sorry—"

He reaches for me, I slip forward and slap my hand full of cake onto the back of his neck and shove the rest of it down his shirt.

Good idea? I don't know, because in seconds, I'm in the air. My hair flopping over my face as Drix carries me over his shoulder. He nears the table, near the pan of cake, and I'm laughing and he's laughing, and then there's more cake in my hair.

I slide down his body and then there's more in my face, and I'm grabbing at it. Smearing it onto Drix's face, down his shirt and somehow there's more cake and more people, and I'm laughing and dodging. It's chaos and joy and freedom and everything I have ever wanted out of life without knowing this was my heaven.

Holiday, Kellen and I opted for showers, and the boys hosed off in the backyard. While the cake fight was freeing and fun, I'm not ready for a cold shower with a water hose. Yes, I am a shower diva.

The water pipes in Drix's bathroom groaned when I turned the knobs in any direction, and there's barely any room to stand between the tub, toilet and sink. It's hard to believe three people share this bathroom. From what Drix has said, Marcus has been staying more nights than going home, sleeping in his room or in the recliner, and that Dominic and Kellen are constants, as well. Six people using this one bathroom. This would be my mother's version of hell.

I've towel-dried my hair, ran a comb through it and have changed into a pair of drawstring shorts and a T-shirt. These are my pj's when I travel, and this is the most down-to-earth outfit that's left in my suitcase. After Holiday's message that Drix had made it into the program, that they were throwing a party and she wanted me there as a surprise, I drove straight from the airport.

A quick look in the fogged mirror and I blow out a breath. For the first time in over a week, I see me staring back— except for the color of my hair, but it's as close to me as I've been for too long. My hair isn't so curled and full of product that it feels like cement, no makeup and my eyes are staring back at me from behind dark-rimmed glasses.

It's after ten, and there's lots of loud conversations filling the house. I step into the narrow hallway, and Dominic, Kellen, Marcus and Holiday are seated at the small table in the kitchen. Dominic deals out cards, and Thor is curled up asleep near the table on a folded blanket that serves as his bed. I turn my head, and Axle and Drix are talking in the living room.

The futon is pulled out, and Axle looks like he's about to drop. Holiday said he and Drix had a long day on a project, and I know from the nights Drix and I have talked on the phone after those long days, he's exhausted. I bet they're both ready to go to bed and that Drix is dead on his feet.

Axle reaches into his back pocket, takes out his wallet and hands Drix something. The tattooed man who's only a few years older than Drix has a serious expression as he speaks, and Drix nods with every word. They clap hands, go in for a hug, and then Axle tilts his head in my direction. "Night, Elle."

"Good night," I say.

Drix leaves the living room, closing the door behind him, and not a second later, the light that had been shining from beneath the door is gone. Drix is so massive that there's no way for him to pass me in the hallway without his body squeezing against mine. He stops in front of me and lifts a lock of my semi-dried hair between his fingers. "Hey."

"Hey." I'm not ready for this day to end, but I spot the weariness in his dark eyes. "I guess I should be heading home."

"I thought you said you're going to be alone there."

"I am, but I'm used to it."

Drix twines the lock around his finger and gently tugs. "You can stay."

"You're tired."

"I am, but I'm not ready for you to go."

I'm not ready to go either. "Kitchen, then, or garage?" Though I'm not in the mood for cards or for music. I had hoped we'd snuggle up together in the worn recliner in the living room and watch TV, but I can't blame Axle for wanting sleep.

"Want to see my room?"

My heart jumps out of my chest so hard, so fast that there

was a bit of pain with the adrenaline rush. But then there's a sense of confusion and emptiness. "Where is your room?"

Drix reaches up, and there's a string hanging from the ceiling I hadn't noticed before. He pulls, I step back and a ladder appears. "Let me go up first so I can turn on the lights. You can leave your bag in Holiday's room."

He climbs, and I rub my hands against my cotton shorts. I have never gone up a ladder, but I will not be a wuss, and I will not ask for help. I can do this without tripping, falling, then busting my head open. This is absolutely possible.

Drix disappears into the blackness of the attic, and I suck in a deep breath and trail after. I steady my bare feet on each wrung before hiking up to the next one. Ascending into darkness is a bit disorienting, and when I make it through the hole, Drix says, "Stay there."

Cracking and footsteps against wood and then there is light. Christmas lights. Hundreds of them hanging along the ceiling and wall of the attic. Red and blue and green. It's a wonderland in spite of the beams of raw wood.

Drix offers me his hand and helps me make the transition from the ladder to the attic. He then places his hands on my hips to settle me on the plywood path that leads to his bed and dresser in the corner. Heat runs along my skin with his touch.

I'm able to stand upright, but Drix has to angle to the side so he doesn't hit his head on the ceiling of exposed sheets of plywood where the tips of roofing nails stick down toward us.

He releases my hips and takes my hand. Drix goes before me, and I walk behind on the wooden path, and when he reaches his bed, he drops down onto it.

His bed is two twin mattresses stacked on top of the other,

with no box spring, and it is covered by dark blue sheets, a red-and-black-checkered quilt that appears ancient and a single pillow with no case. On his dresser is a digital alarm clock, a stack of binders from my father, guitar picks, a pair of drumsticks and the leather band he had worn the first day he came to my house.

Drix turns on a window AC unit, and it hums as it blows in cooler air. "Want to sit?"

I tuck my hair behind my ears and readjust my glasses. I do, but I don't. I want to sit with Drix, lean into him, have his lips touch mine and get lost in his embrace. I want his arms around me. I want to tell him my deepest thoughts in the darkness. I want him to bear his soul, and I want to feel his breath along the curve of my neck as he speaks. I want him to tease me, I want to tease him back. I want us to whisper in the dark like I imagine lovers do.

Lovers. That's the part I'm not ready for and why I don't want to sit. Drix is experienced, and I'm not ready to be any more experienced than what I currently am.

Drix is still watching me, waiting, and I comb my fingers through the ends of my hair. "Why do you have two mattresses?"

"Because a box spring doesn't fit through that hole, and we found two mattresses at Goodwill. We figured two would give me some support. What's going on in that brain, Elle, and don't tell me nothing."

I sigh, and with it, I sag. Drix takes both of my hands and guides me to stand between his legs. When he looks up at me, those dark eyes are so full of concern that I become a puddle. All the muscles in my body that had gone rigid, relax.

"Talk to me," he says in that smooth voice of his.

I open my mouth to speak, but it's too dry, and my words feel too stupid. I've been alone with Drix in a hotel room so many times and have never felt as inadequate as I do now, but Drix told me he loved me, so is there an expectation with that declaration?

"We can go back down." He starts to stand, and my heart picks up speed because that is not what I want.

"I don't want to have sex," I spit out, and Drix pauses in this weird midstate of standing and sitting, and his face is so totally screwed up that I have to bite my lip to keep from laughing.

He falls back to the bed, and his thumbs brush over the tops of my hands. "Is this because you saw Axle give me a condom?"

I choke. On what, I don't know, and I hit a hand against my chest to stop the strange sounds from leaving my body. "He gave you a *what*?"

Drix yanks an orange square from his back pocket, and I swear I could cook a five course meal off my face. He tosses it onto the dresser. "Won't lie, I've had more fantasies than should be legal about ways I'd like to touch your body."

Flames. Flames are now shooting off my cheeks, and I can only stare at his hand still holding mine and I can stare at the floor, because the floor doesn't care I'm currently a mess.

"But as much as I'm attracted to you, as much as I would love to lay you down next to me and become one..."

I swallow because that all sounded so good and so terrifying.

"I don't want to make love to you."

My head shoots up, my eyes find his, and there's a stupid part of me that wonders if I should be insulted. "Why?"

"If I promise not to bite, will you sit with me while I tell you?"

He tugs on my hand, I give, and he slips up the bed to lean his back against the wall. I have a choice. To settle between his legs or sit beside him. In seconds, I run through a million pros and cons, and I ignore them all as I climb up the bed and lean my back against his chest.

Drix wraps both of his arms around me, and those strong steel bands are the best comforting blanket I've ever known. He kisses the side of my head, and he pulls me back until there's no space between us. My temple is against his, and when he tilts his head, he nibbles on my ear, and my entire body comes alive.

"I thought you said you wouldn't bite," I whisper as my skin tingles.

"You want me to stop?"

"No." This is what I want, what I desire. Just this—Drix and me together.

"Still want to know?" he asks.

Now that the fear has faded and I'm safe in his arms, my question doesn't seem nearly as important, but I love listening to Drix talk, and I love it when he wants to talk to me. "As long as you still want to tell."

"I do," he says. "I don't mind telling you. You might be the only person who thinks anything inside me has some worth, even the ugly."

"Nothing about you is ugly," I say. "Now tell me."

HENDRIX

IF ONLY THAT WERE TRUE. SO MANY OF THE things I've done in life are ugly. The drinking, the drugs, my carelessness in playing with girls' hearts. All of it baggage that weighs me down and I've carried it around me with me day after day and night after night.

Elle leans her body into me, and she lays her hands over my arms as if this is exactly where she wants to be. This is where I want her to be. Her soft body in my arms, her sweet scent surrounding me. Even in the forest, even on those nights that my soul would pause and take a breath, I didn't know peace, but this—this is beyond peace. This is heaven.

"My dad had Axle at eighteen," I say. "His mom was eighteen, too. Neither of them wanted him, but they had him anyhow. They married, stayed together for two years, then divorced and fought over who had to watch him next. Then, because my father likes making mistakes, a few years later, he hooked up with a girl after a concert, and they created me.

They didn't know each other's names. Hell, I don't think either of them were sober."

That's the true love kids want to hear about when they ask how their parents met.

"Seven months later, I popped out. Because my mom had a few personal issues and a few outstanding warrants for DUIs, Dad had main custody of me, but he split it with Mom without the courts knowing. She'd watch Axle and me, and when it was Dad's turn, Axle watched me. Dad hooked up with Holiday's mom, she was born, and eventually Holiday's grandma started watching over us some, too, but she was too old to keep up with any of us—Holiday included. But she made sure we ate, and she taught us how to read music."

Elle brushes her fingers along my arm as if that can help heal the gaping wound bleeding on my soul. "Seven months?"

"I was a preemie. Twenty-nine weeks. I was in the NICU for two months." My eyebrows draw together as I search for the courage to tell Elle the truth. "I was born addicted to heroin."

She sucks in a breath and sits up. I give her room to bolt, but instead she turns so she can look me in the eye. She caresses my face with a gentle touch that belongs only to Elle. "I'm sorry."

"It's not your fault."

"No, but someone should be sorry."

My mother never was. Neither was my dad. Elle's words cut so deep that it's hard to keep from feeling. I rap the back of my head against the wall, but Elle reaches around my head, becoming a barrier between me and the wood. She leans in and kisses my cheek. Once, twice, each one coming closer to my mouth until those sweet lips feather against mine.

"You were a fighter from the start, then," she says.

A fighter—from the start. "That's one way to look at it."

"It's the only way."

"I don't want to be my dad, and I don't want to be my mom. I'm the luckiest son of a bitch on the planet that I didn't make a baby before I was arrested. I promise you, I will explore and worship your body every way you'll allow and how you ask, but I've been given a second chance, and I will not mess that up."

Elle sits on her knees in front of me and frames my face with her hands. "I told you weeks ago we're in control. Amazing things are going to happen. I can feel it. Can't you?"

Baggage. It's heavy and dark and slows me down. My doubts, my fears, my worries all jammed in and close to overflowing. All of it things I believed I needed. Carrying it with me minute to minute, second to second, crushing my back, bones and soul.

Baggage.

After a year of being away, I don't need those bags anymore. I thought I did. I thought it all still fit, but it doesn't. I changed—my body, my mind, my direction.

Baggage.

It's time I leave all of that baggage at the curb. I don't need any of it anymore. Seven months in juvenile detention. Three months in the forest. One year of therapy. One year of figuring out who I am. One year of making me a free man.

Yes, amazing things are going to happen because that's what happens when you find your wings and finally fly.

ellison

DRIX RUNS HIS FINGERS THROUGH MY HAIR, and it's the most glorious feeling. "I want to kiss you, Elle."

"I want you to kiss me." So much.

"I want to touch you, too."

I edge closer and Drix wraps an arm around me. In a heartbeat, I go from in front of him to lying beside him. My head is on his pillow, and he's on his side staring at me like I'm the most beautiful girl in the world. Without makeup, without contacts, with glasses, a scar over my eye, with every imperfection that makes me, me—and he finds me beautiful.

"You say stop, we stop," he says, and I nod. "You're in control."

I slip off my glasses and hand them to Drix. He takes them, reverently folds them closed and places them on the dresser. The world faraway blends together into blurs. The Christmas lights no longer single bulbs but balls of lights that merge into one another. But Drix's face is clear, and I skim my fingers along his jaw.

There's something magical about the moment before kissing. The excitement and seduction of the anticipation. How Drix's dark eyes drink me in, how my every inhale is of his spicy scent. How the pads of my fingers are so sensitive that I can feel every individual blade of his evening shadow. How Drix's hand slowly slips along the curve of my waist and every single one of my cells is filled with electricity.

My heartbeat starts off slow, but every touch, every caress, every moment that passes causes it to skip several breathtaking beats. Drix's hand drifts up my side, along my arm, my shoulder and then lightly traces my cheek.

He leans downs. A breath in, a breath out and then Drix's lips are on mine. A sweet taste, a pleasing pressure. A beautiful song and melody played against a steady beat building with time. Hands in hair, stroking along the back, a shifting of bodies and his lips move to my neck.

A gasp of air, sensitive skin being explored, hot breaths and Drix covers his body with mine. His shirt is gone, mine is tugged up. Some clothes still on, and hands wander for new paths. The gravitational need is for him to move closer as this new and fantastical warmth soaks into my bloodstream.

It's a slow rhythm at first, but as we kiss, as we touch, the rhythm increases. It plays, it persuades, it coaxes me to give and explore more. My mind is a haze, my thoughts happily scattered, my body a million frayed wires. It's too much and it's not enough, and as our breaths come out faster, our kisses become hungrier. Then there's this amazing pressure and then there's release. A sweet release. It's like floating on air, it's like a feather in the breeze, and I hang on to Drix and he hangs on to me as if we're both scared of falling away.

Drix kisses me as he rolls so that I'm tucked tight close to him. I'm sleepy, he's warm and the air blowing on us is cold, but I should move. I should go. That's what a good girl should do—run home. But instead I settle my head on his chest and listen to his strong and steady beat—I listen to his heart.

"Stay, Elle," he mumbles. "Stay with me."

I nod against the bare skin of his chest and let my thoughts drift from one to another, a dream, but not a dream. "I love you, Drix."

I love him.

HENDRIX

A VOICE PULLS ME OUT OF THE DEEPEST SLEEP of my life. So deep of a sleep that I lie still and listen to the music playing over and over again. Some lyric from start to finish going on its third round. My phone. Someone's calling me on my phone. I jerk, forcing my limbs to come to attention, and Elle lifts her head and blinks at me with a groggy expression. "What's wrong?"

"My cell." I reach over and accept without looking at the caller ID. A total of ten people have this number, and every one of them is someone who expects me to answer. "Yeah?"

"Is this Hendrix Pierce?" comes a woman's voice.

Elle shifts off of me, slipping her arm away from my chest and her leg from being twisted with mine. The cold air bites at my skin, and I hate any physical distance between us. She and I are close now, closer than before, and having her near feels right and helps make me feel whole.

I rub my face and glance at my clock. 9:30 a.m. It's a Friday and because we finished the roofing job last night, I'm taking today off before we start again on Saturday. Axle will already be gone, though, out giving quotes to potential customers.

In the attic, the Christmas lights still glow, but the colors are muted by the sunlight streaming in from around the window unit. "This is him."

"Mr. Pierce, this is Kathleen Jansen with Henderson High School's Youth Performing Arts Program. How are you this morning?"

"I'm good. What can I do for you?"

Elle raises her eyebrows and mouths, "The campaign?"

I shake my head and mouth back, "Youth Performing Arts."

She smiles, and I take her hand in mine.

"Mr. Pierce, I'm the head of admissions with the program, and I was wondering if you received your letter?"

"Yes, and I intended on returning my acceptance letter today."

"Is it possible for you and your guardian to meet with me today? You can tell me what time works best for you, and I'll fit it in around my schedule."

Warping of my intestines. "My guardian is at work today, and I doubt he'll be able to meet. Do you mind telling me what this is about?"

A pause on her side and Elle wraps her fingers around mine.

"I'd prefer for us to talk about this in person."

And I want to talk about this now. "Ms. Jansen, I'd appreciate it if you'd please tell me what's going on."

"Mr. Pierce, first off, let me tell you what an amazing talent you are. I was at your audition, and you are one of the most phenomenal musicians I've had the honoring of hearing."

It's pretty words, but it feels like she's pushing me toward a mean side of a sharp blade.

"But unfortunately, the list of students accepted has been leaked from the board of trustees to some of the parents, and we have a situation on our hands. Parents are concerned about letting someone with your record into the program. They feel that their children will be in danger if they attend school with someone with a violent past."

Violent past. "But I've paid for my crimes."

"I know." There's a plea in her voice. "But with you being such a high profile person at the moment, the parents are more focused on your past and not who you're becoming. Please know there are those of us who do believe you have changed and that you have a wonderful future in front of you."

I stand, releasing Elle. I wait for the anger, but there's no anger, just pain. A ripping of claws at my insides, and I look down expecting to find blood.

"I hope you understand, but we are a private school, and we rely heavily on donor support. We have had many people promise to pull their financial support of our institution if we allow your entrance into the school. Due to the outpouring of parental concern, our board held a special meeting last night, and they have decided to withdraw their offer of admission to you."

I spin, hoping somehow doing so will rewind time back to five minutes ago, but it doesn't. "But I got the letter yesterday."

"I know, but the list was leaked after the acceptance was sent. We knew we'd have a couple of upset parents, but we were not prepared for the onslaught of concern. We honestly thought that parents would be proud to have someone from the governor's program at this school, but, unfortunately, they're more focused on your past crimes. As I said, Hendrix, you're extremely talented, but we cannot allow you admittance."

She continues to talk. Words of apology, hopes that I'll continue my music career at my local high school, and when she runs out of words, she goes silent, waiting for me to tell her I understand, but I don't. I hang up and drop to the bed, head in my hands.

Baggage. I guess there is some baggage I can never escape.

Ellison

I BLINKED AND THE ENTIRE WORLD TILTED ON its axis, and the continents have disappeared. Hemispheres have shifted. Summer has become winter. Day has become night.

We're downstairs again and Drix is someone else. He's closed off, he's pacing, and when my cell vibrated with a text from my parents to video chat with them soon, he told me I needed to leave so I could talk to them. In a matter of mere minutes, I've changed my clothes, and I'm back out in the hallway. Holiday is there, waiting for me, wide-eyed. "What happened?"

"The youth performing arts school withdrew their offer."

Holiday spits out a few unintelligible words, then tries again. "Why?"

"Because of his past. Where is he?"

"Out back. He went out back."

I'm down the hallway, out the door, and the sunlight that hurts my eyes feels wrong. It shouldn't be a blue and happy day. Not when Drix is in pain. He closes the trunk of my car that's parked next to the garage and glances up at me. "I put your bag in."

My stomach sinks. He really does want me to leave, and that crushes my heart. Last night we were so close, and now it feels as if there are oceans between us. "You want me to go?"

He rolls his neck. "Are you going to video chat with your parents at my house?"

I can't. He knows I can't, and somehow that makes me feel ashamed. As if I'm not proud to have him by my side, but I am proud. "I can tell them we're together."

"And then what?"

I stay silent because I don't know what would happen next.

"You think they're going to let us date? You think they're going to let you walk into the next fund-raiser with me on your arm instead of Andrew? You think I'll ever be able to hold your hand, twirl you on the dance floor, kiss you in front of anyone?"

Tears fill my eyes because I know the answer, and each of his questions is like falling through a mirror into broken glass.

"For the rest of my life, I will always be the guy who robbed a convenience store. I will always be my past. I will always be my mistakes. I will never be anything more."

"That's not true!" I exclaim. "You're more than that. You're so much more!"

"And only five other people see that. I'm changed because of your dad, but I'm also damned because of your dad. I will always be the mistake."

"You are not a mistake!"

Drix swears and my lower lip trembles. He strides around

the car, and I expect him to keep walking, past me and into the house, but he doesn't. Instead, he gathers me into his arms. One hand pressed against my back, the other guides my head into his chest. I collapse into him, holding on as tight as I can because he needs me and I need him. We need each other.

"I don't know how to fix this," I whisper, "but we're stronger together, Drix. I promise we are. Please don't give up on us. Please don't give up on yourself."

"I don't know," he says into my hair. "I don't know where to go from here. I don't know how to be the man you deserve when we can't even be seen together in public. I don't know who I am, especially when I'm never going to be anything more than who I was."

My cell vibrates again and I know it's my parents. It's their insistence to see me, to know I'm okay, to know that I'm following orders like the good little daughter they want me to be.

Drix kisses the side of my head, steps back, and it feels to dismissive. "You need to go."

"I'll stay," I say.

"I don't need your parents breathing down my neck because they figure out we're together. I've got enough problems, and I don't need you adding to them."

His words punch me in the stomach, and I wait for the apology, but one doesn't come. There won't be one, because he means what he says. Our relationship is a problem. He has said it time and time again—I'm dangerous.

"I gotta go," Drix says. "I just...got to go."

He tosses my car keys to me, and he leaves. Across the yard, jumping the fence and disappearing into Dominic's garage. My knees go weak as that felt very much like a goodbye.

A hand on my shoulder and Dominic's standing beside me. "Go. He needs some time."

"I want to help him."

"Trust me to take care of him." He squeezes my shoulder.

From the house, Thor barks and whines from the back door. Drix. He wants Drix, and he doesn't understand why he's being left behind.

I use the remote of my car to unlock the doors, and Dominic heads after Drix. Hopelessness floods through me, but I take a deep breath to try to ward it off. The world has to be better than this. There has to be an answer.

I ease into the front seat, turn on my car, drive out of the backyard and onto the street. Music plays on the radio. It's Drix's favorite station playing a song I never knew before I met him. Drix had a future in music, and just as quickly as it was given to him, it was taken away. It's not fair. None of this is fair.

I pause at the stop sign at the corner and as I'm about to take a left...

"Elle."

I jump. My heart races to my throat, and with shaking fingers, I turn to find blond pigtails, a Spider-Man beanie and an Avenger's T-shirt. It's Kellen, and I sigh with relief that I'm not being kidnapped. "What are you doing here?"

"I snuck in when you unlocked your car. I overheard what Drix said. I overheard what happened, and I don't want Drix to lose anything more. I don't want him to lose you. I don't want you to leave him because he didn't get in."

He's not, but as I go to open my mouth to calm her fears, Kellen says, "Drix didn't do it. He didn't rob the convenience store. Drix isn't guilty. He's innocent and I need you to believe me."

HENDRIX

DOMINIC HOLDS THE PUNCHING BAG, AND I HIT it again and again and again. Blood drips from my knuckles, the skin on my hand peeled back, battered and raw. Throbs, but doesn't hurt nearly as much as losing my spot at the performing arts school. Doesn't ache nearly as badly as seeing the disappointment consuming Elle.

Less than twenty-four hours ago, I felt like I could offer her the world. Now I got nothing, and I'm always going to be nothing.

A shadow lurking in the doorway and I ram two jabs and then a left hook into the bag. Dominic steps back with the force, but then pushes the bag back toward me. I wipe at the sweat pouring from my brow and ignore the blood dropping onto the concrete.

"Drix," Kellen says, and her voice has a shake to it.

I love Kellen—heart and soul, but I can't do this right now.

I glance over at Dominic, begging for help. I don't know how to make her feel better when my world is in flames.

"We'll talk later," Dominic says. "Drix needs a few more rounds."

"I'm sorry, Drix," she continues. "I'm sorry they took the spot away from you. I'm sorry you and Elle are fighting, and I'm sorry you took the fall for me."

Buzzing in my head as I turn to look at her. I never thought she'd admit it. After talking with Dominic, I buried that notion and laid it to rest. She walks toward me, that limp more pronounced today. Maybe because I'm searching for it.

I'll never forget the sight of her bleeding in my arms. Dominic had come to our house seeking refuge, and he had handed her to me so he could wrap a towel around the wound. Embedded in my memory was how pale she looked, how the bone stuck out of her skin, the blood pouring from her body and how I watched her chest to make sure she was still breathing. We were kids, babies even, and none of us should have had to deal with that type of carnage.

"I know Dominic told you," she says. "It's what you two do. You share. You two are close, and it's okay he told you and I'm sorry."

I wipe my blood and sweat against my jeans and go to wrap her in a hug because that's what we both need. Life has been too cruel to us both. "It's okay. It's done. I'll learn to live with the rest."

She sticks out a hand, stopping me from coming forward. "It's not okay. You were happy. Despite all that has happened, you were happy, and I heard what you said to Elle. I heard you say no matter what you do, you'll never be allowed to be with her, and that's not okay, so I told her."

The world comes to a grinding halt as I tilt my head. "You told who what?"

"I told Elle you didn't rob the convenience store."

Dominic steps beside me in complete bewilderment. "What did you tell her?"

"I told her we need help, and that I haven't told you everything." She hesitates and twists her fingers together. "I'm being blackmailed, and I can't live like this anymore."

ellison

I PULL INTO THE SEMICIRCLE AT THE FRONT OF our house. It's a combination of pure joy and seasickness when I spot the old red Mustang parked to the side and a hulking figure on the front steps. Beside him is a brown bag I'm betting is full of doughnuts.

It's Henry, and if Henry's here he knows Mom and Dad are gone. Odds are he also knows I should have been home and I wasn't. Placing the car in Park, I read his calculating stare. I'm so busted.

I'm out the door and he's off the steps. "Where the hell have you been?"

"At a friend's house." It's not a lie.

"I've been here since eight in the morning, so try again. I texted your dad, waving the white flag, asking if I could visit you at home since, according to news reports, you were home. He told me yes. He told me to stay with you as long as I wanted because you were alone, and he mentioned you were freaked out by being alone because of some media breach. He said you were heading straight home from the airport last night. Guess what happened when I got here? You weren't the one who was surprised."

"You could have called."

"Didn't think I'd have to since your parents thought you were home. So spill, Elle, and tell me the truth because I don't do lies. Not even from you."

I dig my suitcase out of the trunk, find my house key, walk past Henry and unlock the door. "I spent the night with my boyfriend."

My back heats as I walk in and turn off the alarm. Henry's rage is red-hot and could possibly melt skin off bones. He slams the door behind him. "What did you say?"

"I stayed the night with my boyfriend." I leave my suitcase at the bottom of the stairs and head for Dad's office. I'm not sure if I have the courage to stand still, nor do I believe I'll have the bravery to do what needs to be done if I wait.

Henry's footsteps are so heavy behind me I can't help but wonder how exactly he goes into enemy territory without announcing his arrival from a mile away. I reach Dad's office, and enter knowing that I'm about to commit an act of treason so great that if my father ever found out, he'd probably strangle me.

"That wasn't funny, and what are you doing in here? Isn't walking in here without permission breaking a seal in hell?"

"I wasn't joking, and I go in here all the time." Not for snooping, but I do.

"I'm sorry, I don't think I heard you correctly. I think you said you have a boyfriend and you stayed the night with him."

I drop into Dad's chair, and like it was a few weeks ago, there's Drix's binder. I pick it up, place it on the desk and begin flipping through it. "Do you need your hearing checked?"

Henry's talking, yelling actually, and I'm not listening. I'm scanning one page, then the next, searching for something, anything that can help. Drix didn't do it. He didn't rob the convenience store, but Drix took the plea deal, according to Kellen, because he didn't see any other option.

Lying—Drix said sometimes it happens because it was the only way to survive two bad choices. I glance up at Henry and interrupt the string of words falling out of his mouth. "Do innocent people get railroaded into plea deals?"

He balks as if he was in the midst of being run over by a Zamboni. "What?"

"You worked internships in law offices and for the district attorney. Do innocent people get railroaded into accepting plea deals?"

Henry curses under his breath and drops into the chair on the other side of Dad's desk. "You think you're in love with the boy from your dad's program, don't you?"

"Not think." This incredible feeling in my chest that flows to the tip of my toes has to be love.

"You told me you weren't interested in him."

"At the time, nothing was between us, but stuff has happened since." I suck in a breath because admitting this to my cousin in broad daylight makes it real. "I love him."

Henry looks like I shot him. "Do your parents know?"

I shake my head. "I was informed to stay away from him."

"Sounds like you listened."

Sure does. "Does it happen? The railroading?"

Henry's lips flatten. "Yeah. It happens. District attorneys are under pressure for convictions. Someone is arrested, evidence points in their general direction, a plea bargain frees up time, takes some burden off the overwhelmed prison system, and it gives district attorneys the statistics of convictions they need when people are up for reelection. I still have enough optimism left in me to believe that no one is trying to put an innocent person away, but I do think they find just enough evidence for guilt, and they go for the easy win."

"What about the attorney of the person accused? Shouldn't they help if people say they aren't guilty?"

"Good attorneys are expensive. Hell, bad ones are expensive. Public defenders are swamped. They have way too many cases than they can handle. In some states, they barely have an hour to spend on their clients' cases before going in front of a judge. A lot of times they'll recommend the plea deal because they need to focus on crimes with bigger penalties— like life in prison or death. If you're talking about this kid from your dad's program, I can see why a public defender would have pushed the plea deal. This kid didn't even serve time in real prison."

Didn't even serve time in real prison. A part of me wants to scream. "Drix didn't do it."

"Are you sure? If I was interested in a pretty girl, I'd claim I was innocent, too."

"He's not the one who told me. Someone else did."

Henry's talking again, and I'm ignoring him again, and I flip the page. My lungs squeeze all the air out of my chest. It's a still frame image from the security camera.

It shows a guy. Drix's height, but not quite Drix's build.

Drix's type of style with a T-shirt and jeans. Ball cap on his head hiding the color of his hair, sunglasses over his eyes, bandana hiding the rest of his face, boots on his feet similar to his.

Proof. I need proof. I stare at the picture, searching for something, for anything to help prove his innocence because even though he hasn't admitted it to me yet, I know he didn't do it. I understand he was someone different before the arrest, but all that he's said since I've known him…it makes sense.

Another pass. I start at the cap, down along the face, at the T-shirt, along the arms, and my entire body twitches. "There's a tattoo."

"Are you listening to anything I'm saying?"

"Drix doesn't have a tattoo." I tear the picture out of the binder, slam it shut and then put the binder back in the stack. I'm on my feet, and Henry's moving right along with me.

"Stop."

But I can't stop. I'm out of Dad's office and yanking my keys out of my pocket, but a hand on my wrist jerks me back. "Elle, you have got to listen to me."

Henry's expression causes me to go dead in my tracks. "What is it? What's wrong?"

"I need you to stop and think before you go blowing up your world."

It's not my world that's falling apart. "What are you talking about?"

"You are going to sit and talk with me. When we're done you can go off and do what you need to do, but not without talking to me first, do you understand?"

Henry is protective, overly so, but he's also my guardian angel. As he stares down at me, he's not the army boy spewing directions. He's my brother, and he's trying to tell me there's danger ahead. "Okay."

My stomach drops when he releases me and heads to the kitchen. It's there that the most serious talks happen, and something tells me, my life is about to change.

HENDRIX

KELLEN SITS ON TOP OF THE PICNIC TABLE, DOM-inic leans his back against the corner of my garage, and I complete our group as I stand with my arms crossed over my chest. Kellen's stoic while spilling what she's kept inside for over a year. Yeah, she's fragile at times, but she's also incredibly strong. It's her strength that Dominic and I often forget.

"Who did it?" Dominic's asked the question probably a hundred times, and each time his voice goes a pitch lower and more deadly. "Who robbed the store?"

Kellen glares at her older brother. "I'm not telling until Elle finds proof Drix *didn't* do it, and then we go to the police. This guy is dangerous, and I will not have the people I love hurt."

The last part stirs that dangerous thread in me I'm always on guard for. "You're more scared of him than of me going to jail?"

Kellen yanks her hat off and circles it in her hand. "He said he'd hurt people. Physically."

"And you believed this bastard?" Dominic shouts.

A sickening wave washes over me as she nods. Dominic is feared on these streets. He protects her in their home. If she's scared of someone hurting Dominic, then that someone threatened murder.

Dominic pushes off the wall. "That's bull. I protect you. You know this."

"Sometimes I protect you, too," she whispers.

He begins an eloquent swearing rant, and I step in, taking a seat on the table beside her. I catch his eyes and subtly shake my head. She doesn't need our anger. She needs our help. "Walk us through what happened. Start with after you took your dad's gun."

"I only brought it because I was scared of walking late at night in the neighborhood. There was that girl that was raped a week before."

"You shouldn't have been out," Dominic says.

"You were bleeding," she snaps. "From your head. I went to get medical supplies for you. I thought you were dying."

"You went to steal from the store," he bites back.

Her chin yanks up, and she swallows as she tries to gain her composure. "Just medical supplies. That's it. I was going to lift some gauze and rubbing alcohol. That's it. I swear."

"Then what about the cash I found? What about the story you gave me? What happened to Dad's gun?"

Moisture lines the rims of her eyes, and her knee begins to bounce. I place a hand on her knee, it steadies, and after she takes in a long steadying breath, I pull back and she begins again. "I was scared to tell you the truth. I knew you'd go after him, and I didn't want you to get hurt. You get hurt enough, and I'm sick and tired of being the reason why."

"That's my job! I protect you. Period. You don't take falls for me."

"You—" I pin Dominic with my glare "—let her talk. Keep going, Kellen. What happened when you got to the store?"

"He was there, and he saw me in the aisle trying to lift."

"And you weren't any good at it," Dominic mumbles.

She doesn't say anything, because her brother's right. "He offered to do it for me."

"For what price?" I ask.

"He said no price."

Dominic and I share a long look because we raised her better. Anything given in this neighborhood comes with a high payday. Debts aren't something you want to owe.

"I was scared for Dominic," she says, "and I wanted those bandages. This guy told me to wait outside and make sure no one else came in."

"You mean you became his lookout."

"For bandages! I had my back to the store so I didn't know what was happening until the gunshot. I checked my back and the gun was gone. I realized he lifted it off of me, and I was scared, so I ran. So fast, so hard, but then he found me the next morning. He told me I was an accessory, and he gave me some of the cash for my part in the holdup. He told me if I ever told anyone, he'd hurt me and he'd hurt the people I loved. I don't care if he hurt me, but I do care if he'd hurt you guys, and I knew he could. I know he still can, but if we get proof, we can send him to jail, and then he can't hurt anyone anymore, and then Drix can get his life back."

I rub my hands together and lower my head. Problem with all of that? Whatever asshole is threatening Kellen has something right. There's a good chance she could be arrested for accessory, and that's a problem for me. With how Dominic is looking at me, he's thinking the same thing.

It's like every time we try to dig out of a hole, someone's shoveling more crap on top of us. There will never be a way out.

Ellison

LIKE I WAS TEN, HENRY POURS HIMSELF A GLASS of chocolate milk and then does the same for me. "I can't remember the last time I drank chocolate milk," I say.

"I'd bet it would be the last time we were in this kitchen together." He pulls out a chocolate doughnut with sprinkles, puts it on a napkin, then slides it in my direction. He gives himself the one that's overflowing with pudding.

I stand where Drix stood weeks ago. Henry is in my position. I stare at him, taking a mental snapshot because this is what I have dreamed of for years, my cousin returning home. "Are you here to stay?"

"I'm here for you. I've been keeping up with the news. Lots of pictures of you, and not one of them is your real smile."

I shrug off his truth. "You missed my birthday."

"I sent you a text."

A phssh sound leaves my mouth. "I deserve more than a text."

"My superior would be pretty pissed if I walked during an assignment. Considering I was protecting someone important at the time, I felt needed."

I playfully roll my eyes at his logical explanation. "Fine."

"I'm here now. Maybe by the end of today, you'll smile for real."

"I'd smile more if you, Mom and Dad would figure out your problems and you'd come here to stay when you're in town."

Henry rubs his biceps and leans forward on the counter. "My problem with them is my problem with them, not yours. I've learned a lot once I took a stand, and one of those things is the risks are bigger for you than they ever were for me. You need to be careful. Your mom and dad don't like betrayal."

"I'm assuming you're referring to dating Drix behind their back?"

"I'm referring to the fact you've got one more year until you graduate from high school. You want to break out of your bubble then, I'm game. I'll even give you a place to crash when you do, but you still have one year of school. That means one more year of control over you. They play nice as long you play nice, but cross them, and they'll crush anything you love."

My mind swirls because his description doesn't come close to describing Mom and Dad. "It's not Dad's fault Drix was arrested and not his fault Drix felt he had to take the plea deal."

"I'm asking you to be careful. Think about what you're doing before you do it. You have a habit of rushing in. Don't be so eager to give or receive the truth. Most times, it ruins lives."

Ruins lives. I have a hard time believing that. The truth is powerful, and the truth only makes us better. "What did you do, Henry? What is it Mom and Dad are so mad at you for?"

"For owning my life."

"What does that mean?"

"It means you need to think before you leap. Once you go too far, there's no going back, and take a good look around because all you see is what you have to lose."

A hole forms in my stomach because I don't want to lose anything. But mostly, I don't want to lose Mom and Dad—not like how Mom, Dad and Henry have lost each other. We may not agree on everything, but they're my parents. They love me and I love them. "Will I lose you?"

"Never." But he immediately focuses on the two untouched glasses of chocolate milk. "I ship out tomorrow."

I hate those words. Hate them more than anyone can know. "How long?"

"Six months."

My chest aches, and I ease onto the stool beside me. There's not enough time to soak in all that I need from him before he leaves.

"I came by thinking we could eat doughnuts, order pizza for lunch and binge watch *Star Wars*."

I nod through the pain. "Then that's what we'll do."

HENDRIX

THE SUN BEATS DOWN ON ME. FIRE IN THE FORM of rays. I'm on the roof of a house that's two stories at the front, and thanks to the walk-out basement, I'm three stories high from the back. One slip of my footing on the slanted roof and I'd better hope Axle added me to his health insurance. Otherwise, he can leave me on the ground to die.

I pound one nail after another into black shingles. Sweat pours down my back, and along my brow. The perspiration has dripped and dried several times, and it's only noon.

"Drix," Axle calls from the ground. "Take a break."

I stand tall, and my entire back aches from being bent over for hours. Sad part? I don't want a break. I want to keep pounding in nails. I can't think then. Too focused on keeping my muscles moving. Too busy settling into numb. I do well in numb, and physical activity brings me to that state. Marching in a forest, pounding in nails. Guess it's good this works for me as this is the best I can hope to do with the rest of my life.

"Drix," Axle shouts again, and I head for the ladder. One step down after another. On the ground, I head over to a towering maple. Once in the shade, I unhook my work belt, drop it off to the side, plant myself next to it, and pull my cell out of my pocket.

Elle. Her name falls into the hollow pit in my chest. I haven't heard from Elle. In her defense, I haven't reached out to her either. I said some cutting words, and I don't know how to take them back. That's wrong. I do, but I've never been good at apologizing. That means sucking up my pride, and my pride is all I have left.

But I think of her in my arms, her soft skin, her smile, her laughter…her trust. She deserves better than me, yet I flip my cell around and turn it on. Yes, she deserves better, but it's me she's going to get. Texting would be easier, but I'm used to things being hard. Wouldn't know what to do with myself if anything in my life was smooth and painless.

I push Call and place my cell to my ear. One ring, then another. When the third ring hits I lower my head. Asshole. Why do I always have to revert to being an asshole when life goes to pieces? I go into voice mail. "It's me. Leave a message."

A few seconds go by. Long enough I'm surprised I didn't get kicked out of the call, but I finally speak. "It's me. I'm sorry. I was—" hurting "—wrong."

"See, I told you it wasn't so hard."

My head snaps up, and Elle is gliding toward me with a bottle of water in her hands. She's gorgeous as always. Blond hair pulled up into a messy bun, those sexy dark-rimmed glasses on, intimidating blue eyes on me and a dangerous smile that could get me into all sorts of trouble I wouldn't mind being in with her.

I go to stand, but she waves me down. "I've watched you from my car for the past hour. You need a break."

She sits beside me and offers me the water. Dehydrated, I suck it down so fast the bottle crackles. It's cold and refreshing and I have a fresh wave of energy. But the energy is from Elle because she's contagious.

"How did you know where I was?" I ask.

"I stopped by your house this morning, and Holiday told me where to find you. I hope you don't mind, but I need to talk to you, and I didn't want to do it over the phone."

I crack my neck to the side because that sounds like breakup words, and I deserve it. Saying I'm sorry isn't enough. Nothing in my world is enough. The other day was the second time I sent her away. At some point, she was bound to break.

"I wasn't mad at you." I scratch the back of my head as if that can force my mind to come up with better thoughts. Something more poetic than the dirt inside me. "I was…"

"It's okay," Elle says.

It's not. "What do you need to talk about?" Might as well get it over with.

She straightens the rings on her fingers. "Why didn't you tell me?"

Don't have to ask her what she's referring to. "Besides the fact it would have sounded like I was giving you a line so I could try to get into your pants?"

She tilts her head in acknowledgment. "But what about later? When things started getting serious? Why didn't you trust me? Why did it take Kellen asking for my help? Why didn't you?"

"Until recently, I thought Dominic did it. I got this stubborn side of me where I don't want the people I love to go to jail. I already served the time. I'm already screwed. There's no reason for that robbery to mess up anyone else's life."

"Is that why you accepted the plea deal? For Dominic?"

Yes and no. "I accepted the plea deal because they found me on the ground passed out behind the convenience store with the gun used in the robbery in my hand and because the surveillance video showed a guy with my build and my height. The damn shirt the guy was wearing in the surveillance video was balled up next to me as well, as was the hat and the bandanna."

"Could they not argue it was planted on you?"

He shrugs. "The police said I passed out while changing and that the reason I didn't have the money is because someone else probably stole it off me after I passed out. I accepted the plea deal because the public defender assigned to me had no clue what was going on, and I was going to be charged as an adult if I didn't plead guilty. I had two bad choices, and I picked the one that stunk less."

She reaches into her purse and extracts a folded-up piece of paper. "I found this in Dad's binder about you."

I open it, and it's a picture I've never seen before. A still frame image of the surveillance video. I was only shown certain parts of the video and certain pictures. Elle reaches over and a painted fingernail points to the forearm. "Whoever did it has a tattoo. You didn't do it, and now we have proof."

My eyes narrow in on the tattoo of a vine and a cross on

the forearm. Red-hot rage explodes through me, and I'm off the ground.

I'm going to kill him.

I'm going to go to real jail this time, and it's because the bastard is going to be dead.

Ellison

DRIX IS GONE, GOING FOR AXLE'S TRUCK, AND I spin, scanning for help. "Axle!" And then I'm chasing after him. "Drix, stop. You have to stop! Axle, please!"

The driver's side door is open, but before Drix can jump in, Axle grabs hold of Drix's arm and slams him into the side of the truck. "What are you doing? We're on a job!"

Adrenaline courses through my veins, and the fire shooting out of Drix's eyes causes me to step back. The rage in him, the madness, the set of his jaw, the entire way his body is poised and ready to strike like a snake full of venom— I've never seen this before. Never in Drix. Never in another human being. This is beyond anger. This is raw and bloody and the most terrifying thing I've ever seen.

Drix rams the picture into Axle's chest. "Holiday's boyfriend committed the robbery. He framed me and he's going to pay."

With one arm still wrapped around Drix's biceps like it's

a metal vise, Axle yanks the keys from Drix's hand, then opens the paper.

"The tattoo on the arm," Drix spits. "It's *Jeremy*."

Axle drops Drix's arm and a sentence full of f-bombs. "Where'd you get this?"

"Me." I step forward. "Kellen asked me for help, and I found this in Drix's file."

Axle's eyes go ice-cold. "Your dad knew Drix didn't do it?"

I shake my head so quickly that pieces of hair fall out of my bun. "No. No way. He had nothing to do with the arrest or what the DA offered. Dad only got involved once there were candidates for the program. He trusted the DA to make the right conviction."

"We never saw this picture," Drix says. "We didn't know it existed."

"We didn't ask." Axle scrubs a hand over his face. "I was stupid, and I didn't ask. But we have to be smart about this now. We have to figure out how to clear your name, how to do it clean, and we have to figure out how to keep Kellen safe. We need a lawyer. A good one."

"And how are we going to pay for that?" Drix snaps.

"I don't know," Axle shoots back, "but I'll figure it out."

"My dad," I say, and they both turn to me as if they had forgotten I was there. "We'll go to him. He'll help us. I know he will."

The anger rushes out of Drix's face. "We can't go to him. We aren't supposed to be together."

Fear and anxiety go around and around causing nausea, but I have no choice. At my core, I'm my father's daughter. "Dad set up that program to give a voice to the voiceless. He would be angrier at me for saying nothing and saving myself. This is important. You're important. No matter how angry he'll be at me, he loves me and he'll forgive me. My future, no matter what, is secure. This is about you and your future. This is about making sure you get all you deserve."

HENDRIX

ELLE HAS THE NICEST CAR I'VE RIDDEN IN. Leather seats, air-conditioning that works and an engine that doesn't sound like it's about to rattle out of the frame. It's a smooth ride, and it's been a silent one except for her fingers that tap against the steering wheel at stoplights. She's nervous. So am I. No telling how talking to her father is going to go down, but the rolling in my gut keeps screaming it'll be bad.

She pulls in her driveway, skips the right that would take us to the front of the house and goes around back to park in front of a massive garage. The smooth engine shuts off, and it's absolute quiet.

"You don't have to do this," I say.

Elle looks over at me, and those normally intimidating blue eyes are soft. "This is how I was raised. My dad taught me to fight for people, and you're someone worth fighting for."

Fighting for. I've been in fights my entire life. None of them worth being in. All were with my fists, and if Elle wasn't in my life, there's a good chance I would have continued down that road, and I'd be fighting Jeremy with my fists again.

I love Axle, but when he told me to accept the plea deal, that was worse than being kicked in the balls. Worse than having my head torn off my body. Worse than having my heart ripped out of my chest as it still beat. My brother told me to give in. He told me we couldn't win. He told me not to fight.

Something broke in me then. Something that has kept me from feeling whole. But sitting here next to Elle, understanding that she will bear the wrath of her family to fight for me—emotions build up and threaten to bust past my skin.

I cradle her face with my hand, and she leans into me. "Thank you for this."

"They're probably going to ground me," she says, and that smile she tries to give me is one of the fake ones. "Will you wait for me? There's a good chance I might be thirty."

I caress a finger over her lips to ease the fakeness away. I prefer the real her—even if it's the side of her that's sad. "We'll make this work. Your dad is a good man, and I'll spend as much time as I can proving to him I'm worthy of you."

"We should go in." Her mouth pulls down, and it breaks my heart.

Her backyard is big, green and lavish, but what catches my eye is the white gazebo next to the weeping willow. Picturesque, private and perfect. Elle and I need an escape. We need to, one more time, live in our own world.

I exit the car and reach Elle's side as she cracks the door. I open it the rest of the way for her and offer her my hand. She gives me a shy grin as she accepts, and I knot my fingers with hers. I close the door, then stare down into her eyes so she knows I'm dead serious. "When we get past this, I want you to go on a date with me."

Elle shines. "Was that a question? Because I'm not sure I heard the question mark at the end. In the real world, people ask for dates. They don't assume dates."

She's killing me. "First apologizing and now asking...you're high maintenance."

Elle laughs, and I pull on her hand. "Come with me." Before we go in and place ourselves in the head of a salivating lion.

We walk across the grass, hand in hand, and Elle points out where Henry had built her a tree house when she was ten, where her father had taught her to hit a ball with a bat and where her mother used to lie with her on afternoons and read books on lazy summer afternoons.

Under the cover of the weeping willow, I tell her how Axle taught me to play the guitar, how the drums came naturally and how when Holiday's grandma said I wasn't being an ass, she'd teach me piano. I tell her that we throw cake at each other on birthdays because I first did it on my birthday when Holiday was getting on my nerves. She threw cake back. A tradition was born.

We talk, we laugh and for a few minutes it feels like two teens wasting away a summer afternoon. Warm breeze, blue sky, birds singing to one another, and we move to the shade in the gazebo where Elle caresses my arm as we sit on the wooden bench.

"Someday, I'd like you to be the one to walk me into a fund-raiser," she says, and her voice has a soft whimsical feel as if we've been transported to another time, another place.

"Does that mean I have to wear a tux?"

She winks. "Definitely. You're stunning in your suits, but I've dreamed of you in a tux."

"We need to work on your fantasies. Mine include less clothes, not more."

Elle turns red, but she smiles—the real one. "You have your fantasies. I have mine. But imagine it, you and I walking in together. I'll be in a long flowing dress, you'll be all adorable in black, and then we'll dance. Then you'll have that snapshot in your mind forever of me in a beautiful dress and of us dancing."

I can see it. It's not hard to do. If she only knew how many snapshots of her I have in my mind already. But I hear what she's saying. She wants to spend time with me as her man in public. She wants to be with me in public during a dance. She's about to walk through hell for me, and I can do this for her.

A gust blows through the gazebo and strands of her hair blow around her face as I stand. With her hand still in mine, I squeeze. "Dance with me, Elle."

Elle is blinding. Her eyes, that smile—a sun that's the center of my world. She stands, and in the middle of the gazebo, she wraps her arms around my neck, and we sway from side to side. I then do something I hardly ever do—I sing.

Low, soft, right in her ear and we move with the beat, move with the melody. I sing of flying, wings and how some loves are meant to be. And my favorite part of the song, the part where the beat picks up, the part where the rhythm changes, I spin Elle. A turn for every tap on the snare drum. Then there's a dramatic pause where there's no beat, no voice, no music, and I dip her, holding my breath as she looks up at me with so much love, my heart is overflowing.

I bring her back into me, and where we should keep dancing, we instead hold on to each other. Her head tilted up, my hands framing her face, a lick of her lips in invitation and I kiss her. Easy and slow. A memorization of how soft she is, yet strong to the core.

There's a burn, a match that's been struck. Mouths moving, her hands along my back, fingernails tickling along the skin of my neck, and her body pressed to mine. The fire runs hot, starts to consume, but this isn't the time, and it isn't the place because this kiss is a promise.

A promise that no matter the consequence, I'm not going anywhere. A promise that I love her. A promise that someday I'll be the man with her in the middle of the dance floor. Me in the tux. Her in the beautiful dress.

I gently kiss her lips one more time, then pull back. I don't tell her I love her because my kiss said it all. She doesn't say it back because the deep blue of her eyes tells me all I need to know. I enfold her into me again, wrap my arms strongly around her and close my eyes.

I will hold her again, I will be with her again, and when I do it, I'll be a man truly free of his past.

Ellison

MY HANDS ARE COLD. FREEZING. YET, CLAMMY.
Drix is following me through the house. It's empty as it typically is after a long trip. Mom and Dad prefer to have downtime. A few moments alone after they've had to be perfect for such a long stretch.

When we first walked in, I heard Mom moving about upstairs, and I stayed as quiet as I could so she wouldn't poke her head out to greet me. I don't need her disappointing stare. I don't need her blocking my path to Dad. This is between me, him and Drix.

Outside Dad's office, I suck in a deep breath, but there's no calming the waves of nausea crashing in my stomach. As soon as one wave fades, another one crests. But this is the right thing to do. Dad will see this. He'll be mad at my lies, but he'll eventually forgive me because that's who my father is at the core of his being—he's love.

I knock on the door, Dad gives affirmation to enter, and

Drix places his hand on my neck. I briefly close my eyes with the touch of reassurance. Then his hand is gone, and I walk in. Dad smiles. It's big and it's wide and it tells me how much he missed me. "There you are. I told your mom you wouldn't be gone long. Where do you want to go to dinner? Your choice. Maybe even a movie if there's anything out you want to see…"

But his smile fades, slips right off his face as if someone had used an eraser. Drix has entered, and I keep walking because if I don't, I might lose my nerve. I sit at one of the chairs across from Dad, perched at the edge, because that's where I feel like I'm teetering.

"Hey, Dad."

Dad keeps his eyes purely on Drix as Drix stands behind the other empty chair.

"What can I do for you, Hendrix? Not sure if you knew, but my wife and I just returned from a long trip. Typically I wouldn't take impromptu meetings, but I know you wouldn't have stopped by if it wasn't important."

"It is, sir. I found out some information, and I came straight here from a job site to see you."

Concern for Drix worries Dad's forehead, and it gives me hope. This is my father—the man who cares. "Elle, thank you for letting Hendrix in. Do you mind giving us a few minutes?"

Here comes the part where I throw myself off the ledge. "Actually, I'm involved in this."

Dad's eyes snap to me, and it's hard to not shrink. "What do you mean?"

I tuck a strand of hair behind my ear, then readjust my

glasses. I should have rehearsed this for about a year because I don't know how to lead off. Should I start with how I've been seeing Drix behind their back since May? How I've fallen in love with him and him with me? Should I tell him how I was at Drix's house and a friend of his told me Drix didn't do the crime? Do I tell him I snuck into this office, went through his private files and removed proof that Drix is innocent?

I raise my chin. I'm in free fall and prepare myself for impact with the ground. "Drix didn't rob the convenience store." I remove the picture from my pocket, unfold it and lay it on Dad's desk. "This is a screen shot from the surveillance video, and the person who robbed the store had a tattoo. Drix doesn't have any tattoos."

My father stares at the photo, and his frozen expression is terrifying. "You pled guilty."

I glance at Drix out of the corner of my eye, and I admire how cool, calm and collected he seems sitting in the chair opposite of me. "Yes, sir, I did. But I pled guilty because we couldn't afford a lawyer, and they were threatening to charge me as an adult if I didn't accept. My brother and I decided I couldn't take the risk of me going to adult prison. We felt the evidence was stacked against me, but that picture proves I didn't commit the crime, and if you allow me to explain, I can tell you who did do it."

"Where did you get this picture?"

Drix goes to answer, and if I know him, it's to cover for me, but Henry is wrong. The truth is important. "I found it." No sense stopping now. "When I was searching through Hendrix's binder here in your office. Someone told me he didn't do it so I searched for answers."

His eyes flicker between us, and I can tell he's doing the math in his head. He's figuring out I haven't stayed away from Drix and that Drix hasn't stayed away from me. It's time to own my choices. "Just so you know everything, Drix and I are together."

A tick of Dad's jaw. "Together?"

"Dating, sir," Drix answers before I can. "We see each other after the events and have seen each other a few times outside of the events, as well. I apologize that we've done it behind your back. I promise, anything going forward, will be with your permission."

Now he doesn't have to go that far.

The cords of muscles in Dad's neck protrude, and my heart picks up speed. I hold on to the arms of the chair for support.

"I need you to leave, Elle. Go to your room and don't come out until I tell you."

"Dad—"

"Go," he snaps, and the anger that blares from him in my direction makes me feel as if the two of us are strangers.

I dare to look over at Drix, and he subtly inclines his head for me to go. I do, feeling like I'm abandoning him. My father starts yelling before I even have a chance to close the door.

HENDRIX

GOVERNOR MONROE ISN'T YELLING AT ME AS A politician, he's yelling at me as a father, and I remain silent and take it. I never had a father who fought for me. Never had a mother who was willing to go a single round on my behalf either. I may not like being on the receiving end of a verbal lashing, but I respect him for loving his daughter.

"I have showed you nothing but respect." He's not yelling anymore, but agitated as hell as he flings a pen across his desk. "How could you not offer me the same?"

Governor Monroe leans back in his seat, every muscle still tense, and the silence between us stretches. I count in my head, like the beats of a bass drum, and when enough time passes, I realize this isn't another rhetorical question. He's waiting for an answer. "You're right, and I'm sorry. Elle and I should have never kept our friendship and relationship a secret."

No change in expression, and I read the writing on the

wall. Doesn't matter if we went to him, he would have forbidden it. So this begs the question if I really am sorry for going behind his back, because being with Elle is one of the best things that's happened in my life.

"You have a right to be angry with me on how I've handled my relationship with your daughter, but with all due respect, it doesn't erase the fact that Elle did find that picture, and it proves I did not commit that crime."

The governor stands and walks over to a bar area. Instead of pouring himself liquor in a glass like I've seen a million times on TV, he grabs two bottles of water from the mini fridge. He hands one to me and then sits in Elle's seat.

I'll admit it, this puts me more on edge than walking through the slasher room at a haunted house. He rests his water on the desk and leans forward.

"Start from the beginning. Every detail you can think of that leads up to the crime and what happened after. If you had Cheerios for breakfast, I want to know. Don't leave anything out. No matter how insignificant. And don't sugarcoat anything either. You were high that night. I saw the toxicology results. I know you went through withdrawal. I know we gave you drug and alcohol counseling. I need to know everything. The absolute truth."

Sincerity. It's etched on the lines around his eyes and mouth, and into the way his body is angled toward me. Since I met Elle, this is what she's been explaining to me. How her father cares and is in power to help others. A sensation of awe and confusion rushes through me.

"No one but you and your daughter has ever been willing

to help me before. I..." It's difficult to sort through the hit-in-the-head blur of thoughts. "I don't know what to do with it."

The governor stares straight into my eyes. "You accept the help. As I said, start from the beginning. I need to know what I'm up against."

ellison

DRIX: YOUR DAD ASKED ME TO GIVE HIM TWENTY-FOUR hours to think things through and he'll get back to me on how to handle everything. He also asked me to stay away from you for a while. He's mad and he has a right to be. He knows I'm texting this to you, but then I'm going to respect him and not contact you again until he gives me permission. We're strong enough to see this through. Are you with me?

Me: Yes.

Drix: I love you. Remember that.

Then there was nothing. We're nearing the twenty-four hour mark and that quiet is a dark space that's filled with shadow monsters and hollow pits. Dad won't talk to me. Mom can barely glance in my direction. The house is full of staffers, and there's this low buzz of panicked energy among them all. Bees on the defensive as their hive is about to be endangered.

I sit on the top step of the stairs with my cell in my hands in the vain hope Drix will contact me again, but he won't.

Not until my father grants him permission, and from the pissed-off flare my father's ignoring me with, I'm thinking that permission will come in never.

Patience. This entire situation is going to require a massive amount of patience, and my father is a good man. I have to have faith this will work out.

Clicking of heels and my mother rounds the corner from the hallway and appears in the foyer. At the bottom of the stairs, she looks up, and when our eyes meet sadness rolls over me. From the way she falters, it appears that same sadness crashes into her.

"We need to talk," she says. I stand, head to my room, and Mom's footsteps follow.

I sit at the top of my bed and hold a pillow to my stomach as Mom closes the door behind her. She's dressed in a black pants suit, her blond hair is slicked back in a bun, and she's perfection. Always perfection and I start to wonder if she ever feels exhausted.

I expect her to remain standing, to lecture me on all that I've done wrong and then leave. Instead she sits on my bed with her back toward me. She surveys my room that hasn't changed since we redid it when I turned fifteen. Soft light green paint, white crown molding, framed pictures of wildflowers on the wall. Besides my laptop on my dresser, there isn't much of the room that speaks to my personality, but then again, at fifteen, I thought this is who I was. Maybe I was that person, but I'm not her anymore.

"You have put your father in a terrible position," she says. "If he announces Hendrix Pierce is innocent, that he accepted the plea deal because he couldn't afford a decent lawyer and his public defender was too busy to help, it will appear as if Hendrix was railroaded into accepting the deal so that the district attorney could raise his conviction rates."

I hang on tighter to the pillow. "Railroaded is how he felt."

"Maybe that's the case, but do you not see how this will ruin your father's career?"

I don't see. "Dad didn't arrest Drix, he wasn't the public defender, and he wasn't the one that offered the plea deal. All Dad did was create the program, and the district attorneys across the state were responsible for recommending teens. That's it. This isn't Dad's fault."

"No, it's not, but that's not how people will see it. The media won't care your father was trusting the district attorneys with the recommendations. They'll want to know why your father wasn't a private detective and sleuthed out every fact and clue for every teen in the program."

A strangling in my stomach. "That's ridiculous. No one will blame him."

"You can't be that naïve. You hung out with a boy on a midway for a matter of minutes, and look how the media behaved. They love a scandal. The media could care less your father has saved lives. All they'll care about is that an innocent boy was punished for a crime he didn't commit, and they'll care your father was the person in charge when it happened. They'll try to search for any angle to crucify your father. They'll speculate that he told the district attorneys to railroad good potential candidates so he could have a successful program. They'll tear that program apart and take your father's career along with it in the process."

I drop the pillow and lean forward on my knees. "But the

program *does* work. Drix will tell everyone that. He says the program saved him, and he's so grateful to Dad for being chosen. I know Drix will tell people Dad had nothing to do with being arrested and the plea deal and—"

"It doesn't matter." She cuts me off. "The truth does not matter—it never does. The only thing that matters is the headline. No one reads the retraction. They'll look for every potential evil in every detail. Have you not figured it out? This country doesn't want heroes. Not when it so thoroughly enjoys kicking a villain."

A bit of crazy nibbles on the outside of my brain. "So you're saying what? That we should do nothing? That Drix will live the rest of his life with the world thinking he's a criminal? That he should lose his shot with the youth performing arts school and whatever other opportunity in his future because the system is broken?"

Mom's eyes are so cold I shiver. "He never had to tell anyone what he did. That was his decision. His records were sealed."

My hands slam on the comforter of my bed. "Dad asked him to!"

"No one can prove that, and he could have declined. Hendrix Pierce is busy blaming the entire world for his problems when the truth is he could have fought for his innocence. Before that he could have chosen a better life. He has to take responsibility for his choices. He was passed out drunk and high at that store. He is not as innocent as you think."

"Are you kidding me? Nothing you said matters. Drix is innocent and I can prove it!"

"At the expense of your father's career?"

"You don't know that's what will happen!" I shout.

"And you'd be willing to possibly throw away your father's career to find out? Over a boy you've seen while on campaign trips? Over a boy you've seen a few times at his house? You've known him months, and we have given you life. We've given you a great life. A perfect life. You're seventeen, and you have no idea what real love is. Nor do you have any idea what the real world is like. It's cruel and unforgiving. Do not make emotional decisions that will ruin the lives of the people you love."

The blood drains out of my face. Did Drix tell Dad everything? "He told you I was at his house?"

"I knew," she seethes.

My heart stops beating, and I experience the sensation of my mind leaving my body. "You knew?"

Mom closes her eyes, sucks in a deep breath, and within seconds her polished mask is back into place. "Of course I knew. I'm your mother. But I kept it to myself. I thought it would be harmless. Plus, you two were being discreet. I was a teenager once, Elle. I understand having a crush, and I also understand flames like this burn out fast. I also understood you needing your space, but I draw the line at self-destruction. None of this matters now. Hendrix is downstairs meeting with your father, and your father is explaining the situation to him."

They must have brought Drix in through the back. The urge is to jump up, rush downstairs, but I understand now why Mom is here. She's keeping me from charging in and making a mess.

"I will say this," Mom says. "He's more mature than you.

He's very respectful, and he understands that the world can be a cruel place."

My stomach drops. "What does that mean?"

"It means that he is, at least, listening." The cell in Mom's hand chirps. She checks it, then sighs. "Your father wants you to come downstairs, but before you do, I would like you to change, put in your contacts and please fix your hair. There are people in the house, and I expect you to start acting your age. I won't ask nicely again. Then please do me a favor and try to be more like Hendrix and start listening and doing what you're told."

HENDRIX

I OPEN THE DOOR TO GOVERNOR MONROE'S office and there's a flash of blond in front of me. "Let me speak to him, Dad, please. Just a few minutes."

I slip my fingers around Elle's wrist, keeping her from storming in and saying more. She halts in my grip, and her eyes widen. A caress of my thumb against her pressure point. "I was coming to find you."

Her head whips toward her father who's still sitting behind his desk, and he nods his approval. Elle goes off balance. Last time the three of us were in this room together, her father was going nuclear.

"When you're done talking to him, Elle," the governor says, "go back to your room. I'll find you when I'm ready to talk."

Elle mutters an agreement, then we leave the office, and Elle closes the door behind us. She stares at me and I stare at her. Her blond hair is brushed out and styled, the colored contacts are in her eyes that make them a brighter blue and makeup covers her freckles and scar. It's Elle, but not Elle, and I wonder if she feels numb when she dresses up to be someone else.

Because that's how I want to feel—numb. No, I take that back. I don't want numb anymore. When I returned home from my year away, numb is what I thought I wanted, but then Elle entered my life, and she helped me feel. The one thing about highs is that there are lows, and this low…it's painful.

"Do you want some lemonade?" she asks, and a ghost of a smile plays on her face.

Lemonade. Someplace inside, I chuckle, but it's buried down so deep that it doesn't reach the surface. "Yeah."

Quiet and pensive, we head to the kitchen. When we reach it, she begins the task of finding glasses, going to the fridge and pouring the yellow liquid. As if it were May again, I stand on one side of the island, Elle on the other. Two glasses of lemonade, but this time, neither of us drink.

"We don't need Dad," Elle says. "I've been thinking about it. We can ask the district attorney to reexamine the video. Tell him to look for the tattoo. We can—"

I cut her off. "The program worked."

"I know."

She doesn't. She can't. She wasn't the one who wandered around for years so angry at the world that hitting, hurting and making myself bleed was my only solution. She wasn't the one who hurt everyone in her path like a renegade hurricane. She wasn't me, and she doesn't know what it was like to wake up on a cold morning sober and breathe in clean forest air, to feel the dew on my face and clothes, watch a sunrise and know that this day I was born. That this was the day I promised myself I wouldn't be the asshole again.

"You don't. Not really. You can take my word for it, but you can't know it worked because you didn't go through it."

"I'm not arguing the program—" she starts, but I cut her off again.

"Marcus changed, too. He was doing drugs and committing crimes. He wasn't deep in a gang yet, but he was close. Since the program, he's been hanging with us and staying sober."

"Yes, but that doesn't affect you clearing your name."

"I try to clear my name and I'm a bastard," I challenge. "Because everything your dad said is right. I take a puppy out of a hotel, and I had to publicly apologize. Your dad had to pay for damages that weren't there. I go forward with this, and the program's future is in jeopardy. Your dad's job is in jeopardy. I can't do that. I can't be the person responsible for taking away the program that saved me, saved Marcus and saved every person in the program. If I clear my name, I'm the bastard who stole hope from anyone else screwed up like me."

Elle silently watches me. She's the beauty with a short temper when the world sways the wrong way. She's the girl on the edge of becoming a woman who believes she can change the world. I don't doubt she can, but it won't be with me. Too many things stacked up against me and sometimes failure is unavoidable.

She taps her finger against the counter. "It doesn't have to be this way. It doesn't have to be all or nothing. There has to be another way."

"Tell me what the other choice is, and I'm game."

She blinks rapidly with tears, and anger reddens her cheeks. I understand the feeling because it's the damn story of my life.

"Two bad choices," I continue. "Choice One: I stay silent, and I'm a criminal for the rest of my life. Covering for a crime done by my sister's asshole boyfriend. Choice Two: I speak up, and the program that saved my life dies, and your father's career is crushed. Anyone like me who needs the help won't receive it. They'll be damned the moment they enter the system."

She wipes at the corner of her eyes, and her pain is killing me. "That is a worst-case scenario. You don't know if that's what will happen. Besides, my mom and dad can take the heat. They'll figure it out. They'll make it work."

I crack my neck to the side. "And what if they're right? I can't take that risk."

"Why?" she shouts, and that sends anger shooting down my spine.

"Because I'm not a bastard anymore," I snap. "Because there are hundreds, maybe thousands more people whose lives can be saved if I stay silent."

Her head flinches back. "The greater good? Is that what you're suggesting? That your life, your future, means less than anybody else's?"

Because I lived so much of my life only for me... "Yes."

"I don't accept that."

"It's not yours to accept or not accept. This is my decision."

"What about your sister? Are you going to let her continue to date Jeremy? If you do nothing, they'll stay together. If you do nothing, he'll be preying on other people like Holiday and Kellen. He's sick, and he needs to be behind bars."

The muscles in my face contort at the sound of his name. First thing I plan on doing is outing that bastard to my sister. "Hundreds of teens just like me can be saved, Elle. How do I walk away from that?"

She mashes her lips together as she tries to fight the tears, but each tremble of her mouth vibrates through me. My own sorrow, my own grief begins to weigh me down.

"What about us?" she asks. "What happens to us?"

My throat tightens, and I clear it. She dreamed of me by her side, and she painted such a beautiful picture that even the part of me that remains in stone softened to the idea. But I was stupid for dreaming. Stupid for even thinking I had a chance with her. "Your dad said after the election we can see each other again, in private. If we do what they say, then he'll consider letting us be seen together in public."

"Consider? What do you mean *consider*? Me and you being together is not his decision to make. That is between me and you, and me and you alone."

She's hurting, I'm hurting, and I close my fists, then force them open. "We're trapped. I've told you from the get-go we're trapped. We don't get to make a single choice in our lives. We're puppets who thought for a few seconds we didn't have strings."

"Because you're letting them tell you what to do!"

"Two bad options, Elle! Which one is it? Whose life do I destroy? Yours? Mine? Because those are my choices. I claim my innocence, I lose you, too, because your father will never let me see you. I'm choosing. I'm choosing to save people like me, and I'm choosing to be with you."

My own eyes burn, and I swear while turning away. I look

out the window at the gazebo and her dreams. I lost mine, but this is my only shot at helping her reach her dreams, and maybe that will be enough to push me through life. Nailing in shingles, twelve-hour days, being weathered in the heat and cold. Maybe then I'll get to be with Elle for a few more months. Maybe a thousand more lives like mine will be saved, and they'll walk out of the program with a real blank slate and a real new future. Maybe Elle will have all she wants and more.

"If I stay quiet, your dad is going to let you apply for the internship and allow you to take the coding classes at school." Because I learned fast once he started talking that I held his future in my hands. There's not much that can be done for me, but I had no problem using that leverage to help someone we both love—his daughter.

"Why?" she whispers.

Because I love you.

"You're important," she says. "Your life, your future, is just as important as mine. Just as important as everyone else's. This isn't okay."

It's not, but two bad choices.

Silent tears stream down her face, and the sight makes my soul bleed. I want to hug her. I want to hold her. I want to tell her everything is going to be okay, but I don't know if it is. "I promised your father I'd tell you, then I'd leave. Once the election is over, I can see you again."

Elle covers her face with her hands, and I shut my eyes because I thought I was done hurting people. Her hands lower, she grabs hold of the glass of lemonade and throws it. The glass shatters, falls to the floor, and liquid drips down the wall.

"He's wrong," she says. "And so are you."

I am, but either way I chose, I was wrong. At the garage, a car honks, and my time is up. That was the agreement. I had as long as it took for the driver they hired to take me back to my house on the other end of town. "If you'll still have me, I'll see you in November. If not, then know that no matter what—I loved you."

And I leave, breaking both of our hearts.

Ellison

"WHEN DID YOU STOP CARING ABOUT THE voiceless?" I barge into Dad's office and could care less how many people are in the room. "My entire life, that's what you ingrained in me. That we are blessed and our job is to help those in need. When did you change, or have you been lying to me the entire time?"

Dad's not behind his desk but perched in the front of it, and he merely raises his eyebrows at my entrance. "I'm not discussing this with you until you've had time to calm down. The past twenty-four hours have been emotional for all of us, and we all need to take a few minutes, regain our composure and discuss these events when we're all thinking rationally."

"Are you admitting then you made an emotional decision? That you were wrong about asking Drix to give up his entire future because you're scared what might happen to yours?"

Dad gets up then, walks straight to me, and my heart stutters when he grabs my arm, shoves me out into the hallway and closes the door behind him. He towers over me, still gripping my arm, his fingers biting just enough into my flesh that it makes me go mute.

"You're my daughter, you're hurting, and I'm sorry for that, but you will never disrespect me like that in front of people again, do you understand?"

My father has never done this and I'm sick.

He shakes me. "I said, do you understand?"

I nod, because I can't find my voice.

He releases me then, places his hand on my shoulders and squeezes. Not in a painful way, but in the way he's done a million times, his reminder that he loves me. This switch-up between anger and love is so confusing I'm dizzy.

"What's happening is terrible, but you have to accept Hendrix's decision. He sees what's best, and I need you to see what's best, too."

"You're letting Drix down. You're supposed to protect him."

"Why can't you see I'm protecting all the people who wind up in the school-to-prison pipeline? If this goes public, I guarantee this program will go up in flames. Sometimes, you have to make a sacrifice in order to win. Hendrix is willing to make the sacrifice. He understands one loss, when so many others will be saved, is a steep price, but one worth paying."

I shrug off his arms and step back. "That's easy to say when you aren't the one paying the price."

"I have paid the price. Multiple times in my life I've made sacrifices to get where I am now. Hendrix is smart, resourceful. He will do well with his life. If I didn't believe that, I wouldn't ask that of him. In a few months, a few years, when I can, I'll help him."

I stare at my father with new eyes. Eyes that are born out of hard emotional labor. Will he help Drix? The man I thought he was would have, but I'm starting to believe that I created a make-believe image. "You were my hero."

Without waiting for his response, I turn and walk away.

One time, as a child, I remember being separated from my parents at a craft festival. I saw a stuffed animal I wanted, so I went one way, and without realizing it, they went another. For a span of a minute, I had complete joy, but when I glanced up to ask my dad if I could have him, I had this instant of intense fear. I was lost.

The same soul-crushing, mind hysteria sensation I'm experiencing now is the same feeling as then, but this is much worse. I'm within the walls of my home, yet I'm lost.

I round the corner to head to the stairs, and my stomach twists in such a way that my head begins to throb. Henry. I need Henry, but he's gone. Out of contact until he contacts me, and if I could call him, he'd be in some country, overseas feeling useless as I cried. I need my cousin, my sole ally, but he's gone.

I'm lost and alone.

"Elle."

With my hand on the stair railing, I glance over my shoulder. Cynthia slinks out of the dining room, a thumb drive in her hands. She extends it to me, but what keeps me locked in place is how her eyes shift left and right, as if she's about to give me a bomb. "Take it."

"What is it?"

"Copies of Hendrix's file."

I blink, then survey the room to see if I'm somehow being tested. "So?"

Cynthia's hand shakes as she strokes her bangs away from her forehead. "No one knows I've done this. Your dad will be angry, but I spent a lot of time with Hendrix, and he's a good kid. He deserves better."

I agree, but my father doesn't. "What do you expect me to do with this?"

She pushes it closer to me. "I don't know. Give it to Hendrix, maybe. Convince him to change his mind."

There's no changing his mind, but I take the thumb drive anyway because I can tell how much this gift is costing her. "Thank you."

"I'm not done," she says, and that catches me off guard.

"There's more?"

"About you." She swallows and flips her cell around in her hands. "The leaked pictures and information about you and Andrew, I know who's been doing it."

I suck in a deep breath. A win. A win that feels too late, but I need a win. "Who?"

She bites her bottom lip, then looks me straight in the eye. "Me. I've been the one leaking the pictures and the stories, and I did it because your father and mother told me to. They knew you and Andrew would be popular with the media and that it would lead to positive press and win voters. They've staged everything, and Andrew's known the entire time. Hendrix isn't the only good person getting a bad deal. You also deserve better. Much, much better."

HENDRIX

I HAD THE RENTED CAR AND DRIVER DROP ME off at the front of my neighborhood, at the convenience store I was convicted of robbing. Seemed poetic. Like an Eminem lyric. Raw, bloody, straight to the gut.

Heat comes up off the pavement, making the already sweltering night suffocating. The neighborhood's dark. Decrepit row after row of broken houses and hopelessness. Enter all those who are destined to fail and be doomed.

Like a lighthouse shining from the Dead Sea, my house glows. Lights from the living room and the garage a beacon. My family's in the garage—Axle, Dominic, Kellen and our newest addition, Marcus. Loud laughter rolls down the driveway and echoes into the night. It's my family, almost all of my family, but almost isn't good enough. Not anymore. Not after what I lost today.

A shadow of a person moving behind the blinds in the living room and instead of heading around back to where life might be easy, I go for the front door. Inside, Thor greets me in that way only a dog can. With complete unconditional love. A quick scratch behind the ears, but then I ignore the ball he drops at my feet.

Holiday grins at me from the recliner. "Hey, Drix. Where've you been? Kellen says she saw one of those fancy town cars pick you up. Does that mean you had a campaign function today? If so, how's Elle?"

In the middle of the living room, I stare down at Holiday. I'm not even two years older than her, but she's still my little sister. I'm the one who poured milk in her cereal for her when she couldn't carry a gallon jug. I'd sit for hours and play with her, whatever game she wanted, when she was sure her mom was going to show and she never did.

I'm the one who messed up by focusing more on myself than on anyone else. I've broken a few hearts tonight. It's time to break one more. Maybe someday, she'll forgive me. "You need to break up with Jeremy."

Her smile falls, and her chin juts out as she goes into fight mode. "You need to butt out."

"He treats you like crap."

"He loves me."

"He doesn't love you. He does his best to own you. Those are two different things."

She pushes out of the chair and to her feet. "I'm not talking to you about Jeremy."

Sounds good to me. "Then let's talk about you."

Holiday leans into me, all pissed-off rage. "What about me?"

"You aren't alone."

Her eyes narrow like she didn't understand me. "What?"

"You aren't alone anymore. Me, Axle, you—we never had roots. We were weeds trying to survive growing up in the cracks of the concrete. All of our parents? Worthless. But sometimes we had each other. I get that, as a kid, that wasn't enough. I understand wanting something solid. I understand wishing that there was someone out there who wanted and loved me. I also understood being pissed off that person after person had that stability and I never did. I understand feeling alone. I understand making stupid choice after stupid choice, searching for something to fill the hole that sucked the life out of me."

"What does that have to do with Jeremy?"

"Everything! You're trying to fill that hole, and you're filling it with some asshole who makes you feel loved for thirty seconds, then makes you feel like dirt for ten so he can control you with a snap of his fingers. That's not love. Love is Axle working ten hour days to put food on the table, but still paints your room when he gets home at night. It's me moving the furniture in your room every other day until you're happy. It's us. It's this family."

"But what if you leave again?" she yells so loudly I go completely still. Holiday shakes from head to toe. One convulsion after the other. "What if you leave? You left and Axle was never home and Dad's gone and my mom's gone and Grandma hasn't remembered who I am in years. Everyone I love goes. It's what happens and he's been here. He only leaves if I tell him to leave, and I don't want to be alone." Holiday slams her hand against her chest. "I don't want to be alone."

Her hurt rattles through my body and ends up slicing open

a portion of my already battle-weary soul. "I'm not going anywhere. I'm home. I'm staying home. I'll stay here for as long you need, and if I'm not around, I'll be there the moment you need me. I love you, and I love you enough to tell you you're ruining your life. I love you enough to beg you to break up with that asshole, and if my love isn't enough, that's fine, but love yourself. Love yourself to not let some bastard continue to treat you like crap."

I yank the still frame image from the convenience store shooting out of my back pocket, unfold it and shove the picture into her hands. "That's the person who robbed the convenience store. That's the bastard who framed me and sent me to jail. Take a good look at the tattoo. That's Jeremy. I told Axle I'd keep my mouth shut about him, but I won't anymore, and I'm pushing hard. It's him or me, Holiday. I can't stand by and watch this guy slowly kill you anymore. And so you know, I hope to God you choose me."

Because that's my only proof I have of my innocence, I grab the paper from her, and as I circle the room for a place to go, the walls close in.

My room no longer belongs to me, but to Elle. If I go up there, the memory of holding her in my bed will crush me. The rest of this house belongs to Holiday. She's the one who needs to feel like this is her home, she's the one who needs the stability.

Me? I belong on the streets. A buzz of my cell, a quick look, and it's Cynthia asking me to give her a call. Screw that. I'm done being anyone's dancing monkey. At least for tonight. I drop the phone on the futon, and I walk out the door. Thor follows.

Ellison

ON MY BED, I CLOSE THE WINDOW THAT CON-
tained Drix's information. I had been scrolling the pages, reading the police reports, the district attorney recommendations,
but then stopped because also included were Drix's therapist's
notes from Drix's stay in juvenile detention. Won't lie, I'm curious, but with the changes he went through in a year, Drix
had to have poured out his heart and soul into the program
and into therapy. Reading anything, even if was meant for my
father's eyes, would be invading Drix's privacy.

I twirl a lock of my hair around my finger and pull. There's
pain along my scalp, but it's nothing like the shredding of my
insides. They used me. My parents used me.

Drix is right, I'm trapped. I'm a puppet, and I not only had
no idea I was being moved along the stage against my will,
but I've discovered the constricting feeling in my lungs is me
being strangled by the strings.

One year left of high school. Four years of college. My

head pounds, and I lower it into my hands. How many decisions in my life were truly mine? Or have I been so easily manipulated my entire life?

Good try at archery, Elle, but wouldn't you much rather try ballet? The Beta Club is an honor, but wouldn't you feel that your time would be better served if you tried your hand at drawing? You're such a pretty girl, why wouldn't you want to help on the campaign trail?

Good girl listening to us. Good girl. We love you, Elle. So proud and we love you.

Did they? Have they ever? Am I only loved if I succeed? Because that's how it's always felt. I want their love. I have needed their love, but what has their love cost?

Me. It's cost me myself.

I flinch with the ache that rolls through my body and rock to try to ease the pain, but it doesn't ease. It only grows.

Even though I know that my plea will be swallowed into the text black hole, I send it regardless because I need to be heard, even if it's just to myself: They used me.

Used me. Their daughter. A pawn in their bloody chess game.

My cell rings, my heart stutters, and I immediately accept the call. "Henry?"

"What happened?" his question swift, the demanded answer implied.

"Where are you?"

"Still on base. We're grounded due to equipment malfunctioning on our transports. Don't know for how long, though, but that doesn't matter. Talk to me."

Talk to him. He and I, we've talked for years. Him trying to ease me past my sheltered world. Me trying to convince him to return home. "What did you do? When you fought with Dad and you left, what did you do?"

Silence on the other end and I'm so tired of people thinking I can't handle the real world. So far, my fake world has been brutal. The real world honestly can't be worse. "Tell me or I'm hanging up."

"I did what your parents told me to do," he finally says. "Until I didn't."

"What does that mean?"

Crackling on the line and I look at my cell to see if we're still connected.

"Henry?"

"I don't want to disappoint you." That quiet voice doesn't belong to a soldier, but to a tired boy.

"You won't."

"I screwed up, Elle."

I release a long breath. "So have I. Maybe I need to know I'm not alone in messing up." Silence again and I internally will him to talk to me. "Please."

"After Mom and Dad died, I trusted your parents. Bought into everything they said. I did what I was told, when I was told. To me, your dad was a god. He made it out of my small town. He made it out of poverty. He made it out when my dad didn't, and moving in with you and them was bittersweet. I missed my parents, but I knew if I listened to your dad, I'd become successful like him.

"So I did it all. I went to college, I took classes to prepare for law school and worked the internships your dad arranged—even when I had no interest in any of it. I had become a zombie in my own life, letting your mom and dad make every decision along the way. One day I woke up, and I didn't like what I saw in the mirror, but I didn't know how to change. I didn't know what to do."

I understand that feeling more than he could comprehend.

"I was miserable. I felt empty. There was this gaping hole in my soul, and all I wanted was to fill it. That hole was cold and it was bleak, but I didn't understand this hole because beyond the loss of my parents, I had it all. So I tried to fill the hole."

I almost don't want to know, yet I ask, "With what?"

He sucks in a breath. "Drugs."

My eyes close and my heart hurts. "I'm sorry."

"So am I. I got lost. Bad."

"Mom and Dad were mad at you for the drugs?"

"Yes, and no. They were disappointed, but they were supportive. They were the ones who approached me about my problem. Turns out they'd been monitoring me at school somehow. Your dad flew up toward the end of the semester, told me that I was coming home for summer break and that he was going to pay for rehab. The first few weeks of withdrawal were at a private hospital, and then I had private therapy while I was at home."

I nibble on my bottom lip as I replay my memories of that summer. Mom and Dad told me Henry had a short summer internship. When Henry was home, he was moody and emotional. Godzilla stomping through Tokyo. "It sounds like Mom and Dad were good to you."

"They were," he admits. "I can't argue that your parents never cared for or loved me, but there are some loves that are smothering. Some loves are selfless on the outside, but completely self-serving on the inside."

"I don't understand," I whisper.

"Taking the drugs was my choice. I know that. No one else is to blame. But when I realized that there was a hole I was trying to fill and that hole was because I was living a life that didn't belong to me, I went to your dad and told him in order to survive, I had to change. I told him I needed to drop out of college. I tried to explain that I was more like my father and preferred to work with my hands. I told him I wanted to attend a trade school, and he didn't agree."

There's a lump in my throat, and I squeeze my eyes shut because I don't want to cry anymore. I'm so sick and tired of crying. "They kicked you out of the house because you quit school?"

"He told me I had no idea how to run my life or what I wanted, and he told me to look at my recent choices as proof. Don't get me wrong, he had a point, but that therapy worked. I knew I couldn't make the right choices while living a life I hated. Your dad was angry, I was angry, and I'll admit the fight got out of control. We both said things we regret. The fight spiraled, and your dad gave me an ultimatum—I return to college, a different college, but a college of his choice—or I leave...so I left."

"Why didn't you tell me?"

"I was ashamed of the drugs. Each and every time you looked at me, I saw love. I lost my mom and dad to death. I lost my second mom and dad to their control. I couldn't lose you, too. I'm strong, Elle, but I'm not that strong. You're the only family I have left."

Unfortunately, I'm feeling more and more like an orphan with every minute that passes.

"I have regrets—the drugs, some of the words I said to your dad, but I don't regret leaving, taking control of my life and joining the army. I love my life now, and I'm stronger because of it, but I'm scared for you. I'm watching as your parents tighten their grip on you like they did with me. I'm terrified what's going to happen to you when that hole becomes too big and you feel like it has to be filled or you're going to die. I never want you to feel as lost as I did."

He's too late. That dark abyss he's talking about—I'm already in free fall.

My cell vibrates in my hand. A quick glance at the screen and my forehead furrows.

Drix: This is Holiday. Call now. It's Drix. There's trouble.

Dizziness overtakes my brain. "I've got to go."

"Wait, Elle."

"I'm serious. I have to go."

"I know, but listen. I'm here. I may not be reachable sometimes, but I'm always here. Whatever you need, I'll help. I promise."

A traveling soldier living on base. There's only so much he can do, but his offer is a lifeline that I grasp on to. "Thank you. Be safe."

"Always." And then he's gone.

I breathe in deeply to try to push all the dull and sharp aches and pains away, then dial Drix's number. Holiday answers on the first ring. "Elle?"

"It's me. What's going on?"

"I messed up." She pauses, chokes on a sob, then continues, "Drix is in trouble. He showed me the picture of Jeremy robbing the store, and I got mad and Drix left. He's gone and left his phone, and nobody can find him. I was so hurt that I confronted Jeremy. It was stupid, but I was mad and I wasn't thinking and I told him Drix had proof he robbed the store. Jeremy got angry and he asked if anybody else knew and I freaked. I knew I couldn't drag you into it, so I told him Drix found the proof on his own and Jeremy lost it. He grabbed a gun out of his dresser. He's going to kill him. I know he's going to kill him. The boys are out looking for Drix, but we need more help. We need the police, but the boys are scared to call. We don't know what type of problems that will cause for all of us, specifically Drix and Kellen. The system doesn't work for people in our neighborhood, but it works for people like you. Please, Elle. We need your help."

I turn my head away from the phone, and I dry heave.

Please, God, no.

HENDRIX

I THROW THE DRIFTWOOD DOWN THE MUDDY creek, Thor chases, then drops into the dirt and gnaws on the wood. He gets the concept of catch. It's the returning he hasn't mastered yet.

It's a long walk to the creek, yet it wasn't long enough. Don't know how many miles it will take to get the demons clinging on to my back off. Maybe those demons are there to stay. Maybe they've just been quiet, riding in silence, waiting for the right time to rear their ugly heads. Mostly, tonight, they whisper…failure.

I attempt to ignore the whisper and instead listen to the gentle lapping of the water. Success. Failure. What does any of that mean?

Failure? Forever being the guy everyone will judge first as a criminal. Five steps behind on the game board because of a past I can't change.

Success? Liking who I became.

The world doesn't view that as a success. The world only values climbing the mountain, getting the win, being in the band that was wanted by music labels. So does that mean my hard-earned success this past year isn't real?

Thor's head jerks up. One ear points up, the other flops down. He tilts his head, and I try to hear past the water and frogs chirping into the night. This part of the creek is more trees than people, which is why I chose it. Closer to the neighborhood, people party, people rebel, people do an illegal deal. But I'm not that person anymore, so I walked farther into the woods. This must be where people like me go to disappear.

Thor's ears go back and he emits a deep growl. He trots over, but keeps low and stares into the woods. A sixth sense of evil runs over my skin—a cold black wind, and the hair on my arms stands on end. Quick glance around. There's nowhere to go besides the water or into the forest, and there's no telling what I'd run into in there.

Someone's coming, a shadow that appears human. A car passes on the road farther up. The headlights hit the trees surrounding us. Jeans, T-shirt, shaved head, near my height and build. A million other guys, but only one has a tattoo of a cross with a vine wrapped around it and would be searching for me.

I lower my head and silently curse my sister. I should have known. Should've have seen her telling him, but I didn't think far enough beyond saving her.

He steps into the clearing and sizes me up. I don't need to do the same. I've memorized every hateful thing about this guy the moment he started dating my sister. Plus, he has a gun in his hand. That makes him the winner by default.

"How'd you find me?" I ask.

"I visited some of your old haunts. Figured you had to be at one of them."

I make a show of looking around. "This wasn't one of them."

"It wasn't, but at the party, someone saw you going in this direction. A guy and his dog. Sounded something old-school."

"Yeah." Once upon a time, I was great at small talk, but I'm not anymore. I should be more scared than what I am, but there's a numbness in the ironic. This kid keeps ruining lives. Fitting that he ends mine. "How's this playing out?"

"You're going to give me the evidence you have, you keep your mouth shut, and then I won't hurt you or your family. Plus, Kellen stays out of jail. If I go down, she goes down with me. Don't lie to me, Drix. There's no way she didn't tell you guys."

Fine. I yank the folded-up piece of paper and throw it at his feet. Jeremy tracks it and hesitates before picking it up and opening it.

"Where'd you get it?" he asks.

"Stole it," I lie. "The governor had a file on me, I flipped through it, and when I saw that photo, I knew you were the one who did it."

"Who else knows?"

"Besides my family? No one. And it's obvious that no one in power knows either, governor's office included, as I'm the one who went to jail."

"How do I believe you?"

"You're not arrested yet. I'm thinking that says a lot."

He twitches. Jeremy has no intention of letting me walk

out of here. I know what he's done, I've cost him his girl-friend, and he's still holding a grudge for that scar on his face from me.

A year ago, I would have welcomed this fight. Now, there's no hunger for blood. "I was arrested for the crime and I did the time. The deal you just offered is accepted. You go home, and I'll go home. You hate me. I hate you. You stay out of my way. I stay out of your way."

"Yeah, I'm not ready for that yet."

Didn't think he was. Thor rubs against my leg as if he's aware what's about to go down. Thor's getting bigger, but he's still a puppy. I should have left him home, but I didn't, so I do the best I can by him. I pick up a small piece of drift-wood and throw it farther down the creek. Thankful he hasn't learned how to come back. "Go get it, boy."

Before I have a chance to see if he does, Jeremy lifts his arm, and there's a bang that vibrates through my entire body.

Ellison

MY BLOOD SWISHES IN MY EARS AND DROWNS out any other noise: the sound of my feet as I race down the stairs, across the foyer, and slide into a wall as I round the corner. My father's office door is open, but he's not there. My mouth moves. My lips and tongue forming words to call out for him. Then I run for the kitchen, and there's a single heartbeat of fear when I spot him sitting at the island.

Dad has the power to save Drix. He has the power to end all of this right now. He has the power to make himself my hero again, but all that power belongs to who I thought he was. This man is somebody else, yet there is a vain hope that the man I admire still exists.

He lifts his head from the binder in front of him, and his eyes meet mine.

"Drix is in trouble and you have to help. The details don't matter, but the guy who really robbed the convenience store found out that Drix knows he did it. He's going after Drix with a gun, and no one can get ahold of Drix."

Dad closes his binder. "What do you want me to do?"

"Call the police."

"And tell them what?"

The answer is so strikingly easy that I feel like an idiot saying it. "The truth. That Drix didn't do the crime. That the person who did is dangerous and is going after him."

"It's a big city. Where do we tell them to look?"

"The creek near his neighborhood. Since being home, his sister Holiday said Drix likes to walk the creek. Have the police go search for him there."

"Surely his family can go look for him."

"They are, but it's not enough."

"How did you learn about this?"

"From Holiday. She called me. She had a fight with her boyfriend when she found out he was the one who robbed the store and—"

Dad raises his hand to cut me off. "You want me to involve the police because Drix's sister had a fight with her boyfriend, a person who may or may not have been the one to rob the store, and now her boyfriend is mad after their fight? Elle, even as emotional as you are right now, you must still have the ability to take a step back and realize how dramatically juvenile this all sounds. Teenagers fight, especially when they think they are in love. They get mad. They say things they don't mean in the heat of the moment."

There's this strangling inside me, taking root in my feet and growing, throttling every organ in my body until it reaches my brain, and then I explode. "Dad! This is a life! We are talking about somebody's life!"

"You're being overdramatic, and you're too close to the situation. Too emotional. This is teenage drama. At worst, the two boys will probably get into a fistfight. It happens."

"It happens?" The world spins. "Jeremy has a gun, and he's gone after Drix. He's shot at someone once before—during the robbery. He'll shoot again."

"You don't know that."

An icy numb enters my veins, and I start to shake, yet my heart picks up speed. "You honestly don't care, do you?"

"I do care. I care about this state. I care about the people in this state. I care about the hundreds of different programs that help thousands of other people. The odds of what you are saying is really happening are slim. Until now, you have always made good choices in friendships so you were saved from severe melodrama. I make that phone call, I allow melodrama, words said in anger between two teens, words that mean nothing in the heat of the moment, to sink my career and what will happen then? The state elects someone who is more interested in lining his own pocket than helping the people who voted him in? Sacrifices have to be made in order for improvement to happen. I'm sorrier than you can imagine that Hendrix is a casualty, but there is no other way. I can't risk my career and the programs I know are working for one person."

"For two people," I whisper. "Hendrix and me. If you don't help him, I will never forgive you."

Dad picks up his binder as if I didn't just draw a line into quick-drying concrete. "You're seventeen, emotional and have your first crush on a boy. You'll see nothing happens tonight. You'll see Hendrix will be fine and will be back out on the campaign trail next week. You two will take few weeks off from each other, and you'll start school. We'll allow the coding classes, we'll win the campaign, and then maybe you'll see Hendrix a few times. But then you'll lose interest in him, and hopefully you'll find focus on this new phase of coding. You might be mad at me for a while, but you'll forgive me, and you'll see your mother and I have been right in the choices we've made for you."

A slice along my heart. That's what my parents have said I always do—start something, then lose interest. I circle the bracelet on my wrist and think of Hendrix's cuff. Axle gave it to him as a reminder that they're family. That they stand beside each other no matter what.

Dad walks past me, and I say, "I'm eighteen."

He pauses and glances at me over my shoulder. "What?"

"I'm eighteen now." Realization rushes over me like sunlight over the cold dark ground that had been blanketed by night. "I can take the coding classes without your permission. In fact, I can do most anything without your permission."

Eighteen—pulled back from starting school when I was supposed to because my mother and father didn't believe I was emotionally ready for kindergarten. Who knows if I was or wasn't at five, but I'm eighteen now, and I'm very capable of making my own decisions.

His skin turns an unusual shade of red. "You live under my roof. I pay for your schooling. For your lifestyle. Until you are financially capable of taking care of yourself, you abide by what I say. You may be eighteen, but your actions over the last few months have shown you don't have the maturity level to handle the real world. You have persistently acted like a child."

In the past, his words would have cut me to the bone, but there's this new power filling me, and it gives me strength and refills the empty well of my hope. "Over the last few months, I have persistently gone after the things in life that matter to me and not to you. All my life, you and Mom have pushed me into activity after activity and demanded perfection. Did you ever stop to think that maybe the reason I kept failing was because your expectations were too high?"

"Don't twist us wanting the best for you into us being bad parents."

"You're missing the emphasis in that sentence—the best for me. Shoving me into activity after activity and pulling me every time I didn't turn out to be the shining star wasn't what was best for me. It made me feel like a constant failure. That I could never measure up to you and Mom."

"What were we supposed to do? Pay for lessons for something you were mediocre at?"

"Yes! That's exactly what you should have done. If I liked doing it. Life shouldn't revolve about being the best, and childhood definitely shouldn't. You should have given me the room to explore who I was without the pressure of succeeding each and every single time.

"Do you not see what your program taught Drix? It taught him that it was okay that he failed because he learned from his mistakes, and it taught him that even after falling so low, that the world welcomes an improved person and will offer him a second chance. If you believe in that program so much that you are willing to risk his life, why would you never offer me or Henry the same second chance? Why do we always have to be the best the first time around?"

The blood drains from his face, leaving him pale, appearing to age him decades before my eyes, and pity fills my heart.

"Make the phone call. You save the greater good when you save one person because then everyone realizes their individual life means something, too. Life has value then."

He slowly shakes his head. "I'm sorry, I can't."

He won't. "Make the phone call or I will."

"You'll sound like a fool rambling to the police. Everything you say will sound like conspiracies from a teenage girl."

So many times I've been called my father's daughter, and I've taken it as a compliment. Thinking it meant I was compassionate to those in need. Maybe that's not what people meant.

Right now, I am my father's daughter because of how my mind is ticking toward calculating and manipulative. "I'm not going to call the police. I'm going to call the media and then send them a file containing everything they need to prove Drix's innocence. I'm also going to tell them you knew the entire time he was innocent, and yet you didn't care. Don't think too hard and too long on this because I do have the information and I will do this. You can send me to my room, you can physically take my cell and laptop from me, and you might keep me from saving Drix tonight, but I promise you, I will personally ruin you if you don't make that phone call now."

HENDRIX

I DIVE FOR THE GROUND AND ROLL. ANOTHER shot and it hits the mud next to me. I'm on my feet, running into the thick of trees. One more round. Wood splinters off the bark of the tree and becomes individual spikes into my skin. Stinging and there are a few trickles of blood, but it's better than a hole in the head.

"Get back here!" he shouts. "Face me!"

But I keep my feet moving, my arms pumping.

"I'll bring this fight to your home! I'll bring it to your sister!"

I halt then. My boots grinding into the dirt. My breaths come out in short, rapid bursts. Getting out from underneath this son of a bitch has to happen because he won't quit. Until I'm bleeding or dead. And even then it won't stop. He'll never stop.

My hands go to my pockets and I silently swear. No cell. Stupid.

"Drix!" he yells into the night, and there is a sound of an animal on the verge of going rabid. Growling and my heart tightens. Thor.

Barking, another growl and Jeremy is yelling at Thor to get away. My feet move again, faster if possible, but toward the noise, toward the sound, toward the one damn thing in my life that's done nothing wrong.

Ferocious growls, a sound of attack, a silent prayer and then another shot, and I'm being torn apart with the high-pitched yelp and whine. Sticks snap in my wake, and tree branches smack my skin as I race back to Thor. Through another bush and the leaves clap and rustle when I break in to the clearing. Jeremy stands at the water's edge, gun trained on Thor.

Red stains his white fur and darkens the black, and the dog limps and whines.

"Thor," I say, and a lump forms in my throat when he jerks his head in my direction. His dark eyes beg me to help.

"You came back for a dog?" Jeremy chides.

I did, because that's the guy I've become—the one who leaves nobody behind.

"You know I'm going to kill you," he says.

Did the math on that one already. I hold my arms out to my sides as I slowly step closer to where Thor, my damn brave dog, is still trying to make a stand. "Then do it."

Jeremy gestures toward Thor. "That mutt mean something to you, then?"

There's an ache in each breath as there's a sickening realization of where this is headed. Jeremy wants to hurt me, and he's sick enough to use the dog to do it. "Just kill me. End this and leave everyone else alone."

"Sure," he says. "Right after you watch as I kill the dog."

Jeremy aims the gun at Thor, and I jump low, tackling Jeremy at the waist, ramming him into the ground. The gun goes off, and the bang's so close that my ears ring. Beneath me, Jeremy flips as he struggles to crawl in the sinking mud for the gun.

I have a fighting chance. Both of my arms wrap around his stomach, and I lift him, rolling us away from the gun. Jeremy lands on top, and before I can shove him off, he lands a punch to my face. My head moves with the impact, and as he goes to reload, I snap out, grab his wrist, hold his arm steady in the air and uppercut him straight in the nose.

Blood gushes, Jeremy loses focus. Pushing past my throbbing fist and face, I strike again, a hook to his head and side. He goes limp, and I kick him off. He grunts, and I'm off for the gun.

Blinding pain in my leg, I yell out, then fall to the ground. A glance back and a stick protrudes from my calf. Mud cakes my body, my arms, slows me as if I'm stuck in concrete. Jeremy staggers past me. He can't get the gun. He'll kill me, kill Thor, hurt my sister.

I grab a hold of his ankle and twist. He goes down, but angles his body to kick his other foot into my head. Stars. I see stars and sound muffles out long enough that I start to wonder if I've been dragged into the water and I'm drowning.

A high-pitched yelp from Thor. I scratch and claw through the haze and blink the double vision away. Thor's dragging himself on three legs toward me, toward Jeremy.

Jeremy army-crawls through the muck, reaches out his hand and grabs the gun. My heart pounds in my chest, nausea rolls in my stomach, and I think of Elle. She has to know I love her. She has to hold and remember that.

Thor whines. I push with my feet to meet him as Jeremy stands and aims the gun. I snatch Thor, cradle him to my chest, roll to protect him, close my eyes and—

"Drop the gun! Hands up! Police! Drop the gun!"

Ellison

I BURST THROUGH THE DOORS, AND MY HEART is so heavy, I can barely stay upright. Since receiving the call from Holiday, I feel like someone has been playing a sickening game of pinball in my chest. They're all there in the waiting room, and seeing them brings such a stark and striking realness to her words over the phone that tears immediately prick my eyes.

"She's here." Axle stands, and Holiday turns away from the shelter of Dominic's body to look at me. Mascara streaks down her face, and her lower lip trembles.

"I'm sorry. I'm so sorry." Her voice breaks. I falter and wrap my arms around my stomach as the sight of her in pain doubles me over. "This is my fault. All of this is my fault. I'm sorry. I'm so sorry."

"Where is he?"

"Down the hallway. Fourth door on your right," Axle says, and the pure sadness, the devastation in his eyes causes me to turn quickly away. "He doesn't have much time, Elle. Drix needs you strong. Kellen's with him now."

Ignoring the nurse behind the desk, ignoring anyone else I pass, I go down the hallway, and when I reach the door, I pause. My hand touching the wood because this isn't how I wanted it to end. This is exactly how I didn't want it to end. There's so much love overflowing in my heart, and when I open this door, that love is going to hurt.

In these short few months, I never knew I could feel so much joy and experience so much pain. But this is living. This is breaking out of the shell my parents created, being more than the paper doll so carefully crafted.

Life isn't running the short and flat open plane. It's climbing the tallest mountain with only my fingertips, and once reaching the top, discovering that this mountain's not the end. It's just the start and that the way down to the next mountain is long and hard.

But even with what lies behind this door, it's worth it. This love, it has been worth it—even if I'm losing a piece of my heart in the process.

I twist the knob, open the door, and Drix's eyes meet mine. Tears swim in them, but they don't fall down his face. He's stoic, yet radiates pain. His back is propped up against the wall, he reclines on a bench seat and in his lap is a blanket and in that blanket is a ball of fur.

My eyes drift to Drix's leg that is bandaged and is stained with blood. Then I'm scanning everywhere, and it seems that every part of him is bloody and battered. "Oh my God, Drix."

"Not me, him," he whispers. "I'm going to live."

Kellen eases past me and the door shuts with a click. All

warmth is stolen from me, and I collapse to my knees next to the bench. I gingerly touch Thor's head. He struggles to open his eyes, and when he sees me, his pink tongue slowly sticks out as if he meant to greet me with a kiss. "Is he in pain?"

"No." Drix's voice is hoarse. "They've given him something to help. The vet says he's not feeling anything."

My throat closes shut, and though I try to fight it, a tear slips down my cheek. "Why can't they save him?"

"Maybe he could have survived the first bullet, but not the second. The police came, and when I heard them call on Jeremy to get on his knees, I loosened my grip, and Thor wiggled out. Jeremy shot him and…" Drix breaks off, and he hits the back of his head against the wall as if that will take away the pain. "I'm sorry I didn't protect him better. I'm sorry."

I wipe at my eyes, yet another tear falls down. "It's not your fault. None of this is your fault." Thor inclines his head into my touch, and I scratch him behind his ear. "There has to be something."

Drix only shakes his head, and that heaviness is too much as I lower my head and kiss Thor. "I'm so sorry. I'm so sorry we couldn't do more."

A knock on the door and a woman with a white coat walks in. She has a soothing voice, a calm demeanor, explaining the extent of Thor's wounds, explaining how it's a matter of time, explaining how she recommends us ensuring that he doesn't feel any pain. We both nod our heads, we both agree, and Drix is careful with Thor as he sits up, and we share our dog on our laps.

The vet prepares what she needs, and we both love on our dog. We both murmur words of comfort, words of love, and then the vet does what needs to be done. First Thor sleeps. Then Thor is in a forever sleep, and I weep.

One hand on my dog, another wrapped around Drix. He has one hand holding our dog, another one around me as he buries his head into the crook of my neck. His body shaking, wetness on my skin, and we hold on to each other and grieve.

HENDRIX

AT THE RECEPTION AREA OF THE VET, THERE'S a candle the staff lights that alerts anyone coming in that a family is saying goodbye to their loved one. It's a sign to keep their voices low, a sign that there are people who are losing a part of their soul. A gentle sign that there are people in the world who understand that not all loved ones and family members stand on two legs. Some stand on four, some are just as loved as any flesh and blood human, and most, if not all, love better than most humans ever can in return.

Because seeing that candle flickering for me and Elle as we left Thor behind meant so much to both of us, Elle strikes a match and lights a candle in Holiday's room. She watches the flame as if maybe it can heal her heart. If it works, I'll watch that flame all night.

Or should I say day. Sunlight cracks through broken clouds, and I shut the blinds. After leaving the vet, Axle forced me to the ER. Took them a while to clean out the stick in my leg and to stitch me up. MRI for my head took time, as well. Elle stood by my side every step of the way. This one is strong. This girl is steel.

I drop onto the bed and rub my face. Protecting my leg, I took a half-ass shower, and I'm ready to sleep for the rest of my life. Elle's also showered, her long hair damp across her shoulders. She wears one of Holiday's tank tops and cotton shorts.

For what easily has to be the two hundredth time, her cell rings, and instead of placing the call into voice mail like she typically has, she powers it off, drops it to the floor and stomps the hell out of it. It's crazy, but it sure as hell isn't the worst thing I've seen in twenty-four hours. "You okay?"

"I think you know the answer to that."

Playing devil's advocate, I say, "Your parents are probably scared. They've always known, or at least thought they've known, where you are, what you're doing—"

"Then I guess they'll figure out how I felt when I asked them to help you, and Dad initially refused."

I raise my eyebrows as Elle's only told me a CliffsNotes version of the events from her side. I want to know more, but I'm too damn tired and Elle's eyes are red from crying, and those dark circles under them are so heavy I'm surprised she's standing. We can talk the sick details later. "Are you going to be mad at them forever?"

"How about I be mad at them for now, and I'll figure the rest out anytime that is not now. All I know is that I'm with you, I'm not sneaking around anymore, and I'm not letting anyone control me. As of last night, my life became my own, and right now, I want to sleep."

"Fair enough." I lie back on the bed, and I never remember a pillow feeling so soft.

It's going to be a few days until I can climb the ladder back to my bed, so Holiday volunteered to switch. She's heartbroken, and I hugged her and told her it wasn't her fault. I also told her I loved her, and I thanked her for having the courage to call Elle for help when no one else did. My sister sobbed then, and I let her. All of us have too many tears we've haven't shed over the years, and it's time we start releasing the pain.

Holding it in isn't working for any of us, and we need to start focusing on each other. Hate hasn't been working out too well either. We've got nothing to lose by trying love.

I stretch out my arm toward Elle, she accepts and lies down on the bed beside me, but that's not nearly close enough for either of us. She flips and molds herself around me, delicately moving as to not press too hard on any of my bruises or wounds.

No painkiller could bring the peace that having her soft body next to mine could bring. No drug, no drink, no other man-made substance can ease all the aches and chaos in my life. Elle is a gift, and it's time I learn how to accept all the serenity she brings to me.

My hand weaves into her hair, I gently knot my fingers into it, and I kiss the top of her head that's resting on my chest. I breathe in her sweet scent and close my eyes. Home. I'm finally home.

"I miss him," Elle whispers.

A flash of an ache in my chest. "Me, too."

"Thank you for giving him a home."

She has it wrong. "He gave me a home. Thor saved me."

In more ways than I can count. The police officer told me he thought Thor was struggling free to go after Jeremy. Another said that last bullet was meant for me and that Thor threw himself into the path of it, but I blink away the burn as I can't think too much about any of that yet.

"He was loved," she says. "There's so many in life who aren't."

So true. Even for humans. "You saved me, too, Elle. Thank you."

"I told you before, your life is worth saving. Always has been and it will always be." Elle lifts her head, caresses her fingers across my face, and she kisses my lips. "I love you."

I love her, too. More than words. More than thought. More than anyone can comprehend. I kiss her in return, a slow movement, and then shift so I somehow fill the slight centimeters between us. The sweet kiss ends, Elle settles her head back on my chest, and wrapped in each other's arms, we sleep.

Ellison

I WEAR A LIGHT GRAY SUIT WITH A FITTED white blouse and black flats. My hair is twisted into a bun, but not one of my patented messy ones. This one is slick, makes me look older and wiser than eighteen, and it's the exact opposite of what my mother's stylist suggests I should wear for the press conference. Several photographers have mumbled between each other about my glasses. They're just jealous because I make glasses sexy, and it must suck to not be me.

But the media forgot about me. My mother stands onstage with my father, behind him in a dark blue dress. I stand in the back of the press conference. Everyone assumes I'm here in support, but I'm not. I'm present to make sure my father upholds his end of the deal...blackmail...forceful persuasion. I'm not too picky on how we call this as long as Drix's name is cleared.

My father comes across as strong and confident as he speaks. Extremely passionate about how when he discovered new evidence that Drix didn't commit the crime that he decided to dedicate himself to helping Drix be exonerated.

But events moved too rapidly, the real culprit learned on the streets that Drix was on the road to proving his innocence, so my father brought in the police. That one act saved Drix's life. Bile just crawled up my throat at the utter disgust of how he corrupted the truth.

What is the truth anyway? The truth that my father was prideful? Full of fear? Would that truth possibly protect the program that saved Drix's life? No, my father's cowardice would have definitely cost something much needed in the world.

As my father speaks, there's a shifting of the media's mood. A winding of a spring, a sprinkling of blood into water full of sharks. They're circling, waiting for the toe to be dipped in so they can attack.

It's a dark sensation, and I rub my arms as if the negativity is a fine ash and soot physically on my skin. My father reiterates how successful the Second Chance Program is, how even if asked, Hendrix Pierce, even though he served time for a crime he didn't commit, will explain to the world how he was on the wrong path and that the program saved his life.

Dad pauses, then steels himself for the coming attack. "I'll now take questions from press."

Hands up, people yelling over the other, and their pure glee of something going wrong, at the hint of a scandal, turns my stomach. There's something terribly wrong with a world that finds joy in other people's mistakes and pain.

Sickened by the sharp teeth and slick tongues surrounding me, the media and my father included, I leave. Out the door, away from the dark room and head for another door that leads me to sunlight. In the back of the parking lot, Drix must be feeling rebellious as he leans against the hood of my car. The plan was for him to stay in my car so that the media wouldn't hound him, but he's probably not as daring as I think. The meat of the story to be feasted upon is inside. Drix, at the moment, is the heart of the story, so of course, no one gives a damn about heart.

Seeing me, Drix widens his stance, and I settle in to hug him between his legs. My head on his shoulder and his arms around my body is enough to wipe away the sludge being in that room created in my veins. I close my eyes and breathe out.

I've lost my home, lost my family, lost my way, but the one thing I've found is where I belong, and it's here, with Drix.

"It's done." I lift my head and stare into his chocolate-brown eyes. "My father has told the world you're innocent."

He closes his eyes briefly, then he looks down at me and caresses my cheek. "I'm sorry it's cost you so much."

I lean into his hand as I love his warmth and his strength. "It hasn't cost me a thing. It broke chains I didn't even know were killing me."

"What now?" he asks.

"Besides changing clothes and getting something to eat?" I shake my head as I honestly have no idea.

The first hint of a smile touches his mouth. "I can't remember the last time I ate."

My stomach growls, and I frown as I think the same thing. "What do you want?"

"There's this place off of Third Street. Has great burgers. Want to try?"

One eyebrow goes high above my bang line. "Are you asking me out on a date?"

A sloppy shrug of one shoulder. "Guess so."

A date, in public. It's like a caterpillar has broken out of its cocoon, has unfurled its wings for the first time, and the movement is a fantastic fluttering in my chest.

"If you want to wait a few weeks to be seen in public with me," he starts, but I place a finger over his lips to silence him.

"No, a hamburger sounds fantastic, but to be honest, I would really love some chicken wings."

Drix chuckles, I smile along with him, and his hands come up from my waist to frame my face. I melt into a puddle when he kisses me.

HENDRIX

October

I'M IN THE RECLINER AND ELLE SITS ON MY LAP. My arms are wrapped around her, but I have yet to breathe for the last ten minutes. I have a new appreciation for Elle and what her life has been like in the public eye. When I joined the campaign trail last May, I thought I understood, but I didn't. Now, watching myself on TV, I feel like an alien in my own body.

Elle lays her hand over mine that are locked around her stomach. I'm on that national news show that appears on Sundays with the ticking clock. They approached me after I began advocating publicly for the Second Chance Program to be given, ironically, a second chance. Right now, the program is on hold, and its funding being threatened.

The old reporter has a deep voice and calming way about him. He earned my respect when he walked beside me in my neighborhood without batting an eye. The cameraman followed us, and seeing how they edited our journey to show my real story freaks me out but, at the same time, moves my heart.

"Oh my God," Holiday says, and pats Dominic's leg multiple times as if he's not also watching with rapt attention. "That's our house. Our house is on national news!"

The reporter is telling the real story—he's telling the truth—and he doesn't mind getting dirty in order to get to the heart of the matter.

Sitting here in this living room, the reporter looks point-blank at me and asks the tough question. "What do you think should happen to the Second Chance Program?"

"I think the politicians who were elected to help the people of our state should stop focusing on party politics, on what gives them more power, and start funding programs that work. The fact the judicial system does not work in favor of those in poverty is an issue, but that issue has nothing to do with Governor Monroe's Second Chance Program. I was wrongly convicted of a crime because I couldn't afford decent representation, but that program saved my life."

The reporter does a voice-over as it shows him shaking hands with Marcus and the other people who went through the program with me. All meeting here in my backyard. The reporter talks about how the political party against Elle's father is holding the funding for the program hostage in hopes it will elect their candidate in November.

It's bull. It's all bull and it's bull I intend to clean up.

Marcus pumps his fist, and we all clap when he comes on-screen. He talks about how the program saved his life, how he did commit his crime, but echoes the same issues that me and the other teens faced…that people with limited resources don't stand a chance within the judicial system, especially teens without advocates. He also emphasizes the school-to-prison pipeline, and that because of the Second Chance Program, he's redirected the path of his life.

We return to the single interview between me and the reporter. "I know you hate this question. It has to be asked, though, but I'll ask it in a different way. Can you tell me about Ellison Monroe?"

On-screen, the right side of my mouth tips up at her name, and in appreciation that he didn't try to dig for info on my relationship with her. When I agreed to the interview, he promised the piece would focus on the Second Chance Program.

"Elle is a force of nature and the smartest, most articulate and compassionate person I know. Beyond my family, she's one of the few people who fought for my future, and she's honestly the only person who truly fought for my innocence. Ellison Monroe saved my life."

A kiss on my cheek from her, and I choke down the emotion building up in my throat. There's a chorus of overly dramatic "ahhs" in the room that leads me to tell them to shut up, and the laughter helps soothe out the moment.

Pictures of me and Elle appear on the screen. Us together with me driving and Elle in the passenger seat of Axle's truck, us eating lunch together at the mall, and my favorite, us holding hands walking down the midway of the State Fair. The snake she won me from Whack-A-Mole is wrapped around my shoulders.

But this reporter doesn't speculate, only talks about how we've been seen together, and about how with one press release we explained to social media and the press that we would never discuss our relationship in public.

He also goes on to explain how Elle was the one who proved to her father I was innocent, but there's no discussion on the fighting that happened between them. I owe much to Governor Monroe and the Second Chance Program, and Elle knows that. Any infighting between her and her parents has stayed completely out of the media.

A few snapshots of Elle by herself, but then of her at a coding competition a few weeks back. The reporter talks about how Elle has stepped back from campaigning for her father and politics in order to pursue interests in her own life.

Then there's video of me in a suit, and I'm talking to the state legislature, of me talking to crowds of people at various events and not one of those was scheduled by the campaign. That's been of my own doing, with a little help from Elle and Cynthia.

"You started out trying to save the Second Chance Program on your own, correct?" the reporter asks.

I nod. "With help from a few people, but, yeah, I decided that one voice can make a change for a whole lot of others."

"Hendrix Pierce has not only made change, but he's inspired others to believe in change, as well," comes the voice-over, and there's video of Marcus and other people from the program meeting with their state legislators, talking at smaller events in their towns and of Marcus speaking in front of a packed congregation at a church.

That church, once learning of his story and of how he's relied on Axle for shelter and support, has decided to help Marcus financially and emotionally.

"Hendrix Pierce's one-man campaign quickly struck a chord with the other nine members of the initial Second Chance Program. Their enthusiasm has caught fire in the state and in the nation. Their passion for this program has sparked discussions about the school-to-prison pipeline, the broken judicial system, and the lack of funding for public defenders."

Back to the interview. "There are many who are saying that you've become the deciding factor in this state's upcoming election. That who will be the next senator is because of the outstanding man you've become out of the Second Chance Program."

"I can't decide any election. That's in the hands of the people. The voters need to do their job, learn about the candidates without being influenced by the media and social media's opinions, and vote. Doing so can save lives."

The piece ends there, the clicking stopwatch comes into view, and the entire room breaks out into applause. When I meet Elle's eyes she kisses me. Full-on, not caring there are easily ten other people in the small and cramped room. I kiss her in return, hands in her hair, and when she pulls back, there's a light in her eyes that makes my heart lift.

We made it, even when the world was falling apart, Elle and I still made it out on the other side alive.

Ellison

EMOTIONALLY EXHAUSTED FROM WATCHING Drix's interview, I park my car around back and sit in the driver's seat for a few extra minutes. I glance up at the towering house and think of all the years my heart leaped when I headed down this driveway. This used to be home to me. It meant comfort and safety and a place to heal. Now I'm overcome with a feeling of dread each and every second I'm trapped in this house.

Blackmailing my parents came with a price—we no longer have a relationship. We decided it was best all the way around for us to pretend through the election that we're still as close as ever, but we don't even talk anymore. We're like lost ghosts roaming past each other in the dark of night.

They, at least, didn't kick me out like they did Henry, and they are still paying my tuition for my senior year of high school. For that, I find the grace to be grateful. It's a lot more than other parents do for their children and a million percent more than they did for Henry.

A buzz of my cell and it's like Henry read my mind. Saw the interview. Maybe this guy isn't so bad. Maybe he'll live.

I snort. Henry and Drix have yet to meet, but this will happen once Henry is in Kentucky again. He's texting so that must mean he's stateside, but whatever the army is having him do isn't in my home state. Do him wrong and you'll have to deal with me.

Henry: So scared...

Done putting off the inevitable, I leave the comfort of my car and enter the house through the kitchen. I head for my room, and as I'm about to turn the corner for the staircase, my stomach cramps at the sound of my mother's voice. "Elle."

I pause and consider still walking.

"Please, Elle," she says. "I miss you."

Those three words hurt, and I turn without thinking how any interaction with her typically wounds more. There's always this small shred of stupid hope that this time we'll figure out how to be a family again.

I blink because Mom's dressed down. Cotton shirt, yoga pants, hair in a ponytail, and she looks younger and more vulnerable than normal. She must be getting ready to work out.

We stare at each other, and I wait for her to speak. I did try to talk to Mom and Dad a few weeks after I forced their hand, but they shut me down. As far as I'm concerned this relationship is their responsibility to repair. When the silence between us stretches, I go to move again, and Mom steps forward. "Wait."

I breathe through my nose to keep myself from getting

angry. If she's truly trying, losing my temper won't help. "What do you need?"

"Your father still might pull off the election," she says. "People are responding well to Hendrix's interview tonight, and that's causing your father's approval rating to bounce."

The muscles in my back tighten. "He didn't do it for Dad. Drix did it to save the program. I'm really tired, so is there anything else you need?"

"Your father would like to speak to you. We both would. We've made mistakes, and we'd like the opportunity to make that up to you."

There's a knot in my chest, and that knot is the representation of all the emotion that's wrenched inside me due to my parents. Do I want to move forward with them? Yes, but I'm still angry. So angry at both of them.

"Come with me to your father's office. Give him a chance to talk with you."

I shake my head because I'm not the one giving again. "If he wants to talk to me, then he finds me. I'm not playing on his turf anymore."

With that, I climb the stairs and head to my room. We've played this game twice since the press conference that ended all press conferences for us. Both times Dad tried to rule me from behind his desk, and both times I walked out. I'm done being ruled. It's time they start figuring me out and try speaking to me on my terms.

Once in my room, I kick off my shoes, go to text Drix, and the pattering of feet causes me to spin on my toes. It's an odd sound in my house, one I recognize, but can't quite place, and I blink twice when a ball of fur bounds into my room.

It's a dog, a big dog, not huge, but not a puppy, and he stops short when he sees me. His fur is all black, he's matted in several places, and my heart aches when I spot his ribs. He begins to pant, a sign he's anxious, so I drop to my knees and hold out my hand. The dog stretches forward to sniff. In seconds, he steps closer. One paw at a time until he's near enough that I can scratch him behind his ears. "You are definitely lost."

"He is," Dad says, and my head snaps up. "I saw him outside of the capitol building this week searching through the trash. I thought of you the moment I saw him."

"Because I'm a lost scrawny mutt in your eyes who needs to be saved by you?"

"Because hundreds, if not thousands, of people passed by this dog this week, and not one person tried to help him, and I was one of them. I heard what Hendrix said about you on the interview tonight, and he made me realize something."

I sit back on my bottom, and the dog lays his head in my lap. I continue to pet him and brace myself for what could be a ripping off of carefully placed bandages on my soul. "Did it make you realize you should have never fought me on Drix?"

"That and that he knew you better than I did. Instead of trying to mold you into something else, Drix saw your strengths in who you are, and that faith in you saved his life."

I stay silent as I honestly don't know what to say. Dad continues, "You would have been the one person to stop and help this dog. No matter how many times I yelled at you, no matter how many times your mother yelled at you, no matter how many times you were punished for your actions, you still would have stopped and saved this dog."

This is true.

"You told me once that every life is valuable. With what happened that night, the lives hurt and lost, that's weighed heavily on me. I don't claim to know all the answers, and I don't know how to fix what I broke, but I do know you would have saved this dog, and now I need your help because I don't know what it entails to save this life."

My heart throbs with each beat. "Bringing this dog home doesn't fix anything between us. It doesn't even start to heal all that's been done."

Dad leans his shoulder against my door frame and shoves his hands into his pockets. It hurts how incredibly sad he appears. "I know, but it's the only way I know how to start trying with you. I love you, and I wanted only the best for you, but I'm realizing I never stopped to figure out that what I considered the best might not have been a match for you."

I'm terrified to forgive him, terrified to hope that maybe my family can be repaired, but here's the thing about forgiveness— I can allow it to take time. I don't have to fake words and actions or offer him a hug or accept all sorts of blatant lies of bygones being bygones. This isn't a made-for-TV movie. This is real life, and sometimes in real life, we take a million baby steps until a wound is healed.

Tonight, Dad is trying, and because of that, I will, too. "Have you fed him?"

"Found some leftovers in the kitchen earlier."

"He needs dog food and he needs a bath. There's some dog food in the laundry room in the bottom cabinet."

Dad pushes off the door frame. "I'll get the food."

I stand and shake my head. "I'll get the food. You'll do the bath. In your bathroom."

He raises both of his eyebrows, and I stare at him to see if he's going to accept being ordered around. To my shock, Dad gives and calls the dog with a whistle. "Let's go get a bath."

They start down the hallway to their bedroom, and I follow. Dad glances at me from over his shoulder. "I thought you were getting the dog food."

"I will, but I want to make sure the dog doesn't eat your face off."

"You don't think I deserve it?"

I half chuckle, and I spot a ghost of a smile on his face. "Maybe."

"At least you're honest, Elle. At least you're honest."

HENDRIX

ELLE LAUGHS AND THE SOUND DRIFTS OVER MY skin. Above us, the night is filled with a million stars, and the cool autumn air nips at my skin. Elle is in a sleeveless gown. Dark blue silk and it's been my pleasure to escort her to my school's fall dance. Without a doubt, she was the most beautiful girl there, and I'm the lucky bastard who got to slow dance with her all night.

I pull off my suit coat and wrap it around her shoulders as we walk across the grass of her backyard toward the gazebo where I held her this summer. Elle pulls it tight, appears to breathe in my scent and then smiles up at me.

Her real smile, the one that owns my heart, the one still reserved only for me.

Elle's parents are gone for the weekend, and tonight, we're alone. I squint as we come closer to the gazebo. Small lights flicker, and I glance over at Elle for an explanation. "Holiday and Kellen may have been helpful tonight."

"Helpful?" My mind tries to figure out what helpful might mean as Elle twines her fingers with mine and pulls me forward.

"Tonight is what I have wanted for so long. For there to be music and laughter and dancing and singing, and I knew I wouldn't want it to end, so Holiday and Kellen helped me, so it doesn't have to end quite yet."

Two steps up into the gazebo and there are lit candles creating a circle. Elle leads me into the middle. On the bench is a basket full of food, a blanket and an iPod with speakers. With a few swipes of her fingers, music begins to play. Soft and low and seductive, and I can't help but smile at the smooth jazz tones.

Jazz, as I'm discovering at my new school, is what I have been born to play. Jazz, as Elle has discovered, is her least favorite music to listen to, but listen she does. To each and every song I play, and she does it all with that amazing smile on her face.

When a public high school in our county heard how I had been offered the spot at the private youth performing arts school and then how that offer was rescinded due to the parents' and board's concerns, they contacted me. They told me about their fledgling music magnet and asked me to be part of the charter class. I agreed, but only with the condition they took Marcus, as well. They did, and so far, it's been one of the best experiences of my life.

"We can dance to something else," I say.

She shakes her head. "We're only dancing to what you have created."

My head whips in the direction of the iPod, and Elle slips

her arms around me in a hug. "I might have called the school this week, and for once, might have used my semi-celebrity status to ask for an early copy, and they might have said yes with the promise I wouldn't release it in public."

My mind is spinning as I listen to the notes, to the chords, to the steady beat, and there's a building in my chest. That's my song. I wrote it from scratch, from my heart, from my soul, and each and every instrument is played by me, as well. This is my song, belongs to me, and I thought it would be weeks before I heard it all together, but Elle has given me a gift. So many gifts and this one nearly brings me to my knees.

Elle beams up at me. "Shall we dance?"

Dance. I don't know how to dance, because I don't know how to thank her, how to let her know how much she means to me. I touch her. My hands along her back, and I lean down and I kiss her. Gently. Lovingly. Reverently.

Her lips move against mine, her hands begin to wander along my back, and tease the hair along my neckline. She presses her body closer to mine, and the flame of desire grows. It burns warmer in my blood, causing me to deepen our kiss.

We kiss more, and we break apart long enough for her to slip my jacket off her shoulders, for the blanket to be laid on the floor and then for those items to cover us up on the cool night as we resume kissing. We continue to explore until we reach a point where Elle decides if we go much further she'll explode.

With a happy sigh, Elle curls into me, and I hold her close. I kiss her lips again, and she runs her fingers along my arm in encouragement. She then rests her head on my chest, and

I listen to my songs and the symphony of katydids and frogs that is our own private orchestra.

"Are you happy?" she asks.

"Very."

"So am I."

Tonight, we don't know if the Second Chance Program will be saved, we don't know if her father will win the election, we don't know if her relationship with her parents will be repaired, and I don't know if I will truly have a career in music.

But there are things I do know. No matter what happens, no matter what dark moments we face, Elle and I have both learned how to stand on our own two feet, and we've also learned that the journey is sweeter when it is shared together.

★ ★ ★ ★ ★

PLAYLIST

"Boulevard of Broken Dreams" by Green Day

"No" by Meghan Trainor

"Take Your Time" by Sam Hunt

"Praying for Time" by George Michael

"Unsteady" by X Ambassadors

"Mrs. Robinson" by Simon and Garfunkel

"Upside Down" by Jack Johnson

"Immortals (featuring Black Thought)" [Remix] by Fall Out Boy

"California Dreamin'" by Sia

"Hazy Shade of Winter" by The Bangles

"21 Guns" by Green Day

"Lift Your Head Weary Sinner (Chains)" by Crowder

"My House" by Flo Rida

"Don't Let Me Down" (featuring Daya) by The Chainsmokers

"Hallelujah" by Pentatonix

"Freedom" by George Michael

"Love Feels Like" (featuring DC Talk) by tobyMac

"Love Broke Thru" by tobyMac

ACKNOWLEDGMENTS

To God

EPHESIANS 4:31-32 "LET ALL BITTERNESS AND wrath and anger and clamor and slander be put away from you, along with all malice. Be kind to one another, tender-hearted, forgiving each other, just as God in Christ also has forgiven you."

For Dave

YOUR PATIENCE AND LOVE FOR ME DURING THE writing of this book is one of the greatest gifts you have ever given to me. You believed in me when it felt like nobody else did. You believed in me when I stopped believing in myself. Thank you for holding me when I cried, thank you for listening to me when I needed to talk, thank you for the times you held my hand when I needed silence, and thank you for giving me your own version of a *Rocky II* speech—the one that made me laugh so hard that I might have woken our neighbors.

I love you, more than any words could ever explain. You are the reason I write love stories.

Thank you to Suzie Townsend, Michael Strother, Margo Lipschultz and KP Simmon. Suzie, your optimism makes me smile and gives me such hope. Thank you for being a shining light. Michael, you're a genius. There are parts of this book that are here because of your brilliance. Thank you for being a part of Elle and Drix's story. Margo, you are the brainstormer extraordinaire! Thank you for all your help! KP—you are the best! Your wisdom and friendship has helped me more than you could ever imagine.

Kristen Simmons—thank you for helping me laugh when everything hurt. I wouldn't have survived this one without you.

Angela Annalaro-Murphy—you have been my biggest cheerleader from the start. I thank God every day for your friendship.

There are people who have consistently encouraged me emotionally and spiritually over the past five years. People who I'm very lucky to call friends. Thank you to Shilo Smaldone, Melissa Steele, Angela Poole, Dana Moon, Colette Ballard, Kelly Creagh, Bethany Griffin, Kurt Hampe, Bill Wolfe, the Mattinglys, my parents, my sister, my Mount Washington family and the entire McGarry "Madness" clan—with a special shout out to Angela, Stephanie and Lisa. It takes a village and I thank you for your love and support.

To my readers: Your continued love, support and faith in me has had more of an impact on me than you could ever imagine. Thank you for reading my books and for being so amazing!